Honors Rendered

The Honor Series
By Robert N. Macomber

At the Edge of Honor
Point of Honor
Honorable Mention
A Dishonorable Few
An Affair of Honor
A Different Kind of Honor
The Honored Dead
The Darkest Shade of Honor
Honor Bound
Honorable Lies
Honors Rendered

Honors Rendered

Commander Peter Wake
Office of Naval Intelligence, United States Navy,
against the Imperial German Navy in the Pacific in 1889

11th novel in the Honor Series

Robert N. Macomber

Pineapple Press, Inc.
Sarasota, Florida

Inquiries should be addressed to:

Pineapple Press, Inc.
P.O. Box 3889
Sarasota, Florida 34230

www.pineapplepress.com

Library of Congress Cataloging-in-Publication Data

Macomber, Robert N., 1953–
    Honors rendered : Commander Peter Wake Office of Naval Intelligence, United States Navy, against the Imperial German Navy in the Pacific in 1889 / Robert N. Macomber. — First Edition.
        pages cm. — (Honor Series; 11)
    Summary: "The 11th in the award-winning Honor Series of naval historical fiction. This time Peter Wake, Office of Naval Intelligence, is sent to the South Pacific to work his covert magic to avert a war with the Germans." — Provided by publisher.
    Summary: "In the eleventh in the award-winning Honor Series of naval historical fiction, Peter Wake, Office of Naval Intelligence, is sent to the South Pacific to work his covert magic to avert a war with the Germans." — Provided by publisher.
    ISBN 978-1-56164-607-4 (hardback)
    1. Wake, Peter (Fictitious character)—Fiction. 2. United States. Navy—Officers—Fiction. 3. Germans—Fiction. 4. Oceania—Fiction. I. Title.
    PS3613.A28H68 2013
    813'.6—dc23
                                                                                2013020654

First Edition
10 9 8 7 6 5 4 3 2 1

Design by Shé Hicks

This novel is very respectfully dedicated to

June Cussen
Executive Editor
Pineapple Press

June is the best kind of editor—a writer's editor.

Over the past dozen years and eleven Honor Series projects, she has gently taught me some of the more subtle mysteries of storytelling with the printed word and of that important person at the apex of our literary world, the reader.

I've always listened to you very carefully, June, and I've learned so much.

Thank you,

R.N.M.

An Introductory Word to My Readers about the Honor Series and This Novel

I believe some background on the fictional hero of the Honor Series, Peter Wake, might be helpful for both new and longtime readers. Wake was born just east of Mattapoisett, Massachusetts, on 26 June 1839 to a family in the coastal schooner trade, and he went to sea full-time at age sixteen. Volunteering for the U.S. Navy in 1863, he became a commissioned officer at the height of the Civil War, and his subsequent career lasted until 1908. He married Linda Donahue at Key West in 1864. The couple's daughter, Useppa, was born on Useppa Island, Florida, in 1865. Their son, Sean, was born in Pensacola in 1867.

After serving as a deck officer for sixteen years, Wake began his intelligence work while observing the War of the Pacific on South America's west coast from 1879 to 1881. He then joined the newly formed Office of Naval Intelligence (ONI) in 1882. As one of the few officers who was not a graduate of the U.S. Naval Academy, his career was constantly at odds with many in the navy establishment. Most of his intelligence efforts were for the clandestine Special Assignments Section (SAS), which worked directly for the Chief of the Bureau of Navigation (parent command of ONI) until 1889. Thereafter, ONI came under the auspices of the Assistant Secretary of the Navy himself. There has never been any official record of the SAS's existence.

The first six novels of the Honor Series were told in the third person, but in the 2009 novel, *The Honored Dead*, a fascinating discovery was described: Wake's collection of memoirs was purportedly found in the spring of 2007 inside a 124-year-old, ornately engraved Imperial Vietnamese trunk, hidden away in the attic of a bungalow on Peacon Lane in Key West. The home was owned by Agnes Whitehead, who had recently died at age ninety-seven. There has been much speculation among Honor Series fans (known as Wakians) about Agnes Whitehead, her relationship to the Wake family, and how she came to possess that special trunk.

With each novel after *The Honored Dead,* another facet of that fictional puzzle is revealed.

The individual accounts inside the trunk (more than a dozen were found) were typed by Wake himself in the 1890s and early 1900s, usually a few years after the events described within occurred. Each account was accompanied by an explanatory letter to his son, Sean, who graduated from the U.S. Naval Academy in 1890, or daughter, Useppa, who became a Methodist missionary. Wake wrote all of this because he wanted his children and their descendants to understand what he endured and accomplished in his long career since the official records on most of it were sequestered in the ONI vault in the State, War, and Navy Building, now known as the Eisenhower Executive Office Building. A note in the Vietnamese trunk requested that none of the material be made public by the family until fifty years after the death of his children. Sean died in the Dutch East Indies in April 1942. Useppa died in Havana, Cuba, in February 1947.

Sean Rork, an Irish-born boatswain in the U.S. Navy and best friend of Wake, served with him in the naval service until 1908 and shared ownership of Patricio Island, on the lower Gulf coast of Florida. He was eight years older than Peter, whose son was named after him. During all those years in ONI, Rork officially functioned as Wake's petty officer aide but was in actuality his close partner on intelligence missions.

This particular volume of Wake's memoirs was written in 1896, seven years after the events in the account. The warnings about Kaiser Wilhelm's global ambitions contained at the end of this account fell on deaf ears in Washington at the time but were proven sadly correct in 1917 by the infamous Zimmerman Telegram. One can't help but wonder how history would have been changed if Wake's advice had been heeded twenty years earlier.

The individual accounts inside the trunk (more than a dozen were found) were typed by Wake himself in the 1890s and early 1900s, usually a few years after the events described within occurred. Each account was accompanied by an explanatory letter to his son, Sean, who graduated from the U.S. Naval Academy in 1890, or daughter, Useppa, who became a Methodist missionary.

Wake wrote all of this because he wanted his children and their descendants to understand what he endured and accomplished in his long career since the official records on most of it were sequestered in the ONI vault in the State, War, and Navy Building, now known as the Eisenhower Executive Office Building. A note in the Vietnamese trunk requested that none of the material be made public by the family until fifty years after the death of his children. Sean died in the Dutch East Indies in April 1942. Useppa died in Havana, Cuba, in February 1947.

Sean Rork, an Irish-born boatswain in the U.S. Navy and best friend of Wake, served with him in the naval service until 1908 and shared ownership of Patricio Island, on the lower Gulf coast of Florida. He was eight years older than Peter, whose son was named after him. During all those years in ONI, Rork officially functioned as Wake's petty officer aide but was in actuality his close partner on intelligence missions.

This particular volume of Wake's memoirs was written in 1896, seven years after the events in the account. The warnings about Kaiser Wilhelm's global ambitions contained at the end of this account fell on deaf ears in Washington at the time but were proven sadly correct in 1917 by the infamous Zimmerman Telegram. One can't help but wonder how history would have been changed if Wake's advice had been heeded twenty years earlier.

It must be explained here that Wake was a product of his times, and his descriptions of people and events may not be considered "politically correct" to our modern sensibilities. For a nineteenth-century man, he showed remarkable tolerance and perspicacity in his political-cultural observations, however, and many of his predictions came true. Much of Wake's rather arcane knowledge was gained through an international network of intriguing individuals he met both in the U.S. and in distant lands during his assignments. He kept a lasting correspondence with them all, which proved to be quite valuable in his work. He also had a mutually productive friendship with two worldwide fraternities that were somewhat politically incorrect and incongruous—the Jesuits and the Freemasons. Indeed, few military men of the period had as diverse a selection of intelligence sources as Peter Wake.

I have corrected only the most egregious mistakes in Wake's grammar and information and have kept his spelling of foreign words, though they may be debated by twenty-first-century scholars who have the luxury of more thorough education than he had in the languages.

In This Novel

Honors Rendered is set in early 1889. Commander Wake is in the South Pacific, having been given a daunting mission by the outgoing president, Grover Cleveland. Newly elected President Benjamin Harrison takes office in March, but war is brewing and Cleveland is desperate to avoid its start during his last days in office and its stain on his legacy, for he fully intends to return to the White House. But that hope may be too late.

In the far-off Samoan Islands, the obsolete U.S. Navy is defying the rapidly expanding German Empire's march across the Pacific and its subjugation of the Samoan people, who have been allies of America and Great Britain. National honor and economic advantages are at stake for both Germany and the United States. The tension is mounting. Neither side is backing down. Warships of both navies are faced off against each other. Across Europe and America, everyone is waiting for the single misstep that will ignite a world war.

Wake's orders from President Cleveland are deceptively simple. He is to quietly find a way to defuse the confrontation and prevent a war. But should his efforts prove unsuccessful, then Wake is to use his clandestine skills to win the war quickly in Samoa before it can spread into global war. This isn't Peter Wake's first impossible assignment, but it may well be his last. The stakes are enormous.

An Important Note about Reading This Novel

After you finish a chapter, I strongly suggest that you peruse that chapter's endnotes at the back of the book, where you will find interesting background details I've discovered while researching this project. My goal is to educate as well as to entertain.

Thus, with the Honor Series, we have the unique opportunity to see inside the events, places, and personalities of a critical period in American and world history through the eyes of a man who was there and secretly helped make much of it happen.

Onward and upward, for us all . . .
Robert N. Macomber
The Boat House
St. James, Pine Island
Florida

Dying a Deniable Death on the Far Side of the World

Falealili Bay, Upolu Island
Kingdom of Samoa
5:15 P.M., Sunday
10 February 1889

I ended up being the last one to run across the beach to the jungle. My mistake.

Straining to lug a seabag laden with weaponry and gold coins, I tried to get off that beach as fast as I could. There was safety in those green shadows fifteen feet ahead of me. Fifteen feet. Five strides. Ten seconds.

In the bushes ahead of me, I heard David Aukai growl something in Hawaiian that sounded like an oath. One of the Melanesians yelled in his Tok Pisin lingo for me to hurry. From somewhere to the left, deeper inside the forest, Jane yelled, "They're shooting at *us* now!"

Turning for a quick glance at the enemy, I saw two flashes of light winking at me from the German warship. She had emerged from behind the small island offshore and was close along the reef now, right where the schooner had been before exploding. At the same instant I saw the guns' flashes, sand erupted all around me.

I could tell by the sound that they were using those new Maxims that fire incessantly by an automatic recoil mechanism. I'd heard the damned things being fired at a gun range in England two years before by Hiram Maxim himself. The humorless irony of being killed on a beach in the South Pacific by German sailors using an American-designed machine-driven gun sold to them by the Brits wasn't uppermost in my mind at the moment, however. Survival was. I dropped the seabag and ran for my life in the loose sand.

But I was two seconds too slow.

Five feet ahead of me, a guava tree's limbs were being snipped off their slender trunk by the bullets whizzing past my head. It was a menacing little sound. *Zzzttt, zzzttt! Zzzttt! Zzzttt!* A veritable snow of pastel green leaves floated down. The distant machine gun continued to spit out death, searching for me by depressing the elevation.

The round that finally caught me went low. Smashing into my right hip like a sledgehammer, it spun me around like a rag doll. I was slammed down onto a black lava rock, my twisted body landing on my right shoulder, hip, and leg. Just short of those bushes.

The German gunners traversed to the right, hitting the seabag a dozen times with little thuds. I imagine that at their range they thought it was a man. Then the geysers of sand and sea shells swept along the beach to the right, away from me, searching for more targets to kill. Seconds later, it swept back to the left, toward me.

Jane screamed at me to get up and run. Aukai crawled low through the bushes toward me. I tried to crawl toward him so he wouldn't be exposed on the beach, but I couldn't move. My entire right side chose that moment to mutiny, refusing to follow my brain's most adamant orders. Instead, an excruciating wave of pain doubled me up.

I'm quite familiar with pain. I've been shot and stabbed before.

It is a natural result of working in this business long enough for those odds to play out. The worst was that time in Africa, but I was fifteen years younger then and much stronger in body and spirit. This time, the pain was different.

I remember Hiram Maxim proudly explaining what his gun could do to the human body. Maxim's gun fires the new experimental British .303 bullet. It's relatively small in size compared to others but propelled by a huge amount of powder, producing an effect on the body far bigger than its dimensions would indicate.

This one had ignited a pain like a white-hot electrical charge, shooting fire up and down my spine, the pain radiating into my guts. I couldn't breathe or even cry out, it was so overwhelming, so consuming.

I had to move, but first I had to assess my wounds, for there were several on my right side—forehead, shoulder, hip, knee. All had impacted that sharp rock, but the hip was the major worry. That's where the round had entered.

Reaching down, I tore away the hole in my trouser to check the extent of the wound. Blood poured over the beach, becoming a congealed, dark-brown lump of sand. Feeling around my hip, I had the odd sensation of large pins pricking me. That's when I smelled the rum.

It dawned on me with stunning incredulity that the round had hit the flask in my right hip pocket. That had slowed the entry and spread out the impact. I held up the mangled flask and saw a jagged hole right through. The round was still in me but maybe not deep.

Why couldn't I move? I tried again but still couldn't move the leg, for that electrical charge instantly stopped any effort. I lay there, paralyzed.

The Maxim gun's rounds were getting closer, bursting in short groups, then the gunner sped up the traverse and centered on the beach around me again. Aukai moved back from the edge of the bushes as rounds whizzed inches above him. Good decision. If he'd made his dash to help me, he would have been hit in the face. Then we'd both be lying there in the sand.

The rounds went left, away from me, but I didn't feel relief. Seeing my friend nearly get his head exploded into a red mist inflamed me with fury. David Aukai was a genuinely good man. He'd already saved our lives from a German maniac on the steamer from Hawaii.

Anger took command of my brain, crushing the white-hot pain, overpowering the fear. No, it was more than mere anger; it was rage now. Cold, hard-as-steel, pain-numbing *rage*.

A civilian reading this account will probably imagine my rage was directed at the men who were shooting at me. But it wasn't. The German sailors were just minor cogs in the wheels of war, sent into action by politicians in Samoa and Berlin. They were only doing their job. Like me. And like my friend Captain David Aukai of the Hawaiian Royal Guard.

No, my rage was directed squarely against certain men in my own government. Condescending politicians, just like those in Berlin, who had never faced absolute terror in their lives. They'd spent years reveling in the game of nations, debating over cocktails at the Willard Hotel whether to make a military threat here, a political treaty there, a commercial agreement somewhere else. Loving their power to buy and sell distant territory and native peoples and counter the European colonies. Loving it all the way up until the consequences turned harmful to the country—and mortal to their own careers.

Sitting in a comfortable office in Washington, they'd solemnly sent me on an impossible mission to clean up the mess they started. And now I had failed only thirty seconds after finally making it to the island. The only Americans who would know of my efforts and failure were those politicians.

Fortunately for them, I was about to disappear, dying a conveniently deniable death on the far side of the world. My children would never know how and why it had happened. They would be told I was lost at sea on a native scow somewhere in the

Pacific while on a routine courier assignment.

Clenching my guts against the spasms, I gripped my hip and clamped down on the wound to stop the flow. I could feel it oozing around my fingers. But I wasn't thinking about my body. My mind focused on the scene in that plush office—six long weeks and ten thousand miles earlier—remembering each sanctimonious face in that room.

And I swore right then and there on that blood-soaked beach that I would not die. No, I would live. And when I got back to Washington, I'd find every last one of those men again—and make *them* taste terror.

2

The View from Washington, Six Weeks Earlier

Office of William C. Whitney, Secretary of the Navy
Room 272; State, War, and Navy Building
Washington, D.C.
10 A.M., Wednesday
20 December 1888

The moment I entered the office, I instantly knew something was terribly wrong.

It was only a fleeting glance on their part before they looked away from me. But it was long enough for my eyes to meet theirs and see the abject fear that filled them.

This wasn't the first time I'd encountered such a look, either there or at the impressive white presidential mansion across the park. Executive political leaders, like the frightened men before me, occasionally are forced into summoning professionals like me to rectify situations they've badly bungled. Usually, this is after the situation is out of control. The catalyst for the summons is that very worst fear of these politicians: that their private bungling is about to become publicly known and reviled. The natural consequence of these summonses is that my life—not theirs, of course—is soon placed in mortal peril.

Such is my way of life, for I work in the shadowy field of naval espionage. It is a profession normally disdained by such refined gentlemen as those who now surrounded me. Looking at their tense faces, I inwardly sighed, wondering what sort of mess I was about to be cast into this time and, far more important, just how I would eventually get out of it in one piece.

I'd been summoned only a few minutes before. The breathless young runner handed me a folded note from my superior, Commodore John Grimes Walker, Chief of the Bureau of Navigation, the most prestigious bureau in the United States Navy.

It was a typical Walker missive: *P.W., Report to SecNav now, R.G.W.*

That was it. No explanation. No indication of how to prepare. And no toleration of tardiness.

One never dawdled upon receiving such a note from Walker. You could wonder the reason and the consequences of your summons on the way but never delay your appearance. So off I went, my mind swirling, trying to figure out what new and weighty repercussion had surfaced from my recent operations against the Spanish in Cuba. It hadn't gone well. I was lucky to survive and salvage most of what I'd been sent to accomplish. My reputation among the few higher officers who knew of the mission was not in the best of shape.

My place of work when I'm not out in the field is the Palace. That's what its inmates of lesser import call the 553-room, seven-floor, French Second Empire–style structure, a notorious boondoggle commonly recognized as the State, War, and Navy Building. There are 151 fireplaces in the Palace, but unfortunately none are near enough to warm up my office in the least. I would have greatly appreciated even a mild coal fire on that cold December morning.

My office is a windowless lair on the fourth floor, hidden behind the Office of Naval Intelligence. To quickly get to the Secretary of the Navy's office in Room 272 down on the second floor, not far from the entrance nearest the Executive Mansion, requires an immediate tactical decision: Use the modern elevator or descend the old-fashioned way via the marble stairs.

I chose the latter, which was slightly slower but far more reliable.

And that's why I was a bit breathless myself when the flag lieutenant to the secretary announced my entry into the *sanctum sanctorum* of the United States Navy. Even with all my guesswork on the way, I wasn't ready for who was in that room or what they had in mind for me.

Commodore Walker was standing near the door. His forked beard, about which there was many a jest behind his back, undulated comically as he observed in a perturbed tone, "Well, here he is, Mr. President. Gentlemen, this is Commander Peter Wake, senior officer of the Special Assignment Section in ONI." Walker waved a hand at me, then said to the president, "I believe you've met him before, sir."

The considerable bulk of President Stephen Grover Cleveland was stuffed into a green leather armchair, casually positioned in front of Secretary of the Navy William Whitney's desk. The president nodded slightly at me and Walker, then resumed his study of the large map of the world on the opposite wall. I followed his gaze and registered the region it was aimed at: the Pacific Ocean.

That meant Samoa.

Hmm. No wonder the atmosphere in the room was tense, almost despondent. Things weren't going well in Samoa for us. In fact, they were falling apart. German and American warships had been facing off against each other for months. Both countries were sending reinforcements. National honor was at stake for both.

Difficult questions were being asked in both capitals and around Europe.

Would the United States actually stand by its commitment to the Samoans and defend them against the Germans, who were determined to add those islands to their rapidly expanding Pacific empire? The Brits, for once, were favorable to our view. That was a product of their long history in the Pacific and a new anxiety building among their public toward Germany's domination of Europe. On both that continent and in America, citizens read each lurid press report with a mixture of pride, anger, and worry. It had been seventy-three years since the world had last seen a global war, and a new one was about to ignite over some ridiculously insignificant islands on the far side of the world.

For the last six months, while I'd been focused on Cuba, Lieutenant Raymond Rodgers and his staff, officially known as the Office of Naval Intelligence and commonly known as ONI, had been working hard to gather information on "the enemy," as the Germans were now being categorized among navy men. I wasn't a part of that effort and only knew what I'd heard around the offices since my return from Cuba in October.

While I stood there waiting for the president or somebody to speak to me, I quickly dredged up my meager understanding of Samoa. A year earlier the Germans had deposed the legitimate native king, Malietoa Laupepa, a devout Christian who admired and befriended the United States and thought we would really do what we'd promised years before: defend him and his country of islands against just the sort of aggression described in the treaty that gave us a coal depot at Pago Pago.

He was still waiting for us when the Germans exiled him by force to an even more insignificant island speck in the far distant German Marianas Islands. Laupepa was replaced on the throne with a pro-German man, a chieftain named Tamasese. The German navy then led the fight against the inevitable Samoan reaction, a rebellion against the German takeover. Tamasese was just a figurehead, naturally. The real men in power in Samoa were a German army captain, Eugen Brandeis, "senior advisor" to the new king, and the German consul, Herr Knappe.

Among non-Samoan residents, the new regime had a lot of support, for the German presence in Samoa was overwhelming. Of the two hundred foreigners in Samoa, most worked for a large company officially known as Deutsche Handels und Plantagen Gesellschaft der Sud See Inseln zu Hamburg, universally known in the German Pacific as the "Firm." It operated cotton, sugar, and tobacco plantations in the region, using imported semi-slave labor furnished by a notorious system called "blackbirding."

The Polynesian culture of the South Pacific refused to understand or participate in European notions of work ethic or private property rights, so plantation labor would have to come from another culture that was more malleable. Blackbirding was the answer, and it had gone on for years, fraudulently conniving Melanesian natives from the Solomon Islands and New Guinea to work in the Firm's plantations for three-year terms in exchange for paltry wages, most of which were lost to the company store in the first month. The worst abuses—outright capture, murder, and torture—had been mostly stopped in the British islands years earlier, courtesy of the Royal Navy, because of the considerable missionary influence in London, Paris, and Washington. The British and French had started to regulate the labor trade, and the tales of horror were diminishing in those colonies.

But the German Pacific was different. The Firm had no such ethical qualms and regarded blackbirding a perfectly acceptable practice. The stories coming out of the Firm's plantations were not for the faint of heart.

There were only a few Britons and a handful of Americans in Samoa, traders and missionaries mostly. Most of them were not enamored of the new Germanic way of life in paradise. Some were downright hostile to it.

And what of the U.S. Navy, the only real instrument of American honor and resolve in the Pacific? We didn't have much of a naval presence in Samoa at all, but what we did have hadn't been idle in the last three months. That was entirely because of the senior naval officer present, an old friend of mine, Commander Richard Leary. He was captain of the gunboat *Adams*, the lone American warship in the southwest Pacific Ocean.

Leary heartily disliked the German practice of bombarding innocent Samoan villages. He had taken a very special dislike to the German naval commander in Samoa, Commodore Fritze. In addition to his flagship, the corvette *Adler*, Fritze had two other warships on station in Samoa to shield his country's interests against the irritating presence of the *Adams*.

The fact that he was hopelessly outnumbered didn't stop Leary, however. He placed his ship directly in the line of fire when Commodore Fritze was about to begin bombarding the civilian town of Mauna, to punish them for furnishing men to the Samoan rebel cause. But Leary didn't stop there. He literally trained his guns on the German warship and sent Fritze an ultimatum: Stop the atrocity or be fired on by the United States of America.

Adler was alone that day. The fight would have been a ship-on-ship duel—and a bloody fight to the death for the Americans, who were hopelessly outgunned. Obviously, Commander Richard Leary took our treaty obligations seriously.

Fortunately for everyone, Fritze had the good sense to back down. Diplomatic protests flurried to and fro, and the press on both sides of the Atlantic spouted forth with inflammatory headlines and essays. In an effort to deal with the escalating crisis, European and American politicians dithered, conferred, consulted, and pontificated, then dithered some more.

Meanwhile, back in paradise, my friend Leary wasn't done. He repeated his previous performance several times, frustrating the Germans and nearly getting himself and his men killed in the process. Then Leary, an Irish-American and therefore doubly dangerous when he truly believed in what he was doing, became even more creative. When the German navy began using night signal rockets to communicate with their landing parties ashore, Leary sent his own rockets up into the Germans' signals, effectively confusing their messages. When I heard that at ONI, I had no doubt Richard Leary was having the time of his life and could just picture him spoiling for a fight.

When word of all this made it back to naval headquarters in Washington, Leary became a hero to the naval officers and a huge headache for the politicians. Leary and the *Adams* were ordered out of Samoa and off to Hawaii, then San Francisco. The gunboat *Nipsic*, under the command of Commander Dennis Mullan, was sent to replace them in Samoa. *Nipsic* was even smaller, older, slower, and weaker armed than *Adams*.

Now it was Mullan's turn to be out there alone against the Germans.

3
Friends and Foes

Office of William C. Whitney, Secretary of the Navy
Room 272; State, War, and Navy Building
Washington, D.C.
10 A.M., Wednesday
20 December 1888

The big factor in everyone's mind was the Royal Navy.

The British had long-held ties to the island groups surrounding Samoa. By all accounts, the Brits ashore had supported us informally in the tensions with the Germans there, so we knew they were sympathetic. The Royal Navy also had warships from its Australian Station in the area and thus the means to render more than just sympathy.

But the Germans weren't some badly armed, ragtag native uprising that would crumble after a few salvoes or machine-gun bursts without any serious danger to the sailors. Fighting the Germans would be real combat. On a global scale. Would the British risk that and support us militarily?

The majority opinion at ONI was no. It wasn't because the Royal Navy couldn't take on the Germans, though. It was primarily because of Queen Victoria.

The sovereign of the largest empire on earth, on which the sun never set, was half German on her mother's side. Her beloved late husband, Albert, for whom Victoria had spent the last twenty-seven years in formal mourning, was also German. Two of her daughters married Germans, and the newly installed, thirty-year-old kaiser of Germany, Wilhelm the Second, whose colonial ambitions helped engender the predicament in the first place, was Queen Victoria's very first grandson, who proudly proclaimed that he was her favorite grandchild and that his love for her knew no bounds.

There was also the not-so-little matter of the war scare the year before with Canada and Great Britain over fishing rights on Canada's eastern seaboard. Even President Cleveland was stirred to make bellicose statements to defend American fishermen. In fact, Walker himself led an ONI reconnoiter of the Royal Navy bases in Canada to assess strengths and vulnerabilities should actual war break out. Fortunately, that idiotic political situation had calmed, but ill will was still felt among the British.

So due to all this, nobody in Washington had any illusions that the British queen would side with the Americans against the German Empire and her own family blood. No, the U.S. would be on its own, militarily and politically, and the Germans knew it.

Such was the extent of my understanding about the United States' Samoan imbroglio. I was still waiting for somebody to speak to me, so I relaxed from my position of attention and stood with hands folded at my back, surveying the room.

Secretary Whitney was seated behind his desk, which was completely covered with its usual piles of envelopes, notes, documents, dossiers, maps, and photographs. The clutter extended to a sideboard and file rack alongside. Unlike my office on this cold morning, there was a roaring fire at each end of the room, with crackling pine logs scenting the warm air. The chandeliers, paneled walls, priceless paintings, magnificent ships' models, and plush carpets all bespoke power and engendered respect for the occupant. At that moment, however, my impression of the room was of a maudlin air formed by the silent demeanor of the pensive men inside, as if they were too scared to say what they were thinking. Instead, they all mimicked the president and concentrated on the wall map.

At forty-seven, Whitney was two years younger than I, with a boyish face that frequently displayed his pleasure with the luxuries and ceremonies of his position, but his furrowed brow made him look ten years older now. He was the first to look away from the map, swiveling his chair toward me. Leaning forward, his hands tented upward as a platform for his chin, he studied me as a scientist might an intriguing but poisonous insect. I got the impression he didn't want me there.

The chair next to the president's was occupied by an equally unsmiling Mr. Thomas Bayard, the nation's illustrious secretary of state and a man to be reckoned with in Washington. Some said he ran the administration—or thought he should—since he came from a long line of aristocratic wealth and power. Secretary Bayard deigned to glance my way, then returned to join the group's gaze on the Pacific. He didn't seem favorable to my presence either.

Unsurprisingly, the senior admiral of the navy was not in the room. Everyone knew that seventy-five-year-old David Dixon Porter couldn't stand Secretary of the Navy Whitney, and now that the Democratic administration's days were numbered, Porter didn't think it necessary to devote much time to his official civilian overseer. Porter was an unabashed Republican who lumped the Devil, Democrats, heinous criminals, and the Pope all in the same category, and he didn't mind telling people so.

Twenty feet away in the far corner of the large office, I spied a bad omen. A very bad omen. Slouched in a cane-back chair and watching the proceedings with faint bemusement was Mr. Smith, his first name unknown to me. He was a plump man with a permanent sneer and one of those pointy goatees I associate with Mississippi River shysters and Washington lawyers. I'd last seen him in September, when I got those damnable orders to go inside Cuba and rescue two men from a Spanish dungeon. Mr. Smith—an alias if I've ever heard one—gave me some unwritten private orders after the official ones were issued. Those orders proved to have interesting political consequences.

Smith was ostensibly an "executive department operative" in the Cleveland administration, a rather grandiose term for a political hack. His sole claim, from what I could tell, was that he had the ear of those with influence in the president's inner circle.

I saw him perhaps five times in my life, at meetings where unpleasant subjects were discussed. He listened but never spoke at those meetings. Afterward, he would collar his target in a passageway and conveniently impart his personal instructions or warnings without witnesses.

Well, I thought with a sense of relief, at least nobody in the room was looking at Cuba, the Bahamas, or Haiti, all of which were scenes of my operations during the preceding months. Good. I began to feel less anxious about being in trouble for past endeavors and mishaps.

Finally, with funereal solemnity, Whitney broke the silence while staring at a paper on his desk. I tried but couldn't make it out upside down.

"Commander Wake, we are in desperate times. You are being sent on a very delicate and dangerous mission to the German-held islands in the Pacific."

The Germans controlled hundreds of islands in the Pacific, but I knew which one he meant. Damn it all. It *was* Samoa. I hadn't been in the Pacific for five years, since my mission in Indo-China in '83. That assignment started as a routine courier mission and ended as a convoluted operation that ended through sheer luck in a relatively successful outcome. But why me? I'd never been to Samoa except for a brief coal stop while transiting the Pacific to and from Indo-China.

"Samoa, sir?" I asked, trying to sound professionally enthusiastic.

"Yes. You will receive your official orders in a moment, but we want to give you some insight on what we expect from you on this mission. You will leave today, immediately after this meeting. This will be your last opportunity to ask questions so listen carefully."

This was sounding bad, just like the Cuba assignment. I stole a look at Smith, who returned one. He was the only one in the room smiling—yet another ill sign.

Whitney paused and looked up at me, cocking his eyebrow expectantly. I gave the reply expected of all naval officers. "Aye, sir."

He spun his chair around and looked at the map, turning his back to me. I heard him quietly say, "Very well. You may begin, Commodore."

4
Disturbing Intelligence

Office of William C. Whitney, Secretary of the Navy
Room 272; State, War, and Navy Building
Washington, D.C.
10:15 A.M., Wednesday
20 December 1888

Commodore Walker bellowed to the anteroom for Lieutenant John Parker, who I knew to be ONI's resident expert on Samoa, to enter the office. The lieutenant arrived instantly and walked to the other side of the room, where a large-scale chart of the Samoan Islands was pinned to the wall.

Evidently, Parker had already briefed the others, for they showed no surprise at what he said next. However, I most certainly did, for the Samoan situation was even worse than I'd thought.

"Commander Wake, four hours ago a communiqué from Consul Blacklock, our diplomatic representative in Samoa, arrived at the State Department via a fast steamer to the cable station at New Zealand. One hour ago, a cable from Commander Mullan of the *Nipsic* arrived at ONI by the same route. Both communications say the same thing—the situation in Samoa has grown dramatically worse in the last several days. Actual war between the German Empire and the United States is imminent."

Parker's voice dwelled on the last sentence, then he went on.

"Two days ago, the Samoan rebels soundly defeated a well-armed column of German sailors and marines, here at Fangalii." Parker pointed at a place on the north shore of Upolu Island, near the capital village of Apia. "The Germans lost almost half their men. Estimates are around a hundred killed and wounded, but it may be more. The leader of the Samoan rebels is a chief called Mataafa. He's a supporter of the deposed king, Malietoa Laupepa, whom the Germans have as a virtual prisoner at one of their other islands in the Marianas group. Some are describing the aftermath of the battle as a massacre, including decapitation of the German dead by the Samoans."

President Cleveland slowly shook his head and groaned. Ignoring the interruption, Parker resumed his briefing.

"Mataafa is a renowned warrior but has no modern military skills and is not the one who coordinated the successful attack on the Germans. That person appears to be an English-born man by the name of John Klein, who is a naturalized American citizen and a war correspondent for Mr. Pulitzer's *New York World* newspaper. In addition to Klein's commanding the Samoan forces in the field, he has encouraged other foreigners in Samoa to fund and provide necessary modern munitions to the rebel army.

"Those efforts at encouragement have yielded positive results. Most of the Americans in Samoa, along with some of the British traders, have been openly supporting the rebels by purchasing arms and ammunition and smuggling them to Mataafa in clear defiance of the Imperial German Navy. Last week, a British merchant ship, the *Richmond*, got no fewer than twenty-eight thousand rifle rounds to Klien and Mataafa.

"The German commodore, Fritze, and the consul, Knappe, are stunned and angry by their defeat. They particularly blame the Americans. They have vowed revenge and total war on the

Samoans, their supporters among the foreigners, and anyone who gets in the way of a total defeat of Mataafa—a thinly veiled reference to us."

I glanced at my companions. Now all eyes were on Parker. The lieutenant cleared his throat and continued. "As of noon yesterday, the Germans have formally declared war against the Samoans in rebellion. All attempts at maintaining the façade of fighting Mataafa by proxy, through supplying and reinforcing their puppet king, Tamasese, have stopped. The Germans have directly taken over Apia completely.

"The Imperial German flag is now flying over Tamasese's palace at Mulinuu, just west of Apia. After the declaration of war, Knappe and Fritze immediately shut down the English-language newspaper, imposed martial law on the island of Upolu, and sent marines and sailors ashore to patrol the area around Apia. One of their main goals seems to be to harass and intimidate the local American and British citizens into leaving.

"Meanwhile, the Samoans under Mataafa are begging for the United States to honor our treaty obligations from eighteen-seventy-nine and liberate the islands from German occupation. The foreign missionaries are requesting help as well. Their mission stations are overcrowded with refugees and wounded. Rumors are flying in Apia about what might come next. One of them is that the Germans have told Tamasese to proclaim that the U.S. Navy's coal depot at Pago Pago on Tutuila Island has been appropriated by his government and will be turned over to the German Navy. The next closest coal depot is at New Britain Island in the Solomon Islands, but that is German-controlled territory. That leaves us the coal far to the north at Honolulu or down to the south at New Zealand. New Zealand could be a problem if the British government enforces its probable neutrality in the event of war between the German Empire and the United States. Tahiti is French, and we think they'd let us have some coal there."

Parker put a finger on the chart. "And now to current German naval operations."

I stepped closer to see.

"The revenge against the Samoan people for Mataafa and Klein's victory was quick. The German Navy spread out among the Samoan Islands and has already shelled several villages with an unknown toll of casualties. German marines have landed at Savaii Island and Tutuila Island. At Tutuila, they are reported to be at Pago Pago, near our coal depot. That is all we know of the disposition of their forces."

"Where is *Nipsic?*" I asked.

"She was at Tutuila, sir. But Commander Mullan's cable reported that, in response to requests for help, he is steaming at full speed to the village of Laulii." Parker pointed it out on the map. "He intends to interpose *Nipsic* between the German commodore's flagship, *Adler,* and the village in an effort to stop the Germans from bombarding civilians there, including some American missionaries and British citizens."

So Mullan was repeating Leary's efforts? A courageous decision.

"Any news yet?" muttered Secretary Bayard.

"No, sir," said Parker. "I just checked again. We've heard nothing since Commander Mullan got under way and don't know the outcome. The only fast vessel in the area has already steamed at full speed to Auckland to get the State Department and navy messages to the transoceanic cable office there to be transmitted here. That vessel is steaming back, but the transit time is such that we won't hear anything for at least a week, probably much longer. The weather is an unknown factor also. The Southern Hemisphere's hurricane season has begun."

Bayard grimly looked at President Cleveland and shook his head but said nothing. No one did until Commodore Walker asked, "Given all that you know of the men and events in that area, what is your professional opinion of what the situation is there now, Lieutenant?"

Parker said what I was thinking. "Sir, I am afraid that, given the recent German announcements and actions, it must be assumed that *Nipsic* and *Adler* may have already engaged. And *Nipsic* is no match for *Adler.* . . ."

Looking down at the floor, President Cleveland mumbled something under his breath, then said in a distant voice, "Go on, Lieutenant."

"Aye, sir. Since Commander Leary and the *Adams* departed the area two and a half weeks ago, *Nipsic* is the only naval vessel we have there. It is unknown if *Adler* was alone at Laulii, but the other German warships aren't far away in any case. So therefore—"

Cleveland turned away to look out the window. Parker stopped and waited. Cleveland turned back and nodded to continue.

"So therefore, sir, vis-à-vis the United States Navy, the Imperial German Navy dominates the western Pacific Ocean."

5
A World at War?

Office of William C. Whitney, Secretary of the Navy
Room 272; State, War, and Navy Building
Washington, D.C.
10:20 A.M., Wednesday
20 December 1888

P arker looked at Walker, who added further information.

"Commander Wake, Rear Admiral Kimberly received telegraphic orders half an hour ago to consolidate all available elements of the Pacific Squadron in Apia—that will be *Trenton* and *Vandalia*. Once there, he is to first and foremost ensure the safety of American citizens and other non-German foreign citizens. After that is accomplished, he is to stop German depredations upon Samoan noncombatants through a demonstration of strength. The admiral has been ordered to stay in battle-ready condition at all times, in case of German attack, but not to attack first."

Walker stepped over to the large wall map. His next words came out in an angry growl. "Our problem, gentlemen, is twofold.

First, all of our ships are wooden, with obsolete engines and guns. None are a match for any of the European fleets. Secondly, the squadron is scattered across the Pacific at this moment."

He pointed to the isthmus. "Admiral Kimberly has arrived in Panama but is without a ship. His flagship, *Trenton*, is down here, in Callao, Peru. *Vandalia* is in refit in the yard at Mare Island."

"Wait a minute. I thought we had more ships than that out there," said Cleveland.

Whitney answered, "We do, Mr. President. But they are small and even more useless than *Trenton* and *Vandalia*. Good only for impressing natives."

Walker resumed. "*Dolphin* is relatively modern, but she's just a dispatch vessel. Besides, she's in the Mediterranean, heading home from the Pacific. *Alert's* a small gunboat and incommunicado at sea, in transit to Honolulu from the east. *Monongahela's* a storeship and repairing at San Francisco. *Adams* is at sea, in transit to Honolulu from the southwest. Her orders are to continue to San Francisco due to her dilapidated mechanical condition.

"It will take five weeks to get *Vandalia* done with refit and all the way out to *Nipsic*. Six to seven weeks to get *Trenton* out there, at the earliest, without weather or machinery delays."

A double knock sounded at the door, which opened as Lieutenant Raymond Rodgers entered the room. Commodore Walker turned and asked, "Ah, yes, Mr. Rodgers. He is our coordinator of naval intelligence information at ONI, gentlemen. Mr. Rodgers, what's the latest you have on the status of German naval activity in Europe?"

Rodgers had the answer ready. "Most are in home port, sir. A three-ship squadron is visiting Oslo, bound for Sweden next. They have two ships down in the Med, preoccupied with the Russians and Italians. No sign of movement out of the area by them.

"However, several of their more long-range ships are provisioning right now, sir. One of their newest got under way out of Hamburg this morning. According to Lieutenant Buckingham's information, which is from a reliable source, she is heading for the Pacific. She's the new cruiser *Blitz.*"

Ben Buckingham was the ONI man in Berlin, with primary responsibility for intelligence on the German and Russian Navies. He was very good at his job.

"Characteristics of *Blitz?*" asked Walker.

Rodgers opened the valise he'd carried in with him and pulled out a thin, large-format book. I recognized it as the 1885 ONI report on *Foreign Ships of War*. It had been compiled by ONI naval attachés on European navies and by ONI officers in overseas squadrons around the world. I'd contributed to the Spanish naval section.

Reading from the book, Rodgers reported, "*Blitz* was commissioned in eighty-three, sir. She's twin screwed, steel hulled, light, and fast—sixteen knots. Main guns are one four-point-seven inch and four rapid-fire, three-point-seven inchers. All are modern Krupps with high explosive shells. She also has two very large spotlights, one large bow torpedo, and four machine guns. A formidable enemy—newer, faster, bigger, and better armed than even *Trenton*, the best ship in our squadron, sir."

"Range?" asked Walker.

"At ten knots her range is twenty-five hundred miles, sir."

"Probable route?"

Rodgers had it all ready to recite. "Coal at Corunna, Spain, then head to Cameroon in German West Africa and recoal and reprovision there. Then it's around Cape of Good Hope to Dar Es Salaam in German East Africa, where she'll fill her bunkers and stow all of the extra coal she can on deck. From there, she makes the long haul to Finschaven in German New Guinea, where I think they'll have a collier waiting with Australian coal. Then it's over to Samoa to begin operations against us. Estimated date of arrival in Apia is the twentieth of February at the earliest.

"That's only if her boilers can stand the strain, though, which I seriously doubt. Buckingham hears that she's steaming the whole way to keep up the speed, so I think they'll have to stop for a while in East Africa and clean out the boiler tubes. She's new and the machinery's in good shape, but the tropical waters will play havoc on those condensers."

"So if all goes well for the German ship, she'll arrive in Samoa about the same date as our flagship?" asked the president.

Walked answered for Rodgers. "Yes, sir. And I'm sending orders this day to the *Chicago* and *Boston* to head that way too, but it will take longer for them. *Chicago's* on a training cruise along the east coast. *Boston* has been struck with yellow fever at Haiti and is currently headed for New York."

"I see," said the president flatly.

"You are sure no other German ships are en route from Germany at this time, Lieutenant?" asked Whitney.

Rodgers hesitated, then said, "Well, sir, as of this morning's cable from Lieutenant Buckingham, he's heard that other German ships are preparing for sea, but he has no definite intelligence on which ones or where they're headed. He indicated he should have that by tomorrow."

The president glared at the wall map. "Hmm. Lieutenant, these other warships that are mobilizing . . . could they be a raiding squadron headed for our East Coast?"

An enemy raiding the coast was one of the nightmares the army dreaded since they were responsible for coastal fortifications. They were modernizing their heavy artillery but were far from done. Our harbors were essentially undefended. I'd noted that Secretary of War Endicott, in charge of the army, wasn't present at the meeting and wondered why.

Again, Walker stepped in and answered for his subordinate, sparing him the burden of giving the president bad news. "Yes, Mr. President, that's a definite possibility. The memoirs of the Confederate ocean raiders are required reading for all officers in the Imperial German Navy, so they know of the successful Confederate raid on the New England coast in June of sixty-three. They have long planned a worldwide *guerre de course* strategy against their European adversaries' trade routes and coasts, so we must presume they'd do that to us too."

Walker glanced at me. "And, as you may remember, they have that island in the Caribbean they are trying to build into a naval base. Commander Wake is the one who brought that to our attention. Commander, please fill in the others."

Everyone looked at me. I kept it short. "Last year the German Navy decided to build a naval base in the Caribbean. They chose a small island near Dutch Curacao called Klien Curacao, or Little Curacao. This year they occupied it and have built some basic structures and deposited some coal, and they have a detachment trying to build some docks. The Dutch have objected but haven't done anything. Our last look at it was in September, and there wasn't much there."

"And they've obviously thought about the future. It's close to the French canal in Panama," observed Whitney. "Not to mention their commercial enterprises in Venezuela and Colombia."

"Exactly, Mr. Secretary. It's only twenty miles off the Venezuelan coast, about three days' steaming upwind of the canal or across the wind to Haiti or Cuba."

"So once they build that place up, they could use it to raid us?" asked the president.

"That'll be a while, Mr. President. That island is dry, with no wells or water supply. It's low and unprotected against storms. There is no harbor. To make it a viable base will take years and a lot of money and effort. Any raiding squadron will come from Europe."

Bayard held up a hand. "But, wait, we're getting ahead of ourselves, gentlemen. They wouldn't raid our coast unless they knew there'd actually been a naval battle." He addressed Walker, "And they can't know that ahead of us, can they?"

"No, sir. The nearest cable office to Samoa is in Auckland, New Zealand. If there was a battle, either the U.S. or British consul would charter a vessel to get the word to Auckland straight away, as would the Germans. So if we don't know what happened between *Adler* and *Nipsic*, I don't think the Germans do either."

Bayard thought about that. To the president he said, "Good. So there's no basis of fact yet to justify alerting the army and state militias to man our coastal forts, is there? That would cause panic."

Cleveland didn't sound as confident as the secretary of state. "Well, no, apparently not, Tom. Not yet, anyway. What do you hear from your people in Berlin?"

"The German government is irate with American meddling in Samoa, and the German press is calling for the defense of their national honor."

"Yes, but what about Bismarck and this new kaiser fellow."

"Bismarck and Kaiser Wilhelm the Second don't get along. Bismarck will cut your throat commercially and politically, but he doesn't want war. It's bad for business. The problem is the kaiser. Kaiser Wilhelm's young and ambitious and a naval enthusiast. He's only been on the throne six months and already wants a navy to equal the Brits'. And he feels like he has to show he's a tough warrior, like his grandfather. He's listening to the press and ignoring Bismarck's advice. There are rumors that old Otto may be leaving the government soon."

Lieutenant Rodgers chose that moment to pull out another ONI book, the *1885 Coaling, Docking, and Repairing Facilities of the Ports of the World*, and turned to a dog-eared page.

Commodore Walker nodded his assent, and Rodger addressed the president. "By the way, sir, if *Blitz* has to make any significant repairs, she'll be out of luck once she's beyond German East Africa. The German Navy hasn't built up its Pacific shore bases to handle major repairs yet, so it'll be dependent on those of other countries. That's always a serious detriment to wartime operations."

I had to admit, Walker was a master at handling politicians. Clearly, he'd orchestrated his lieutenants' briefings. Rodgers' last comment offered a slim reed of hope, brightening the president's dour face a bit, while simultaneously reminding his audience of *our* need for repair facilities at distant stations.

The lieutenant continued seamlessly on the same topic. "Because of the royal connections, we don't think the Brits out there will deny them help at Singapore, but the actual Royal Navy officers, most of whom don't like the Germans, probably won't be enthusiastic about it. I imagine the Germans might experience some delays if they used Singapore. They know that reports about any repairs will get sent to us."

"Will other Europeans out there help them?" asked the president.

"The French will certainly deny the use of their facilities at Saigon, but the others won't. The Dutch East Indies base at Batavia would be open to them. But I think the Germans would use the base at Manila. It's more remote to our eyes than Singapore. They're very friendly with the Spanish right now."

Yes, that made sense, I thought. The Spanish were adversaries of the United States over Cuba. It was the old story: The enemy of my enemy is my friend.

Just in case these ignorant landlubbing pols didn't get it, Walker stepped in and threw cold water on the conversation by stressing our own strategic naval support needs.

"We have the same problem, gentlemen. Modern navies require modern support. Mare Island is our only major repair facility in the Pacific, and that's almost seven thousand miles away from Samoa. Honolulu is friendly, but it can only handle minor repairs and coaling. We have no colonies or large commercial support in that entire hemisphere.

"Any conflict with the German Empire is likely to encompass the entire globe, and the Germans have colonies or a strong commercial presence—and therefore at least a minimum of support for their warships—in Africa, Asia, and the Pacific."

President Cleveland murmured, "A world at war." He waved a hand at Walker. "Alright, I've heard enough about all this. I have another meeting in a few minutes, so let's get on with it, Commodore. But before we give Commander Wake his orders, I want to know something from him."

"Aye, sir." Walker turned to the two lieutenants. "Mr. Rodgers and Mr. Parker, you are dismissed."

Once Commodore Walker had closed the door, all eyes shifted to the president.

"Commander Wake, the assignment you are about to get will be voluntary on your part. It will be very difficult and extremely dangerous. It's my understanding that your children are grown and that you have been a widower for some time now. Is that correct?"

Old memories flooded my mind. Sweet and sad. Yes, I'd had a family once. Now I saw my children only occasionally. They had their own lives and work. I was left with no one to go home to. I'd found love with a woman during the previous summer while in Haiti. It was the first I'd really had since my wife, Linda, had died in 1881.

I was certain the lady felt a strong bond too, but our future foundered on the rocks of her decline of my marriage offer. She loved me, she said, but couldn't marry me. Not with the life that I led. That heartbreak had been just three months earlier.

I felt my cheeks redden. The pent-up emotion and despair about my personal life was always just below the surface lately. I dared not let it show, lest I fall apart—not in front of these men.

Aware they were all staring at me, I let out a breath and answered the president's strange question. "Yes, sir. My two children are grown. My daughter, Useppa, is a Methodist missionary in Key West, and my son, Sean, is in his third year at the naval academy. And yes, my wife Linda died from a cancer almost eight years ago. I've never found anyone to marry since then. Well, nobody who wanted to marry me . . ."

The president regarded me grimly as he shook his head. "I don't mean to pry, Commander, and I am truly sorry for your loss. As you know, I am a newlywed—only two years now—and I can't imagine life without my Francis. It must be very hard."

He paused, deep in thought, then bobbed his head decisively, as though he had waited until then to make the decision to give me the assignment.

"I just needed to know more about the man I am sending into harm's way. That man needs to be undistracted, completely devoted to the assignment. A lot will depend on you. But you've done well in the past, and I know you are the right choice for this assignment. So, Commander, here are your orders."

Like a judge about to pronounce sentence upon a condemned man, Grover Cleveland cleared his throat, straightened up in the chair, and faced me squarely.

I looked him in the eye and braced myself.

6
The President's Plan

Office of William C. Whitney, Secretary of the Navy
Room 272; State, War, and Navy Building
Washington, D.C.
10:25 A.M., Wednesday
20 December 1888

The president smiled for the first time that morning. It was his patented politician's smile, guaranteed to melt the hardest of his opponents' hearts.

"Commander Wake, among those few who know, you have quite a reputation. You used considerable ingenuity in Haiti with that Russian lunatic and his aerial warship a couple months back. I was impressed. And you did it again on the mission inside Cuba in September. You've had quite a year, haven't you?" He laughed at my reaction. "Oh, don't look that surprised, Commander. Yes, the rumors are true. I actually do read the reports that come to my desk."

Everyone in Washington knew Cleveland worked long hours and thoroughly examined every report that arrived on his desk. The lamp lights in his second-floor office at the Executive Mansion were frequently seen burning brightly at midnight. The president even put in a full nine hours of work on the day he married twenty-one-year-old Francis Folsom two years earlier. I thought that was a bit much, but it did show his sense of duty regarding the job.

The president's pleasant manner disappeared in a flash, for the compliments were over. He leaned forward in his chair, his eyes as serious as his next words. "Ingenuity is what we need in Samoa. But it must be *quiet* ingenuity. Understood?"

No, I didn't at all. But it wasn't the moment for a question, so I said, "Yes, sir."

"Well, I thought you would, since you've got more foreign clandestine experience than anyone else around here. So here's what you're going to do, Commander Wake. You're going to go into the German Pacific, not as a U.S. naval intelligence officer but in a covert role. You will represent yourself as a Christian missionary from Canada looking into the problem of the slavers who are still blackbirding those colored people to the German plantations. That charade will lend you a modicum of safety and entrée into the white society there, without the liability of your true nationality and profession."

He was speaking louder with each sentence, clearly pleased with his idea and getting more enthusiastic as he progressed. I, on the other hand, was stunned at the stupidity of the notion that an anti-blackbirding Canadian missionary would be welcome in the German Pacific, but I couldn't interrupt Cleveland right then. The man was, after all, my commander-in-chief, at least until March, four long months away.

"Of course, Commander, your real intent will be to find those influential German inhabitants who are willing to take action against their own leaders in Samoa to stop this dangerous nonsense of taking over everything and everyone they see in the Pacific. You'll have to figure out a way the German leaders can keep their honor intact, obviously, but the Germans need to stop this bellicosity themselves internally. Understood?"

I was beginning to understand, and the more I heard, the more I didn't like it, not one little bit. Me, a missionary? That ridiculous farce wouldn't last a day. The first biblical question would wreck me. I am a Christian, yes, but not as well versed in the Bible as a clergyman.

Let me say here that Grover Cleveland was an honest, hardworking man who tried his best to be a good president. He and Whitney had not been neglectful of the Navy, though I believed they could have done far more. I respected him professionally in spite of the dark rumors about his past personal behavior, particularly during the war of the Southern rebellion.

But he, like many politicians in the capital, was completely ignorant of the outside world. Only a couple of years before his ascendancy to the presidency, he'd been sheriff and mayor of Buffalo. In fact, Cleveland had never even visited Washington before his inauguration, much less anywhere beyond our country. He had no idea what he was talking about when he spoke of the world.

Well, that was to be expected of a president, but what really angered me was the way the others in the room were acting. They were nodding sagely with each presidential assertion. Not one of the sycophants was objecting. Even Bayard, who had a detailed understanding of the world, was going along with it. And Walker, who knew more about world affairs than almost anyone else in the U.S. government, wasn't objecting to this pie-in-the-sky twaddle. Apparently, the unpleasant duty of bringing reality into the meeting was going to have to be done by none other than *me*.

The president had asked whether I understood, and he wasn't going to like my answer. I steeled myself to burst the presidential fairy tale asunder and suffer the certain consequences.

Just then, I saw Walker glowering at me. I knew that look well. Walker was one of the few senior men at headquarters who had my total respect. He gently shook his head once, a subtle signal not to do what he knew I was about to do.

I took a breath and turned to the president, who was starting to glower at me himself. I'd kept him waiting too long for my reply.

"Yes, sir. I understand."

Walker nodded slightly. The president slapped his right hand on the chair's arm.

"Good, Commander. Now . . . here is the second part of your orders. If there is *absolutely no way* you can defuse this thing by getting Teutonic tempers to calm a bit and we do find ourselves in a real shooting war with the Germans out there, then I want you to use all of the ingenuity you've got inside that brain of yours in the other direction."

"Sir?"

"I want you figure out a way to sabotage the German fleet and make sure we can destroy them at the outset. If we can't stop it from happening, then I want this war localized to Samoa and decisively won in the first two days. If things are still boiling when he finally gets there, Kimberly will have orders to assist you in any way he can."

"Aye, sir."

"This is free rein to come up with some good results, Commander. But I want it all done as quietly as possible. Your own life, this country's honor, and the lives of a lot of good men on both sides will be in the balance. But there is precious little time and no room for failure on this." He sighed. "Well, that's it in a nutshell, Commander. Do you have any questions?"

Oh, yes, I had about a thousand questions, none which the president probably had answers for. He was spared that embarrassment, however, by Commodore Walker announcing, "Mr. President, Commander Wake and I need to go over the details in my office. As you said, sir, there isn't much time and he has a train to catch. May we have your permission to leave, sir?"

Cleveland became the enthusiastic politician again.

"Yes, quite right, Commodore. We will leave you experts to your work. Good luck, Commander, and I hope to see you when you return. If it's after the Harrison inauguration in March, I would be greatly pleased to have you come visit me at my apartment in New York. I look forward to hearing the whole inside story of how you accomplished your mission!"

"Aye, aye, sir," I replied, already feeling Walker's tug on my sleeve, pulling me toward the door.

As I exited, President Cleveland was still wedged in that chair, surrounded by his now chattering entourage. Mr. Smith was still in the far corner, his hooded eyes watching me carefully.

It made me sick in my stomach.

7
Orders

Office of the Chief
Bureau of Navigation
Second Floor; State, War, and Navy Building
Washington, D.C.
11 A.M., Wednesday
20 December 1888

alker sat down heavily at his desk and let out a groan. "Glad you kept your mouth shut in there, Peter. If you had told the president what I figured you were about to, it would've made my job much worse."

"Worse, sir?"

"You'll be getting out of here, but I'm the one who has to stay and deal with these political people for the next several months while I get the navy ready to handle this crisis. God help me."

"With all due respect to the president, sir, it's a damned stupid idea."

"Yes, of course it is. He came up with it himself. So here's what we're going to do. Like naval officers have done for a hundred years in this city, we're going to say 'Aye, aye, sir' and make him feel good, and then we're going to ignore that damned stupid idea and do what we know should be done.

"I'm certainly not going to have you go out there as some Canadian parson, blundering around asking questions about native slavery and wasting valuable time. No, you'll be a well-off, greedy American businessman from Baltimore who disagrees with the American government's meddling in the Pacific. You are out there scouting for good investments among the plantations. That'll get you in with the Germans just fine and not get you sidetracked into their labor problems. You'll tell them you have money to invest and want it to make more money and that international politics aren't your problem. How's that sound?"

"Much better, sir. But it'll be more expensive for the department to fund. I'll have to travel like a rich businessman."

"I know, and it's worth it. This is a priority mission, so there'll be no penny-pinching by the bookkeepers down in the accounting office."

"Thank you, sir. Now, about that part of the plan where I try to convince the Germans to turn on their own government and stop a war. . . . That's doesn't sound very realistic either."

"I agree. You can still infiltrate their community as a businessman and see what's what, though. Do a reconnaissance of their military and naval assets. But forget trying to coerce or induce the German planters out there to get Knappe and Fritze to stop their warmongering. That's a waste of time, and time is something we don't have. No, Peter, your main mission is simple: Sabotage the ships in the German squadron. Parker will give you a dossier with information on the ships and captains. You will have to come up with a way to get it done."

"Aye, sir."

"I understand Rork's down with tropical fever?"

"Yes, sir. Recurrence of malaria. He's sick in bed at the Navy Yard for the next couple weeks. I'll be on this one alone."

Sean Rork is a boatswain, commonly known as a bosun, in the navy. He's been my dearest friend and professional colleague for twenty-five years. Each of us has skills that complement the other. I wasn't looking forward to doing this without him.

"Well, more's the pity because you'll not have a team like you had in Cuba. We have no ONI assets in the Pacific either. Hopefully you can buy some assistance from locals, but other than that, you'll be on your own. Remember that."

"Understood, sir. What's my route there?"

"One-thirty train to New York, which you've already booked for that meeting with your friend José Martí tonight, so you can still do that. Send me a cable from New York with what you learn from Martí. The Cuba-Spain situation has subsided for the time being, but I still need to keep my eye on it. You're packed and ready to go, right?"

"Only for a two-day trip, sir, not for several months overseas. I'll need to get home quickly and stow my gear, then get back here for the train. It's going to be tight to make the train."

"Quite right, of course. Hmm. We'll have the secretary's landau get you over to your lodgings and then to the station to catch the train, which we'll have held if you're running late."

Walker roared to his clerk outside to get Secretary Whitney's landau up to the entrance immediately for Commander Wake's use. That order was sure to raise eyebrows in the anteroom. I wondered how he would explain it to Whitney.

He handed me an envelope, which I opened. It was full of greenbacks. Then he handed me a small pouch. It was full of small ten-dollar gold pieces. Next he gave me an envelope full of train and steamer tickets.

"Five thousand in bills, two thousand in gold for your mission expenses. By the way, it's all signed out to you, Peter. After this is over, you will be required to remember and report where it was all spent, submitted in the standard notarized statement to the accountants.

"Now, listen. Don't stay out too late with Martí tonight, for tomorrow morning at five o'clock you're catching the express train from New York to Chicago. From there you take the Central Rail train to St. Louis, then the Union Pacific to San Francisco, arriving late on the twenty-seventh.

"No need to go to Mare Island. They are receiving orders as we speak for the ships refitting there. Upon arrival at San Francisco, you will immediately board the steamer *Australia*, bound first-class for Honolulu at Hawaii. She's reputed to be fast, so you should arrive there on January fourth. So far?"

"Understood, sir."

"Good. Commander Leary and *Adams* may possibly still be there then, if his engine problems have gotten worse. Here is a message to give him."

He handed me a plain, sealed envelope.

"They direct him to return to Samoa under sail and support *Nipsic* and our American citizens ashore. You may also give him all of the information you've received today. If he's not there, leave it for Leary with the officer in charge."

"Aye, sir."

"From Honolulu, the *Australia* will head south to Auckland, New Zealand, arriving sometime around the eighteenth. From there you'll have to find your own transport to the Samoan islands. Assuming you can find passage aboard a modern fast steamer, you could be there around the end of January.

"You will immediately begin your mission. If by some great miracle there is no active war when you arrive, you will still sabotage the German squadron and render it ineffective. Got that? Don't wait for a war to start. Disable their ability to attack us."

That was a direct contradiction of President Cleveland's orders. "Sir, that's not what the president ordered. He said that if the war had *already started*, then I was to sabotage the German ships."

"He also said to win the war decisively in the first two days, Peter. That's what he wants—to win the damned thing straight away and get it over with, so it won't spread around the world and a German squadron raids our East Coast ports. That means the German ships will have to be already sabotaged to render them ineffective so we can destroy them. No fair fights in a war."

"Sir, if *Nipsic* and *Adler* have not engaged and there is no active state of war between us and Germany when I arrive in Samoa, my sabotaging their ships will be the very act of war that will start it."

Walker's forked beard wagged in concurrence. "Yes, you are correct. It would be an act of war that would ignite the whole thing—so don't get caught. Do a false-flag ploy, like you did in Cuba. Or arrange it to look like routine machinery failure. Or get 'em all drunk as coots on that terrible hooch they have out there. Sitting here at a desk in Washington, I haven't the faintest idea how to do it out there, Peter. But you're good at improvisation and will have to come up with a way."

He leaned forward. "Look, Peter, I am *not* going to wait around hoping for the best, pinning our chances on Bayard's striped pants set to defuse this mess that they started in the first place. That squadron has to be neutralized, and you have to be the one to do it."

Walker was warmed up to his subject. The "striped pants set" was a derogatory term used by naval officers to describe career diplomats. It was usually accompanied by a reference to them "making the world safe for cocktail parties."

"Aye, aye, sir."

"Besides, it'll already be a shooting war," he said grimly. "Probably already is. If that's the case, your job will be much tougher—but still the same."

I nodded. It would be tougher. Probably impossible.

Commodore Walker stood and reached out his hand. "It all comes down to you, Commander Wake. Buy us the time to get Admiral Kimberly and the rest of our ships there."

Though his tone was strong, his eyes were sad. I had served under him for seven years. He was one of perhaps three men in Washington who knew the intimate details of my victories and failures. While others above and around my station in life had periodically praised me or forsaken me, Commodore Walker was the one superior who'd always stood by me.

I replied, "Aye, aye, sir," and shook his offered hand.

After scribbling a hurried note to Rork at the Navy Yard sick bay that I was headed for Samoa, I was riding in cushioned comfort inside the secretary of the navy's official landau as it clattered along at full speed through the streets of Washington to my lodging across the Potomac at Boltz's Inn on Chain Bridge Road.

Two days later, having met with José Martí in New York City and learned some noteworthy information from him regarding Cuba, I was aboard one of those new luxurious train carriages I'd heard about but never seen, swaying and rumbling my way westbound across the magnificent North American continent.

Two weeks later, I was happily lounging in my first-class stateroom aboard the fast passenger steamer *Australia* of the Oceanic Steamship line. My stateroom was positively opulent, especially when compared to my usual spartan accommodations in a man-o'-war. We surged across the vast North Pacific Ocean toward the fabled isles of Hawaii. The ocean proved worthy of its name—a rarity in the winter—and the ship provided delightful companionship in the form of the officers and my fellow elite passengers.

Even the captain, Henry Clay Houdelette, was an intriguing soul, having been knighted as Sir Harry Houdelette by none other than King Kalakaua of Hawaii for services rendered to the king's family while passengers aboard the year prior. Sir Harry had many sea stories with which to regale his charges, having been at sea for nearly thirty years, since the age of sixteen, in every ocean of the world.

One of the passengers was of particular note and never suffered for want of companionship. She was a charming widow who soon formed a daily entourage of admirers trailing her from deck to salon to dining room. Occasionally, I was one of them.

It was a most enjoyable journey from New York to Honolulu and, not knowing if I would experience something like it again in my life, which promised to be shortened soon, I took care to appreciate every bit of it.

As a matter of fact, several times during this intriguing trek around the globe to reach the war zone, my appreciation reached the level where Commodore John Grimes Walker became the subject of a deeply heartfelt private toast at the railing while I watched the sunset.

And only with the good stuff, naturally.

8

A Lecture on American Liberty

Royal Hawaiian Hotel
Honolulu, Kingdom of Hawaii
3 P.M., Friday
4 January 1889

As a successful businessman, I was of sufficient social import to be invited to various soirees, dinners, entertainments, and card games aboard the steamer. This continued at Honolulu, for I was asked to accompany several of my genteel shipmates to a tea party at the Royal Hawaiian Hotel, somewhere near the palace of the king. There we would meet the movers and shakers of Honolulu society.

Hawaii is the cosmopolitan crossroads of the North Pacific Ocean, and the arrival of a passenger steamer ignited the populace to an expenditure of energy both curious and predatory.

It was a beastly hot day, and the light breeze on the water didn't reach far into the town. Bare-chested, brown boys darted to and fro, carrying baggage, trying to look important in front of their peers. Ragged Chinese street vendors hawked trinkets in atrocious English, their tone almost bored, as if they realized the futility of it, for no one was buying. White women strolled by carrying parasols to protect their pasty skin and melting face powder, accompanied by stern-faced white dandies in linen suits with sweat stains darkening their armpits and backs. All of them were clearly trying to impress the visitors with the local level of sophistication.

A solitary, middle-aged, white policeman, his skin broiled to an almost African shade, stood arms akimbo under a faded pith helmet as he surveyed the action from the shade of a porch. He watched the native boys with particular closeness, lest some light-fingered thief among them be tempted by the naïveté of the newly arrived tourists.

Here and there a real Hawaiian man could be seen. They are magnificent men, having about them an aura of latent malevolence, should they choose to employ it. Most are a head taller than the whites and much broader in the shoulders. That day they preferred to remain apart as they watched the bustle with a mix of curiosity and regret on their massive mahogany faces.

I saw a few of the Hawaiians dressed in Western-style suits. They looked utterly miserable. Most Hawaiians were attired in the only sensible rig for the tropics: the native costume of loose cotton robes or shirts in various pastels. I noted seeing no Hawaiian women near the customs building, which I found odd and vaguely disquieting.

Our motley procession of Americans and Europeans finally arrived at the Royal Hawaiian, a three-story, stone-block edifice with beautiful frame verandahs on all floors. The lobby was on the second, entered via a pair of curving stairs from the courtyard. On the front of the third story was a huge emblem of the royal crest of Hawaii, which lent a regal air to the place.

We ascended the sweeping circular stairs to the second-floor verandah. There we were ushered from the dazzling brightness outside into the cool hotel's interior with smiling hospitality by a line of servants. Each bowed and greeted us with *"Aloha!* Welcome to our island kingdom!"

I was impressed by this pleasant demonstration of island patriotism. I was even more impressed to find that Honolulu possessed modern metropolitan amenities. There was a telephone at the front desk and electrical lights on the walls. Honolulu was proving to be a study in contrasts. Eager to meet the upper crust of such an intriguing place, I entered the hotel's tea room, ready to be impressed again by our hosts, who I assumed would include some of the famous royalty of the islands.

As it turned out, however, not a single one of these swells was a true ethnological Hawaiian. In fact, most of the political and mercantile leadership were Americans, along with a few Brits. Many of them were born in Hawaii to missionary parents. This privileged class influenced everything by owning everything of commercial value.

As an aside, allow me to introduce them briefly as I met them that day, for they have recently been the subject of considerable attention by the world's press.

We will start with a certain Mr. Whitney, no apparent relation to the secretary of the navy. He was the congenial manager of the *Hawaiian Gazette* and took pains to speak to me, the rich American investor, about the wonderful things that were happening in Honolulu. The *Gazette* is the official paper of record for the king's governmental announcements. It is also largely considered the public voice and advocate for something called the Hawaiian League (more about this later). Whitney introduced me to the others in rather glowing terms. Money can do wonders for one's reputation.

George W. Merrill, a former district attorney in the state of Nevada, was the amiable fifty-two-year-old American diplomatic minister to the Hawaiian kingdom. I liked him, but since he was a political appointee, I surmised his days in Honolulu were probably as numbered as Grover Cleveland's in Washington. Conversely, the rest of the array of personages before me were men whose stars were just ascending. Their days and future prosperity seemed well assured by a sort of mutual protectionism that I deduced immediately.

Lorrin Thurston, born in Hawaii and grandson of the first two Christian missionaries on the islands, was an energetic young lawyer, politician, and the king's interior minister. Only thirty years old, he was said to be the most powerful man in the king's cabinet, and he certainly looked and acted the part. Expressive eyes, balding pate, and full, dark beard made him seem a common, everyday type, but then you heard him speak and realized that here was a serious decision-maker.

Sanford Ballard Dole was a forty-three-year-old gentleman with commercial interests around the islands, as well as a prominent member of the legislature. He already possessed the patrician face and graying hair of a man ten years his senior. Shrewd eyes peered out at you above an intimidating mass of mustache and beard, which was forked like Commodore Walker's. Unlike the bushy mane covering his jaw, his hair topside was under complete control. Confined by oil and carefully combed, it was parted straight as an arrow right down the middle. Born in Honolulu of missionary parents from Maine, Dole was the real power in Honolulu, as evidenced by the deference shown him by all of the other residents of Honolulu.

Thirty-nine-year-old William Castle was yet another Hawaii-born white at the gathering. A graduate of Harvard Law School, Castle was a former attorney general of the kingdom. His trimmed beard and spectacles bespoke a sober and considered man, which was echoed in his pronouncements about the excellent future of the islands.

The opinion that Hawaii was logically the next point of expansion for the American nation was shared by everyone I listened to in the room. A more optimistic group on the subject I've seldom found.

Most, if not all, of the aforementioned gentlemen appeared to be members of the civic group incongruously called the Hawaiian League, which apparently had few if any real Hawaiian natives in it. From what I could tell from the conversation buzzing about me, the main fame of this organization was that on July 6, 1887, they forced King David Kalakaua to amend his governing constitution, literally at gunpoint by a white businessmen's militia company known as the Honolulu Rifles. The existing constitution dated from 1864, during the reign of his predecessor.

The businessmen's complaints focused on the wholesale corruption and ineptitude within the king's cabinet, not to mention some of his notions regarding bringing back traditional dances the missionaries deemed licentious. A dance called the *hula* was referred to with special scorn.

The Hawaiian League's demands having been reluctantly agreed to, the king lost most of his royal authority. In addition to the loss of his personal power, the king's friend and prime minister Walter Murray Gibson—supposedly the worst of the previous crew—and his entire cabinet were removed from office. Hawaii ended up with a new constitution, written by the leadership of the selfsame Hawaiian League, albeit one that greatly empowered the legislature and new cabinet.

Hawaii was moving forward. It shed its autocratic past and became a modern constitutional kingdom, like that of Great Britain, which sounded like a good thing to me. But as I listened further to the chatting men, I learned that this new constitution contained some insidious provisions. Similar laws have lamentably come into use in several of our American states, notably in the South, since the decline of Republicans in the legislatures. With the increase in Democratic political control has come anti-Negro legislation, designed to minimize their participation in society and government. The gains made for black Americans, at the cost of thousands of their fellow citizen's lives, have been lost.

In the new Hawaii, dark-skinned natives found themselves in a similar situation. Foreign residents were allowed to vote, but not a single Asian person could. American, European, and Hawaiian males had the franchise—but only if they satisfied the wealth requirements: an annual income of at least$75 or ownership of private property worth at least $150. And that was only if they wanted to vote for members of the lower chamber of the legislature. To vote for members of the upper chamber, called the House of Nobles, required an income of at least $600 or property worth at least $3,000. Thus, many of the native Hawaiians became excluded from participating in the new government of their own country.

All of this political modernization and native exclusion reminded me of the French in Indochina and of what I'd heard of the German intentions in Samoa and their other colonies across the Pacific. It was the European concept of using the world for the economic betterment of the home country while ostensibly Christianizing and bringing the natives into our culturally advanced nineteenth century. "The white man's burden," some in Europe were calling it. This sort of attitude ignites my personal opinions on the subject—I'm dead set against it and despise those who espouse such arrogance.

Despite mounting evidence to the contrary, I hoped our United States was on a morally higher plane and would refrain from joining Europe in subjecting the darker races around the world to an alien cultural and political regime.

Coal depots and naval docks leased from an independent and willing island chief were one thing. It was quite another to assume responsibility for governing entire uneducated, un-Christian peoples. There was no logical reason for us to be mired in that quagmire, which would be a major monetary drain on our public treasury and a never-ending hemorrhage of our soldiers' and sailors' blood. Witness the incessant cost to our British cousins everywhere in their empire.

It was very evident from what I heard that afternoon in Honolulu, however, that it was a widespread belief among the American residents that Hawaii should be under the U.S. flag, first under the guise of a protectorate. I wondered how much the potential for completely untariffed sugar sales in the United States entered into their thinking, for sugar was an expanding industry and the sweetest teeth in the world were in North America. Hawaii already had a special trade treaty with the United States regarding the importation of sugar from the islands with little or no duty tax and wanted an even better deal in the future.

No wonder then about the pale complexion of those around me who were running the show in Honolulu. Mostly born there, they considered themselves the new Hawaiians and the generation that would bring a better future to the islands. This future was to be *sans* those parts of the traditional culture that offended them, like several of the dances.

Oh, yes, quite proud of themselves they were. They displayed no hesitation or embarrassment in proclaiming their accomplishments in de-Hawaiianizing Hawaii and making it more like Philadelphia or Boston. The ultimate goal, said one of them candidly, was to become the first overseas American colony.

Well, that did it. I quietly pointed out that the United States didn't have or need overseas colonies. Feeling that this didn't explain my point well enough, I not so quietly followed up with the observation that the concept of colonial empires was an old European one and contrary to the new concept of American-style democracy and individual liberty.

When I finished my lecture, I saw that the room had grown quiet and everyone was staring at me. And not kindly either.

9

Crown Princess
Lili'uokalani

Royal Hawaiian Hotel
Honolulu, Kingdom of Hawaii
3 P.M., Friday
4 January 1889

They had evidently heard similar arguments before, for one rather large-bellied man had a ready reply, which he accentuated by periodically stabbing the air with an unlit cigar.

"I understand that you are an investor, Mr. Wake, and you're looking for a money-making locale that will give you a good return for years to come. Well, let me tell you that this is the place and now is the time, for times are changing. We already have American innovation and energy at work here, and soon we'll have American political stability and American commercial power. Yes, sir, it's a fact that someday our American empire will be just as large and rich as the British one. Real democracy? We'll have that too—but an intelligent version, tailored for these islands."

I had several counters to this notion, but right then the lady passenger who had charmed her fellow travelers all the way across the Pacific arrived at our circle of gentlemen, which now included Dole, *et al.* It was a good thing she did, for my blood was up and I was about to launch into a more detailed sermon on American culture and history, which I knew would refute my verbal opponent's arrogance and his complete dismissal of the natives' wishes. The pause caused by her arrival allowed me to belatedly calm down and realize that my intended rant would most certainly not have served my façade. Culturally disinterested businessman looking for ways to make money don't care about natives, their traditions, or their freedoms.

The lady who saved me from making this blunder, Mrs. Jane Cushman, was a raven-haired widow who had retained her facial beauty and hourglass figure, knew it full well, and utilized her assets very effectively. She had what I call "pixie eyes" of a deep blue color, which contrasted attractively with her long hair. Those eyes could captivate a man by showing great whimsical delight or heartbreaking sadness. Her age was somewhat difficult to determine, but my estimate was early forties. Nothing was denied her aboard the ship, and I could see that she was enjoying a similar ease ashore.

Mrs. Cushman came from San Francisco, where her late husband was in cargo shipping and chandleries. Her widowhood had lasted for three years so far, and she showed no signs of wanting to end it, for she was left with quite a sum, by all appearances of attire and manner. Jane Cushman had it all and wanted little. Well, except for a little adventure.

During the passage, she'd told me over a glass of pre-dinner Bordeaux that she had been exploring the Pacific for the last two years. Originally, the journey was an exercise in replacing grief with activity, but then traveling had gained a hold of her and sprouted an interest in seeing new places and people.

"I love to get away from the societal prison of the city and *live* life, Peter. Oh, I know that is not the masculine expectation for us females, but I consider the sedentary lifestyle to be nothing more than a slow death," she said to me that evening. This was a sentiment that I and most seamen understood completely. The more I listened to her, the more I found myself becoming intrigued by Jane Cushman.

My interest was further piqued by her recollections of a visit to Samoa the previous year. She had met King Tamasese, the German puppet; Commodore Fritze and Consul-General Knappe; and many others in the German community there. During other conversations on the ship I gently prodded the lady to share her impressions, which were surprisingly positive regarding Berlin's intentions in the Pacific.

Jane had also visited Hawaii several times and provided me with a general knowledge of the situation in Honolulu before our arrival. She knew many of the attendees at the tea that afternoon and had a positive sense of them too. Judging from her attitudes toward the personalities in Samoa and Hawaii, I imagined her late husband had had a similar outlook on the members of the Hawaiian League.

But there was one man in Honolulu she'd told me about on the steamer who wasn't at the party. She mentioned him now, as her arrival at my circle interrupted the conversation and spared me from ruining my pretended role.

"Let's go over to Washington Place, Peter," Jane whispered in my ear. "John Dominis isn't here at the hotel, so he's probably over there. That's where he lives. I just heard that his wife, the sister of the king, is out of town, so he's probably lonely for some company. I think you'd enjoy meeting him. Come on. This party is getting boring and it's a pleasant day and a short walk."

She was right about the tea party and the weather, so I acceded to her suggestion and off we went, arriving five minutes later at a lovely two-story, white mansion known as Washington Place, on Beretania Street, not far from Iolani, the king's royal palace in Honolulu. Washington Place was in the Southern architectural style, with verandahs wrapping around both floors. Two royal guards met us at the front lawn and allowed us entry, confirming that Mr. Dominis was in residence. On the walk over, Jane had given me a more detailed background of the man.

Dominis was the son of John Dominis Sr., a Croat-Italian sea captain who arrived in America from Trieste during the Napoleonic upheavals. There he married a girl named Mary Jones and continued his profession on the sea, eventually moving wife and son to Honolulu. Dominis the elder built the mansion before his death at sea in 1846. His wife, Mary, now an elderly widow, still lived there. The son, John Owen Dominis, grew up in Honolulu and became friends with the Hawaiian royal family while still a youngster, even to the point of betrothing one and thus becoming a prince consort to Crown Princess Lili'uokalani.

As of my visit, Dominis had been married to Crown Princess Lili'uokalani, the sister of King Kalakaua, for twenty-six years. According to Jane, it provided a very nice income, for he had been governor of Oahu Island and was currently a lieutenant general and commander-in-chief of the royal guards. Dominis also served on the health board, education board, and immigration commission, and he was commissioner of crown lands. Jane said that fifty-five-year-old John cut quite a figure in his official uniform and regalia. I noted that her voice got a bit husky as she said that.

Seconds later I met the man himself, attired in a red-sashed, bemedaled, and starred dark blue uniform, similar to that of a British lieutenant general. The neatly trimmed full beard and receding head of hair, both suspiciously devoid of any gray, completed his martial bearing. He stood nearly at attention on the front verandah of Washington Place, having been alerted to our arrival. Jane was her effervescent best as she greeted him warmly and introduced me.

As I spoke to General Dominis, a foreign military officer, his eyes never leaving me, strode out from the interior of the mansion onto the verandah. With parade-ground precision, he silently took his position one step to the right and rear of the general, who then made him known to me.

"Mr. Wake, this is a military consultant, Colonel Ludwig Starkloff."

I nodded and Starkloff stamped to attention, executing a curt half bow. I had to fight the instinct to come to attention and salute. Instead, I slouched even more, waved a hand at him, and drawled out in my most lackadaisical American English, "Hiya, colonel. Nice to meet 'cha."

I got a muttered *"Guten tag, mein herr,"* in return.

In contrast to the affable General Dominis, the colonel was a sour-faced, middle-aged fellow in the light gray uniform of a Prussian cavalry colonel. It was the full formal rig, complete with staff tassels, various medals, saber, and ornately decorated *picklehaube* silver helmet and top spike. I recognized the regimental insignia—the Prussian Third Cuirassier Cavalry, a legendary military formation and some of the most feared cavalrymen in the world.

Starkloff's sole facial hair was a thin goatee perched on his stalwart jaw, which was accompanied by a badly healed, purple dueling scar that ran from the corner of his mouth all the way to his left ear. His entire visage was one of barely restrained aggression, totally incongruous with the lovely, sensual gardens surrounding us.

Beyond his brief bow, Starkloff showed no emotion, staring right through me, for I was just a soft-willed businessman and therefore no threat. The only perception of humanness I saw in the man was when his gray eyes suddenly lit up upon noticing my female friend. The slightest ghost of a smile crossed his mouth and softened his features, but only for a second. Then it vanished.

Jane showed no such stoicism, however, and fairly bounded up the last few steps to the colonel and gushed, "Oh, Ludwig, what a pleasure! I didn't know you'd be here. I thought you were in China!"

The colonel didn't gush at all, but his white cheeks turned pink. "Ya, I vas in China but only for one month. Und now, I haff returned to my advisor duties here, with zee Royal Guards of Havai-ee."

Hmm. It dawned upon me at that point that I had been

somewhat duped by dear Jane in her spontaneous suggestion at the tea party to come over and meet John. Her gay greeting with the Prussian colonel had a twinge of fear in it, as if she didn't expect him to be there. Her embrace of Starkloff went well beyond that of simple acquaintances. The subsequent mutual gaze spoke volumes. Dominis looked surprised at both of them. Something was definitely afoot, and charming Jane was a bit more complicated that I had imagined.

And things were about to get even more interesting.

Mary Dominis, dressed in subdued formal attire, made her appearance on the verandah and was introduced to me. She smiled and said, "Welcome," but displayed no such hospitality to Jane. In fact, she paid no attention to her.

Jane seemed oblivious to the gracious matron of the house as well. It was an interesting exhibition of silent female confrontation, reminding me exactly of when my late wife, Linda, and I once met a woman of ill repute on the street in Pensacola. Linda's hand had gripped my arm protectively and pulled me closer to her, and she had maintained a silent gaze at the woman while I politely said hello. In the present situation, that same dismissive gaze was on the face of Widow Dominis and directed at Widow Cushman.

In the midst of all this, a maidservant padded out to the verandah and quietly informed Dominis, "Her Highness is on her way, sir."

A moment later, yet another lady arrived, this one dressed in a formal pink gown with diamond necklace, blue sash, and glittering insignia. Crown Princess Lili'uokalani presented a stunning image. There was no doubting she was born to wealth and power, for her confidence positively radiated around her. The princess had smooth olive skin over a full figure, but her smile turned into a smoldering scowl when she saw Mrs. Jane Cushman. Evidently, my lovely widow acquaintance was *persona non grata* among the royalty of Hawaii.

I wondered why, when the clear object of her affection was the Iron Colonel? Could she be a past paramour of the general? Or was it a preemptory attack on a potential foe by the local ladies? For her part, Jane tried unsuccessfully to look innocent of all unspoken charges as she curtsied to Her Highness.

General Dominis, surrounded by three mistrustful women, his stalwart Prussian colonel, and one bewildered American businessman, now proceeded to try to salvage the delicate situation. He did so by using me to deflect any verbal slings from mama or wife, as I was introduced to Her Highness.

"My dear, this is Mr. Peter Wake of Baltimore, a businessman who is aboard the *Australia* en route to Auckland and the South Sea islands, looking for good investment opportunities. And you both remember Jane from her visit last March. She is aboard also and brought Mr. Wake by to meet us."

Turning to me, Dominis said, "Mr. Wake, may I present my wife, Her Highness, Crown Princess Lili'uokalani, of the Royal House of Kalakaua of Hawaii. We all welcome you to our home here at Washington Place and to the Kingdom of Hawaii."

Neither of the local ladies made a sound or movement. For a second, there was an awkward silent tableau, like actors pausing for effect on a stage. Starkloff gazed straight ahead, as if he was searching for enemy artillery; Madam Mary regarded her son quizzically; Princess Lili'uokalani openly seethed at Jane; and my pretty widowed companion looked at me pleadingly⸺or was it with embarrassment?

General Dominis looked at none of us but seemed newly interested in the pink flowers of a frangipani tree nearby.

"Thank you, General," said I, trying to break the tension. "And please excuse our unanticipated intrusion into your beautiful home."

Then, to add a bit of cover for Jane, I put my hand affectionately around her shoulder and added, "My dear Jane and I came here in a moment of spontaneity. It must be your wonderful weather that made us forget our manners and appear without invitation, and I do apologize again for our imposition. We can see you are about to go out."

He smiled at my gesture and seized on it like a drowning man grasping a raft.

"No imposition at all, Mr. Wake! Glad to make your acquaintance. My mother, wife, and I, along with the good colonel, are just leaving for an official function with Bishop Koeckemann at the cathedral, so I regret not being able to spend time with you right now. I would've enjoyed hearing your opinions about the current political happenings in the United States."

He spread his hands in regret, then snapped his fingers. "But wait! I happen to know the steamer isn't leaving until tomorrow morning. Do you good people have plans for tonight? How about attending the ball at Iolani Palace? Eight o'clock. His Majesty will be attending and you can meet him. I will have invitations delivered to the ship."

Jane squeezed my arm and hugged me in delight. "Oh, thank you for the invitation, General. What do you think, Peter? Do you want to go and meet a real king?"

"Sounds delightful, my darling," I replied, though I'd met kings before and found that most are highly overrated dunces. "We'll be honored to attend, General Dominis. Thank you for the kind invitation."

"It will be entirely my pleasure, Mr. Wake," he said, darting his eyes for an instant at Jane. He then turned to Starkloff and said, "Colonel, please be so kind as to tell my adjutant to have a carriage pick up the lady and gentleman at their ship at eight o'clock."

That got a click of heels and a "Wery gut, mein general."

And with that bit of social subterfuge on my part, Jane and I made our good-byes. We wasted no time beating a hasty retreat through the manicured hedges of tropical flowers to escape from that frosty verandah.

The long, hot walk back to the docks was done in contemplative silence. I found the new impressions of Jane intriguing. There was far more to her than she had presented on the ship. Somehow, there was a dark component in the mix.

The darker components of human nature are major factors in my line of work. If they are yours, they must be hidden; if they are someone else's, they can be used for advantage; if they are your target's, they can be exploited. I sensed that time would soon tell regarding Jane's hidden side.

When we arrived at the waterfront, the good lady touched my arm and we stopped. Her pixie eyes were filled with tears, though I couldn't determine their authenticity.

"Thank you for that very subtle kindness, Peter. I'm sorry for that entire uncomfortable scene and that you had no chance to talk to John or Ludwig. I didn't even know Ludwig would be there. I know he's a fright to look at, and most people think him hostile and sullen, but he's really a nice man inside, once you get to know him. I crossed the Pacific with him once, several years ago, and got to know him well. In fact, I learned a bit of German from him."

Several years ago? Was it before Mr. Cushman died? Interesting.

She added more. "I didn't know the princess would be there either. I'm afraid that John's wife has taken to an uncalled-for disliking of me and can be quite rude."

I looked at the lady as innocently as I could, then lied through my teeth to her.

"Dislike *you*? Why, Jane darling, I can't imagine why Crown Princess Lili'uokalani, or anyone else, would ever dislike *you*."

The pixie eyes opened wider, creasing into a smile. She hugged my arm, pressing her bosom against me, the sadness gone and all joy now.

"Oh, Peter. You really are such a kind dear."

After ensuring my friend's safe return to the ship, I made my way to the U.S. consulate, where I asked to see the senior man on duty.

He was a clerk. I explained that I had an urgent communication for Commander Leary of the *Adams* and asked if he was in port.

The reply was in the negative, and I learned that *Adams* had arrived at Honolulu on the twentieth, the same day I got my orders, and departed a week later for San Francisco.

That meant that Leary never got the message from Commodore Walker and wouldn't get the one from me. Such is the state of our naval communications in the Pacific. The modern convenience of transoceanic telegraph cables—so common elsewhere to the point that warship captains are tethered to the instant wishes of headquarters in Washington—have not yet crisscrossed that vast expanse of ocean. So I did it the old-fashioned way and left Leary's orders from Commodore Walker in their sealed envelope at the consulate, to be delivered to *Adams* if she returned.

Thus ended my hope for an easy mode of transport to get directly to Samoa.

10
Cocktail Intrigue

*The Iolani Palace of His Hawaiian Majesty, King David Kalakaua
Honolulu, Kingdom of Hawaii
8:30 P.M., Friday
4 January 1889*

The native Hawaiian majordomo—all six-foot, eight-inches and 350 solid pounds of him, decked out in a magnificent uniform of red and gold—stepped into the entryway between the Grand Hall and us assembled guests in the Throne Room. He slowly brought a heavy, brass-trimmed teakwood staff down on the polished wood floor of the Grand Hall three times. His deputy, less ornately uniformed and far smaller in stature, then stepped forward and sounded a conch shell in three long wails.

The chattering faded away and all faces—some with glistening expectation and others with tired practice—turned toward the entry. It was soon filled by a white-haired Anglo chamberlain in formal tails, his chest bearing two rows of medals. He waited dramatically for several seconds, his stern visage commanding attention. Finally, he nodded across the Throne Room and through the open doors to German bandmaster Henry Berger, whose Royal Hawaiian Band musicians were formed up on the verandah just outside.

All in the room stood respectfully still, those in uniform ramrod straight, as the band struck up "Hawai'i Pono'i," the Hawaiian national anthem composed by the king himself. Afterward, three trumpeters stepped forward and blared forth a flourish.

Then, in a British-accented stentorian tone, the chamberlain announced, "Exalted ladies and lords of the Royal House of Kalakaua; your Excellencies, the Honored Nobility of Hawaii; distinguished foreign guests and friends; and beloved people of Kingdom of Hawaii: I have the privilege and honor to present to you His Hawaiian Majesty, David La'amea Kamanakapu'u Mahinulani Nalaiaehuokalani Lumialani Kalakaua, son of High Chief Caesar Kaluaiku Kapa'akea, and now Head of the Royal House of Kalakaua, Sovereign King of all of the islands and people and seas of the Kingdom of Hawaii, in our Pacific Ocean of this Earth, under our merciful and just God in the heavens around us."

The crimson damask curtains parted at another doorway to show two giant Hawaiian soldiers, each holding a tall *kahili* staff of polished brown *koa* wood, topped with colorful feathers—the ancient symbol of royalty in the Hawaiian Islands. Their staffs had been crossed, but now they were brought to the present-arms position, the feathers flurrying with the movement.

Behind them stood a refined man in dark blue uniform with what must have been ten pounds of European royal decorations spread across the tunic. He was a bit older than I, dark-complexioned and -haired, with a bulky build. He wore a moderate mustache and long, flowing sideburns that ended abruptly at a clean-shaven chin. The expression on his face was one of solemnity as his intelligent eyes scanned the room, seeming to evaluate every one of us for potential amity or latent enmity.

Standing next to him was his queen, Kapi'olani, a middle-aged lady gowned in white and crimson, with a strand of pearls adorning her chest. She also took in each guest with a sweeping glance from perceptive eyes.

The royal couple made a most extraordinary first impression upon me, nothing like what I'd expected after hearing the businessmen's opinions at the afternoon party. They were neither ignorant nor decadent.

The attendees bowed and curtsied as the king slowly entered and stood before the dais, upon which sat two gilded crimson thrones. Now that he had shown his serious side, King Kalakaua waved a hand at his subjects and displayed a disarmingly genuine smile. He was joined by the queen, and soon the room was filled with buzzing conversation as a receiving line formed to their left and hundreds of people lined up to meet them.

Unlike my earlier social encounter in Honolulu, many in attendance at the palace were native Hawaiians. All were attired in European dress and conducted themselves with the utmost decorum. Was it fantasy on their part? An attempt to emulate Europe? Or was their behavior a natural progression to civilized modernity in an effort to hold their own in an increasingly complicated and competitive world? I thought the latter.

Civilized modernity, indeed, for the gala that evening could very well have been a regal soiree in London. Except for the brown faces, the conch shells, and the *kahili* feathers, the entire affair, from displays to clothing to procedures, was pure British.

This surprised me not at all, since the Brits had been the principal advisors, both political and religious, to Hawaiian royalty in the early days of the kingdom some seventy years earlier. The very flag of the kingdom included the British Union Jack dominating the upper left quadrant, with the rest of the ensign horizontal red, white, and blue stripes.

The personal ties between the royal houses were still quite strong. Queen Victoria and King Kalakaua were said to be close friends and constant correspondents. Just a year and a half earlier, Queen Kapi'olani and Crown Princess Lili'uokalani had represented the Hawaiian royal house at Queen Victoria's Jubilee celebrations in England, where they were welcomed warmly and seated beside Victoria and her family.

The political complexion of the advisory influences in Honolulu had changed in recent years, though, for now German traders and American missionaries and businessmen were the principal advisors to the government. In spite of that, or maybe because of it, the appearance and customs of the Hawaiian monarchy remained staunchly Britannic.

I was not one of the people in line, having no urge to listen to inane chatter for half an hour just to shake hands for five seconds with the king. Instead, while Jane was busy conversing with several ladies about the latest New York copies of Parisian fashions, I partook of a decent rum flip and professionally surveyed the surroundings. The stone-built palace was pleasant and spacious, well made in the neo-Florentine architectural style. But it was clearly not designed for defense, for it was too open and had no defensive barriers or positions, other than the eight-foot-high wall surrounding the palace grounds.

On the other hand, the protective detail was far more professional than I anticipated. They were a platoon of Royal Guards from the adjacent barracks-armory known as the Halekoa, or House of Warriors, about a block away to the north. That structure was built for defense, being a parapet-topped, one-story fortress with several two-story towers. All of the walls had cross-shaped firing slits, giving the place the image of a thirteenth-century Norman fortress.

The only artillery pieces I observed were two pairs of old Napoleon, smooth-bore field cannons on display in the garden and two modern, breech-loading, brass ten-pounders on the far side of the grounds. I surmised the Napoleons were there mainly for ceremonial duties since they were essentially useless for anything else. The two breechloaders were relatively modern but not enough to defend against a modern military attack.

Many of the guards were intently watching the perimeter while others watched the guests near the king and queen, ready to intervene if needed. Those inside the palace were all armed with Colt revolvers in flap holsters, the outside soldiers with twenty-year-old Springfield rifles. A few had new Winchester repeater rifles. The uniforms were similar to British Royal Marines: dark blue tunics and white trousers with white patent leather crossbelts and ammunition pouches and white helmets. The private soldiers were all natives. The sergeants were a combination of whites and Hawaiians, as were the company-grade officers I saw scattered about.

Standing near the bar, I was speculating on how the kingdom would defend itself from European attack when an ample-sized lady with a strong Boston accent sidled alongside and whispered to me in a huff, "Well! Now I know we've descended back into the depths of savagery in these islands. First, the king not only allows the return of that heathen *hula* dance, he encourages it! And now I hear that he's invited that Scottish lout Stevenson to call upon him here at the palace when he visits Honolulu. Have you heard that information also, sir?"

The matron was holding a glass of orange juice quite daintily, but her expression was one of outrage. I figured her to be with the fundamentalist missionary faction, even though she'd obviously been committing the sin of gluttony during her long life.

"Stevenson?" I asked. "Sorry, madam, but I am new here and don't know whom you speak of."

That set her off on a diatribe. "Oh, you must've heard of him. Robert Louis Stevenson, the Scotchman who wrote that Devil-pleasing book they call *Doctor Jekyll and Mister Hyde*. It was printed two years ago, and the paganish sorts back home have been all agog over it. And that's not his only one. He wrote a trashy book called *Treasure Island* a few years back."

She huffed in indignation and added with a nod to our royal host, "King Kalakaua fancies himself a good judge of such things and thinks Stevenson is a literary mastermind. The so-called Christian king can't wait until the writer arrives on his yacht in two weeks so he can fawn over him. The newspaper says the king wants to have him here in the palace to discuss books!"

Another huff vented out of her thinly pursed lips. "Well, I do say! Why would any decent person want to talk about the rubbish that Scotchman writes, especially with the diseased, old, sordid reprobate himself? And, of course, you just *know* how those writer types are, with their disgusting views and habits. No telling what he'll do in this climate with our natives when he sees a hula dance."

"Hmm . . . ," I muttered noncommittally while searching for an avenue of escape.

She leaned closer and poked a fat finger at me. "I've even heard that Stevenson is completely *addicted* to strong spirits."

The lady chose that tardy moment to get a whiff of my rum flip and realized, with undisguised horror in her widened eyes, that I wasn't a fellow pure-orange-juice drinker but quite obviously a degenerate pagan like her foes. There was a little gasp, and suddenly it grew cold in our corner of the room. Having educated me on the cultural deficiencies of His Majesty and the rumored lifestyle of Robert Louis Stevenson, my righteous companion began glancing about for greener pastures.

Providentially for both of us, she saw a kindred soul in the distance and informed me, "Oh, there's Mildred. I must tell her about this dreadful Stevenson business! Have a *pleasant* evening, sir." She said that last with mocking insincerity just before she spun on her heel to steam off toward Mildred, probably to tell her about the reprobate she'd just met.

My sense of humor got the best of me. I counterattacked her departing posterior by loudly commenting, "Oh, *that* Stevenson! Yes, madam, I quite agree with His Majesty's opinion. R.L. Stevenson's a great writer. Hope I can meet him when he's here."

Two fellows standing nearby at the bar laughed at my jest, then went back to their conversation. It was a dialogue I found interesting. One of them was a young Hawaiian in an officer's uniform. He was a proponent of a trans-Pacific Greater Polynesia, headed by the enlightened monarch of Hawaii. The other had the flaccidity of age and too much drink and thought the Polynesians of the Pacific no match for the ever-expanding Europeans, of which he was one. I thought this subject potentially educational for me, so I joined them.

"Good evening, gentlemen. I'm Peter Wake of Baltimore, just passing through aboard the steamer *Australia.*"

The young man said, "Good evening, Mr. Wake. I'm Captain David Aukai, adjutant to General Dominis and artillery officer of His Hawaiian Majesty's Royal Guard. This is my friend, Monsieur Jean Touchard, owner of the wine emporium in our city. He is originally from Paris."

We all shook hands and in the next few minutes I heard the background of each man. Touchard had moved to New York in 1872 right after the Franco-Prussian War. After two years in New York City, he headed west to San Francisco for a while, then arrived in Honolulu in '81. His emporium sold French cognac, champagne, and wine. By his attire, I deduced it was doing well.

Aukai was from the big island of Hawaii, and his name meant *seaman* in the native language. He wasn't as large as some Hawaiians I'd seen, but he was more intense in manner and word, and his eyes bespoke a shrewd type of intelligence. He'd been in the army for seven years, had done some training with the Italian army, and was scheduled to visit army posts in the United States the next year, particularly our coastal fortifications. This impressive young man spoke several languages, had been to college, and worked directly for General Dominis.

Touchard inquired of me in fluent American-style English, "So, how do you find yourself in the Pacific, Mr. Wake? It is a very long way from Maryland."

"Looking for good investments. I heard there were good opportunities in Samoa and the islands over in that area. The plantations there are said to be the most efficient in the Pacific."

Aukai's expression tightened. "That is a dangerous area for you Americans to visit, Mr. Wake. Your country and the Germans are about to have a war there. It may have already started, in fact."

I played the naïve *gringo*. "Yes, Captain, I heard. There were rumors about all that ridiculousness when I left the States, but I'm sure it'll blow over and the saner minds will prevail. It's silly for either us or the Germans to have a war about Samoa. We should be devoting our energies to making money."

"Perhaps you are right, Mr. Wake, but many wars have started over making money. Or more precisely, who gets to make the money."

I persisted in my gullibility. "Well, they shouldn't. There's enough to be made for everyone. Say, what have you heard about the situation in Samoa, Captain? I've asked around since we arrived in Honolulu, and no one can tell me anything except that war hasn't started and that the Germans haven't attacked our ships yet."

"Our information is that the Germans and Americans are still in a standoff, but no battle has taken place. I would strongly advise you to forget Samoa. There are many opportunities for investment here in Hawaii. This is a stable and modern country."

Touchard harrumphed indignantly and put a hand on my shoulder. His breath reeked of rum. "Yes, forget Samoa, Mr. Wake. Too many damned Germans down there. They make money, that is true, but how can you live with them? No sense of humor, no appreciation of the finer things in life."

"We have Germans here, Jean," cautioned Aukai. "In fact, over there I see the German consul."

Touchard lifted an eyebrow and wagged his head defiantly. "I don't care if the new kaiser himself is here. I'll say what I want. They have a bad reputation and have alienated the natives in the Pacific. Even that German who played cards with the king is no longer in favor and has left. Maybe the rest of them in Honolulu will go too."

"Why don't you like the Germans?" I asked, guessing the answer.

"I have vivid memories of them overrunning France seventeen years ago, Mr. Wake. They've dominated Europe since then, and now they are trying to dominate us out here in paradise. Hawaii tried to stop them in Samoa in eighty-seven but failed. Afterward, Bismarck threatened to bombard Honolulu to teach Kalakaua a lesson. Your country can stop the Germans now in Samoa, but will you?"

I sidestepped his question with one of my own. "Excuse me. This country, Hawaii, tried to stop the Germans in Samoa? I didn't know that. What happened?"

Captain Aukai explained. "Yes. In early eighty-seven, His Hawaiian Majesty proposed a treaty of friendship with King Malietoa Laupepa of Samoa. It was signed in February of that year. A few months later, His Hawaiian Majesty sent the Hawaiian Navy to Apia, the capital of the Kingdom of Samoa, and offered a mutual treaty of military and political confederation to King Malietoa Laupepa. We tried to form a Greater Polynesia. A good and noble idea, but unfortunately it failed, for the Germans pressured the Samoans against it. And yes, Chancellor Bismarck became angry at what he considered our interfering and made comments that he would like to have his navy bombard us here in Honolulu. I think the presence of one of your warships here dissuaded them."

This was all new to me. "Did you say the Hawaiian Navy? Forgive me my regrettable ignorance, sir, but I didn't know you had a navy."

Touchard, who had been fuming while Aukai spoke, suddenly barged in.

"Ha! Another of that fool Gibson's stupid ideas. A total waste of money and time. Hawaiian *Navy?* The *Kaimiloa* was a rented guano steamer with a couple of four-pounder saluting guns. The whole affair was a sad joke—a joke of a ship with a joke of a drunk named Jackson for its captain and a joke of a mutinous crew. The German Navy laughed them out of Samoa, right about the same time the Hawaiian League ran Gibson out of office here with bayonets. This drivel about Hawaii run by Hawaiians is the biggest joke of all, like that Greater Polynesia business, but Kalakaua still says it like he believes it. The Merry Monarch. More like the merry fool. I am in serious need of a drink."

He'd referred to the "Bayonet Constitution," the derisive term among many locals for the 1887 coup and constitutional rewrite by the Hawaiian League. I doubted that those within the palace used that phrase in public. The reference to the Merry Monarch was in reference to Kalakaua's well-known proclivity for enjoying himself and playing the cheerful host to visitors.

Aukai wasn't amused by the Frenchman's rude cynicism and warned him, "Jean, I think you have had too much and fear the rum has had its way with you. You are sounding discourteous regarding your host. Please comport yourself more civilly, *mon ami*, or leave the palace now."

To me, Aukai said, "Excuse me, Mr. Wake, but I see that I am being summoned by the general. Perhaps we can speak again. I reiterate my recommendation that you stay out of Samoa. Look elsewhere for a good investment."

After Aukai departed for General Dominis, Touchard wagged his head and opined, "A good man, that Aukai, but delusional. He's a true believer in the king's Hawaii for Hawaiians slogan. Somehow he thinks the king can carry it off, even as the missionaries and commercialists take more and more power from him."

"Captain Aukai strikes me as a good man also, Monsieur Touchard. I think Hawaii will need men like him in the years to come."

"Yes, but I wonder how long he will last. Aukai distrusts the Germans just as much as I do, he just won't say it in public."

"Oh, he does?"

"Yes, and he has good reason. Most of *le Boche* have left royal employment, but there are a few still around the palace, like that one."

With disdain, he indicated the musicians on the balcony. Evidently Touchard's anti-Germanism even took in the smiling bandmaster.

The Frenchman then nodded over his shoulder toward the corner where Colonel Starkloff stood, surveying the room. "That man is one of the very worst. Prussian with Russian blood too—a bad combination. He was with Bismarck's bastards in France in seventy-one. And now he is here, hating Hawaiians even more than he hates Frenchmen. Some in Honolulu think he's a German spy, but I do not. He isn't smart enough to be a spy."

As if he overheard us, Starkloff swung his attention in our direction.

"So why *is* he here?" I asked.

Touchard was getting louder with every word. "Because some of the royal household wanted a Prussian to train the guard battalion that protects them, and they persuaded the king to approve it. They do not trust the Americans or British anymore. Starkloff was sitting around in Shanghai, available and cheap, so they got him. He is simply another hired brute in the Pacific—one of many."

"So the German government didn't send him?"

"Oh, no. He is a mercenary with nowhere else to go. Kicked out of the regiment years ago, I've heard, for some honor violation. Wanders around the Pacific telling the locals how to use the new military toys they just bought, but he takes care to keep away from all of the German islands. Honor violation. Can you imagine that, Mr. Wake? I didn't know they even had honor in their army. We never saw it in France. No humor, no honor, no *amour*, no compassion, no refinement, no champagne or decent cognac— and they like to eat that terrible *sauerkraut*. Mark my words, sir. They have dominated Europe for twenty years, they have taken over large parts of Africa, and now they are spreading all over the Pacific like parasitic vermin."

He frowned and sadly said, "They will not stop until they take over the world. Can you imagine Hawaiians eating sauerkraut and speaking German?"

People around us were beginning to notice his harangue, and some were staring. I decided to exit from Touchard and was backing away when he uttered a final comment.

"But Starkloff got his just rewards, courtesy of the American widow. Ah, such delicious irony for the arrogant Colonel Starkloff. Kindred souls—that is what those two are. Both are parasites."

I moved back toward him and in a low voice asked, "What widow?"

HE nodded toward Jane. "The pretty one over there. She got Starkloff's money, and now she has her eye on old Dominis. He should beware of her."

I took a flute of champagne off the tray of a passing steward and gave it to Touchard. "You look thirsty, Jean. What did you mean by 'parasite'?"

"She is a Frisco gold digger, Mr. Wake, pure and simple. That's how she lives."

He said it matter-of-factly, as if it was common knowledge. I wanted to know more, so I prodded him with, "Well, that's a very serious accusation, Jean. I find it hard to believe. That lady over there certainly doesn't look like a gold digger to me. How do you know for sure?"

He laughed sarcastically, his words coming out low now too, for he didn't want everyone to hear his next comment.

"Because she got *my* money six months before she got the German colonel's."

Well, well, I thought, *my time ashore in Hawaii has turned out to be very productive indeed. I'll have to double my efforts to befriend Mrs. Cushman, for she's just the sort of woman who can prove very useful in my mission.*

But that's not what I told the French wine merchant of Honolulu in response to his revelations about Hawaii, the Germans, and the pretty widow, Jane Cushman.

No, to him I merely raised my glass and said, "*Merci beaucoup pour l'information au sujet de la femme fatale, mon ami. Bonne chance avec l'amour et la vie, Monseiur Touchard. Adieu.*"

I never did see Aukai again that evening. After stumbling my way through a couple of waltzes with various ladies, both white and Hawaiian, I made my excuses and returned to the steamer. I would have escorted Jane back to the ship, even looked forward to it, but she had disappeared from sight.

I wasn't concerned about her safety or virtue in the least. It had become quite clear to me that Jane Cushman could take care of herself.

11
The Doldrums

Steam Ship Australia
Central Pacific Ocean
Lat. 5° S, Long. 169° W
10 P.M., Friday
11 January 1889

The equatorial regions of the world's oceans are notorious among seamen for unsettled weather. No steady trade winds blow there. There are only light, unpredictable zephyrs interspersed with savage thunderstorms. The most common conditions are an undulating, greasy sea and a heavily overcast atmosphere. Stars do not shine, and the nights are some of the blackest on Earth. The ocean is no longer blue, nor is the sky. Both are gray, a monotony of color as far as you can see, blended so uniformly that the horizon is lost to sight. This fatigued light washes out even the colors on your ship, for no bright sun brings them out. You are on a gray ship moving through a gray universe.

For ships dependent upon wind, such areas are to be avoided by staying at least twelve degrees north or south of the equator. If transit of the area is absolutely necessary, it is done with as much food and water aboard as possible and by crossing the area at a right angle to reduce the time within. Sailing ships will wallow for days or weeks at a time in the region, waiting for the next thunderstorm to either dismast them or provide propulsion for several more miles.

Veteran sailors have a legendary name for these regions. To think of it makes the toughest Jack Tar shake his head in anxious contemplation. To speak it aloud is considered bad luck and is never done at sea, lest the Devil below hear and think it an impudent challenge to his authority. I hesitate even to write it, but in order to understand what happened there on this voyage, the reader of this account must understand the place that sailors dread: the Doldrums.

As *Australia* steamed south-southwest at fully fourteen nautical miles every hour, the Doldrums lived up to their reputation. But it wasn't just the sky and barometer that were unsettled on this leg of our long voyage, for a strange effect came over the passengers as the heat and humidity pervaded their every waking moment. First class or steerage or forecastle—every soul aboard felt it.

We crossed the Equator at the 168th meridian and entered the Southern Ocean in January, a month into the annual cyclonic season, when immense tropical storms move through the vast uninhabited wasteland of the Pacific. Word spread among the passengers that the low swells we were facing were from a typhoon somewhere to our southwest.

In first class, most of my fellow passengers initially ignored this news or treated it whimsically, concentrating instead on their pink gins and card games. One deck below, in second class, they had fewer diversions. Conversations over beer began to involve weather predictions by armchair prognosticators, with many a prolonged debate on the subject.

Down in steerage, grandiosely called third class, things were different. At the bottom of the ship, the uneasy motion, foul air, and lack of amenities—for both individual and social needs—

fed rumors among those less experienced at sea that the ship was headed directly into a typhoon, where she would ultimately founder. The rumor's real horror was in the statement that there were only enough boats for the elite on the decks above. This led to discontent among the steerage passengers, and no amount of persuasion from the officers and crew could alter their mind-set.

On a ship at sea, even one 376 feet long like *Australia*, word spreads fast, for the gossips have nothing else to do and enjoy seeing others' discomfort at hearing bad news. With iniquitous speed, the word went fore and aft and up through the ship.

A word about tropical storms is in order at this juncture. I think the readers of this account will probably be familiar with Atlantic hurricanes and their mode of travel and circulation, but I should point out that the South Pacific Ocean works differently— just the opposite, as a matter of fact. Whereas Atlantic storms circulate counterclockwise and travel north and west, South Pacific typhoons circulate clockwise and move south and east.

Typhoons in this region are frequently stronger and larger than Atlantic hurricanes, and some scientific minds suggest the reason for this is the huge areas of unfettered ocean. In both the Pacific and the Atlantic, cyclonic storms are engendered at least twelve degrees from the equator. Most reach their most catastrophic strengths between seventeen and twenty-seven degrees from the equator.

The reader will note that on this day, the eleventh of January, our ship was only at five degrees, twenty-five minutes south, far from any potential storm. That meant that the increasing sea swells we were seeing come out of the west signified a large, powerful storm was somewhere to our southwest, probably heading south before it turned easterly. Thus, we were on the weak, safer side, and our course would take us along behind the storm's track.

The barometer glass was a bit low at28.7 but steady, as expected with the evidence around us. The overcast had no large formations indicating an approaching cyclonic system. Thus the situation presented no alarm to me. We were moving through the ripple effect of the storm's seas. The experienced seamen aboard knew this. Not so an increasing percentage of the passengers.

I, ostensibly a landsman from Baltimore, kept my mouth shut on the subject and focused my attention on gaining any intelligence about the situation in Samoa and the other German-held islands. Not much was forthcoming from my fellow passengers, for few had experience of Samoa, and I discovered that there were no Germans aboard in first class, a rare state of affairs. Only one was in second class.

It was opined by the purser that this unusualness was because we were an American ship and German citizens didn't want to be caught aboard in the event of war. Nevertheless, I persisted in my social forays with a view toward subtly gaining something—anything—of value that would assist me once I reached the war zone.

But none could be had, for the Doldrums had done its insidious work. With no breeze, the heat became oppressive in the cabins and salons. That turned minds to a more negative frame, susceptible to pessimistic talk. I began hearing conversational rumblings as the sea swells persisted and those lower-deck rumors ascended into even our privileged area. Stewards denied them, of course, but did so with hesitation, adding fuel to the fire.

The effects were tangible and rapid. Nerves began to become frayed. Slights were imagined and remembered. Discussions became arguments. Silence at the dinner table, once rare, now reigned for longer periods of time. Tense expressions and accentuated tempers led to studious avoidance of politics and religion as banter disappeared altogether. A fight in second class resulted in a passenger being sent to the brig and his victim to the sick bay with a knife wound. Ships' officers traveled in pairs in the second-class and steerage areas, on the lookout to immediately end any altercation before it could turn bloody.

So it had become aboard that good ship on the Friday night when Jane and I shared an after-dinner brandy at the promenade deck railing just abaft and below the bridge. It was a secluded part of the ship, away from the deck lights further aft. Underneath us was the incessant rhythm of water racing along the hull, while above us cinders roiled up from the funnel, little red specks flitting in the dark.

Looking out over the inky blackness, Jane remarked to me about the changes she'd seen among our companions. "They seem on the verge of fisticuffs sometimes, Peter. It's ruining the dinners. What's wrong with everybody? I've done this voyage before and never seen it like this."

"Yes, I must admit that things are a bit tense lately," I replied nonchalantly. "This weather has people on edge, and the sea swells add to it. These rumors about a monster typhoon have made it worse."

She leaned against me when the ship rolled and stayed there. "Well, the behavior I'm seeing is simply *unsuitable* for our class of passengers. One would think they would remember who they are and act accordingly."

I thought that comment a bit disingenuous but glossed over it. No sense in tipping my hand. "Yes, my dear, I agree. They should certainly conduct themselves as their station in life requires. And all this nonsensical worry is spoiling our fun."

We were close enough I could see her face in the gloom. Her eyes showed no reluctance as she murmured, "I don't think we should allow anything to spoil our fun, Peter. After all, I may never see you again after we arrive at Auckland, so this is our time, our moment in history, to live and love and enjoy life. I think you feel the same way, though you try to hide it in public. You can be so detached and cold."

"I thought I've been very friendly!"

"You've been politely friendly, which is not what I'm talking about and you know it. I think you are playing coy with me, Mr. Peter Wake of Baltimore. Is that the way a man acts when he's alone with a woman back East?"

I've been accused by women of many things, but being coy has never been one of them. It was true that I had kept my distance from Jane for the first half of the voyage. I knew she had discreetly spent time with other gentlemen, noting that age, looks, and wedding rings were no barriers to her attentions. I harbored no illusions that the time she was spending with me was anything other than a reconnaissance to ascertain the exact nature of my wealth and the potential for its transfer to her purse. We both had missions to accomplish and were both desperate in our own way and degree.

But the salient factor was that only one of us knew the true nature of the other. My mission was paramount, and the more I knew of Jane Cushman, the more I realized she could be an excellent asset to help me accomplish that mission. But the time wasn't right just yet to make her an asset. That would come later. And it would never be right for her to know me in any way other than as an acquaintance.

I will fully admit, however, that I am not a celibate saint nor immune to the charms of a woman like Jane. My state of mild inebriation and the loneliness of my life were working mightily against me as we stood at that railing, her body molded against mine and her arm around my waist. She knew precisely what she was doing and the result it would produce in a man.

Jane snuggled even closer. "Hmm, I can tell you're no longer coldly detached, Peter. I do believe that I've finally thawed out that blood of yours, darling." She caressed my face, then my throat. Her hand slid south along my chest. "Why, Mr. Wake, you're so hot you're getting positively tropical."

My willpower was fading quickly in the heat. I began to rationalize my weakening defenses. What harm could it really do to give in and enjoy one of life's finer experiences for an evening? It would just be for one night. Besides, I had nothing else to do right then.

"Well, I suppose I am getting a bit heated," I admitted, my hand around her waist and now wandering northward. "After all, we are in the tropics, my dear. One's blood does tend to boil occasionally. And you know the saying: When in Rome. . . ."

Right at that moment, at 10:25 P.M. on Friday, January 11, 1889, is when all of the devious preparatory work done by the Doldrums came to fruition. But not in the way I was anticipating.

12

Lovers' Quarrels

Steam Ship Australia
Central Pacific Ocean
Lat. 5° S, Long. 169° W
10:25 P.M., Friday
11 January 1889

Twenty feet away from us, the gate leading down a ladder to the second-class passenger deck flung open. A bulky man emerged from the ladder onto our deck. He immediately marched directly toward us.

Jane recognized him first and gasped, "My God, it's Ludwig! Why are *you* here?"

Colonel Starkloff was without spiked helmet, uniform, or even a coat or tie. His white shirt was unbuttoned and in disarray, flapping in the slight air caused by the ship's movement. Startled by this apparition from nowhere, I didn't register the large revolver in his right hand until he was a couple of feet away and closing in on us. The barrel was pointed toward Jane.

She, looking at his face and unaware of the danger, inquired in a perturbed manner, "What in the world are you doing here, Ludwig?"

"Ach, you know vhy! I haff come for you, *mein Liebling*," he snarled.

"Oh, for goodness' sake, Ludwig, how very ludicrous. I told you before that we're through. It was an affair, nothing more. I do believe that this awful heat must've gotten to you."

His bulging eyes were two white dots in the dark as he roared out in rage to her, "I am not a fool. You are *mein Liebling*, Jane, und only I vill have you!"

I stepped toward him just as Jane saw the revolver and screamed, "No, Ludwig!"

A shadowy movement come up behind Starkloff, and I presumed him to be an accomplice. The colonel was still the closest threat, however, so I went for his weapon first. My intention was to lock my fingers around the cylinder and prevent it from turning. When done correctly, this will stop the revolver from firing.

My hand was still six inches away from the weapon when a muffled pop sounded, followed by another, then a third. The revolver clattered to the deck as Starkloff lurched forward onto Jane, propelling them both against the railing. Another scream caught in her throat, coming out as a hoarse moan. The colonel fell, grasping at her arms on his way down, until he lay in a twitching pile at her feet.

Not knowing where the weapon was on the deck, I dove on him and pinioned his hands until I felt no movement. There was no sign of breathing. Letting go of his hands, I groped around the deck with my hands until I found Starkloff's revolver. Then I searched him for other weapons but found none. In fact, there was nothing in his pockets except for a gold watch. The revolver was a standard, German army–issue, 10.6-millimeter 1879 Reichrevolver model, which I aimed at my new target, the second man, who had apparently just shot Starkloff.

He immediately raised his hands in surrender, and I was stunned for the second time in thirty seconds. It was Captain

David Aukai. He and I stared at each other as he slowly lowered his hands and put a derringer in a trouser pocket.

I threw Starkloff's pistol overboard. Jane stood there wordlessly, staring at the body at her feet.

Aukai glanced around, then spoke to me in a low voice, "Glad you decided not to shoot first and *then* figure out it was me."

"What the hell are you doing here?" was my rude response, for I was not happy with either the Hawaiian or the German aboard. I didn't need complications like the one that had just arisen.

Aukai said, "What, here on the ship? Well, that's a bit of a long story, Mr. Wake. And we don't have time for that right now, do we? As for here on this deck, it's simple. I heard Colonel Starkloff ranting about Mrs. Cushman in the second-class gentlemen's smoking room. He was acting like a madman, darting around the room, soaked in sweat, waving his arms about, and making the most dangerous threats. Fortunately, no one else was there to see him."

Aukai shook his head. "I tried to stop him from getting up here, but I am afraid he fooled me by pretending to calm down. He'd been drinking schnapps. I tried to get him to return to his cabin and sleep it off, but then he pushed a chair between us and stormed away at a run. I was too far behind to prevent him from getting up the ladder to this deck. Once I got here, I had to shoot him." He turned to Jane. "I had no other choice."

She made no reply, still standing there stone-faced, transfixed by Starkloff's crumpled body. His dead eyes stared out at the sea beyond the railing.

The scene was nothing short of bizarre. Here we were, politely discussing how and why we'd just killed a man on the upper-class promenade deck of the most celebrated liner in the Pacific. I finally came to my senses.

I held out a hand. "Captain Aukai, you saved us. Thank you. We need to talk later, but right now we have to deal with the body."

Aukai took a deep breath. "I suggest overboard would be best.

Grab the legs. I'll get the shoulders."

In seconds it was done. The splash was barely noticeable against the constant rush of the waves. I took Jane by the shoulders and led her aft, toward a doorway leading to the main salon.

"Go to your stateroom right now and stay there. I'll be by in a few minutes, dear."

She walked away in a stupor, still unable to say a word. To Aukai, I said, "I'll meet you on the other side of the ship, down on your deck by the ladder, in ten minutes."

To my surprise, he accepted my order without hesitation. "Yes, sir."

Once they were both gone, I bent over and studied the deck for any sign of blood, almost impossible in the darkness. Since none of the bullets had exited into Jane and I felt no liquid on the deck, I surmised the wounds to Starkloff's back had not produced an appreciable amount of blood. With any luck, no one had heard the muffled shots or seen the scuffle.

I heard approaching footsteps. It was two deck officers. They were in no hurry, just making the hourly turn around the first-class area. I ducked into the doorway to the gentlemen's smoker. The few men still awake were elderly, minding their brandies and cigars and half-asleep. They didn't even acknowledge me as I passed through to the starboard side. I went aft to the ladder, then descended to the second-class deck.

Captain Aukai was waiting there for me. I was struck by how extraordinarily composed he appeared for having just killed a professional military man on a crowded passenger liner.

That bothered me.

13
Complications

Steam Ship Australia
Central Pacific Ocean
Lat. 5° S, Long. 170° W
10:30 P.M., Friday
11 January 1889

The Hawaiian spoke first. "I suppose you are wondering why I am here on this ship, Commander Wake. Due to what just happened, I suppose I have to trust you, so I'll explain."

His use of my rank took me aback. I thought my pretense was secure. He smiled at my reaction.

"I'll start with how I know about you, Commander. After I left you and Monsieur Touchard at the soiree that night at the palace, I talked to Commander Nichols of Her Britannic Majesty's ship *Cormorant*. We became friends several weeks ago, when his ship and a sister Royal Navy ship had a cricket match at Christmas, which was played right there at the Iolani Palace.

"Well, to make a long story short, he was talking to General Dominis when the general summoned me. When I got there, the general asked Nichols to repeat what he'd just said. His words were, 'Why is an American naval intelligence officer in Honolulu? Especially portraying himself as a civilian businessman?' "

"You can imagine General Dominis's thoughts—and mine—upon hearing this. I asked Nichols how he knew you were in ONI. He said he'd had occasion to meet you in Washington and in London and that he'd heard you were involved in a shady operation in the Bahama Islands last summer."

I didn't remember Nichols personally. I'd met a bunch of Brit officers over the last few years. But the information about the Bahamas was disturbingly correct and very confidential. Not many people had knowledge of my experiences in the Bahamas, but I knew that British army intelligence did. I stood there waiting for the inevitable accusation that I was spying on Hawaii. It didn't come.

Instead, Aukai said, "I was directed by the general to ascertain why you were in Honolulu. Some quick inquiries to various sources yielded the benign information that you had not been anywhere other than at an afternoon tea party at the hotel, your consulate, and the palace. I was told that in conversations at the tea party and at the soiree later, you expressed seemingly genuine views that were contrary to American colonization of the Pacific.

"Based upon all of that, I concluded your mission—for it was clear to me that you are on a mission—does not include Hawaii. Obviously Honolulu was merely a stop on your voyage, the destination of which I believe will be Samoa. I further believe you are working against the Germans there. That is what I reported to the general the next morning, just before the steamer departed."

It was neatly said. But a lot was not divulged. I had a couple questions of my own.

"I congratulate you on your efforts, Captain Aukai. Yes, I am a commander in the U. S. Navy and am on my way to the western Pacific. But why are you aboard? And why was Starkloff?"

He was about to answer when we heard footsteps. I saw forms cross in front of a deck light farther aft. Two men in uniforms were approaching. They were the same pair of deck officers, now touring the second-class section. They saw me and changed course for us.

The younger one said pleasantly, "Sir, this is not your first-class area. This is second-class. You can reach your area by going up that ladder."

"Oh, right. Sorry. We were just talking about Hawaii. Beautiful place, you know. Sure is prettier than Baltimore. I'll head up to my room in just a minute."

Both of them were eyeing Aukai sharply now. I could see they were wondering why he was talking to me. Was he a con man after a rich swell from the deck above?

The older officer turned to me and forced a smile, sounding like he'd had this conversation a hundred times before. "We'll see you to your cabin, sir, if you'd like. And just so you know in the future, the ladders down to this deck are restricted to the officers and crew only. There is a sign to that effect on the gate."

"Oh, it appears I have violated some serious rule of the sea. I do apologize, gentlemen. No need to see me up to my room. I'll be heading there shortly."

There followed an awkward silence during which nobody moved. The officers stood there, waiting. I started for the ladder. "Yes, well, it is getting late and I don't want to impose on your valuable time, gentlemen, so I'll head up now. We'll talk at Auckland, Mr. Aukai. I want to hear more about the Polynesian culture."

Aukai was a quick study. He waved good-bye and said, "Yes, I will look forward to it. I can tell you more about my church's work in Hawaii. Until then, have a nice voyage, Mr. Wake."

14
The Offer

Steam Ship Australia
Central Pacific Ocean
Lat. 5° S, Long. 170° W
10:50 P.M., Friday
11 January 1889

My mind was a chaotic swirl, assessing the consequences of all that had happened in the previous half hour. My preoccupation made it all the more of an astonishment when I arrived at the door to my cabin and opened it.

There, clad in a transparent nightgown and sitting upright in my bed, was none other than Mrs. Jane Cushman. Her black hair had always been perfectly coiffed in the French style, but now it was loose, cascading around her shoulders. She made no attempt to conceal her figure inside the gown, and I suddenly realized my gaze was lingering over her while the door was wide open.

I quickly remedied that problem and blurted out the obvious question, "How'd you get in here?"

She laughed softly, with a distinctly naughty inflection. "I've always been amazed at what money can do, Peter. Even just one little dollar. Especially with stewards. I hope you're not offended that I'm here. You didn't seem offended before, when we were out on deck."

This woman's audaciousness was astounding. And if she was this brazen, she was damned dangerous. Had she searched through my possessions? None that were in plain view were incriminating about my true business and intentions. But I immediately worried that the steward had somehow gotten her into the cabin's locked safe. There was more than seven thousand dollars in it and several other things that would be very difficult to explain. Theoretically, only I and the chief purser could get in. Now I wasn't so sure.

"Jane, look, I know how it was with us out there on deck, before Starkloff . . ."

Her face changed instantly. The pixie eyes went from delight to anguish. "Poor Ludwig!"

She started crying, wiping her tears with the bed linen. "Obviously he'd gone demented, but why? I just don't understand why, Peter. He wasn't himself at all. It must have been these awful Doldrums and this appalling heat infecting his mind. It's been so terribly humid, worse than I can ever remember."

More likely it was you, my dear, I reflected. I shook my head woefully, trying to project an air of shocked upper-class innocence and revulsion at the events on deck.

She ran her hands down over her body while looking me in the eye. "Peter, I can't stand this suffocating heat. I actually felt like I was going to die in my clothing. But this feels so much better and cooler. Do you like this negligee? I found it in a Parisian shop in San Francisco. It's very soft, sensual. . . . Come on over here and see how soft it is."

It took all my self-discipline to say, "You should go back to your cabin, Jane. After what's happened, I'm no longer in the right frame of mind for love-making."

Her face changed to a little-girl frown. "No, Peter. I don't want to be alone tonight. You are a widower. I am a widow. We both know about loneliness and heartache, so please don't make me leave now. We can just hold each other, nothing more. And I promise I'll leave before sunrise, so no one will see me here. But not now, please. . . ."

She reached out a hand toward me.

What should I do? What would a widower Baltimore businessman do? It was too soon to end my façade with her and reveal my profession. That would have to wait until we had arrived in Auckland, for I needed her to be desperate for money when I offered it.

The businessman would give in, I decided. That would preserve my deception. But was it safe? No. Jane's behavior and attitude had more than a touch of arrogance in it, which steeled my will. She had the potential to be become, at the very least, a diversion from my mission. At the worst, intimacy might lead to a slipup on my part, compromising my mission.

And the mission was more important than anything else. This one wasn't an intellectual exercise or background investigation or espionage for secret information. I was there to try to stop a war. Or win it.

"Jane, you know how I feel about you, but now you're going to leave."

The next morning, I seized upon an opportunity that presented itself. My cabin steward, an Australian by the name of Wilson who heretofore had been a marginal performer, couldn't hide his smug look as he entered my cabin to deliver my early morning repast.

Wilson had the mug of an experienced drunkard: a red knob of a nose, drooping jowls, and watery, yellow eyes. As he put down the tray holding my coffee and croissants, I saw him studying the bed closely. A sneer was starting to show on his face.

"No, Wilson, she didn't spend the night. I asked her to leave. Now I have to decide what to do about *you* and whether I should inform Captain Houdelette of your misdeed."

Before he could answer, I walked over to him and pushed his sleeve cuff up his arm, exposing a faded tattoo I'd caught a glimpse of when I saw him staggering by the grog shops on the Honolulu waterfront. The tattoo was a large D on the top of his right hand, near the wrist. It had obviously been the object of some incompetent attempts to change it into something less shameful. But the D was still visible.

"So you were in the Andrew, weren't you?"

The sneer disappeared completely. In its place was a look of terror, for I was dead-on in my accusation. I'd used the old British sailor name for the Royal Navy, showing him I knew the meaning and origin of that tattoo. His reaction told me his present superiors didn't know about his past. It wasn't the time to let up. I needed to have him in total fear of me.

"Oh, yes, you were a Royal Navy man, at least until you deserted. Then they found you, tattooed you, and sent you to Australia on one of the convict ships. Let's see, they ended the practices of branding and convict exile in the mid-sixties, so you must have been one of the last to be sent out here. You're old enough that I'll bet you have stripes on your back from your first desertion, before they banned flogging in the fifties, don't you? They didn't brand you back then for the first offense. So you were a serial rabbit." Rabbit was an old term for a man who ran every chance he had. Wilson shrank back from me, his eyes darting toward the door.

"I figure you must've worn very long sleeves your whole time aboard, trying to hide that tattoo. But the heat and drink in Honolulu got to you, and you pushed them up just enough for me to see it. I wonder what the captain would say about that tattoo and how you got it."

I said the next with a sneer of my own. "You're not the sort of man who should work in first class, are you, Wilson? In fact, you shouldn't even be aboard this ship or any reputable passenger ship at all."

I'd hit the target with every verbal shot.

Wilson reverted to naval discipline and jumped to attention, blabbering, "Oh, sir, I am so sorry! I do most sincerely apologize. The lady said she was your fiancé, sir. And, you see, I just thought that, well . . ."

"Exactly, Wilson. You just thought wrong though. The privacy of my cabin was intruded upon. Your thinking was colored, no doubt, by the bribe she gave you. I wonder what the captain will think of that. What other misdeeds have you done for bribes? What personal possessions of the passengers have you looked through? And what all have you stolen from them?"

"Please, sir, I beg you not to bother the captain with this matter. I made the wrong decision, as you say, sir. Please don't report me. I need this work."

I let him stew for a few more seconds, then said, "Hmm. I'll make my decision regarding you when we reach Auckland. Until then, I expect outstanding attendance to my requests. That may mitigate my anger with you. Understood?"

His relief was pathetic. "Understood very well, sir. I am at your service, sir."

"Very good. Then listen carefully, for I have a simple task for you. You know that I am an American business investor looking at plantations here in the Pacific. Well, I want to know about some fellow passengers. I believe they may be competitors, and in my business I need to know about the following: What do they have for baggage, clothing, and money? Whom are they sharing time with while aboard, both in the salon and in their cabins? What documents do they have? All this is to be accomplished by you alone, with no one else aware. *No one.* Got it?"

His answer was a reticent, "Yes, sir."

"The first is a man named David Aukai, a Hawaiian fellow down in second class. The second is a German named Ludwig Starkloff, also in second class. The third is Mrs. Jane Cushman, on this deck. You will report your findings to me tonight at ten o'clock here in this cabin."

Wilson's brow creased in worry. "Sir, I work in first class exclusively. I don't have access to the second-class cabins. I don't know how I . . ."

I'd thought of that. It was probably true. So my next comment was pure bluff.

"That is another lie, Wilson. You can figure out a way, since you used to work in

second class before you were promoted up to this deck. I will see you at ten tonight."

I left him standing there, mouth agape, and walked out the door for my morning stroll.

15
A Hawaiian Enigma

Steam Ship Australia
Central Pacific Ocean
Lat. 9° S, Long. 171° W
10 P.M., Saturday
12 January 1889

That day, my path did not cross Jane's. Apparently, anger or shame kept her out of the public areas, which was counter to her routine.

I didn't seek out Aukai since I wanted to get Wilson's information prior to my next meeting with the Hawaiian. Instead, I spent the day seeking shade in a deck chair, reading a travelogue of the South Sea Islands.

That evening, at precisely the appointed time, a newly respectful Wilson arrived in my cabin and delivered both fresh towels and the report I had ordered. He began with a loaded question.

"You gave me a tall order, sir, but I got it done and found out some interesting things. Do you want to know how I did it?"

I could tell he wanted to impress me by reciting his detective skills, but I was tired and not in the mood for that game. "No, not particularly, Wilson. Just get on with it and tell me what you found out about Cushman, Aukai, and Starkloff."

"Aye, aye, sir. Oh, I mean, yes, sir. Well, if I may, sir, I'll start with the Hawaiian kanaka fellow, David Aukai."

He used the prevalent term by whites for a native islander of the Pacific, and his tone echoed the barely subdued condescension many felt toward the locals.

I nodded my assent and Wilson started. "He's a bit of an odd fellow indeed, sir. Seems he isn't a second-class deck passenger at all but is down in third with the common steerage passengers. Bunks in with two other chaps. That's the way it usually is out here. Only the royal kanaka folks stay topside; the rest of them stay down in steerage. Understandable, really. Most of them just don't know how to act around ladies and gentlemen, you know. Never had the upbringing, I suppose."

I glanced sharply at him.

"Ah, yes, sir, sorry for getting off course. Back to the point: He's been seen acting friendly with your Mr. Starkloff up on the second-class deck several times since Honolulu, both at Mr. Starkloff's cabin in the mornings and out on deck in the evenings. Been run off twice by stewards and officers to get back down below where his type belongs."

"Acting friendly with Starkloff? No arguments, no animosity?"

"Animosity, sir?"

"No ill will, tension, hostility between them?"

"Oh, nary a bit, sir. Thick as thieves they were, according to me mates that saw them. Oh, don't worry. I didn't tell me mates anything about why I wanted to know, just steered the conversation in that direction, so to speak. I can be quite cagey when I need to be. Had to be in the navy."

"Go on, Wilson."

"Yes, sir. Well, a quick look-see through his cabin turned up this in his waste bin, sir. It was scattered amongst the other rubbish, but I pieced it together and thought you should see it."

The steward handed me a sheet of ship's note paper torn into three pieces. I assembled them and read the missive that was scrawled in a quick hand.

DAVID,
SEE ME ON BACK DECK AT 5.
TOMAS.

"Who is Tomas?" I asked.

"Did some work on that, sir. At a little after five o'clock last night, Aukai was seen at the railing right aft with a man named Tomas Pietra, a second-class passenger who's been aboard since San Francisco. Evidently, he's some sort of scientific man from somewhere in the northern part of Italy. The two of them talked pretty closely for a long time. Aukai dashed below to third class just as the officers were coming 'round aft on their hourly tour."

The name Pietra didn't ring a bell. "Only met once?"

"So far's me mates know, yes, sir."

"Has Aukai associated with anyone else from any deck?"

"No, sir. Stayed mostly away from the social affairs of his own class. Only been with those two gentlemen, Starkloff and Pietra, one deck up."

"I see. What about his belongings?"

"Steerage don't have a safe in their cabins. Not much in the way of possessions. Nothing out of the ordinary, just clothing, toiletries, some small American currency, all stowed nice and neat in the cabin's drawers. But I did find out something curious-like. He's keeping four cases in the purser's locked stores, sir. Not sure what it means, though." His face was screwed up in a pensive attitude, which looked painful for him.

"And why is that curious, Wilson?"

"Purser's office doesn't usually store things for steerage passengers, sir. I assume there was some inducement involved. By the way, I can't get into that locker, sir. Only the chief purser has the key."

Captain Aukai had four cases under lock and key by an arrangement with the chief purser? I silently agreed with Wilson: It was curious. I had an idea that what he had in those cases was similar to what I had in my cabin safe, some of which would make a very loud noise.

I found it salient that Wilson's inquiry had not revealed that the Hawaiian was a military officer. Clearly, he had taken pains to conceal his profession and thus was traveling under pretenses like me.

"What's his profession?"

"The stewards think he's a native preacher." He shrugged. "Maybe there's Bibles in kanaka-pidgin writing inside them cases."

I nodded. "Yes, good point, Wilson. He's probably a preacher."

The major question in my mind was not whether Aukai was an espionage agent—that much I felt was certain—but whose side was he on? Was he operating against the Germans for his king, David Kalakaua, out of a Hawaiian fear of a Teutonic invasion or coup d'état? Or was he operating as a double agent *for* the Germans, against Kalakaua, in an effort to extend their Pacific empire over the Hawaiian Islands?

If he was the former, he might be an ally. If the latter, definitely an enemy. Either way, I needed to know, for I had a premonition that Aukai was headed to Samoa also.

And therefore he would be a significant factor in my mission.

16
A Naval Demonstration

Steam Ship Australia
Central Pacific Ocean
Lat. 9° S, Long. 171° W
10 P.M., Saturday
12 January 1889

I had no more time to dwell on the Hawaiian at that moment, for I didn't want to alert Wilson to the man's importance. "Very good so far, Wilson. Now what about the others?"

"Yes, sir. Let's do Mr. Starkloff next, sir. Very interesting gentleman, indeed. I found out that he has kept company with none other than Signore Tomas Pietra. Yes, sir, that would be the very same gentleman the kanaka lad's been talking to. Mr. Starkloff's played poker and smoked and of course, has been drinking with Mr. Pietra almost every night since he came aboard in Honolulu. By the by, Mr. Starkloff can stow away a fair load of liquor, sir. Mostly gin with a wedge of lime."

The web gets more tangled, I thought. *Why is Thomas Pietra the nexus between the German and the Hawaiian?* "Go on."

"Well, a look-see at Mr. Starkloff's cabin turned up some unusual things, sir. He's obviously a senior military man. Some sort of German uniform—quite full of baubles and dangles, it is. Never wears it, but it's there in his hanging locker. No documents in his cabin beyond an old letter in German. Not much money stowed away in his things and not even many clothes. The gentleman travels light, indeed. Everything squared-away proper, neat enough for a Sunday inspection.

"His downside seems to be imbibing, sir. He drinks that gin to great excess in the evenings, loses a lot in cards and then complains about it, and doesn't talk at meals. Can be quite rude after drinking. Scares the stewards quite a bit, sir. Got a nasty scar on his face and bellows orders to them like a bosun to a 'lubber. They don't like him a bit."

The memory of his bulging, enraged eyes came to mind. *Rude's not the half of it, Wilson. You should see him when he's homicidal.*

"You said he's a military man. Any weapons?"

"None I saw, sir. But I think you needn't worry about him none, 'cause I didn't find any business papers at all. I think he's no threat to your commercial endeavors, sir. He's just another old soldier wandering around this part of the world, hiring out to the local chieftains to kill off their rivals. There's a bunch of them over here in the western side of the Pacific."

"No social interaction except for Pietra at the evening card games?"

Wilson's leer came back. "Well, not much in public, sir. But late at night's another matter. It would seem the gentleman's done a bit of prowling in search of companionship. On Thursday night, from midnight until five in the morning, he was in Madam Cushman's cabin, up here in first class."

That was the night before our confrontation on deck. I recalled Jane's reaction to seeing him come toward us in the dark. She'd acted as if she didn't know Starkloff was even on the ship. Plainly a lie for my consumption. A well-presented lie. Their past affair had been rekindled. Why? Why had she acted so deceptively? Why not admit their tryst—they were both single and unattached. Was she duping him for money again?

"How often did he spend the night in her cabin?"

"Mr. Starkloff visited the lady's cabin only once since he's been aboard, sir. She never spent the night down in his."

Wilson read my mind and shrugged. "Night stewards notice a lot of things, sir."

"Yes, evidently. Anything else on Starkloff?"

"Only that he hasn't been seen today or this evening, sir. Not in his cabin or in the public areas. The officers are searching for him now."

I was surprised it had taken this long for Starkloff's disappearance to be noticed. At least there was no indication of any witnesses to his demise.

I tried to appear ignorant, mystified, and intrigued. "That *is* odd, Wilson. How does a man disappear on a ship? You can only walk so far in either direction. Could he have gotten drunk and fallen overboard or gotten lost?"

"That's what I think, sir."

"Yes, well, he'll probably turn up worse for wear down in the steerage or cargo hold or whatever they call that place down there, after waking up from getting drunk on gin. I agree with you. I don't think he is a competitor or worry to me. Or Aukai, for that matter. It pays to be careful, though, and I'm glad to have your information. On to the last person now. What about Mrs. Cushman?"

"May I have permission to be candid, sir?"

"Yes."

"Mrs. Cushman is more of a known factor, sir. She's been with us on several voyages and has proven to be quite popular, both publicly and personally. Lovely lady. Treats the staff aboard quite nicely too. They're all aware of her . . . peculiarities, shall we say . . . but because they like her, they keep quiet."

"Peculiarities?"

"Her friendships on board and certain things from her past,

sir. In fact, I am aware of her maiden name, which, in light of the German gentleman aboard now, may prove interesting for you. This tidbit came about rather roundabout, for I had occasion to serve as steward to a society lady acquaintance of hers last year. I inadvertently overheard a conversation about Mrs. Cushman. The society lady's comments were not very nice."

The man could certainly ramble. "What the hell is her maiden name, Wilson?"

"Oh, sorry, sir. Her maiden name is Moltke."

"Moltke? Are you sure? She has no accent at all."

Wilson was clearly pleased with himself and the reaction he'd gotten from me.

"I am very sure, sir. Moltke's what I heard. But Moltke was an adopted name. It turns out that her mother was a woman named Margaret Burt, originally of the West Indies. Mrs. Burt was some sort of relative—don't know how—of the English wife of General Helmuth von Moltke, head man of the whole German army."

Von Moltke. An honored name in the world. The celebrated old general, an icon of the Prussian army, had just retired as chief of the general staff in August at age eighty-eight, after sixty-two years in uniform. He was still a force to be reckoned with. He and Otto Bismarck were the two men most responsible for the unification of Germany, its domination of Europe, and the new worldwide German Empire. Moltke was one of the late Kaiser Wilhelm's favorites as well. The new Kaiser, Wilhelm the Second, on the throne since June, was only twenty-nine years old and wanted new blood in charge of the army.

"And this lady's specific comments about Jane Cushman were?"

"That before Mrs. Cushman married Mr. Cushman, she'd adopted the name of her relative's famous German husband, then used it to gain access into social circles in San Francisco. That's how she hooked Mr. Cushman, who was much older."

That she was a gold digger, I knew. "So what was her real original family name? Was it Burt?"

"Don't know, sir. The society lady didn't bring that up. And, of course, I wasn't in a position to inquire."

"When did you hear this conversation?"

"On a voyage last spring, sir. April, I think. Auckland to Honolulu. Both ladies were aboard."

"Who exactly was this society lady?"

His blotchy face got redder. "Well, sir, she's a quality lady. I don't like to . . ."

"Who the hell was she, Wilson?"

"A lady named Wellsingham, sir. Very highly regarded in the upper levels at Sydney, I'm told."

"And how did Wellsingham know about Mrs. Cushman and her *peculiarities?*"

Wilson had started fidgeting with his hands, nervous under interrogation. He let out a long exhale before replying. "Not sure, sir, but from the gossip among the bar stewards, I heard that Mrs. Cushman had an affair with Mr. Wellsingham. This is confidential, between us, isn't it, sir?"

I ignored his plea. "When was the affair?"

"My impression was it had happened just before the voyage. The stewards heard about it from the lady's maid, who heard a hell of a row between Mr. and Mrs. Wellsingham about it."

"Anything else of pertinent value about those three?"

"Nothing I can think of, sir."

It was time to sow some false trails. "Anyone else aboard who is looking into investing in Samoan plantations? Any Canadians, in particular?"

"None that I know of, sir. They say there's going to be a war between America and Germany there, so I doubt anyone wants to invest money there."

He looked at me warily, the tone of his comment almost a challenge to explain my interest in Samoa and my fellow passengers. Wilson may have been crude, but he had the quiet shrewdness regarding human nature born of years of survival on the lower deck. He knew I wasn't what I purported to be, but he wasn't sure at all of what I really was. It was time to reinforce my pretense.

"Sometimes wars bring big profits to those who buy early, Wilson. Canada won't be involved in the war. Her Majesty will be neutral and her subjects will reap the rewards. It's a good time and place to be Canadian." I flashed a knowing grin and a wink.

Wilson smiled in understanding, now convinced that I was, in actuality, a wily Canadian businessman merely portraying myself as an American. "Ah, very good point, sir."

"You did well, Wilson. I'm starting to feel as if I should amend my initial assessment of you. But time will tell. Do *not* let me down between here and Auckland, or you will regret it."

Reverting to his former self, he knuckled his brow in the old sailor salute. There was a twinkle in his eye. We were kindred souls, one con man to another, both subjects of Her Majesty, Queen Victoria.

"Aye, aye, sir!"

Not a moment after Wilson departed from my cabin, I felt the rumble of the ship's engines subside. *Australia* was slowing, which I thought unusual in the middle of the ocean. Something must be wrong.

I went out on the darkened deck outside my cabin and looked about but saw no one but Wilson. He was standing at the rail, peering out into the gloom. I stood beside him and searched the sea until I could make out the bow wave of a ship. Lit up by the luminescence of the ocean, it was a glowing white line of froth in the night.

Wilson turned to me. "Speak of the Devil and he shall appear, sir. I know that ship, recognize her anywhere, even on a black night like this. She's the *Olga*. Imperial German Navy gunboat. Makes sense, since we're not far from Samoa now and they're checking all foreign-flag ships for gunrunning to the rebels. Come up from astern with no lights until they're right alongside. Showing a bit of a warning, as it were."

I dredged up the details on *Olga* from the ONI file I'd memorized. At 2,400 tons, she was classified as a corvette, larger than a gunboat. And the three-masted, twin-funneled, iron-hulled, and heavily gunned warship was more than a match for our ships in the Pacific.

"Now, Wilson, how do you know it's a warship, much less a German one? I can barely make her out."

"We used to put into Pago Pago, sir. That's an excellent harbor at the Samoan island of Tuitila. The Americans have a little naval coal depot there. We'd see *Olga* there all the time. But now, because of the war and all, we don't put in there anymore."

The corvette was rapidly gaining on us. Her features were clear to me now but not her intent. I asked, "Think they'll board us?"

"No, sir. No worries. They just want us to know they're here. They know we're not stopping at Pago Pago anymore. If we were a smaller ship headed the other way, they probably would board and search us. They've caught some British-flagged ships running guns lately."

One of those new electric searchlights—our navy had only a few and those were on the newly commissioned ships—suddenly pierced the night from the German ship. Its beam circled around until it focused on *Australia*'s bridge for a second before it traveled down the length of our hull. Wilson and I were momentarily enveloped in white light.

Just three months earlier, I'd had a Spanish cruiser do the same thing to the American steamer I'd taken refuge aboard when escaping Cuba. I shuddered inwardly at the memory and willed myself to stay calm.

"So tell me, Wilson, this just a show of force, way out here in the middle of nowhere?"

"Exactly, sir. They just want to demonstrate to us who *owns* this part of the Pacific Ocean."

I had to admit to myself, as I stood there looking over at the corvette, the Germans' demonstration of naval force was quite effective. She was very close now, and I could make out details, for our captain had illuminated our electric deck lights.

A crowd of officers was on the corvette's starboard bridge, pointing toward us. Below the bridge, one of the secondary batteries—a 3.7-centimeter rapid-fire gun—swiveled from its fore and aft stowed position until the barrel was aimed at us.

I thought that a bit much. They certainly were carrying this demonstration business too far. The damned thing might accidentally go off.

I heard someone approaching on our deck. It was one of our young officers running forward to the ladder leading up to the bridge. He looked scared.

Just then, Wilson yelled with disbelief, his carefully cultivated syntax of a gentleman's gentleman vanishing into the slang of the lower deck.

"Bloody friggin' hell! The bastards're gonna fire into us!"

I whirled around and stared at the warship's bridge, now even with ours and a mere fifty yards away. The water between us was a roiling white caldron from the colliding bow waves. *Australia's* steam horn sounded in a long wail of warning.

The situation was getting completely out of hand. Both ships were moving at least ten knots. One mistake from a helmsman on either vessel could lead to disaster in seconds. I could hear our officers shouting from the bridge. The liner's course altered to starboard, away from the warship.

I stood there, astonished, and watched as one of the German officers raised an arm and dropped it.

Boom!

17
A Descent into Hell

Steam Ship Australia
Central Pacific Ocean
Lat. 9° S, Long. 171° W
10:30 P.M., Saturday
12 January 1889

"Jesus, Mary, an' Joseph too!" cried out Wilson as he ducked behind a boat davit.

My reaction was less polite as I waited for the pain to come.

There was no explosion aboard *Australia*, however. They'd fired a blank charge.

As I breathed a deep sigh of relief, a disembodied voice came across the waves through a speaking trumpet. *"Ahoy to zee steamer* Australia! *Ve are zee Imperial German Navy varship* Olga! *You are in zee operational area of the Imperial German Navy, vhich is conducting vartime maneuvers und a blockade of zee waters around zee islands of Samoa. You are ordered to heave to und vill comply immediately! You vill stand by for a boarding party und have your cargo und passenger manifests ready for inspection!"*

The steward stood up, staring wide-eyed at the warship

alongside. I put a hand on his shoulder to get his attention and said calmly, "Steady on, Wilson. You're a navy-trained man. You've heard guns go off before."

"Aye, that I have, sir," he said in a voice an octave lower than his previous outburst. "And bigger ones than that little peashooter. The Heinie bastards just took me a bit by surprise. They never did that before. Show-offs—that's all they are. Why, they've never even seen a *real* warship, like Her Majesty has. . . ."

I smiled at the deserter-turned-patriot's new anger. "Good. Now listen carefully, Wilson. I want to know what or who the Germans are looking for when they come aboard. Report to me in my cabin as soon as you know. If I'm not there, leave a note hidden in my underwear in the bottom drawer. Got that?"

"Aye, sir. I'll chat up the duty steward for the bridge watch."

He soon disappeared as passengers filled the deck in various stages of undress. Soon the deck was full of indignant people in night clothes and robes sputtering at this "gross breach of law" in stopping us. Several opined that our captain should ignore the warship and steam on, since we were an American ship with American passengers and nobody in the entire world dared touch us.

I, on the other hand, knew the Germans were within their international legal rights. They had declared the area a war zone and instituted a blockade and could search any ship they wanted. I'd done the very same thing during the war on the coast of Florida and had searched many a Spanish-, British-, and French-flagged vessel.

The big question, which was voiced by a knowledgeable few around me, was whether the United States and Germany were at war yet. If we were, then the ship and all Americans aboard could be legitimately detained as enemy noncombatants. Every cabin would be searched. Every safe would be opened. This logical train of events would have a very nasty ending for me.

Once they saw the contents of my cabin's safe, I would be arrested as an enemy spy. Visions of Teutonic efficiency came to mind. I'd probably be hanged immediately as an object lesson.

Both ships had slowed almost to a stop now, and the crew of *Olga* had launched a steam cutter. It started puffing across to us, and I noted there was a senior officer in charge and his men were armed with pistols and rifles. Another boat was being launched. I took that as an indication that we were, in fact, at war. This was no mere manifest examination. There were enough men in both boats to seize the *Australia* and search her thoroughly.

Returning to my cabin, I did a quick assessment of where to hide my things. They would search all of the public and private spaces aboard of both passengers and crew. The holds would be searched as well. Where would the Germans not look? Then it came to me. I would have to hurry.

Pandemonium was everywhere as officers and stewards sought to calm the passengers and assure them this was only a routine stop. The upper-class folks weren't buying that explanation, and some began loudly complaining in a mix of panic and anger.

I made my way aft through the crowd, lugging two bags on my shoulders and trying to be inconspicuous. One bag was a large black canvas affair I'd purloined in Cuba months earlier in order to transport Rork's and my personal weapons—and some very interesting intelligence documents—off the island. Now it contained my naval uniform and personal weapons. The other bag was a smaller one containing the money.

Curiously, the commotion diminished the farther I descended in the ship. I wasn't stopped by anyone. I suppose the officers had enough to do. By the time I reached steerage, some of the dwellers there were laughing about the whole thing. From what I could hear, they weren't worried a bit about the Germans and considered it just another intrusion by authorities into their lives. The only difference was that this time the authorities wore different uniforms.

Having never been down there, I wasn't sure where to go, so it took several false leads to discover the hatchway to the engine spaces on the deck below steerage. Finding the correct one, I descended the ladder—no easy matter with my load—and ended up in a dimly lit space crammed with tubing, moving wheels and arms, and a giant shaft. It was disengaged. The ship was completely stopped.

To the surprise of a grimy oiler lubricating his beast's massive cylinder heads, I squeezed around him and walked forward toward the boiler rooms. Passing a couple more of the black gang, so-called because of the soot and grease that impregnates their skin, I left them behind and entered the after-boiler room.

The reader may wonder why my presence was not challenged verbally by these men. The answer is that there are no conversations in engines spaces. The incredible din of noise and the commotion of mechanical actions make it impossible and dangerous. Communication in such areas is by short shouts and gestures.

In the after-boiler room, the duty fireman was busy studying his gauges, and the stokers were taking a break. I cannot adequately convey the heat of a boiler room on a ship in the tropics, except to say that Dante's version of hell is but a health spa in comparison. I passed through briskly, searching to port and starboard for the access hatch I knew should be there. It wasn't. *Australia* had a different design scheme.

Finally, I found it in the small passageway between the after- and forward-boiler rooms. On both sides there was a manhole hatch in the bulkhead. I chose starboard and opened it. By the dim illumination of the passageway, I could barely see inside. For good reason, it was coal black in there, for it was the main starboard coal bunker. The hatch was a secondary access point to the bunker. The main access points were in the boiler rooms.

I climbed in and closed the hatch door enough that it would appear secured to a man walking in the passageway. Inside, I felt my way in the dark along the longitudinal bulkhead to the right. The bunker was half full. I slipped several times as I walked across the top of the pile. The boilers on the other side of the iron wall were roaring, the reverberations in the bunker pounding my brain. Since the moment I'd entered the engine room, I hadn't heard a thing except the incessant cacophony of the machines. Sight and touch were my remaining navigational senses.

The coal was the hard stuff from Newcastle in Australia, which supplies the entire Pacific with coal. Covered with soot, I would look a mess when and if I ever emerged and got back to my deck, which would prove a challenge to explain.

I never saw light from the main bunker hatches where the stokers worked. That was good. It meant that the pile was to the overhead, filling the space between me and the main hatches. And that meant it would take a while for them to dig their way in this far to feed those hungry boilers.

Burrowing in a couple of feet, I placed the bags down in the coal, then covered them up. Making my way back, I scrambled over the pile, my left hand constantly on that bulkhead, as I strained my eyes searching for the glimmer I hoped would show me the access hatch. It couldn't be much further. Yes, there it was, up ahead. The darkness was just the faintest shade lighter. Perhaps fifteen feet to go.

Then I stepped on something soft . . . that moved.

I fell backward in panic, recoiling my hands to my side so I wouldn't touch whatever it was. I gasped in a cloud of coal dust, choking me and heightening my terror. It seemed too big to be a rat. What was it?

An instant later I knew. It was a hand, groping and then grabbing my right arm. I felt a man's breath in my face and could hear some sort of screaming, the words completely incomprehensible in the din. Was he a stowaway? One of the black gang working in the bunker?

I pushed him away and resumed my crawling toward where I hoped the hatch would be, keeping my left shoulder right along the bulkhead. I saw the outline of the entry up ahead and doubled my efforts. Close to my right, I sensed he had the same goal. If he got there first, he could lock me inside. There was no way to open it from the bunker side.

I reached out with my right hand to find him in the dark. I

touched his left shoulder and seized a bunch of his clothing. He was wearing some type of coat with soft material, which I found odd for a stowaway or member of the black gang. An officer?

Jerking him backward, I brought my arm forward again, then rammed my elbow back toward where I estimated his face would be. I was rewarded with the crunch of my bone smashing into his nose and mouth. I turned and hit him with my left fist, not making a solid contact, but glancing off what felt like his forehead. Then I scrambled for the hatch and rammed it open.

My nose and mouth were full of coal dust by this point and I could barely breathe. I desperately pressed through the opening into the comparative light and air of the passageway, ready to kick the man should he try to drag me back inside the bunker.

Falling out of the hatchway onto the deck, I ran out of strength and lay there for a moment, trying to get air in my lungs as I coughed up strings of black sputum coming out of my mouth and nose. I cursed myself for not covering my face with a kerchief before entering that place.

A hand appeared on the lip of the hatch, the fingers frantically trying to gain a hold. I knew I had to stand up and end it right there, killing him before he could attack me or escape or some crewman saw us. He would never get out. I would slam the hatch shut on him, sealing him inside that black hell to his ultimate doom.

I got up on my knees and reached for the handle. Another hand appeared, then the top of a head. The hair was gray with a bald patch. Both my hands were on the hatch now, and I growled in an effort to gain strength enough to crash it closed before the man could fully emerge.

His shoulders were out, and I saw that his face was a blackened mess, the blood looking like oil streaming out of his crooked nose. He was older than I, much older. In his late sixties, at least. It wasn't making any sense.

He looked up at me, putting a hand out in terrified supplication. He saw death coming and shut his pale eyes. I hesitated, then saw a soot-grimed white collar that wrapped right around his neck. The coat was a dinner suit jacket. In the gloom, there was a tiny golden reflection on the lapel.

It was a cross.

18
An Unequal Confrontation

Steam Ship Australia
Central Pacific Ocean
Lat. 9° S, Long. 171° W
10:58 P.M., Saturday
12 January 1889

I felt sick to my stomach. Why was a clergyman in the coal bunker just as the Germans were boarding the ship?

I pulled the man out and lowered him gently to the deck where he could lean his back against the iron bulkhead. Examining him, I saw that my elbow had broken his nose and cut his upper lip, the blood matting with the soot to form a black paste across his face. He was stunned, not saying a word as I ran my hands around his head, searching for any other wounds. There were none. His neck wasn't broken; his arm and legs functioned. I pushed his nose back in line, and he grunted in pain. I needed to get us out of there before an engineering officer showed up.

"I'm sorry I hit you, sir. I didn't know who you were. I'll get you to my cabin in first class and get you cleaned up properly."

He still said nothing, but the daze was fading and his eyes were starting to focus on me. Probably, he'd gotten a minor concussion from the blow and was now coming out of it. I lifted him up, made sure he was steady on his feet, then led him aft through the passageway.

In the after-boiler room the stokers were back at it, shoveling coal into the furnaces, their bodies glistening in the firelight. I kept my body between the parson and the stokers, hoping to shield his face from them. It worked. Like stokers everywhere, they were too absorbed in their work, stupefied by the repetition, their muscles going through the motions as if they were living extensions of the mechanic beast they were feeding.

Our luck ran out in the engine room as we passed the condenser. A junior officer spotted us. "You there!" he shouted, barely understandable in the roar of the machinery.

I picked up our pace and called over my shoulder to him, "Sorry. Got lost and went down the wrong ladder. On our way back now. Very sorry!"

He had a wary look about him and was still heading our way. I decided to give him something else to think about and brought a nearby lever down to close a valve. It appeared to be on the water feed to the condenser. At least I hoped it was, for that would have immediate effect.

"Stop!" the officer shouted, just as a scream pierced the racket of the engines. It was steam escaping a safety valve in the feed line. I'd picked correctly. I pushed my companion faster to get away.

Someone nearby yelled out, "Condenser!" and I saw a movement toward where we'd just been. They were converging on the feed line. I pushed the parson behind a main bundle of tubing as two oilers came running by. The officer wasn't in sight, presumably directing the efforts to rectify what I had put asunder.

That gave us time to reach the ladder. By then the parson had regained enough strength to climb, and we emerged from the hell below into the relative calm of the steerage deck. As we passed by a table outside the mess room, I spied a wide-brimmed hat, which I promptly appropriated and jammed down on my new acquaintance's head to better conceal his wounds.

Pretending he was incapacitated by drink, I led him up to my deck, one friend helping another, with apologetic blather to the curious looks received along the way. No one stopped us or inquired closer, for the main event aboard was occupying their attention right then. Everyone was echoing the news.

The Germans were aboard and searching the ship.

I sat the man on my bed and wiped his face with a damp cloth from the basin. It took a few minutes to clear it of debris and soot and blood. He still hadn't spoken, but his gray eyes locked on mine with unnerving intensity. After I removed the mess from around his mouth, the lips moved, tentatively at first, without sound.

Then he spoke, in a deep croaking bass, tinged with anger. "Who are you?"

"Peter Wake from Baltimore. A businessman heading for Samoa. I needed to hide some confidential business documents in the bunker. I thought you were about to attack me, so I hit you. I'm truly sorry for that, Reverend. Who are you and why were you in the coal bunker?"

His smoldering gaze never wavered. He replied only, "John Irons."

I tried to deduce more about the man, mentally reviewing what I knew. He was medium height and thin, in his sixties. He had the flat speech of the Midwestern states. First-class passengers were given a list of their social equals. The name Irons wasn't on that list, so I presumed he was in second class or steerage. He was dressed well, as if he'd been at dinner before going to the bunker. There was no wedding ring or jewelry of any kind except for the small cross pinned on his lapel. It was a Protestant cross.

I held out a fresh, damp cloth for him. "Here, you might

want to use this. Look, I am so sorry, sir. I didn't realize you were a clergyman. I really did think you were about to attack me in the dark bunker, so I hit you first. Please accept my apology. Do you have family aboard? What can I do to assist you, sir?"

He took the cloth and wiped around his eyes. Coal dust had filled every wrinkle in his exposed skin. It would take a long bath, several towels, and a lot of scrubbing to remove it. I caught sight of myself in the mirror above the wash basin. Suddenly, I realized that I looked pretty frightening myself.

I tried friendly humor. "Our appearance will be a bit difficult to explain, won't it? Takes a lot of scrubbing to get coal soot out of your skin."

He coughed, black sputum and mucus dripping from his lips and nostrils. I handed him another cloth, my last. He leaned over to look at himself in the mirror.

At last, he spoke to me. "I'm alone on the ship. Second-class cabin, number fifteen. I need to go down there and wash up."

"I'll take you there."

"No. You are still filthy. You'll attract too much attention." He looked down at himself. "I'll leave my dirty coat here. Get it cleaned and sent to my cabin later. I can make it there on my own."

"Reverend, I must insist on helping you."

"I said *no!* Get out of my way. I'm leaving."

Clearly, my attempts at contrition weren't working. Reverend John Irons wasn't impressed, and he was very much a threat. He could tell the ship's officers that I'd been hiding something in the coal bunker, after he removed whatever he'd hidden. It was time to change tacks with him.

He rose from the bed. I stepped between him and the door.

"No, you need to remain here a little longer, Irons. I was candid with you. Now you need to be candid with me. Why were *you* in that coal bunker?"

"Get out of my way."

"I'll be glad to as soon as you answer truthfully. I don't trust you not to report me to the ship's officers or the Germans, Irons. And until I do trust you, I'm not letting you go anywhere."

He didn't back down. "What are you going to do if I don't tell you? Kill me?"

I put my face in front of his and said the words I knew I had to say.

"Yes, I will. It'll be easy. The crowd outside this cabin has cleared. It's dark and no one will see your body go overboard. It will take me maybe twenty seconds."

He stepped back, evaluating me. I didn't see fear. I saw cool analysis. When he finally spoke, it was in a monotone. "You aren't a businessman at all, not the way you just threatened to kill me, a clergyman. Most men couldn't do that, but I can see in your eyes that you've killed before. I know the look only too well. I used to have it too. During the war."

He wasn't a frail old man anymore. Something had entered him, a force, an intimidating energy of some kind that radiated from his eyes. I dared not look away from those steady eyes.

I kept up my bluff but knew it sounded anemic. "Answer my question, Irons, or I'll end the problem."

He disregarded my threat and continued. "Oh, yes, you are definitely a killer. But not a criminal, I think. A military man of some sort. Probably navy, the way you knew what lever to push to draw them away from us down in the engine room."

I didn't know what to say, and he didn't give me time to come up with anything.

"You're sophisticated, so you're an officer. But out of uniform and hiding something in the coal bunker. Which means you are aboard this ship in a clandestine capacity. And that means you are a spy and were concealing something quite valuable to the Germans."

I just stood there, trying not to show my reaction but completely undone internally by this old man with the fortitude of a lion and the discernment of a psychic.

"And of one thing I am certain. You only kill when you have

to, so you won't kill me or even hurt me now. You can't, because you respect life and you respect that little cross and what it stands for."

He slowly nodded in satisfaction as a thin smile spread on his face. "Oh, yes, I've figured you correctly, all right. I can see it all in your eyes. Is Peter Wake even your real name?"

My words came out before I could stop them. "Yes, it is. And you're right about me."

He nodded again and put a thin hand on my shoulder. "Well, don't feel bad. You were outnumbered from the start. I had reinforcements from above. Let me take the time to tell you about me, Peter. I am a Methodist pastor from Ohio, doing missionary work in the South Pacific. A special kind of missionary work."

He chuckled softly at my confusion. "I think God led you to me, Peter. In a coal bunker, of all places! Had to be Him, for what are the odds? You see, as dissimilar as the two of us appear at first glance, we have far more in common than you may know. Sit down, son."

He sat back down on the bed. I took a seat in the chair as he started.

"The reason I saw through you is because I was once the same kind of man. A professional military killer. And once you've become that, it never leaves your soul, no matter where you go or what you do. It can be submerged, but those memories, those visions of what you've done, are always there. Aren't they?"

"Yes, they are . . ."

He then proceeded to tell me the strange tale of the late-in-life redemption and mission of Pastor John Irons, age sixty-six, of Cleveland, Ohio.

19
The Unlikely Missionary

Steam Ship Australia
Central Pacific Ocean
Lat. 10° S, Long. 171° W
11:30 P.M., Saturday
12 January 1889

The war changed John Irons, as it did so many men. As it did me.

I served on the coast of Florida, searching for blockade-runners and raiding Confederate positions ashore. It was a dirty little guerrilla war, with small unit ambushes and lone snipers. Deadly tropical diseases and reptiles were every bit as much our enemy as the Confederates. There were no lines of blue and gray, no bands playing, no advances of territorial control, no cities gained or lost, and no acclaim in the press. Just years of incessant, personal privation and peril.

But Irons had it worse—infinitely worse. A small-town Ohio lawyer who volunteered in the initial wave of patriotism sweeping the north in August of 1861, he was given a brevet commission as a lieutenant in an infantry company and sent to the front lines in northern Virginia. Irons started out as a true believer in the glory of the great cause of preserving the Union and of someday freeing the Southern slaves, and he spread the word among his troops. He continued believing, even after surviving the chaos and carnage at Antietam and Fredericksburg, which resulted more from the stupidity of the army's leadership than from Rebel strategy and tactics.

But the end of his faith in God and the nation's glory finally came on May 2, 1863. That was the day when a newly promoted Captain Irons led his regiment—for all of the other officers above him were dead—on a suicidal charge at the Battle of Chancellorsville. His subordinate officers objected, but he had insisted and employed thinly veiled threats of arrests for cowardice. He had orders from above, he told me sadly, and he was, by God and General Hooker, going to follow them.

So John Irons led his men out past their protective stone wall and into the open, marching toward the enemy. The idea was to blunt the oncoming Confederate charge with a counterattack. It failed. The enemy decimated his men. The sound of the rifle barrage flailing them down was so deafening that no one could hear his commands to retreat, so they fell where they stood, a gory monument to his faithfulness to orders.

Irons told me that killing hundreds of the enemy up until that day hadn't bothered him so much, for he could invent justifications for it. But getting his own men killed—the men from his hometown, his friends and relatives—made him feel like a monster. And, worst of all, he had survived, without even so much as a scratch.

As he spoke, I recalled that same day as well. I reported to the navy as a volunteer officer at the depot at New Bedford, Massachusetts, bound for a billet with the East Gulf Blockading Squadron. I was relieved I was escaping the fate of my friends in the trenches with the army. By that time in the war, we'd lost more than a hundred thousand men in the north. Nobody was volunteering anymore for the army.

The day Irons' faith in God and the United States left him, what was left of his regiment was incorporated into another. They saw action on the third day of Gettysburg and afterward were quietly sent to the rear, guarding the perimeter of Washington for the rest of the war. Incongruously, he obtained a regular commission and stayed in the army after the war, for as he explained to me, he'd become good at killing and he couldn't remember how to do anything else. Being a lawyer seemed hypocritical after what he'd seen and done. Then he added that the real reason was he had nowhere to go. There was no way he could return home and face the families of the friends and neighbors he'd sacrificed at Chancellorsville.

So he went west and killed Indians for the army, hundreds of them, mostly women and children, in raids. His first was Custer's attack at Washita, Oklahoma, in November 1868. Then he went on with Sheridan's Comanche campaign in Texas later that winter. His final fight was in '72 at Salt River Canyon in Arizona Territory.

The day after the fight he woke up in his tent, looked in the mirror, and saw a tired-eyed, fifty-year-old captain—twenty years older than his fellow officers—who cursed his men every day and drank himself asleep every night to avoid the nightmares. He didn't like the man he saw in that mirror. And more importantly, he couldn't find anything to respect in him.

An hour later, a half-breed Apache preacher came into his camp and reported that there were wounded Indian women and children on the road a few miles away.

"Will you help save them?" the preacher desperately asked Irons.

To the surprise of his troops, who suspected an Indian trap, he ordered them to do just that. There was no trap, just a dozen women and children, some dead, some dying. Grumbling the whole time, the soldiers buried the dead and tended the wounded as best they could, then put them on their horses and took them to a nearby Indian encampment.

Two weeks later, Irons left his company's bivouac, rode into Fort Lowell, Arizona, and tendered his resignation to the regiment's dumbfounded commanding officer. Three months after that, he was in a Methodist seminary back East. Two years later, in May of 1875, he was a missionary roaming the South Pacific, redeeming his life through faith and action. His primary quest was to end slavery there, operating in the guise of blackbirding.

Irons was returning aboard *Australia* after a journey to Honolulu for some needed supplies. In Auckland, he would board his schooner—appropriately named the *Samaritan*—and sail for the Solomon Islands.

I could scarcely believe it. Irons was actually doing what President Cleveland had wanted me to pretend to do. Was this whole encounter mere coincidence?

I guessed not. When he answered my next question, I knew it wasn't.

"So the Methodist Church sent you out here all alone to take on the blackbirders?"

"No, they didn't. In fact, they told me not to do it. The church leaders back home said that I should come and preach and minister to the natives, and in that way slowly change the situation with love and kindness and patience. I'm not against that, naturally, for it's Jesus's way, but I don't have enough time left for love and patience to solve the problem. Thousands of innocent people would be taken from their homes and families while I was waiting for love to triumph over evil. So I ignored the bishop's wishes and came out to take on the blackbirders in the only way I know how to do things—directly."

"What does that mean?" I asked, more and more curious about this intriguing fellow who I was beginning to think might be of some use to my endeavor.

"It means I liberate natives at the plantations and sail them back to their home villages and islands. That way they get to live long enough to enjoy some love. Needless to say, that means that sometimes I am compelled to not be meek with my enemies."

"You actually go *into* the plantations and rescue these people? Where?"

"Yes, Peter, I do. I go to the German plantations in the Solomon Islands, New Guinea, the Marshalls, the Bismarcks, the Marianas, the Carolines, and Samoa. The German blackbirders are the worst now that the British have cleaned up their part of the trade. The French too, though it took them longer. These days, the last of these scum and the plantation masters who buy from them are German."

"Ever have to fight them? With weapons?"

"Sometimes, as a very last resort to defend innocent lives. Even Daniel had a slingshot. But I try to liberate people without any violence or clash. I go in quick under cover of night and get the people out before the guards or overseers are any the wiser."

"Don't they know your ship by now?"

"No. They're always looking for my last ship or, at least, my ship's last appearance. A sort of legend has started to spread."

"Legend?"

"Oh, some of the local people call me Robin Hood, or as they say in the local pidgin equivalent: Rebbin Hoot."

"How do you pay for all this?"

"I get some money from Anglican and Methodist churches in New Zealand, *unofficial* private offerings from the congregations. That's what keeps the ship provisioned and repaired. I also take legitimate cargo and passengers sometimes to bring some money."

"And the Germans? What do they think of you?"

"Oh, the Germans have taken to calling me a pirate and a thief. Even put their warships on the alert for me. We have to constantly repaint my schooner or switch to another ship to maintain my façade of island trader. The Germans are smart. I'll give them that, all right. It's a challenge to get in and out, and they've nearly done me in a couple of times. But, of course, in addition to my crew, who are all native Christian men, I've got some pretty strong assistance from above."

I judged that the time was right to reiterate my original

question. "So what were you hiding in the coal bunker from the German boarding party?"

He looked at me sharply for several seconds, then answered, "My list of contacts in the islands. And now you know all about *me*, Peter Wake. What about you?" His face relaxed. "You never refuted my assessment of you. By your age, I'd say you're probably a full captain by now. That's a pretty high rank to be traipsing around the Pacific. I would think usually they'd use a younger, more junior man. Your mission must be an important one, indeed."

There are times in my profession to maintain a façade, bluffing your way until the end to buy time for escape or victory. And there are times to recognize an opportunity to gain a man with unique assets as a valuable ally. That takes a certain amount of candor on your part, for once insightful men see through your pretenses, further deception merely erects walls of distrust. John Irons was one of those men, and this was one of those times.

"I haven't reached the rank of captain, John. I'm still just a commander. Never attended the academy, so my career's been stunted—no major commands, no public accolades. I do quiet work, behind the scenes, and get things done without attribution. Like you, I started out as a volunteer officer in the war, then got a regular commission after the surrender and stayed in. And, yes, my mission is important."

"The war in Samoa, isn't it?"

"Yes."

He wagged his head slowly, taking it in. "So what did *you* put in the coal bunker that was so important?"

"My personal weaponry and uniform and some money."

"Well, I'll be. God does work in mysterious ways, always at least ten steps ahead of my feeble mind. It looks like we have more in common than I even guessed."

"That we do," I said. "And I'm thinking that perhaps we can help each other."

Irons' brow furrowed. He thought for a few seconds, then said warily, "Maybe, but it depends on . . ."

We were interrupted by three loud thumps on my cabin door. They were followed by Wilson cracking the door open and peeking inside.

"Oh, very sorry, sir! Didn't know you had company. Sorry to disturb you."

"No. Come in, Wilson," I said. "Give me your report. It's all right. You can speak in front of this gentleman."

He stepped inside and closed the door, unable to conceal his surprise at the grimy appearance of Irons and me. "Well, sir, the Heinies—excuse me, sir, I mean the *German* gentlemen— have shoved off. *Olga's* gone about and she's heading northerly. Quartermaster says that course'll take her to Pago Pago."

"What were they looking for?"

"Hard to tell exactly, sir. Me mate who's the duty steward topside says they did a quick look-see at the cargo manifest but didn't do any searching in the holds. He says they spent more time on the passenger list. Asked straight away about Mr. Starkloff, sir. Asked for him to be brought to them, but the gentleman still hasn't been seen. They were a bit peeved on that and went to his cabin."

"Did they take anything from the cabin?"

"Ah, I asked me mate that very same question, sir. He said they didn't take nothing big enough to carry outside a pocket. So if they did, it was small."

"Did they ask for anyone else?"

"No, sir. Just him. But according to what the steward says the duty quartermaster told *him*, the senior German officer did point a finger at Mrs. Cushman's name when he saw it. Started jabbering kind of excited-like at his junior in their own lingo. None of our lads could tell what they were saying, though. None of them speak that German stuff. I only know they never asked for her or went to her cabin, just started talking after seeing the lady's name. Aboard maybe thirty minutes, mostly searching Mr. Starkloff's cabin, then off they went in their boat. Our captain's glad to see them gone, that he is."

"Thank you, Wilson. You did fine. That'll be all for now."

"Aye, sir."

After the steward had exited and closed the door, Irons raised an eyebrow and said, "I see you have a spy network already going on this ship. You don't waste time, do you?"

I shrugged. "It's important for me to know who's who and what's happening."

He cast a troubled look toward me. "May I presume the steward was speaking of Colonel Ludwig Starkloff, the Mad Prussian of the Pacific?"

"The one and only. Know him? His cabin is in second class at the after end."

"I know of him, but he doesn't know me. Rumored to have ice water in his veins and no visible sense of humor. He's done some mercenary work for the colonials in my area, training the plantation guards and local native militia they call *schutztruppen*. Didn't see him aboard, but then I've been staying in my cabin most of the time. I take it you are acquainted with the colonel?"

"Somewhat. Met him at Washington Place and at the palace in Honolulu. He is a former paramour of the lady Wilson mentioned. She's up here in first class."

"I don't know of her. Should I?"

"No, I think not. Now, let's talk about that mutual assistance between us, John. How can I help you?"

"I can't think of a way you can, Peter."

"How about three hundred dollars in gold? That would fund your ship for a year at a minimum."

"In exchange for what?" he asked cautiously.

"Passage from Auckland to Samoa."

"Not going to Samoa, Peter. I'm leaving the same day we arrive in Auckland, hopefully within the hour, and heading northwest through the Coral Sea to the German-held Solomons. I have an important rendezvous there. No deviations, I'm afraid. I suggest you take the mail steamer from Auckland to Samoa. It's a British ship, the Union Line, so they're probably still going there, unlike these American steamers. You'll be there in a week, maybe eight days."

The situation in Samoa had clearly degraded, as evidenced by *Olga*'s boarding of the *Australia*. An American arriving on a steamer would be immediately suspected. I did some quick estimations. It would take a week and a half to sail to the Solomons. The Solomons were about a week's sail due west of Samoa.

"No, we need to arrive in Samoa quietly, at night. Very quietly, John. We can't arrive there publicly on a steamer."

"We?"

"There will probably be two of us, possibly three."

"Please tell me the guest list does *not* include Colonel Starkloff?"

"The colonel is definitely not on this list."

A knowing look crossed his face. "Quietly arrive at night, eh? Well, that's no different than my usual arrivals in Samoa. But delivering three *palangi*—that's the Samoan word for white people—surreptitiously, right under the eyes and guns of the Germans, is far more difficult than only one person."

"How about *five* hundred dollars in gold?"

He thought that over briefly. "Hmm. That would enhance even more my missionary rescue work. I think the Lord would be pleased."

"So, you'll sail us to Samoa after the Solomons?"

He gave me a paternal smile. "You know something, my new friend? Your namesake nineteen hundred years ago was a seaman like you, and he was known to be a pretty persistent fellow too. Just remember that Saint Peter's persistence led him right smack-dab to into the heart of evil in Rome and, ultimately, his death at the hands of Nero. Don't say later that I didn't warn you."

I conjured up recitations from my old biblical studies class forty years earlier at Teignmouth School in Massachusetts and wagged a finger to disagree. "Ah, but we must remember that Peter didn't die until he was an old man, and all that time in captivity he accomplished a great deal, so I think I've still got a few more productive years to go. I'll take my chances on avoiding a modern-day Nero in the Solomons and Samoa."

Irons' face crinkled into a grin. "*Touché*, Peter. All right, then. I suppose I can give you and your friends a ride into the heart of evil in the South Pacific, my friend. *Samaritan* could use a decent refit, and I could use a real sailor aboard for a while. I hope your navigation is as good as your punch."

"Thank you, John."

"Say, now that we're friends and no longer foes, could I trouble you for the loan of a clean shirt to wear for the journey down to my cabin?"

20

At the Bottom
of the World

Waitemata Harbour
Auckland, New Zealand
8:15 A.M., Friday
18 January 1889

The city's main wharf was an enormous affair, with half a dozen large finger docks jutting out into a very crowded harbor. The anchorage was filled with foreign merchant ships laying to their hooks, including many under the German flag; British warships steaming by; interisland schooners and brigs beating up the channel; and small boats everywhere. Auckland was the British empire's main base in the region. All island trade under the Union Jack went to it, from it, or through it.

To the west was the fishing anchorage, where I was supposed to find John Irons' schooner. Before me lay the town itself, a pretty little place built from brick and mortar as if it were in England, not in the South Sea. Church spires and smoking chimneys were everywhere, steam engines whistled and gasped, and the streets were filled with hectic activity. Auckland was the home of a commercial people busily transforming this rugged place at the bottom of the world into a replica of their homeland so far away. The energy in the air reminded me of San Francisco.

Even for us in first class, disembarkation at Auckland's main wharf was bedlam. Wilson, decked out in his best uniform, with long sleeves covering his hands, led the way down the gangway, carrying my things. He was clearly itching to receive a substantial fee for his services to me. I hadn't rescinded my threat to tell the chief purser about his past life and present behavior, but evidently he thought I had changed my opinion enough that I might even say something good about him to that officer. I found it humorous how he just happened to walk close by the chief purser, who was fielding complaints from exasperated rich people who had somehow lost their baggage.

Wilson knuckled his brow to the officer and smiled politely.

"Good morning, chief! A beautiful day it is in Auckland, sir! As soon as I finish helping Mr. Wake here, I'll return and assist you with these gentlemen."

The purser turned and nodded distractedly to Wilson, then saw me standing there.

"Good morning, Mr. Wake. I hope you enjoyed your voyage with us and will be our guest again."

"Only if Wilson can be my steward, chief purser. He is the best I've ever seen. You are fortunate to have him in your crew. A gentleman's gentleman servant."

Well, that did the trick for both men. The purser had something to smile about in his harried morning, and Wilson positively beamed with pride.

"Mr. Wake, that won't be a problem. We will make sure that Steward Wilson will be your attendant anytime you sail with us in the future. We at the Oceanic Steamship Company are very proud of his skills and glad he's with us. It is nice for you to recognize them. Can we assist you any further, sir?"

By this point the purser was ignoring the complainers and concentrating on me. That is exactly what I'd hoped for,

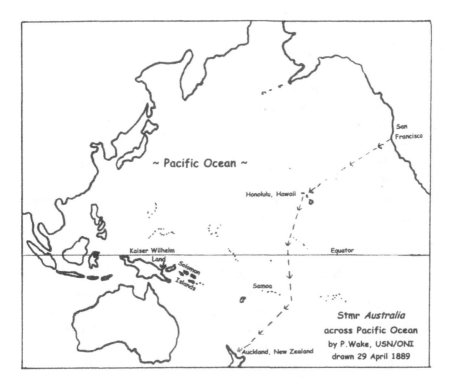

~ Pacific Ocean ~

San Francisco

Honolulu, Hawaii

Kaiser Wilhelm Land

Solomon Islands

Samoa

Equator

Stmr *Australia*
across Pacific Ocean
by P. Wake, USN/ONI
drawn 29 April 1889

Auckland, New Zealand

because there was a reason beyond the accolade for Wilson in my comments. I had something I needed the purser to do.

"Yes, there is one small thing. I need to get through this customs rigmarole quickly, for I have people who have appointments with me this morning at the Hotel Victoria. Obviously, I am not a smuggler and the line and inspection would be a waste of time. If it's no bother, can you assist with expediting my passage through the customs hall?"

Pursers who work regular routes usually have friendships with the customs people. It was so in this situation, for the officer immediately said, "Not a problem or bother at all, sir. Please follow me."

Five minutes later, I was on the other side of the customs hall by the cab stand, thanking the purser. No one had searched my baggage, my passport was duly stamped, and my secret things were still secret. The only question to me by the officials was a pleasant query as to my address and length of stay in Auckland.

As the reader by now knows, I had no address in New Zealand and had no intention of staying, but one look at this little piece of England in the Pacific told me there must be an exclusive hotel named after the sovereign, so I nonchalantly told the customs man, "Why, the Hotel Victoria, of course. And I'll be here about a month or so, looking to invest in one of your enterprises, until *Australia* and Wilson here return and can take me home. She's the only way to cross the Pacific."

That got an appreciative reaction from the purser and a wink from Wilson and satisfied the official. I was about to bid farewell to the purser, give Wilson some money, and hail a hansom cab when I spotted dear Jane being interviewed by a customs officer. She appeared distinctly perturbed. I heard her say something to the man about being "just a widow all alone in the world who doesn't understand all your laws."

"Say, chief, could we assist Mrs. Cushman on getting through the officialdom without further delay? She's a lady in distress and needs some help. I'll give her a ride to the Victoria Hotel once we rescue her from Her Majesty's customs."

"Not a problem, sir. I'll speak to the senior man."

My entourage and I were soon standing with Jane in the portico of the building, the chief purser beaming at having impressed two first-class passengers, Wilson summoning a porter to carry the lady's baggage. The customs man suddenly came up and said, "Please pardon me, Mrs. Cushman, but in all the rush you never did give me your address in Auckland. *Pro forma,* of course." He looked at her apologetically. "I just need it for the form, ma'am."

Her hesitation reinforced what I'd suspected. I stepped forward and quickly filled the pause with, "You told me at tea yesterday that you are staying at the Victoria until your steamer to Singapore comes in, Mrs. Cushman. I am staying there also. May I have the honor to invite you to accompany me there in my carriage?"

She didn't miss a beat. "Yes, of course, the Victoria. Whatever was I thinking? All this commotion has me a bit frazzled. I just don't deal with commotions very well, I'm afraid. If my dear, departed husband were still alive, he would deal with all of this. But I'm alone now. Sadly alone. Thank you, sir. You are a gallant gentleman, indeed."

With a sniffle at the memory of her departed husband, Mrs. Jane Cushman—alias Jane Moltke, alias who-knows-what-else?— then swept out of the portico on the arm of the attentive chief purser, followed by a customs official carrying a pink hat box, a gallant, rich Baltimore businessman carrying one of her bags, a subservient ship's steward with my two seabags over his shoulder and one of her suitcases in his hand, and a bewildered porter lugging a mound of other baggage. It was quite a parade.

Wilson hailed a cab and supervised the stowing of all of the gear on the luggage rack. In addition to a tip, I gave an item to him, with instructions for his final service to me.

Once we climbed into the back of the cab and were alone, Jane began gushing her thanks for being so kind and apologized for avoiding me on the ship, but I stopped her. It was time to be blunt and use a verbal stick to tear down her façade.

"Jane, listen very carefully. Your immediate future depends on your understanding exactly what I'm about to say. I helped you back there in customs not because I like you. I don't. I used my influence to get you through because you are going to do some work for me. You will be paid for that work. Paid very well, in fact. It will not involve compromising any virtue you may have, but it will involve using your considerable talents at charming men and eliciting information."

She started to puff up in indignation.

"Stop the act, Jane. I know about your past endeavors and your present circumstances. I know you have barely a cent on you and not a clue as to where you're laying your head tonight, much less live next week. Your much-grieved-for husband actually left you next to nothing, and you've used that up already. So while you pretend to be the merry widow traipsing around the Pacific on holiday journeys, you're really desperately looking for another husband. A rich, old one. But, alas, so far none will put a ring on your finger."

She steamed silently at me. Now was the time for a hint of a carrot.

"I also know that you've been chummy with the Germans in the Pacific, occasionally passing along what you hear about the Brits, the French, and the Americans."

The bit about the Brits, French, and Americans was pure guesswork on my part, but she confirmed it when she didn't protest. I then added, "And that, my dear, makes you potentially useful to me."

There was the slightest flicker of her eye, showing she realized that I might be useful to her. But I needed her to know who was in charge of our relationship and that I wasn't like the other men in her life. Back to the stick.

"So now, Jane, you have a choice to make. You either practice your talent for making friends and obtaining information for me as a paid double agent and tell me what the Germans are up to, or I'll have the fun of turning you over to the local constabulary for thievery and murder."

That surprised her. She blurted out, "I am *not* a thief or a murderer!"

I kept my voice infuriatingly level and devoid of emotion. "I agree. You probably aren't. But I'm afraid that it certainly does look that way at first glance. In fact, there is an expensive gold watch hidden away in your luggage, that ridiculous-looking pink hat box to be specific, that belongs to a certain German colonel who mysteriously disappeared aboard the steamer one night. The watch even has blood on it. Poor Starkloff, whom several people know you had a relationship with, is presumed dead by the ship's officers. The reports are being written up this morning for the official court inquiry. So you see, my dear, unfortunately for you, everyone will assume you are not only a fraud and a gold digger but a murderess. Try to charm your way out of *that.*"

"My God, what kind of man are you? You must've taken Ludwig's watch from his pocket that night and slipped it into my hat box this morning!"

She certainly did have a quick mind. That was exactly what I'd done. By instinct, I'd taken it from Starkloff's body just before dumping him overboard. The blood, of course, was some of mine.

"That is very cynical of you, Jane *Moltke*. Ah, yes, my dear, I know about that too. You purport to be a distant cousin, only by marriage, of General Helmuth von Moltke. And by coincidence, dear old cousin Helmuth is the very same general who approved of the dismissal of Colonel Starkloff from the Third Prussian Cuirassier Regiment for violations involving honor. So your family disliked the colonel too. A woman spurned by the colonel, from a family disgusted by the colonel. My goodness, your motives to kill Starkloff are adding up, aren't they? Tell me, did you kill him for his money, or out of vengeance, or perhaps to keep his mouth shut about your true state of wealth?"

I shrugged. "If the authorities ask me—and they will once

they read my letter—I can only tell them the truth. I've heard you are a female shyster on the prowl for rich men's money across the Pacific. You even tried with me. And I think you are certainly capable of killing the colonel."

"They won't believe you at all."

"They don't have to. They'll possess the vivid evidence of the crime. You see, Jane, the hat box is no longer in your possession. I took it off the cab's luggage rack and gave it to Wilson. He has specific instructions. As we speak, it is being wrapped in parcel paper. In one month, it will be mailed to the chief constable of Her Majesty's New Zealand Police. Inside the box is the letter from me explaining your relationship with Colonel Starkloff, your predatory affair with Monsieur Touchard of Honolulu, and your attempt to swindle me as well. That parcel will get mailed unless Wilson gets a code word not to mail it when *Australia* returns to Auckland on February twenty-first."

She was a tough bird, all right, struggling to maintain her composure and contain the combination of anger and fear showing on her face. "What *exactly* do you want me to do, Mr. Wake?"

"Simple social interaction, really. You are going with me to Samoa by a rather circuitous route. There, you will see your old German friends and make new ones. You will tell me what you learn from them. I will pay you. It won't take long, and by the time we're done, you will have enough money so you won't have to worry about your future lifestyle anymore. You'll get four hundred and fifty dollars in gold by the end of March, with two thousand more in six months' time, deposited to your bank account in San Francisco."

Her tone lowered as her eyes narrowed into slits. "I know *what* you are now, Wake. But *who* are you, really?"

"A person very much like you, Jane. I worked my way up from the streets and became a successful businessman from Baltimore. Now I need information about the plantation and political situation in Samoa."

"So, you want me to do a honey trap?"

That was an interesting slip of her tongue. It is a term usually used by espionage professionals and criminals.

"Precisely, Jane. How far the relationships progress is your decision—I just want the information from them. *Confirmable* information. Ah, there's the police station now. I know there will be a telephone there. I could call to the shipping line's shore office and pass the word to Wilson to send the parcel today. You can feel free to try to run away, if you wish."

I leaned forward and called up to the driver. "Could you pull over here?"

Turning back to Jane, I announced, "You have thirty seconds before I stop wasting my time with you and cut my losses. What do you want—lots of money and the good life, or a cell in the women's section of the Auckland jail?"

"You've done this before, haven't you?"

"Just about four months ago, in Havana, to be exact. She was a regular prostitute, dressed up to portray a lady so she could pass along foreigners' pillow talk to the Spanish. I convinced her to work for me instead. You, on the other hand, are genuinely a high-class person and are getting *a lot* more money for far less time and effort."

I heard her groan. "You cold-blooded bastard. You've got me. I'll do it, but know that I hate you for it."

"Good decision, Jane. Hate me all you want. Just get the job done."

21

Surprises

Her Majesty's Post Office
Auckland, New Zealand
9:20 A.M., Friday
18 January 1889

I had four main objectives upon arriving in Auckland. First, convert Jane Cushman into my subordinate. Second, find Captain Aukai ashore, whom I'd not seen since that eventful night aboard, and discover his mission and whether it might be a useful adjunct to my own. Third, check for cable messages from Washington. Fourth, get aboard the *Samaritan*, which was to sail with the ebb later that very morning.

Objective one was accomplished, though I didn't trust Jane one iota. I'd hoped to accomplish objective two at the customs hall, but the situation with Jane evolved too fast. I didn't dare leave her alone to search for Aukai there. It looked like that opportunity had vanished. So objective three was next on my list. The driver took us to Her Majesty's Post Office, into which I brought a reluctant Jane with me, tightly held arm in arm, as two close friends should be.

There were two cables for me. They had come across the Atlantic, passed through the continent of Europe to Cairo, thence on the British cable system to India. From there they passed over to Singapore and on to Australia, finally ending in New Zealand. It is a miracle of modern science that never fails to fascinate me. Almost-instant communication with the other side of the world. How times have changed.

The first cable was from a Mr. Sage in New York. That was the January *nom de ruse* for Commodore Walker at headquarters. It changed every month. The cable was dated the fifteenth of January, three days earlier, and addressed to Mr. Kessle, my alias for January.

Memorization is a crucial skill in my profession, and I mentally dredged up the January code to decipher the cable, which was mercifully short. In outward appearance it was an apparently innocuous message about the price of copra and potential investment possibilities, in keeping with my pretenses. The real message was:

—X—NO   WAR   YET—X—CONTINUE MISSION—X—REINFORCEMENTS ENROUTE—X—

This explained why *Olga* didn't search our steamer more thoroughly. The second message was dated January third and sent from Charleston. It was from Mrs. Wexford, the alias of my dear friend and colleague Sean Rork, who I thought was still sick at the Washington Naval Yard with a recurrence of malaria. It was in plain language.

—X—YOU THINK I WOULD LET YOU HAVE FUN W/O ME?—X—ON THE WAY VIA SAM TUB NJ—X—ARV LATE FEB—X—

"Sam tub" referred to American sailors' name for their warship, one of Uncle Sam's tubs. "NJ" must refer to the *Trenton*.

So Rork was heading for Samoa? Not surprising. He'd no doubt been upset at being left behind without so much as an adios in person from me.

As a senior boatswain, Rork has myriad connections in the navy's web of long-serving petty officers. Petty officers are the ones who actually run the navy and get things done. Somehow he'd finagled his way aboard a ship and was heading south to Panama, a place he knows well. We'd worked there several times to keep track of the French canal effort.

Sean Rork is an interesting study, and I think a word about him is called for at this juncture in my account. Born in Wexford, Ireland, he's been at sea since a boy. Jumping ship in New York, he joined the United States Navy in 1861 and has been a bluejacket ever since, with more seamanship skill than any admiral and more espionage cunning than all of ONI put together.

Physically, he is unique. At fifty-seven, he is eight years older than I but has the strength of a thirty-year-old. Courtesy of a sniper five years earlier in Indochina, he has only one hand, his right. His left hand, from the forearm outward, is an India rubber appliance created by petty officers in the French navy just for him. It looks eerily genuine and is formed into a grip suitable for grasping an oar or a bottle or a belaying pin.

The truly remarkable aspect of his left limb is the fact that the appliance hides a wicked-looking marlinespike inside, which is securely anchored to a wooden base. It is the perfect weapon for our type of work: lethal, silent, and fully concealable. Rork merely unscrews his rubber hand with two twists, and there it is. There have been several occasions when it has proved useful, including as a "motivator" in convincing recalcitrant ne'er-do-wells to speak the truth. Rork is very proud of his spike.

All is not rosy, however. Being Rork's commanding officer, as well as his best friend, does have its challenges. He is adamantly prejudiced against all things English, an understandable product of his Irish boyhood. On the other hand, he is incorrigibly attracted to ladies, usually those who work along the waterfronts of the world. And they are even more attracted to him, a hopeless Irish romantic who can charm his way into any girl's heart or other places. I've seen the rogue melt hard-hearted females on four continents with just his lopsided grin.

His speech gets the best of him sometimes, however. For Rork regrettably reduces other ethnicities to a slang designation, many times in profane terms, though I must admit he is working hard to clean up his language. He no longer uses "spic," "dago," "wop," "fuzzy-wuzzy," "greaser," and many others, though "frog-eater" still slips out when referring to the French and "kraut-eater" for the Germans.

Rork is fond of spirits, particularly "the sailor's nectar," rum. We share that vice and have sometimes ended up the worse for it over our twenty-five year of service and friendship. But now, at our now advancing age, we have both slowed down our consumption considerably.

A lover of music, he can play the harmonica and guitar and tap out a Celtic beat on a drum. He reads novels by Loti and Dumas and Stevenson and has lately taken to reading the Bible, of all things.

As to his liabilities, his greatest is a lack of patience. My friend's tolerance wears thin with the more intellectual aspects of our profession; he usually suggests the use of violence long before I deem it necessary. Fortunately, old-school naval discipline is alive and well with Rork, and he does restrain his Gaelic proclivity for fighting when I tell him the time for that has not yet arrived.

But this much is certain: When violence is necessary and you're in a life-or-death fight, Sean Rork is the one man in the world you absolutely need to have beside you.

And so it was that I rejoiced inside at the good news that he was coming.

Jane, meanwhile, had been unhappily standing there at my side, not understanding the meaning of the cables or my pleasant reaction to them. It was then that a serendipitous turn in our fates occurred.

She nudged me and said, "Isn't that the man from that night on the deck with Ludwig?"

It was indeed. Walking into the telegraph office was Captain David Aukai, dressed in a linen suit with straw hat, the very picture of a successful island trader.

I held back from approaching him, preferring to see what his business was about. Aukai knew his way around, heading directly for the manager's office. The manager's secretary, an officious-looking young man, greeted him by name and immediately ushered him in.

Seconds later, the secretary was out front at the telegraphist's desk, searching the slots in the shelves that lined the wall. He extracted two telegrams and took them into the manager's office. A full five minutes later—I timed it—the secretary returned with an outgoing message for the operator.

My surveillance turned out to be too intense, however. The secretary noticed my interest in his activities. He made another entry into the manager's office and a moment later emerged with Aukai at his side, both of them looking at Jane and me.

I handed the man at the desk where I was standing my quickly worded cable to Mr. Sage. To the outside world, it said that I'd found some commercial investment possibilities but hadn't made up my mind yet. To Commodore Walker, it said that I was in Auckland and bound for Samoa.

Aukai dismissed the manager's secretary and made his way to us.

"Mr. Wake, Mrs. Cushman, how good it is to see you both.

I trust the rest of your voyage was more pleasant than our last encounter?"

Jane nodded warily as I responded. "Yes, Mr. Aukai, it went nicely for me. Jane and I didn't have occasion to see each other again on the ship but just ran into each other at the customs hall. So we shared a cab and took this opportunity to send off some telegrams. Where are you heading now?"

"Why, the coincidences seem to abound this morning, Mr. Wake," replied the Hawaiian with an amiable air. Then, with a close scrutiny of me, he said, "I'm heading the same place you are and by the same conveyance. John Irons is an old . . . acquaintance . . . of mine too."

I felt Jane fidget. I suppose I fidgeted myself, as I commented as casually as I could at this unforeseen turn of events, "Ah, well, that is good news. Our journey will be made even more pleasant, Jane."

"*Our* journey?" asked Aukai.

"Why yes, sir." I gestured at the lady. "Jane wanted to see her friends in Samoa again, but that steamer has already departed, so she is taking passage on the *Samaritan* as well"

"Then how very fortunate we are, Mr. Wake," said Aukai with a curt bow toward Jane but not much sincerity in his tone. "Shall we be off? The tide waits for no man or even a beautiful woman."

She noted his compliment with a forced smile.

"Do you have your own transport?" I asked.

"No, the wagon I used to get here had to leave, so my baggage is piled over there, near the door."

"Our cab is waiting outside, and we have room for you and your baggage if you wish," I offered.

He accepted. At the cab, I put Jane inside and went around back to assist in loading Aukai's things, which he trundled out on a dolly. They included the four cases Steward Wilson had reported. Each was about three feet long, two high, and two deep, looked watertight, and had substantial latches. Too small for rifles, too large for pistols.

Ignoring Aukai's polite objection that he could handle them himself, I shouldered one of cases up to the driver. It was heavy, at least sixty pounds. Nothing moved or gurgled inside. The carriage's stern sagged down even further when they were loaded. Up on the box seat, the driver shook his head in displeasure.

"So why are *you* heading to Samoa?" I whispered.

"For the same reason you are, Commander: to stop the Germans."

So I had been wrong in my assumption of the man's intentions. He wasn't going to merely observe events in Samoa and report them to his king back in Hawaii. Captain Aukai was heading there to fight.

"But this isn't your war, Aukai."

He effortlessly lifted a case up. "Oh, yes it is, Commander. Your American confrontation is recent, but my fellow people of the Pacific have been fighting the Germans for some time now. Yesterday it was the Melanesians at New Guinea and the Solomons, today it is the Polynesians of Samoa, and tomorrow it will be us in Hawaii. Is it not better to stop them before they reach our islands?"

H had a valid point regarding strategy, but the actual combat would be a far different matter. The Samoans had no artillery to speak of and were relying primarily on insurrectionary guerrilla tactics. And though they weren't losing, they weren't winning either. Even Aukai's European training and Hawaiian determination would be hard pressed against the modern military might of Germany in the Pacific.

He interrupted my thoughts with an observation about my companion.

"By the way, Commander, contrary to your explanation earlier, I get the impression Mrs. Cushman is less than enthusiastic about traveling to Samoa."

I tried to dismiss his comment with humor and a wink. "Yes, well, I suppose it wasn't totally her idea. I wanted some feminine company, and she does know people there. But these war scares have her warming to the idea a bit slowly."

He saw through that easily and cut right to the point. "I would think that her friends there are among the German elite and that certain information she might obtain through her friendships would be of use to you. . . ."

And to you, I thought, wondering whether he would attempt to co-opt Jane away from me and use her for his own agent. Hmm, so much for maintaining a semblance of secrecy. Aukai was definitely a man to be reckoned with. No, more than that— he was a man I needed to have on my side. I didn't want him as a hindrance and certainly not as an enemy.

"Very perceptive, Captain Aukai. Yes, it's always useful to have friends who know what's going on and pass it along to you."

We finished loading to last of his things and were about to enter the carriage, but I stopped him. "Not to be rude, but since we're being candid, what's in the cases?"

He grinned. "Some things the Germans won't like at all, if they live through them." My quizzical expression prompted him to add, "Some of Alfred Nobel's latest creation, Ballistite."

Ballistite? I could scarcely believe it.

From the Scotch whiskey–loosened lips of a Brit army officer in a Washington barroom the year before, I'd heard vaguely of Nobel's new invention. It used camphor in some way to make explosives far more stable when transported than any previously known composition. Details about Ballistite were known only inside the Italian army, to whom Nobel was contracted. From another European source, I learned that the French, whom Nobel used to work for, were attempting through nefarious methods to obtain the scientist's formula. From our ONI naval attaché in London, I heard a rumor that the Brits had already done just that.

So how had a Hawaiian, of everyone in the world, laid his hands not just on the formula but on four cases of the actual explosive? Then I remembered the conversation that evening at the Iolani Palace in Honolulu. Aukai told me that he'd trained with the artillery branch of the Italian army.

An admiring grin spread on my face, and I offered my hand. He shook it as I said, "Well, well. So it seems the Germans won't be the only ones with high explosives in Samoa. This is shaping up to be quite a journey, captain. And I think we'll get along just fine. Please call me Peter."

22

A Not-so-Good Samaritan

Waitemata Harbour
Auckland, New Zealand
10 A.M., Friday
18 January 1889

The moment I saw our schooner crew at the landing, I rethought my decision to use Irons' ship for transport to Samoa. A more cutthroat mob I've seldom seen. They were a mix of every color and age but had several things in common—filthy rags for clothes, unkempt bodies emanating a disgusting aroma discernible for fifty feet, a wide assortment of scars and tattoos, and the dead-eyed look of men who were capable of anything.

The ship's launch was no better when it came to inspiring confidence. It had never seen paint; the mast was cracked, and the lug sail ripped. Half the oars were crudely made sticks with boards nailed on the ends. The bilge had six inches of slime, and the floorboards had long ago rotted. I doubted it would make it out to the schooner.

We were spotted by the crew as we walked along the wharf,

trailed by the driver and some men we contracted there to carry our considerable amount of cargo. Five crewmen stood or sat on bollards, eyeing us suspiciously.

The oldest of them—maybe forty, possibly sixty—with a scraggly beard fully a foot long descending from a pimply, pock-marked face, hailed us in French-accented pidgin English, the *lingua franca* in that region of the world.

"*Masta! Pipel long* Samaritan?"

I caught only the last word. "Sorry. What was that?"

"He's speaking Tok Pisin," said Aukai. "That's the pidgin of the Melanesian people of New Guinea and Solomons. He asked if we are the people belonging to *Samaritan.*"

"Yes, we are," I answered the man, wondering how Aukai got so fluent in a Melanesian language.

"*Dispela* Samaritan." The fellow pointed to a two-masted schooner out in the anchorage, then thumped his chest. "*Boskru,* Bosun Jack!"

Our porters and driver tried to suppress their mirth at Jane Cushman's reaction to all this. It was a combination of revulsion at the sight of Bosun Jack, anger at me, and abject fear for her life. I must confess I was feeling somewhat the same emotions right then.

Aukai showed no such hesitation. He strode forward, shook Jack's hand, and launched into a rapid patois of his own. "*Stret. Gutpela, Bosun Jack. Kago tumas go long sip. Isi isi wantaim kago, Jack. Isi isi wantaim misis putim sip.*"

Aukai saw my confusion. "I told him he is a good man, to take our cargo to the ship and be careful with it. Also I said to be careful with Mrs. Cushman when they put her on the ship."

"Oh. Thank you. You're pretty good at this lingo."

He laughed. "I've been there before, several times. You'll pick it up quick enough, once we get to those islands and you hear it all around you. Tok Pisin is a phonetic language using local words, with some German, French, and English, and a little Portuguese added for spice. It was started many years ago on the plantations so all of the various groups of imported laborers could have a common language. We have a pidgin in Hawaii too. Different from this, though. Ours is Polynesian and English with a little Japanese thrown in."

While Jack and his men loaded our cargo, Aukai commented to me, "These men really are the perfect crew for our purposes, Mr. Wake. All Melanesian locals. No one would suspect them. Though few know it by his manner, John Irons is a very smart man."

With that strange statement made and my internal questions about Aukai mounting by the minute, my companion plunged into helping load the launch, which was settling farther and farther down into the water. Soon my attention left the Hawaiian, for the boat was taking on an alarming aspect of instability, with only inches of freeboard left.

Things were looking dicey, and we hadn't even left the dock.

From our conversation onboard our steamer *Australia*, I had presumed that John Irons, born and bred a landsman, had engaged a captain to command his schooner, *Samaritan*. However, in what was becoming a disturbing habit on this mission, upon reaching the schooner I discovered that once again I was wrong in my assumptions.

Bosun Jack explained this to me while we were rowed out to the anchorage. Aukai was the intermediary. The translation into English of Jack's tortured speech had it that Irons had no captain in his employ. Instead, once arrived in the Pacific he had applied himself to learn seamanship and navigation and was the chief in all respects among his savage entourage. But it immediately became clear upon rounding the stern of the ship that the one thing he had not learned how to do was to maintain a vessel properly. Or even minimally.

Samaritan was a one-hundred-foot, ninety-five-ton, flush-decked schooner. She was also a decrepit, unseaworthy mess and as filthy as her crew. Ragged sails, black with mildew, slack rigging, gouged topsides with open seams, rusting chains and hawse pipes—all this assaulted my naval eye. Much worse than her appearance was the stench, a gagging mixture of charnel house and cesspool. It wafted out of the ship herself and was so thick you could taste it.

What kind of vessel were we boarding? And how could any Christian from a civilized place claim to be her master and call her *Samaritan?* In fact, *Samaritan* was not even the name I saw primitively painted on her transom. Her name board said *Profit,* which I deduced was a temporary *nom de ruse.*

Gaining her deck and casting a dubious look around, I found no comforting sight to counter my original opinion of her. Not a thing was seamanlike. Or missionary-like. Suddenly, terrible scenarios filled my imagination. Was Irons actually some sort of confidence man who lured passengers aboard a derelict hulk to rob them?

I tried to logically think of a way out of this situation. I had my weapons close and thought Aukai would too. We could fight our way back into the boat and row ashore or at least to another vessel.

Glancing around the deck, I studied the crew going about their duties. No one indicated criminal intentions. If anything, they looked bored. No, I decided once I'd calmly assessed the crew, they weren't pirates, at least not toward us. And Irons was just a religious zealot with the best of intentions, funded meagerly. But the schooner was another matter. She engendered zero assurance in her ability to depart the harbor, much less cross the open ocean. Immediate danger having been dismissed in my mind, I reconsidered my transportation options to get to Samoa.

There were none. No steamers were currently heading for my destination. No schooners or larger sailing ships either. Time had become my main enemy, and I was wasting it in New Zealand. Damn it all. I could see no alternative but to try to make it to my objective aboard whatever transport was available and could float.

Irons didn't greet us. I was told he was in his cabin and would see us later at dinner. Apparently, there was no man designated as the mate. Bosun Jack was thus the senior man present and stood by the main cargo hatch, self-importantly assigning us our accommodations.

With a knowing leer, he gave Jane his own cabin, belatedly adding that he would be sleeping on deck. Aukai and I got the "*kaikai ruum*," which Aukai translated somewhat grandiosely, with a mocking tone, into "dining salon." It turned out to be the ship's food storeroom. I thought bitterly of how far I had come down in the world, in only four hours, since my luxurious first-class cabin aboard *Australia*.

Once below decks, Jane, whose reaction to all this had morphed from wary reluctance and horror into an outright visceral hatred of me, grabbed my sleeve in the narrow passageway and snarled in a very unfeminine tone, "If that repulsive brute Jack so much as touches me with a finger, I'll kill him where he stands. And, Wake, you'll be my second target."

Having said that, she produced a small derringer from a heretofore unseen side pocket in her skirt and, by the faint illumination of a deck light overhead, brandished it in front of my nose. The piece's muzzle appeared to be a thirty-two caliber, big enough to kill. Before I could conjure up any response, she opened the hatch—door would be far too grand a description—to her new abode, let out a blue oath at the sight, and threw one of her bags inside.

I decided that nothing I could say would improve my position or her attitude, so I retreated to my "dining salon," ten feet away. It wasn't far enough. I could hear her swearing in German and English for the next half hour, her rage mounting with every second as she dumped one after another of Bosun Jack's vermin-infested belongings out into the passageway in an effort to clear a space for herself.

We weighed anchor at eleven and rode the strong ebb under all plain sail through the islands off Waitemata Harbour. Once out of the shipping traffic, the topsails and outer jibs were set and we squared away on a northerly course with a light wind over our port quarter. Bosun Jack was in charge on deck during all this, John Irons being still out of sight below. The crew was competent, I was greatly relieved to see, handling the lines with a minimum of commands, and we had no problems with our departure.

The harbor patrol cutter sailed close by and received a half-hearted wave from Jack, who failed to dip our tattered British red ensign, as expected by custom and law. The cutter men hardly noticed. In their eyes, we were but one more tramp trader, bound for the islands with a cargo of household trinkets to sell to the dumb kanakas for double their value. The real smugglers were inbound from the Dutch or French islands.

Seven hours later, the schooner was broad-reaching in a good westerly breeze, making a fair speed through the Hauraki Gulf. Far off on the port side, a copper sun melted below Kawau Island as Jane, Aukai, and I stood on deck by the main shrouds, each of us lost in thought.

I intensely wanted to expand my precious conversation with the Hawaiian since I wanted to know more about his past and needed to know more about his future plans. I especially wanted to learn his plans for that Ballistite explosive to ascertain if I could merge them with mine. But with Jane and him chatting about the places they'd seen in the South Pacific, there was no privacy to broach my professional questions, for I dared not include Jane too closely in the details of my endeavor. Later, perhaps, I could interview Aukai in our shared "cabin."

A few minutes after the sun disappeared, just as the sky was entering its most colorful phase of pastels, one of the more villainous looking of the crew—I later learned his name was Kan, of what mix of ethnicity I never discovered—came up from below and approached me.

Kan had a markedly disgruntled air to him, which was enhanced by his frightening appearance. I recognized his type well, for I've made the unfortunate acquaintance of similar pitiless men around the world, some of whom were trying to kill me. One does not relax in such company.

Lanky, with the ropy musculature honed by a life at sea, this fellow was evil personified, his violent potential readily apparent and barely contained. Black, piglike eyes were set in olive skin over a crooked nose and stubbled chin, with decayed yellow teeth prominently displayed. Like Starkloff, he sported a badly stitched, livid, purplish scar from the outer edge of his right eye around to his right ear. I doubted he got it in a formal duel, though. I easily surmised it wouldn't take much rotgut to make him oblivious to pain and malevolent to anyone in his path.

Kan would've alarmed my friend Sean Rork, and that's saying something. Rork has a saying about men like Kan: "Only way to deal with buggers the likes o' them is kill 'em quick-like. Anything less than that jus' aggravates 'em."

"*Kaikai redi nau,*" Kan grunted dismissively in my direction. It was accompanied by a look that indicated his indifference toward me as a man or a potential adversary.

"*Go daun Kapten ruum,*" he commanded, then stood there unblinking, waiting for us to obey.

It took me a moment, but I deduced his meaning. Determined to make the best of our situation and not allow the fellow to think he had the upper hand, I announced to my fellow travelers in the most pleasant tone possible, "Evidently dinner is served, and we are to have it in Captain Irons' cabin."

I extended my arm to the lady of the ship. "Shall we go, my dear?"

For my efforts, I received a scowl from the lady and a comical nod from Aukai. So much for civility in the face of adversity. Oh, well, all you can do is try.

As of yet, none of us had actually seen Irons aboard or been invited to his *sanctum sanctorum*, so the crewman led the way down the ladder, past our accommodations, to Irons' cabin in the stern. When we reached it, Kan gestured toward the door but stood back from it, indicating with a grunt that I should enter the cabin, which I then did.

As bizarre as was our introduction to *Samaritan* that morning, what happened next surpassed it. Suddenly, the seemingly extraordinary events of that morning made perfect logical sense. More than that, I now knew they were part of a brilliantly executed plan on the part of our host to further his perceived Christian mission, of which I also was now an integral—and unwilling— part.

23
A Leap of Faith

Aboard the Schooner Samaritan
Northbound, Hauraki Gulf
Off North Island, New Zealand
7 P.M., Friday
18 January 1889

John Irons stood as we entered his sanctum, which was only moderately less disheveled than the rest of his ship.

"Welcome aboard *Samaritan*, my friends. Please forgive me for not being on deck to greet you earlier, but I was consumed by affairs needing my immediate attention. I also regret that you had to be subjected to this outward façade of the ship and crew with no explanation of why we look so shabby. The false name and appearance are, unfortunately, a necessary charade, given the stealthy nature of our work. They allow us to sail unnoticed among the many others of our class in this part of the world."

There was a little chuckle as he permitted himself a small boast. "I am glad to say that our deceptions have worked so far. Otherwise, I wouldn't be standing here before you, for the German officials consider what I do to be piracy."

His face took on a frown. "My one regret this evening is the state of your lamentable accommodations. I am truly sorry for them. Your presence aboard departs from our customary practice. We never have white passengers from civilized countries—our usual passengers are those sad natives we rescue from blackbirding, and they recognize our pungent odor, for this was a blackbirding ship until six months ago. These newly freed men understandably prefer to never be below in such a ship again for the rest of their lives."

So that was it! The stench seemed so familiar to me. Now I knew why. I'd smelled it during the war when I'd captured a slaver trying to escape the coast of Florida.

Irons focused on Jane. "In normal circumstances, I would offer my cabin to the lady, but this not a normal ship. I am extremely sorry to say that I cannot give up my cabin, for there are operational necessities that have a greater priority—a matter of life or death for us all—than comfort for a lady, even for one as lovely and genteel as you, my dear."

She eased her scowl slightly, and he went on. "However, let me assure you that right now your accommodations are being made as comfortable as possible, with bedding and pillows. Your belongings are safe and secure from any theft by the crew. Though they certainly don't look it, my men are far above that sort of behavior.

"Now, should we be stopped by a patrol, you may remain on deck as regular passengers. Your story will merely be the truth of the matter: You are three independent travelers who have contracted with me for passage to Samoa since you have business there and missed the regular steamer. We may be searched, so if you have any items that could pose a danger if found during a detailed examination of the ship, please give them to me. They will be kept hidden in a very secure location aboard. When you leave the ship, you can have them back. Are there any questions?"

The lady and the Hawaiian had none, but I had a long list.

I started out with, "Is this the ship you've been using in your work? How long? Even with the charade on deck and below, don't the Germans know of her and you by now? How can you sail unmolested through the heart of the German Pacific Empire in her?"

As I spoke, I saw his eyes light up with smug satisfaction. It came to me then. I knew the answer to my questions and said, "Savvy Read. . . ."

Irons bobbed his head and grinned. "Very good, Peter. Yes, I am doing what Lieutenant Savvy Read of the Confederate Navy did on the coast of New York and New England in eighteen-sixty-three. He captured twenty-six ships. Every third or fourth blackbirder ship I capture or steal, I use as my ship, sinking the previous one. The German Navy is always several steps behind, looking for a ship that no longer exists. The name and appearance of any ship I am using is changed, but I never use one for longer than a month or so at the very most. We're overdue for a change, so we'll be getting a new vessel and sinking this one in a few days."

I remembered that Rebel raid well, for it dominated the attention of the region where I lived and worked. It also dominated my family, for one of those captured ships had been in my father's small fleet of coastal schooners.

Savvy Read shut down Union commerce for weeks, drove up insurance rates, created panic from New Jersey to Maine, and forced the reallocation of army units and naval vessels from their primary duties against the enemy, all without the loss of a single life on either side during the entire operation. Before he was finally captured at Portland, Maine, the U.S. Navy had thirty-eight warships removed from blockade duty and looking for him. Or, rather, for the last ship they thought he was in.

The Navy, to their humiliation, never got him. It was the Maine army militia that earned that honor. Read, sitting in Fort Warren prison at Boston, was awarded the Confederate Congressional Medal of Honor and became a sensation in the South.

Yes, I had to admit that Irons had a clever plan, all right.

Although I noted he never mentioned that no one had been killed in his efforts to free blackbirded slaves. That would've been a bragging point.

And, of course, even Savvy Read was eventually caught. I didn't much fancy being with John Irons when the Germans ultimately got him and charged all aboard with piracy.

Jane wasn't impressed by what she'd heard. "Then you admit what the Germans say is correct. You really are nothing but a pirate, stealing ships and people. And I thought you had a ship named *Samaritan*, after the Bible story, and were doing missionary work. That's what I was told." She shot me a sharp look.

Irons was unruffled by her challenge. "*Samaritan* is the name for me and my work among the dark-skinned people of the islands. The names of the actual ships change. Technically, though, you are correct, Mrs. Cushman. I am a pirate in the eyes of the law. So was Robin Hood. Like him, I do this to help people. I am a pirate who liberates the enslaved."

"Those contract laborers volunteer for their work and get paid for it. That's not slavery," she countered quickly, using the rationale she'd heard from her German friends. "And they're not even Christianized natives. A little work at a German plantation will educate them about civilized ways to live and work."

I didn't have to guess at what was coming. He took a breath, set her in his sights, and let loose. "No, they are not Christians. They are from primitive tribes and don't understand the concept of contract labor or even what a Christian calendar year is, much less how long a contract term of three years is. Hoodwinked into signing their X on a piece of paper, they work under slave conditions, sometimes for five years, and are beaten and flogged for trying to escape or breaking any rule. And the Germans have a lot of rules.

"These people are paid the equivalent of *one* dollar a month in credit, in useless Bolivian currency, which can't be spent anywhere but on the German plantations. Once it's too late and they can't escape from this strange island to which they've been taken—

hundreds if not thousands of miles from their home village—they learn that the cost of their food and board is far more than one dollar a month, and they owe more than they are paid. If they do escape into the jungle, they are hunted down and killed. That, madam, is slavery, pure and plain, and is *not* what is expected of a nation that calls itself Christian."

Madam had no counter to that.

"And what of this crew of yours?" I asked. "You say they're trustworthy."

Irons liked the question. "Devout Christians one and all. Most share a similar warrior past as mine, though from various countries. They have great fun with their outward appearance and the effect it has upon those we encounter."

"Christians, you say? They don't look or act like Christians."

"No, they don't, do they?" he agreed, with a warm smile of pride. "At least not out on deck. But they most certainly are my dedicated brothers in Christ. They have to be, Peter, to be able to do the work required of them, against the incredible odds we face."

This extraordinary candidness on Irons' part didn't make sense to me. I was thinking of Jane in my next question. "You know the Germans would pay good money to know about this ship and her real mission. Why are you trusting *us?* How do you know one of us won't betray you?"

"It's very simple, really. We're all in the same boat, sailing into very dangerous waters, soon to be surrounded by mortal enemies. We have to trust each other."

Irons motioned to a chart table in the corner. Four place settings had been laid out, complete with wine goblets.

"I am sure you all are very hungry. To make amends for your troubles, please allow me to host a very nice dinner in your honor. Our cook fancies himself a gourmet chef, and I must say he is gaining in skill. Tonight he has prepared some of the sea's bounty for us."

He held out a chair for Jane. "Mrs. Cushman, would you care to sit here?"

Once we were all seated, a clean-shaven man in neat brown trousers and white shirt appeared from a hidden door in the forward wall. He carried a tray holding a bottle of Bordeaux. With a start, I realized it was Kan. The beard and filth were gone. I'd been completely fooled. This Kan was a different man entirely in appearance and demeanor.

Irons laughed. "Dear lady and gentlemen, may I have the honor to introduce Kan, our chef? You've already met him."

With the faintest self-congratulatory smile at pulling off his earlier deception, Kan filled our glasses and departed, silent the entire time.

Irons had us all hold hands as he said a benediction. After amens were dutifully echoed around the table, our host held up his wine glass and gleefully explained that it was "liberated" from a plantation in the Solomons. Having lulled us into a sense of well-being, Irons then dropped yet another surprise upon us.

"Please enjoy your wine while I elucidate our basic plan for the next few days. We are sailing to Finschaven on the coast of German New Guinea. They call it Kaiser Wilhelm Land. There we will pick up a man who is important to our mission. Next, we will go to the German Solomon Islands. New Britain, to be exact, which the Germans call Neu-Pommern. At that place we will drop off that same man. After that, we sail to Upolu Island in Samoa, otherwise known among sailors as the Navigator Islands."

24
Coercion

Aboard John Irons' Schooner
Northbound, Hauraki Gulf
Off North Island, New Zealand
7:30 P.M., Friday
18 January 1889

I struggled to keep my words tactful, though I seethed inside. Side trips to New Guinea weren't in my plan. But diplomacy was needed, for I was, after all, essentially in a captive position aboard the schooner.

"John, you never mentioned German New Guinea when I made the agreement for our passage. You said a stop in the Solomons, then to Samoa. I have to get to Samoa as soon as possible. This will add extra time I don't have."

"Yes, I know that. But when we spoke earlier, I didn't know about this problem in New Guinea. I just found out about it in Auckland, and I have to deal with it very quickly. It will take only a couple of extra days, and I assure you we will get to Upolu as rapidly as the wind serves us. Each of us has important things to do there, commander."

When he called me "commander"—it was obviously no accidental slip of the tongue—Jane gave me a questioning glance, her face tightening in anger. *Oh, no,* I thought, *not again.* The woman's temperament was proving to be difficult, to put it mildly.

Having verbally lit that fuse, Irons gave me a fleeting got-you expression, then turned to the lady to make sure her explosion would be memorable.

"Why, Mrs. Cushman, you look as if you didn't know that your traveling companion is a United States naval officer . . . who works in intelligence work, no less. Tell me you didn't believe that 'businessman from Baltimore' story."

When she didn't reply, he said, "Hmm . . . I see you did. Well, since we are headed into a fair amount of danger, I think we all need to lay our cards on the table, so we know who is really what."

The ship lurched from a wave, making the overhead lantern sway wildly as Jane countered Irons' arrogant tone with a frosty reply. "Yes, as a matter of fact, I did believe that businessman story. So no, I did not know the truth about Mr., or should I say Commander, Wake. Or any of you, evidently. It seems I have been lured here under false pretenses and am surrounded by dishonest men engaged in criminal activity."

I thought that statement and her dramatically peevish attitude a bit much coming from Jane Cushman, the feminine predator of the Pacific, but kept silent to see what would happen next in this peculiar scene. Aukai, meanwhile, watched the verbal sparring with open bemusement on his face.

Irons started up again. "*Mea culpa,* madam. Please allow me to make atonement by stating the situation clearly. By now you know about me, a former American army officer turned Christian missionary who now, in repentance for his many prior sins, rescues Melanesian slaves from the clutches of the blackbirders and the German plantations in the islands of Samoa."

He swept a boney hand toward the Hawaiian. "Next, we have Captain David Aukai here of His Hawaiian Majesty's Royal Guards. He is actually an army intelligence officer, charged by his king and your friend Dominis with clandestinely assisting the Samoans to defeat the Germans in their islands and thus halt the Teutonic expansion across the Polynesian Pacific toward Hawaii."

Aukai didn't react to the exposé. I surmised he must have known it was coming. Given all I'd seen of them, I realized that he and Irons were of long acquaintance, if not close confidants. I wondered what else they'd been planning.

The hand gestured to me. "Commander Wake is here to spy on the German military in Samoa and assist his fleet in defeating them, since war between America and Germany may break out at any time. Thank God, it hasn't yet, as far as we know."

He faced Jane. "And last, but certainly not least, we have *you*, my dear lady. A *bon vivant* of high society in the Pacific and friend to the Germans. You have the ability to obtain information considered valuable to the captain, the commander, and myself.

"There, have I stated it plainly enough to your satisfaction, madam? All of the men here are against Germany, and all want the intelligence you gain from your social interactions. Please be aware that this is not a matter of competition among us gentlemen but rather a matter of cooperation."

Then he asked me pointedly, "Am I right, commander?"

I had to admire his nerve and execution. He'd boxed me neatly into a corner, literally and figuratively. Sometimes one cannot select his allies but must take them as they arrive, however unexpected or unorthodox.

"Yes, John," I replied. "That about sums it up."

Irons didn't pause to gloat over co-opting me but said, "I imagine Commander Wake has offered financial consideration for your efforts, Jane, which is fine by me. I would hope that is not your only reason for doing the right thing for your country and your God, but if it is, then so be it."

He leaned forward and suddenly grasped her forearm, making

her flinch. Studying her pretty face intensely, he said, "Now that you know our true identities and intentions, Jane, what side are you on? The side of the slavers and the devil? Or the side of the saviors and of God? I think this would be a very good time for *us* to know *your* exact intentions so that we may govern our subsequent actions accordingly."

By her expression, I could tell Jane comprehended precisely what Irons had said and what he didn't have to say. But she was good, very good, at handling men and adverse turns of fate. The charm I'd seen so often aboard *Australia* emerged in good form.

"Why, of course, I'm on *your* side, John," she cooed as she put her hand atop his on her forearm. "I'm a Christian too. A passionate one. But I've never really thought about the laborers and didn't know some of the things you just brought out. I am not in favor of slavery, if that is what is going on."

"So you have Christ in your heart?" Irons asked.

"Yes, I do. Though I admit that I have . . ."—those dark blue eyes looked into his as she sank her hook deeper—"*sinned.* Oh, Lord, how I have sinned."

I was impressed that she could say any of it with a straight face, but say it she did. Irons showed no such doubt about her sincerity, though. He boomed out, "Very good, Jane. Let the sin go, my dear. You are not alone. We've all sinned."

As he sympathized with her, I noticed his hand withdraw from her clutches. It slapped the table in triumph. "Praise the Lord and down with the blackbirders!" he boomed. Then, in a far more composed vein, he went on. "Now that we all understand each other, I feel free to add some detail about our plans for Finschaven. There will be some grand excitement, my friends, for the man we are taking aboard there is currently a prisoner of the Germans. And you three good people, along with Kan, are going ashore to effect his rescue and bring him out to this ship!"

Former sinner Jane gasped in wide-eyed shock. "My God."

My reaction was less pious. "What the hell did you just say?"

Aukai and Irons both grinned at our responses.

The renegade clergyman—that was how I was thinking of him by that point—tried to calm us down by sounding cheerful, as if it was merely a schoolboy lark.

"David and I have a plan. Don't worry. It won't take long to carry out and no one will be hurt. Nonviolent and quick. You'll all be back aboard in no time."

"You keep referring to us. What about you? Aren't you going ashore to do this?"

"I would do it. However, I recently learned that the German authorities there are circulating a poster with a photograph of me among the natives, seeking informants. So, you see, I dare not go ashore lest someone alert the Germans to our presence. But no worries, my friends. Everything's arranged. I just need some unknown people to make contact, that's all. One of them needs to speak German, which is why Jane is necessary. Perhaps an hour ashore in the dark of the night at most, Peter. It'll be easy."

Easy? I'd heard that sort of nonsense before, usually from brandy-drinking politicos in their comfortable Washington offices just before they sent me heading off on a mission in the more perilous parts of the world. But there was a big difference: We weren't in Washington, and none of this slavery affair was in my mission or interest.

Aukai nodded in agreement as Irons outlined his idea. But I wasn't on board with any of it. "And if I, or Jane here, refuse to go along with this escapade?"

A frown formed, as if I'd hurt Irons' feelings. "The answer to that is quite simple. You, commander, will forfeit your deposit to me of two hundred gold dollars, and you both will be dropped off at the first inhabited island we see. There you can convey to God your excuses for failing to help Him and his enslaved children and also ask Him to get you another ship to take you to Samoa."

A smile replaced the frown. "But, my friends, why should we dwell on such a negative view of this opportunity? A better question to ask would be what if you *do* assist? In that case, your deposit will be returned, the passage to Samoa will be absolutely free, and you, commander, will be five hundred dollars the richer."

Robbery was the plain word for it. If Sean Rork had been with me, the two of us could have seized the schooner and triced up the good pastor and his motley crew to the mast or killed any who disputed us. We'd extricated ourselves from far worse positions over the years. But Rork wasn't with me. I was alone and vastly outnumbered.

No, my lot had been cast, by my own foolish hand, for better or worse with John Irons. The cannibal islands between New Zealand and New Guinea were no place to be marooned. Especially with a woman like Jane Cushman.

She chose that moment to grumble her surrender, "All right. . . ."

The fact that I sounded much like Mrs. Jane Cushman had earlier in the day was not lost on me as I let out a long breath and muttered, "Well, *Reverend*, it appears your coercion has worked. What exactly do you want us to do at Finschaven?"

Based upon my professional experiences, I knew this was the point of no return. My heretofore leisurely journey across the Pacific, spent gathering intelligence and making my preparations for the execution of the mission, was over. I was entering the heart of enemy territory among people I dared not trust. Factors I could not yet anticipate would dictate my actions. The luxury of deliberation in decision-making had evaporated. Time would accelerate.

And every minute of it would be filled with personal peril and international consequences.

25
The Kalabus

Schneider Harbor
Two Miles North of Cape Cretin
East Coast of German New Guinea
2:17 A.M., Tuesday
25 January 1889

The pale yellow crescent of a waning moon was rising above the sea behind us, shimmering in the dank heat of a Southern Hemisphere summer. To the west, the Rawlinson Mountains blotted out the stars like a jungle carnivore creeping toward us in the night. The wind was light from those same mountains, zephyrs sliding down the slopes to ruffle the sea ahead of us, carrying with them the sickly-sweet earthy smells of New Guinea's maze of equatorial tropical forest.

Several times, a squall raced down the mountains, blanketing us with rain for five minutes as it passed over our darkened ship. The northwest monsoon would soon be blowing strong, but for now it was still fitful. Between the squalls, we slid slowly forward, pointing up into the land breeze as high as possible to reduce our silhouette to anyone ashore.

Irons displayed no hesitation or qualms, quietly giving out orders while standing by the wheel. Bosun Jack was at the foremast shrouds, swinging a lead line, the splash of the lead coming once a minute in a constant rhythm. We were close in but as yet still had deep soundings. According to the chart, soon the bottom would rise under us as it met the shoreline.

Directly to our south lay Matura Island, brooding like a mother over the lesser islets lined up in the bay across our stern. North of us was the low form of Gagidu Point. North of that by a mile and a half was the German town of Finschaven, the official capital of the colony. It, along with everything else around the area, was run by the company managers of the Deutsche Handels und Plantagen Gesellschaft der Sud See Inseln zu Hamburg.

"*Wara et fathum. Ananit bilong hat rip,*" called back Bosun Jack softly.

After seven days of hearing Tok Pisin, I could make out his meaning. The water was eight fathoms deep, with a hard, rocky reef bottom.

"*Faiv* fathom. *Kina.*" Five fathoms, with a shell bottom.

"Douse the main and foresail," ordered Irons. "Get the boat ready."

The dinghy towing astern was brought alongside as the schooner started to swing to starboard. Kan, Jane, Aukai, and I stepped carefully down into it and shoved off. Kan and the Hawaiian each took a pair of oars. I sat aft and steered. Behind us, the schooner completed her turn and slid silently out of the bay on the ebb tide, her masts and jib faintly visible against the powderlike scattering of stars between the clouds.

A half mile dead ahead lay a thin horizontal stripe of white beach, topped by the dark jungle and even darker mountains behind. There were no lights showing ashore, and, according to Irons, there were no villages on this stretch of coast except for tiny Buki, a mile to the south. The coastal road from Schollenbruch was a hundred yards inland from the beach. It would take us up to the southern outskirts of Finschaven. The humorist in me noted that the Germanic names sounded ridiculously inappropriate for the tropics.

The plan was that once we arrived at Finschaven, Kan would lead us to the *kalabus*, or German jail for native prisoners. At that point, Jane Cushman would have a critical role, for she was to find and speak to a German sergeant who had, theoretically, been bribed a week before and was waiting for his contact to show up. Then the prisoner would be allowed to escape to our custody.

Aukai and I were along essentially as guardians for Jane. Each of us carried our personal weapons. For Aukai, that meant a Colt revolver and an amputated double-barreled shotgun. I had my Merwin-Hulbert 44-caliber pocket revolver with a "skullcrusher" frame and an 1882-model, seven-round Spencer 12-gauge pump shotgun. We weren't there to defeat the German military, just delay them long enough to make our escape should events turn nasty. Jane had her derringer and Kan had a cane knife that was rusted except for the edge, which had been honed.

The boat grounded. We waited for several minutes, listening and peering around for any sign of movement before getting out. The only sound was the unending buzz of insects, interspersed with chirps and croaks of amphibians and the lone cry of some feline creature. Pulling the dinghy across the narrow sands, we entered into the wall of black tangle and another world.

The jungle was pitch black. No light from moon or star penetrated the roof of leaves. Kan led the way, followed by me, Jane, and Aukai, all of us staying carefully right astern of the one in front. To do otherwise meant instant disorientation in that maze of vine, leaf, and stalk, many of which had thorns or sharp edges.

At last we emerged onto the road, a double-rutted lane that didn't look well traveled by vehicles. There was no pause, for Kan marched northward with the determination of a company sergeant, his foreign entourage dutifully trailing behind.

Kan said not a word of explanation as we lined up prone beside him behind some bushes. He simply pointed to a squat building with no windows and grunted something.

Unlike the other structures we had seen, the building wasn't thatch or crude frame but cement and clay. By the light of a lantern on the front wall, we saw a coat of arms displayed. On a banner over the top was inscribed *Neu-Guinea*. Below the inscription was a black German eagle on a white background, and underneath that was a magnificently plumed bird on a green background. This was an official station of the German colonial police.

Inside there was bright illumination from several lamps. It glowed out of an open front door and lit up the area. I could hear the scrape of chair legs on the floor inside. One, maybe two men were in that room.

"*Jemeni kalabus?*" whispered Aukai.

A grim nod from Kan confirmed it was the Germans' jail.

"*Jemeni bosman?*" asked Aukai, inquiring where the German sergeant was whom we were to meet.

Kan studied the sky for a moment. He grunted again and pointed up at the stars.

"Does he mean time?" I asked.

Before he could reply, Kan held up one finger, but what did that mean? One hour? One night?

"This is absurd," opined Jane as she slapped a bug on her cheek.

Aukai squeezed his eyes shut. Thinking aloud for the right word in Tok Pisin, he muttered to himself, "Ah yes, of course, it is phonetic."

To Kan, he said, "*Wetim aua?*"

Kan nodded. We needed to wait one hour. Presumably for

the change of the watch, when the sergeant would begin his duty.

We spent the hour lying under that bush. I peered out at the building. Other than the fancy coat of arms, it didn't look like much. Maybe we could just go in, overwhelm the guards, and get the man out without the sergeant's help. I turned to the Hawaiian to suggest such an action, but Aukai was sleeping. On his other side, Jane scratched and slapped at insects. I put aside my idea, for I'd have no allies.

Our native companion wasn't sleeping, though. Peering through the gloom with eyes that darted back and forth, seeing everything, Kan periodically would ease himself away with the grace of a cat. Circling around the area, he crept slowly along the ground on all fours, alert for any signs of ambush. Then he would return and resume his silent watching.

At last, I heard the sound of squeaking cart wheels approaching and nudged Aukai. Kan glanced our way and nodded. The sergeant was arriving. A few minutes later the cart, pulled by a scrawny mule, entered the scene. Aboard were three policemen of the Neu-Guinea Polizeitruppe. Two were dark-skinned Melanesian privates, the third an older white man. Kan smiled, pointing at the fourth form hunched down in the back of the cart. Our man.

The two native policemen went inside. I could hear them greeting their comrades in a back room, then the thud of a door closing. Some muted laughter came out of the building.

The white policeman stayed outside. His shoulder boards had some type of ornamentation on them, and he had the three inverted sleeve chevrons of a *vize-feldwebel,* a senior noncommissioned officer. Thus he would be the sergeant in question. Standing next to the cart, he furtively scanned the perimeter of darkness surrounding him, waiting for his contact to appear. He looked nervous, as well he should. He was committing treason.

I nudged the lady. "Time for your skills, my dear. Go charm this fellow in German and get our man turned over to us. I want to get the hell out of here."

She didn't move.

I tried being understanding and supportive. "Look, I'll be standing right behind you, and I'll have a properly menacing look on my face. Aukai and Kan are circling around now, and they'll be in the bush right behind these fellows in case any of them even think about double-dealing us. So let's get this thing done."

That seemed to alleviate her fear somewhat. She stood up, brushing the dirt off her skirt and assuming her usual confident pose. After a deep breath and some muttered curses aimed at me, she emerged from the bushes with an angelic smile, outstretched hands, and the top two buttons of her blouse undone.

It was disquieting easily how she went right into character. Her voice was a combination of shy and come-hither as she repeated the code words Irons had given her, "*Gutenabend, Sergeant. Herr Weiß sendete mich, um Herrn Schwarzes zu erhalten.*"

I recalled Irons laughing as he translated the pun for me at the time: "Good evening, Sergeant. Mr. White sent me to get Mr. Black."

The sergeant was clearly expecting a man to be his contact but was just as clearly delighted to see it was a beautiful woman instead. He sucked in his paunch and puffed up his chest, then visibly deflated when I emerged from the bushes. To dissuade him from any further amorous thoughts regarding Mrs. Cushman, I struck my most threatening stance, with the Spencer shotgun doing most of the intimidation, since it was leveled right at him.

Jane reiterated her speech, this time with a perturbed attitude.

Realizing his momentary fantasy was not going to come true, the sergeant grabbed the shackled prisoner in the cart and pulled him out roughly. The man fell down onto the ground and groaned quietly in pain. The man's hands and feet were manacled, then chained between. He tried to get to his feet but rolled in the dirt, unable to stand. The sergeant chuckled.

The man we'd come to rescue was incredibly black, with matted fuzzy hair like an African's. His only clothing was a breastplate of feathers and bones, with two large boars' tusks prominently rising out of the plate. Instead of a loincloth, he had a two-foot-long, thin gourd sheath covering his manhood, secured by jute strings around his neck. His musculature was lean and scarred, his age somewhere north of forty and south of eighty. That he was a lifelong warrior was obvious. Even as physically defeated by the heavy manacles as he was, I could see the formidable internal strength that showed in those menacing eyes when he regarded the sergeant.

The sergeant swung a glance from the man's sheathed genitalia to Jane and back again, sniggering at her reaction to seeing a truly naked aboriginal. He produced a key and turned the manacles' locks, then jerked the man up on his feet. The prisoner, however, having been confined in such a restricted manner, still could not stand. He fell again, this time in a sprawl.

With a knowing sneer, the sergeant yanked the man up by the armpit and shoved him toward Jane, snarling, "*Ist hier der ihr schwarzes spielzeug, mein libeling.*"

Whatever that meant, it didn't sound good to me and she didn't like it one bit. She walked two steps to the sergeant and slapped him hard across the face, her dainty little fingernails clawing three red stripes across his left cheek.

"*Zuruck in ihren schweinestall, sie gehen schwein!*"

I wished she hadn't done that, for the situation had now escalated beyond words. Eyes bulging in rage, he reached for his pistol in its flapped holster, but I hissed right then and shook my head.

"Bad idea, Fritz. Don't do it. *Nein,*" I told him. He hesitated, but I could see he was beyond reasoning and could explode at any second.

Whatever the entirety of her statement—I did grasp the *schwein* part, which meant "pig"—I thought it appropriate right then to step forward and take over the negotiation with my Spencer. Putting the muzzle of my shotgun in the sergeant's face, I reminded him in English that a gentleman never shoots a lady or even a woman like Jane Cushman. Comprehending the gist of my message, or at least the twelve-gauge's remarkably large business end, he slowly backed away, his hands in the air but his murderous glare still glued on Jane.

Aukai's timing was impeccable, for he chose that juncture to silently approach the infuriated sergeant from the rear. Placing the double barrels of his shotgun against the back of the sergeant's neck, he whispered into his ear, "Shh. . . . Stay calm, sergeant."

Meanwhile, Kan dashed to the aid of the prisoner and scooped the poor man right up into his arms. I was impressed to note that Kan carried him off into the bushes on the Finschaven side of the *kalabus*, the opposite side from where we had come. That would add to the confusion of any Germans who might search for us afterward.

Mrs. Cushman, having made her truculent point, stormed off in the same direction. That left me, Aukai, and the sergeant, whose initial terror of our shotguns was fading rapidly. The sergeant now made me the target of his anger.

I knew exactly what he was thinking by his cunning expression: Would I pull the trigger? I was part of the Samaritan do-gooder Christians, liberating Melanesian savages. But could I kill a white man in cold blood? Would I react fast enough if he went for the shotgun?

I pre-empted his next logical move by ramming the shotgun's barrel into his large belly, doubling him over. In seconds, Aukai relieved him of his pistol, a rusty old affair, and together we used the manacles on the sergeant in the same manner as he did on his former victim, with hands to feet. Since I couldn't understand him anyway, I stuffed his slouch hat firmly in his mouth. He lay in a fetal ball on the ground, moaning through his gag.

Aukai turned and covered the doorway, for the sergeant's subordinates had come out to investigate the yelling. One had a rifle, the other a cane knife, but both had the good sense to hand their weapons to Aukai, who then backed away down the road after Kan and Jane and our rescued chieftain.

By the time we circled back to the south along the beach and reached our boat and companions, I heard three shots coming from the area of the *kalabus*. From the north, I heard answering shots. The sergeant had been freed, and the alarm was being given.

We headed out into the bay. I could see the schooner waiting, half a mile away.

26

Dunkels Geld

Waterfall Bay
Southern Coast of Neu-Pommern
(New Britain Island) Bismarck Archipelago
250 Miles East of Finschaven
4:20 A.M., Friday
28 January 1889

The target was anchored just ahead, her bow to the sea and her stern tethered to the steep shore fifty yards away. She was, like most large vessels in the islands, a schooner. There were no lights showing, which meant to me that all aboard were either passed out from drink or waiting for us in an ambuscade.

Profit was lying hove to out of sight a couple of miles to the west, around Cape Jacquinot, in the care of a skeleton crew of three men. Everyone else from *Profit* was with us, a dozen men and Jane, who adamantly refused to be left alone back on the ship with what she termed "the scum." We'd sailed in the *Profit*'s launch around the Cape and had just lowered the mast and sail. Now under oars alone, we were advancing on our objective.

Aukai and I carried our weapons tightly, pistols in our pockets and shotguns slung on our shoulders. In addition to his white collar and black suit, Irons wore a belt containing twin army Colts, a cane knife, and a dagger.

His crew, led by Bosun Jack, carried all manner of bladed weaponry about their persons, literally armed to the teeth. Several carried a Malayan kris, an assassin's dagger with a serpentine blade, designed to create vicious wounds that would never close. Others carried the bow and tin-tipped arrows of the Komodo people in the Dutch Indies or the stone axes of New Guinea.

We made a piratical, malevolent-looking bunch, all right. No one seeing the likes of us would possibly mistake our cutthroat horde for a congregation of devout Christians embarked upon a Samaritan mission to free the downtrodden. Neither, of course, would the Germans, should we be captured. I had no doubt that they would photograph us in all our regalia just prior to our executions, which would be done within minutes of our being made prisoners. The images would be disseminated to the European press and the local natives as the final evidence to dispel any notion of Irons' Robin Hood legend.

Clearly, this diversion was not my fight. It was, in fact, delaying the actual implementation of my mission and presented every chance of resulting in my demise before I could accomplish a single facet of what I was in the Pacific to do. To say I was disinclined to embark in that launch with Irons is a gross understatement. I was on the verge of mutiny or desertion before our departure from his schooner. One look at my savage companions, however, halted that urge. You didn't want to be considered an enemy by these fellows. And their definition of enemy was a fluid perception, highly influenced by John Irons' mercurial changes of opinion.

So there I was, about to go into combat against a desperate and well-armed foe, completely unlike our freeing of the native leader at Finschaven. All this to steal a ship, no less. That is called piracy everywhere in the world, no matter the motive. And piracy is dealt with summarily when the authorities eventually catch you.

I would imagine that a reader of this account is by now wondering just how and why I came to be in this predicament, when I'd been promised passage to Samoa once we had liberated the native chieftain at Finschaven. I was pondering the same thing at that very moment. As I strained to see in the dark, I found myself mentally reviewing what had happened in Irons' cabin two nights earlier.

We hadn't seen the warrior chieftain—his real name was unpronounceable but his *nom de guerre* was Kilim, and by the story I heard it was a well-deserved sobriquet—once aboard *Profit*, for he disappeared forward to live with the crew. For the next twenty-four hours we sailed straight out into the Solomon Sea to evade the German Navy, whom we assumed were searching for us and their escaped prisoner. Our course was southeast and, courtesy of the growing northwest monsoon season, we were making very good time toward Samoa.

Irons had been silent, brooding internally over some issue, ever since our return from the rescue. At dinner that first night after Finschaven was when I learned what it was and that the *Profit*'s course was about to change.

"Commander, we'll be wearing around to port at the change of watch tonight. New course is for New Britain Island in the Bismarck group. A little necessity needs to be attended to before continuing on to Samoa."

"What?" I blurted, my blood instantly heating up at this treachery. "There's no time for more postponement. Your necessities are not my problem. I need to get to Samoa straight away, as we've agreed to twice now."

Irons huffed and said, "Well, I was going to do this chore *after* I'd put you ashore in Samoa, but that was before you and the lady mangled the chieftain's rescue last night, turning it into an assault on a German sergeant, who had been cooperative before he met you people. Now he has put the word out about us. Remember the gunshots fired by him to alert the garrison? I was aboard here and heard them too, just as I was speaking to a fisherman I've known for some time on this coast."

"So?"

"The fisherman had left Finschaven only hours before, and he told me three pieces of significant news. The first is that he heard rumors that the Samaritans were on the coast somewhere. The second was that *Adler* was in port at Finschaven. She got under way a couple of hours earlier and was headed north, probably to look for us in the Dampier Strait. That was why I immediately got all sail on and headed out to sea, away from the *Adler*'s course. And if anyone on shore saw us leave and noted our course, he'll think we're bound for Woodlark Island or Guadalcanal, maybe Fiji or Samoa."

Significant news indeed, and I wondered why he hadn't said anything about *Adler* earlier. She was, after all, Commodore Fritze's flagship, mounting six modern, 5.5-inch guns, plus another five smaller cannons in turrets.

Irons let his comments sink in, then continued. "So we now have a steam warship looking for us, though in the wrong direction. She left before the alarm was given, but the signal station at Cape Kaiser Wilhelm could let her know, and then she'll come about and head this way. All this means I can't keep this vessel any longer. We need to get a new one immediately."

I ended his sentence. "And after we do that, we'll sink the *Profit* so they'll be searching for a ghost ship that no longer exists."

"Exactly, commander. So there's no time to do anything else, like steer for Samoa. Fortunately, the third thing the fisherman told me was about a vessel that will fit the bill nicely and also provide a nice bit of poetic justice. Right now she's lying at Waterfall Bay, on the south coast of New Britain Island, two days broad reach from here with this wind. The poetic justice is that she's a blackbirder, run by some old adversaries of mine."

"Adversaries?"

"Oh, yes indeed. These two are some of the most dead-hearted characters in these islands, which is truly saying something, for we've got more than our share around here. Captain Gunter Metzger commands the vessel, and Heinrich Grun owns her and several plantations as well. The ship is the *Dunkels Geld*, a blackbird slave schooner that takes Melanesians east to plantations in Polynesia, mostly Grun's places on Upolu in Samoa. We're going to Waterfall Bay to steal her. We should get there Friday night if all holds fair."

"I thought those blackbirder ships were heavily armed."

"They certainly are. But they're used to fighting ill-armed and untrained Melanesians, not three well-armed veteran warriors supported by some very determined sailors and some equally determined natives from shore. Plus, we'll have surprise on our side."

Three? As usual, Aukai was nodding his head in agreement with Irons. They both assumed I would go along. Well, we'd see about that. "I don't get it, John," I said, trying to sound reasonable. "How are you going to pull this off nonviolently?"

He ignored the *you* in my question. "First, we're putting Kilim, the chief we rescued from the Germans, ashore on the west side of Cape Jacquinot after dark. He has been here before, helping me liberate some of his brother Dani Sendani men from New Guinea, who were taken there to work in the plantations.

"Kilim will sneak into the nearby plantation, gather some of them, and walk across the cape by way of the jungle to the beach at Waterfall Bay. The Dani Sendani will be more than ready to help us, for they have very good reason to hate Gunter Metzger. He's the one who tricked them into coming here. Kilim and his men will be our reserves, set up on the beach in case the blackbirders escape the schooner and try to get ashore."

"So how are you going to take the ship?"

"We go aboard by surprise late at night. Look, I know what

you're thinking: Blackbirders are notoriously itchy with their trigger fingers. But they are also notorious for getting drunk at the drop of a hat. *Dunkels Geld's* been anchored at Waterfall Bay for a week, waiting for orders from Grun. They don't party ashore at night, so they'll all be aboard. And by now they'll all be drunk as coots on square-face and cavorting with the local girls they brought aboard."

"Square-face?"

"Rotgut German gin. It's all over the German Pacific. They give it to the locals to make them drunkards and beholden to them. But a lot of the Germans out here are habitual drunkards too."

"So we simply climb up onto the deck and take the schooner?"

"Yes, it's that simple. The native men will occupy the beach and prevent Germans from escaping ashore while we board the ship and capture her. *None* must be allowed to escape us and give the alarm, for the ship must just disappear. Initially, it will be assumed Metzger just sailed her away. Eventually, with any luck, it will be assumed that she was lost at sea. That's not unusual. It's monsoon season now and local storms brew up quickly. Every year several ships disappear during monsoons."

"What will you do with the Germans?"

"Once we take over *Dunkels Geld,* they will be put below and kept there under guard."

"In the same hold where they usually put the Melanesians?"

He smiled. "Precisely. It's ready made for prisoners, isn't it? Don't worry. We'll feed and water them with just the same slop they dole out to the natives. And at some point, well *after* I deliver you to Samoa, I'll put the blackbirders ashore somewhere."

He gazed at the overhead whimsically. "Hmm. Maybe at Manus Island. They took a hundred men from there four years ago and nobody knows where they are. Yes, I think that would be the perfect place for the German crew of the *Dunkels Geld* to go. By the way, do you know what that German ship name means in English?"

I shook my head. Irons looked at Jane and raised an eyebrow, then sarcastically asked, "Jane, you speak German. Would you do us the favor of translating it?"

"It means 'Dark Gold,' " she said quietly.

"Yes, it does, my dear. What a clever pun by the owner, Herr Grun," he mocked. To me, Irons asked, "Commander, I'm counting on you doing me the favor of accompanying us when we take the ship. I can use a steady man with me. But it's your choice, of course."

Again the knowing smile, but this time his eyes weren't joining in the humor. "I think you know the answer already as to what will happen if you refuse my request. No harm will befall you from me or my crew. That I guarantee. You'll merely no longer be part of our happy band of brothers."

"I'll merely be marooned on an island full of cannibals instead."

"Cannibals? Oh, that's the stuff of fanciful novels, commander. There really aren't that many of them around anymore. The locals will still kill you, but you don't have to worry about them eating you afterward."

We were getting close to the blackbirder. Thankfully, no moon was showing and the stars were covered. The sky was black with banks of low clouds. I could barely see the ship ahead, so it must've been doubly hard for them to make out our small boat. In any event, no challenge came from *Dunkels Geld*.

We took no chances even so. Everyone was clothed in black. No one stood up or spoke above a whisper. Our men rowed muffled oars with deliberate strokes. In the bow crouched Bosun Jack, looking like an old hairy bear ready to spring. He had a rusting cane knife clenched in his teeth, a belaying pin in his right hand, and a butcher knife in his left.

I noted that the only people carrying firearms were Irons, Aukai, and myself. And Jane Cushman, with her little derringer.

The crew was apparently not trusted or trained enough to handle guns, which I thought quite telling.

We shipped oars and coasted up to the anchor chain. Bosun Jack leaped for the hawse pipe, rattling the damned thing while the oarsmen held the boat steady. I expected a volley of grapeshot, but nothing happened. Jack poked his head over the gunwale and grinned, then whispered something down to us.

Three of his fellows pulled themselves up to join him on the foredeck. The rest of us pulled the boat along the starboard side of the hull to the forechains, where Irons led the way up to the deck. So far, everything was as quiet as a graveyard. Jane stayed in the boat, per Irons' orders, to help the one man there keep it close against the schooner.

When I reached the main deck, I saw a dozen forms collapsed in various attitudes on the deck, some snoring great blasts, others dead to the world. The air reeked of rum, gin, urine, and vomit.

Peering aft, I saw one figure sitting on deck, leaning back on the binnacle box by the wheel, his head resting on his shoulder. One of our men stumbled on the foredeck near the capstan. Something metallic fell on the deck and woke the man at the wheel. He started to move unsteadily, his hands groping for support to pull himself up. By the time he was able to stand, two of our number pinioned him from behind with a knife to the throat and hand over his mouth. Another man took possession of the revolver in the man's belt. Luckily, no one else woke up.

That was fortunate, as it would've meant a bloody fight, for there were weapons everywhere: axes, machetes, pikes, belaying pins, shotguns, pistols, and rifles, all either on or within easy reach of the blackbirders.

Irons and I carefully walked aft among the sleepers and took a look at our first prisoner. Leaning close to the man's face, Irons examined the now wide-awake German. The man eased his struggles when he saw white men among the pirates who had taken his ship, knowing his chances of survival had grown. Islanders would've cut his throat on the spot.

Irons turned away from the man and whispered to me, "It's not Metzger. He must be down in his cabin. Come with me."

Suddenly, I realized something or, rather, someone was missing. "Wait, where are the native girls?"

"I don't know. Come on."

As I descended the ladder, I saw that Aukai and Bosun Jack were quietly gathering the assorted weapons and laying them in a stack forward. The rifles were Winchester-model 73 repeaters, quite expensive rifles way out in the farthest reaches of the Pacific. Jack's men spread out on the deck and were watching him, waiting for the signal to concuss our slumbering foes with taps to the head from belaying pins.

Now that my eyes were accustomed to the surroundings, I registered that this German-owned and -operated schooner was completely unlike *Profit*. This one was in good condition and well maintained. The crew was in good physical form and clothing and not nearly as dirty as the Samaritan men.

It was pitch black below decks in the officers' cabins. Irons and I made our way slowly down and aft, finding the way with our hands more than our eyes. We came up to a closed door and opened it slowly but it still creaked, one of those long, high-pitched sounds impossible to conceal or ignore. The faintest shading of light in the room entered through two stern port windows, enabling us to see a large bunk along the transom. Several forms were on the bed. In the middle was a large one with pale torso and legs; on either side of him, smaller dark figures.

The pale form grumbled something vile at us in German. Irons instantly leaped upon the man, sticking the point of his dagger deep into the man's open mouth. Both girls screamed. I took one of the girls by the arm and slung her out of the bunk. I reached for the other but she made haste to join her sister native in running out of the cabin.

Returning my attention to Irons and his victim, I heard the reverend say, "The Samaritans have just taken this ship, Herr Metzger, and are going to use her for the blessed work of the Lord.

There is no use arguing or fighting. Do you understand me?"

Metzger tried to nod affirmatively, but the dagger prevented it so he grunted out a "Ya." Irons murmured back, "Smart decision, Gunter."

That situation well in hand, I lit a lamp and made my away around the other cabins, glad to find them deserted. I then helped Irons escort a lashed but still naked Captain Metzger up onto the main deck.

The ladies shrieking from the cabin had been signal enough for Bosun Jack. The entire blackbirding crew was duly conked on the head before they could even figure out what had happened. By the time Irons and I arrived back on deck, they were trussed, gagged, and nicely arranged in rows by the hatchway over the laborers' quarters, the cargo hold, where they were unceremoniously slung down into confinement. Several of their foreheads were a bloody mash, but as well as I could see, all appeared to be breathing. Metzger glanced around incredulously on his way to the hold.

The half dozen females on board, all of whom were also *sans* clothing, didn't wait for transport to shore. Without delay, they jumped overboard and swam the distance, still crying and shrieking in their tribal tongue.

The traffic in swimmers was two way. Kilim appeared aboard, looking frightening in his war getup of painted face and body, feathered breastplate with boars' tusks, shell beaded headband, and outrageous penis gourd sheath and armed with a stone-age ax and a dagger of sharpened leg bone, along with a small bow and arrows. Having done his job to secure the beach, he now came back to his friends Irons and Bosun Jack, who greeted him with embraces and some congratulatory Tok Pisin.

It was astounding to me that Irons' bizarre plan had actually worked, considering the human material he had to work with. Now all we had to do was cut the stern cable to shore, weigh anchor, and sail back around to *Profit*. There we would transfer our supplies to the new ship and sink the old one in deep water.

But then one of our men pointed out to sea. On the dark horizon, near Cape Jacquinot, I saw an even blacker spot moving. A ship. A speck of light sparkled at us from it. Aukai blurted out, "That's the *Profit*. She's signaling us. Something's wrong!"

27

In the Presence of Mine Enemies . . .

Waterfall Bay
Southern Coast of Neu-Pommern
(New Britain Island)
5 A.M., Friday
28 January 1889

I rons started issuing orders to us. "Bosun, get the jibs up now! Cut that stern cable, Captain Aukai. Jane, stand aside there. Get some men and haul away on the hook, commander. No, belay that. Cut the thing away."

Bosun Jack was up in the foremast crosstrees. He called down, confirming it was the *Profit*, sailing under plain lower sails toward us. She was close-hauled and making good speed from a gusty squall crossing the bay.

Ten minutes later, both ships luffed into the wind, hailing distance apart.

"*Yu mekim wanen hia?*" called out Irons in Tok Pisin to his men aboard *Profit*, meaning "What are you doing here?"

"*Stimsip! Belong Jemeni pait stimsip!*" came back the excited reply. I got that part: They'd seen a German war steamship. *"Adler stimsip? Westap?"* asked Irons. "Where?" *"Ya, long Malakua!"* the man answered. Then he went into the details, his rapid speech beyond my capacity to decipher. Aukai did it for me. Yes, it was *Adler*, near the village of Malakua.

As both crews hauled the schooners close alongside each other, Irons got a further report from his man. Afterward, he blew out a breath and said to me quietly, "We've got trouble, Peter. They spotted *Adler* across Jacquinot Bay near Malakua village. It's about seven miles away from where *Profit* was anchored near the cape, which is about ten or eleven from here. *Adler* was getting up steam at anchor. Our boys saw the sparks from the warship's funnel and sailed here straightaway to warn us. She was slowly moving east, toward us, when they last saw her."

"Then she was there when we anchored *Profit* on that side of the cape, hours ago."

"Yes, she must've been there and we missed seeing her in the dark. Probably not showing lights at anchor, watching the coastline. But I don't think she saw us then either, or she wouldn't have waited 'til now to get up steam. No, someone on shore spread the word we're here and it finally reached one of their informants, who alerted *Adler*."

Aukai sounded nervous for the first time since I'd met him. "I thought *Adler* was up in the Dampier Straits."

My mind conjured the chart of the area. "If it is her, then she never went to the Dampier Straits. There wouldn't have been enough time to go there and then come here."

I asked Irons, "How do your men know that ship is *Adler?*"

"Merchant ships don't usually put in at those little villages like Malakua. And few steam at night this close to the coast. Too many reefs. It's a German warship, all right. *Adler's* the right size, but it doesn't matter what her name is."

Bosun Jack landed on deck with a thud and asked if there were orders. *"Oda, Captem?"*

Irons paused in thought, then said, "All right, everyone, listen up. We'll keep the schooners rafted together, put all sail up on this one, and steer southeast toward those islands." He pointed to a group of hilly islets to the east. The horizon was just starting to lighten behind them.

His voice was calm as he went on. "We'll have to get our things out of *Profit* quickly as we sail along. We'll sink her in deep water, then hide this ship over there, behind the hill on Mocklon Island, the biggest one. Commander Wake, take a man into *Profit's* bilges and start opening her up immediately with axes. Captain Aukai, get your explosives and our other things on this ship right away. Just dump everything on the main deck here, for you won't have much time at all. We need to be behind that island in less than an hour. Much less."

Jack repeated the orders in Tok Pisin, setting the crew into motion with some men lashing the hull together, others setting the fore, main, and forestaysail and others leaping over to *Profit* to begin the transfer. His idea seemed impossible, for *Adler* could do twelve knots under steam, more if she used her sails to assist. That meant she would be at Cape Jacquinot in forty-five minutes.

In the cargo hold, Captain Metzger, who had evidently heard the entire thing while loosening the gag over his mouth, chose that moment to bang on the underside of the hatch with his head and shout, "Let us out now und I vill let you go on your way in the other schooner."

Irons lifted up the small companionway set into the larger hatch. Metzger popped his head out, swaying unsteadily on the ladder since his arms were still tied behind his back. Irons smiled at him benevolently and murmured, "Time to go to sleep, my son." Then he took a hatch batten and smacked it down on the German's head.

"I should've done that in the first place," he muttered as Metzger's body thumped down into the hold.

Thirty minutes later the *Profit*'s main deck was awash. Aukai's detail was still throwing things onto the new ship when Irons told them to jump for it. Bosun Jack reported that the deep sea lead showed no bottom just as the last of the lines were cast off and our former home rolled over and capsized. That was what we didn't want, for trapped air in the hull might keep her a floating derelict, easy to spot in the daylight. It was a tense thirty seconds as she sat there, her spars sticking up at an angle. Then, with a great gasp, the air went out through her hatches and she settled down bottom first, until her mastheads disappeared.

It was light enough to see the shoreline now. Sunrise was in less than an hour. All eyes except the helmsman's were riveted on the horizon behind us to the west. The wind had piped up to a brisk breeze carrying a new squall line from the mountain ridge to our north. We were on a broad reach, speeding forward toward Mocklon Island.

I turned forward and surveyed Mocklon, a dark green lump standing out against the blacker background of New Britain Island. It wasn't a large island, but it looked tall enough to conceal our masts. We had a quarter mile to go to the northern point of the island and perhaps another quarter mile to get situated behind the tallest hill. I did the mathematics: We were doing at least seven knots in the smooth waters of the bay. We were fortunate *Dunkels Geld* was over-sparred with a swift hull—she was built to carry perishable human cargo—so that meant maybe another two minutes to the island at the most.

I heard someone groan and spun around. The seaward sky to the west was much lighter now, the horizon a crisp line. Bosun Jack raised his arm toward the cape, grumbling something in his lingo.

Wisps of black funnel smoke could be seen in the sky beyond Cape Jacquinot.

That certainly was fast. *Adler* must have had every sail she owned up to assist her engine. If we could see her smoke, she must be just around the corner.

I suddenly had a chill go through me. What if the warship wasn't *Adler* but the *Blitz?* I remembered the briefing in Washington when ONI reported *Blitz* as departing Germany, probably en route to the Pacific, the first of several modern cruisers being readied at the naval station at Hamburg. She was faster than anything we had in the Pacific. Her main guns were a slightly smaller caliber than *Adler*, but they were new Krupps, with just as much reach. And—the chill returned—she had the newfangled, long-range searchlights and a bow torpedo launching tube to go along with those guns. *Blitz's* arrival in this area wasn't expected until mid to late February at the earliest. But that was just an educated guess.

Irons and the helmsman were staring ahead. The man at the wheel tightened his jaw. Irons glanced down at the deck and shook his head. I turned around to see the problem and felt like swearing aloud. The morning light now showed what we didn't see minutes before.

There was a thin line of white water breaking over reefs all across our bow, a barrier between us and the safety of the island.

"Sharpen her up, man. Sharpen her up! Steer for that gap," Irons growled to the helmsman as he stretched out a thin arm toward an area without white water.

To Bosun Jack, he shouted, "Trim those sheets in right quick, Jack. I see a narrow channel and we'll shoot her through it."

The men ran to their stations, putting their desperation into action as they hauled away on the sheets to bring the great sails tighter inboard. *Dunkels Geld* heeled over on her new course, moving even faster now on a close reach.

I examined the line of reefs. Irons' gap wasn't visible to me. It might or might not have been a possible path through the reefs. Many gaps were only pockets, leading nowhere but into reefs further inside the outer barrier. On the north side of the bay, along New Britain Island, the line of reefs was much clearer. I'd seen and heard them even in the dark, but by Mocklon Island they were less apparent, much lower in the water, so it was harder to gauge. Our altered course added another third of a mile, assuming we would get through. That would be another two minutes.

John Irons was saying something under his breath. It was a prayer. No, it was the Twenty-Third Psalm. Several of his men were repeating it with him in Tok Pisin as their heads swiveled between the scene ahead and the danger behind.

Irons was almost singing it now, his voice strong and clear, the verses interspersed with commands to the crew.

"*He leadeth me beside the still waters.* Get that jib and forestaysail in tighter!"

A sailor with the lead line called out the depth: "No bottom." We were a hundred feet from the reef.

"*Yea, though I walk through the valley of the shadow of death.* Steer small, man. Steer small and high. *I will fear no evil. For Thou art with me!*"

Aukai and I, and even Jane Cushman, were reciting along with Irons. Every one of us on that deck was shouting out the words to heaven above us.

"*Thy rod and Thy staff, they comfort me!*"

We entered the reef line. This was it. We would either crash onto the reef or pass through. I had no idea which it would be.

"*Thou preparest a table before me in the presence of mine enemies.*"

Several of us glanced aft at Cape Jacquinot. The smoke was thicker now. We were running out of time. The warship would come into sight at any moment.

Close around us on both sides I could see water frothing on coral rocks. It was impossibly shallow. Exactly how much water did this ship draw? I didn't know and doubted Irons did either.

I felt a sickening nudge from below. *Dunkels Geld* slowed, straightened upright, and slewed off to the starboard. We were moving at only a knot or two but still moving.

"Got to get the stern up. All hands forward to the bow!" cried Irons before he continued on with the psalm. "*Surely goodness and mercy shall follow me—*"

We stopped completely.

But the ship hadn't taken ground while heeled over. We were

still upright and therefore barely grounded. I looked down into the water. We hadn't hit a rock; it was sand. If we could get her heeled over, we'd get the keel off the bottom and go forward. The worst of the white water was behind us. I looked aloft. One small sail was brailed up on the mainmast, still unused.

Irons stood there, staring dumbly at the island, so close and yet so far. His voice distantly trailed away now into a mumble. *"And I will dwell in the House of the Lord forever. . . ."*

I grabbed his arm. "John, get the main topstaysail set. That'll heel her over farther and get the keel off the bottom."

He wasn't listening to me. His eyes were closed, his lips moving soundlessly, talking directly to God

I yelled to Bosun Jack, in a perch atop the mast. "Set the topstaysail, Jack! Get her heeled over and moving!"

Snapping his fingers, he jumped down to the crosstrees, loosened the sail's furling lines, and shouted to a man on the deck to haul the sheet. The sail came out to the gaff peak and took the wind with the sound of a gunshot. It was too much sail up for normal safety in that rising velocity of wind, and the masts might break under the strain, but despair had driven us well past anything "normal."

Dunkels Geld heeled right over and slid to leeward, bumping along the bottom roughly. The schooner lurched violently into a coral head, knocking several men and Jane to the deck and making the masts sway threateningly—but she didn't stop moving. Gouging her starboard chine along the coral, I was convinced she'd open up, but the schooner held together. It was daytime now and I could see the bottom clearly. The water below us got darker, a good sign. She stopped bumping. We'd reached deep water.

Jack slid down the main boom's topping lift and landed on the deck. Irons was still in blind communion with God, oblivious to what was happening, so Jack asked me, "*Odas?*"

He wanted orders. I had an important one. "Check the bilges."

"Steer for the end of the island," I told the man at the wheel.

Two hundred feet to go. I could smell the thick, sweet scent of jungle detritus now.

"There they are," said Aukai.

Eight miles behind us, the bow of the warship emerged from beyond the cape.

We had one hundred feet to go.

Bosun Jack came up on deck and quietly spoke to Aukai in Tok Pisin.

"Jack says there's water rising in the bilges," said Aukai.

"To be expected," I replied as I glanced aloft to check the wind. Our sails were like huge beacons against the dark background of the green New Britain shoreline. The Germans couldn't fail to see us. Jack followed my gaze to the sails, then nodded his understanding as I ordered him, "Get all sails down—*now!*"

Bosun Jack screamed to his men in their lingo, and they rushed to cast off the throat and peak halyards from the main and foremast. The huge sails lumbered down the masts. The upper staysail sheets were let go as the brailing line hauled it in. Up forward, both jibs slid down their stays.

Shed of her canvas, *Dunkels Geld* slid behind the point of the island just as the warship came into full view on the distant horizon. I couldn't make out her identity, for it was only a second or two. We saw a glimpse of her through the sparse trees on the point; then she was hidden by Mocklon Island's forested hills.

I climbed aloft to the main masthead, which rose to the same altitude as the island's treetops. The warship wasn't heading our way. She was heading out to sea, southbound. At that distance, and obscured by her own smoke, she was impossible to identify.

Was she *Adler* or *Blitz*? *Adler* had one funnel and three masts, two of them with square yards. *Blitz* had two funnels and two masts, with no square yards. It didn't make sense that *Blitz* had made it all the way around the world that quickly, but I just wasn't sure which one I was looking at.

28

Solomon's Gold

Solomon Straits
10 Miles NW of Savo Island
Dawn, Monday
4 February 1889

For a week we sailed southeast, propelled by the mounting northwest monsoon, which had set in and dominated life aboard. Blowing at a steady fifteen knots, more in the frequent squalls, we rolled from one beam to the other along New Britain, east to Bougainville in the German Solomon Islands, thence down that chain to the British end of the archipelago. For that week we saw few oceangoing ships, and those were traders. We dared not touch land lest we be seen too close to our crime and a connection made.

Except for the native laborer quarters in the main cargo hold, *Dunkels Geld* was far better in cleanliness and accommodation than our previous vessel. Jane, Aukai, and I got the officers' cabins, while Irons settled into Metzger's stateroom. All personal items and identifications of the former occupants were put in a weighted bag and thrown overboard. The interior of the after cabins was made as English in motif and ambiance as we could, and the obvious German food, like sauerkraut and schnitzels, was fed to the fish.

The main and fore holds were converted back to cargo spaces. All of the "kanaka beds"—crude shelving formed into five-tiered bunks crammed together—were broken up and thrown overboard. Our German prisoners slept on the deck of the holds. Except for enough to feed the prisoners, the taro-yam mush fed to the "native recruits" was dumped as well. The prisoners were extremely unhappy with their diet and accommodations, but Irons' crew dissuaded any attempt at revolt by an intimidating mixture of glares, drawn weapons, and convincing whispers of the revenge they wanted to wreak upon their captive blackbirders—if only their Christian captain would let them.

The ship underwent a change of outward appearance as well. The first day out from Waterfall Bay, the gilded name of *Dunkels Geld* was ripped from her transom. She now sported the moniker *Solomon's Gold*, painted in careful script by Irons himself, dangling over the stern in a bosun's chair while the wake churned below him. The coach roof of the main cabin was removed and the deck made flush. The large launch was scuttled, and only the small cutter and a dinghy retained. In a flash of inspiration, Irons had a spare topmast spar fashioned as a square yard with a small topsail to go with it, complete with sheets and braces. It was ready to hoist to the foremast crosstrees if needed, so we would become a square topsail-rigged schooner.

Also ready to hoist was a British red ensign with the Canadian crest in the lower right corner. Irons had brought it from the previous ship. He explained that if the Germans inspected us, we would be Canadians from Vancouver. It had worked for him in the past, since most Germans couldn't discern the difference in accents.

Subtle changes occurred with those aboard as well. Irons, who had seemed so calm and almost blithe in battle, now took on a nervous aspect. Leaving Bosun Jack to run the ship, he stayed in his cabin mostly, except for sullen attendance at the evening dinner table. I offered to stand an officer's watch but was petulantly refused, which I thought peculiar given his statement at the beginning of our voyage about needing my skills.

For the rest of the passengers, attitudes transformed for the better, despite the constant rolling effect of sailing dead downwind. Having survived two harrowing ordeals, David Aukai, Jane Cushman, and I became less tense around each other. Jane actually turned cheerful on occasion, usually over wine at dinner. She bestowed her verbal charms on Irons, naturally, as she had from the beginning, but Jane also lightened up her mood enough to smile and laugh for Aukai and me. Though I trusted her not one inch, I will admit I found it pleasant to be in her company. Even a poisonous snake can be beautiful to look at.

Most notably, I finally had an opportunity to privately sound Aukai out about his mission and see if what I was strategizing in my mind was feasible.

"I've been waiting for you to ask about the details of my mission," the Hawaiian acknowledged one night on deck during a brief intermission in the squally weather. "It is simple. The Ballistite is for valuable targets the Samoans choose and will be employed under my direction. My role must remain covert, Peter. Mataafa and the Samoan patriots will be credited with the achievement. Then the Germans will see they are not dealing with a ragtag bunch of ignorant island savages but a disciplined and determined foe with access to modern means of war. The hope is that the Germans will then abandon their conquest of Polynesia."

Aukai wagged his head thoughtfully. "However, I am not certain how much of the Ballistite will remain viable by the time we arrive, for its condition has suffered considerably during transport. You saw that I had to discard an entire case of it already. Too unstable."

"I did. But I thought Alfred Nobel found a way to make it safer than any other explosive."

"He did, but that is under usual transportation and storage conditions, of course. Our journey has been anything but usual, has it not?"

"Land targets or ship targets?" I asked.

"Land would be much easier."

"Yes, but the German warships are serving as their mobile artillery, with devastating effect, from what I understand. The Samoans have defeated them several times on land, but they haven't been able to touch those ships. With that Ballistite, you could rectify that and alter the balance of power."

He cast a dubious look my way. "The German warships have been devastating, yes, but it is their troops ashore who are causing the most terror. No, Peter, I think you are not as much concerned about my fellow Polynesians' liberty as you are your own country's chances against the Germans. You want me to sink their fleet for you so your navy doesn't have to fight them."

"So? My enemy's enemy is my friend, David. We share a common foe. With my knowledge of ships and your explosives, we could end the German squadron in one night, and thus our mutual problem. Don't waste it on land targets. Hit them where they least expect it, in their most powerful asset, the warships. That will send a bigger message than anything else you could do."

His forehead crinkled in thought, and I knew I'd broached his defenses. "How would we go about it?" he asked.

"Small native boats sent alongside the warships, with the Ballistite exploded under their transoms by a timed fuse. The boat crew jumps over as the boat approaches and swims away to the beach. A coordinated attack on the whole squadron at once, for maximum effect."

"You do not even know if your country is at war with the Germans, Peter. You might have to wait for that to happen before you take action. I cannot afford to wait any longer. The Samoans need help now, and my king has ordered me to give it."

"Look, it doesn't matter if the United States is at war with Germany yet or not. As you say, the Samoans are at war, so they can do the job."

I could tell he was in league with it when he said, "You and I would have to go along to make sure it is done effectively."

"Yes, we will. Clandestinely, of course."

A gust of wind hit us, canting the schooner over farther just as a wall of rain arrived. Aukai shouted above the deluge, "I will think upon it." Then he dashed below, undoubtedly to consult his mentor, Irons. That was fine with me, for I figured that, as a fellow war veteran who was clearly a decisive commander, Irons would see my logic and recommend the alliance.

A knock on my door came late that night. It was Aukai, who poked his head in my cabin and simply said, "I agree with your idea, Peter. We'll do it together, against the German ships."

And so it was that the seed of my notion, first planted in Auckland when Aukai told me the nature of his cargo, had at last borne a sprout. Time would tell whether it would grow to its deadly fruition.

~~~

The dawn came quickly but without the positive effects of a rising sun, for it was hidden in the gray and blue-black storm clouds racing from the northwest. The Solomon Straits is a funnel for wind and waves that are built up by several days of foul weather in the northwest monsoon, and the seas were building accordingly. The ship was averaging an astounding nine and a half knots, under reefed main and forestaysail, for well over two hundred miles a day. We'd passed through the German Solomons without incident or inspection and were now approaching a large island named Guadalcanal in the area where the native chiefs were British-influenced.

Irons was back in command on deck, for navigation in the Solomons is immensely difficult. Uncharted reefs, twisting currents, and low visibility played havoc on our nerves and were far beyond Bosun Jack's abilities. Irons had a change of heart and gratefully took my assistance in working out our hourly position and course. He even acquiesced in letting me serve in the watch schedule. I didn't mind at all, for we were all, literally, in the same boat, and steady hands and minds were needed on deck.

Thankfully, though, at our speed we had not long to go in this area. Once through the Solomon chain of islands, our course would shift to due east, through open ocean and free of land-bound dangers. Passing north of the New Hebrides and south of the Santa Cruz Islands, we would reach the large island of Fiji. A day or two later, we would be at the Samoan group.

It was now the morning of February fourth, and I had the deck watch. A man stood at the wheel and another at the bow as lookout. The smell of breakfast wafted from the after hatch, to be flung away on the wind. I was anticipating a decent meal as soon as my watch ended.

"*Spoilim! Spoilim bot!*" the bow man called aft, his hand pointed directly ahead of us. Then he added, "*Daiman!*"

My Tok Pisin was improving. *Daiman* meant "dead man." *Bot* was "boat." I guessed that *spoilim* meant "wreck."

I saw it seconds later: three bodies draped across a raft of debris.

I ordered, "*Olgeta man on dek! Slipim main sel!*"—"All hands on deck to take down the mainsail."

When we came alongside a few minutes later, we saw that the men weren't dead but very close to it. Two were native Solomon islanders, black Melanesians with blonde fuzzy hair, wearing loincloths and nothing else. The third was a young white man dressed in a black cassock. All were hauled up onto the main deck and lay there face down, barely breathing, eyes slitted by crusted salt and cracked lips unable to speak.

Bosun Jack turned the white man over. A silver chain and cross holding a crucified Jesus fell out of his hand.

"My dear Lord, he's a Roman priest!" exclaimed Irons, who knelt down and held the man's head. "Get him to Mr. Wake's cabin," he told Jack. "And get the other two below forward with our boys."

To me he said, "Peter, you bunk in with Mr. Aukai."

29

Rumors of War

Solomon Straits
1 Mile NW of Savo Island
8 A.M., Monday
4 February 1889

The priest opened his eyes an hour later. Looking at Irons and me, he croaked, "*Parlez-vous Francais?*"

"*Juste un peu,*" I replied, saying I knew only a little. "*Parlez-vous Anglais?*"

Irons whispered to me with a wary tinge to his words, "Ah, so he's French . . . which means he's one of the Marists priests. Their bishop—I think his name was Epalle—was murdered here by the Melanesians a few years back. All of the Marists fled the Solomons after that. So why is a French priest here now?"

"My native friends, how are they?" the priest asked me in very good English. Irons frowned when he heard it, his face openly suspicious.

I gave the priest a sip of water. "They are recovering and are up forward with the crew, Father. My name is Peter. What is your name?"

He was alert now, glancing around the cabin and noticing the Protestant cross on the bulkhead. His voice was much stronger as he said, "Thank God for our miracle. My name is Paul Lambert." He managed a smile. "We have been rescued by a sailor named Peter. God's hand is definitely in this."

To Irons he said, "And yes, I am a priest, of the Society of Mary from the island of New Caledonia in the Archdiocese of Auckland. You asked why am I here. I am visiting the Solomons to see if the people have changed their minds and want our help. We were going to Honiara, on the island of Guadalcanal, when the boat was capsized by a wave. You are correct, sir, our order has been gone from these islands for many years, since the bishop's martyred death. And who may you be, sir?"

"John Irons, master and owner of this ship, the Canadian trader *Solomon's Gold*. We'll put you off at Honiara tomorrow morning."

Having lied convincingly to the priest about our identity, Irons then intoned a prayer, including a part about God being good enough to help everybody, even a Catholic priest. Lambert sighed when he heard it but said nothing.

After we left the Marist alone to rest, Irons pulled me aside. "Spread the word to David and Jane. Keep that priest from leaving the cabin without one of us as an escort. We can't allow him to know about what we've done to get this ship or about our prisoners. He wouldn't understand."

That evening, Lambert joined us for dinner. Irons proved not a very gracious host to his fellow clergyman, however. Instead, he conducted a thinly disguised interrogation of the priest. It started with demanding an explanation of why his religious order sent him all alone into the heart of priest-killing heathen islands with only two paddlers in a dugout canoe. "I find that very unusual.

Why didn't they send you with a proper ship and crew?"

"You know, Captain Irons, God sent Paul around the Mediterranean in a small boat. Paul traveled amidst many enemies to spread the Word. And on the way, he was shipwrecked too. Eventually, God even led Paul into the heart of pagan Rome as a lowly prisoner of centurions. So my troubles are minor by comparison."

"I know the Bible's account of Paul's journeys very well, thank you, Mr. Lambert," snapped Irons, pointedly omitting Lambert's religious honorific. "Acts Twenty-Seven, verses one to forty-four. But you didn't answer my question."

Lambert sidestepped Irons' barbs and asked a question of his own. "Your biblical knowledge is obvious, captain. Then you also know the Bible describes the gold Solomon regularly received from Ophir. Six hundred and sixty-six talents of gold, several tons in modern measurement, were brought by a ship up the Red Sea."

Irons interrupted him. "You're wrong. I thought they trained you people better than that. It was four hundred and twenty talents, just under sixteen modern tons. First Kings, nine, verse twenty-eight."

Lambert smiled. "Very good, my son. I stand corrected. You are indeed a biblical scholar. My point was that the name of this ship reminded me of that passage and intrigues me, sir. You say she is a trader. In what, may I ask? Or is this ship looking for gold too, sir?"

There was an uncomfortable silence as Irons glared at him for several seconds, then dug into his food, ignoring the priest and everyone else. Obviously, Irons had a prejudice against Catholics in general and this priest in particular, but I couldn't deduce why. I thought they would've been allies against paganism and blackbirding.

Lambert acted as if nothing untoward has passed and proceeded to converse pleasantly with the others at the table. Charming the lady with compliments and listening to Aukai's tales of Polynesian life in Hawaii, it was as if he'd been with us for weeks.

But it was more than pleasant conversation on Lambert's part. He was using honey to gain information. I could tell that while he spoke, he was scrutinizing his surroundings closely. That he was not fooled in the least by our pretensions was made manifest an hour later.

Irons had delivered his usual post-dinner prayer, including a condescending remark about "Popish followers," then abruptly left the cabin without a word. I heard him clomp up the ladder to the main deck. After the cabin door closed, there was an awkward quiet.

After a while, Father Lambert sadly commented, "May God in His mercy help Captain Irons. I think he has known terrible evil in his life, an evil filled with death. He has taken many lives, and for that his heart is heavy."

Aukai shot him a curious look. "Why would you say that, Father?"

Lambert shook his head. "His eyes. His embarrassment. The tone of his words. Captain Irons says far too many prayers for an innocent man with minor sins of omission. His sins were of *co*mmission and of major import. And I think he is hiding a current sin, a terrible burden on his soul."

The priest turned his eyes to me. "Captain Irons asked why I was here. But I wonder the same about all of you. I am confused by what I see and feel on this ship. That this is a blackbirder ship is apparent. I can smell it. But the captain and crew do not act like blackbirders or even traders." He cocked an accusatory eyebrow. "Nor do you, my friends, act like the usual passengers on transit through this area. So I will ask yet again, why are all of you really in the Solomon Islands?"

My companions nervously looked at me to provide the answer. The pointed question made me quickly evaluate how much the Marist might have guessed about us. Did he recognize Irons as the actual man behind the anti-blackbirding Samaritan legend of the islands? Had he guessed about our captive Germans aboard, only a few feet forward of the bulkhead where we sat at the table? I wasn't sure of anything, so I decided to continue the Canadian façade.

"I'm afraid there's no mystery here, Father Lambert. In fact, I have to admit that our story is rather dull. The three of us are just passengers who, through a serendipitous turn of fate, found this ship, which was heading our way. I'm a trader from British Columbia, looking for opportunities. I haven't found many, so I'm heading home. Mrs. Cushman is a recent widow and, like Captain Irons, is a compatriot of mine. She's going back to Canada also. Mr. Aukai is going home to Honolulu. We came aboard in Townsville, in Australia, for passage to islands farther east of here, where we hope to find a ship heading for Hawaii. From there, it will be easy to get a steamer home to Canada."

I paused, trying to display an appropriately embarrassed mien. "Alas, you are right, sir. The ship was once used in blackbirding but no longer. Captain Irons bought her and discontinued her role in that odious trade. She trades in finished goods only nowadays. Obviously, Captain Irons is a Christian, and you probably know that we Canadians don't countenance blackbirding."

Lambert's face was a mask as he nodded an acknowledgment of my explanation. He didn't ask anything more about us, merely saying, "Yes, of course. Canadians are very good people."

A thought entered my mind, and I changed the topic. "By the way, Father, I am concerned with our passage to the east and whether it will be prudent. What have you heard of the German-American confrontation in this area? Is it war yet?"

"Yes, regrettably I think it has come to war from what I heard when I was at Noumea, on New Caledonia, just a few days ago. The newspaper there reports that the Germans are boasting they will chase the Americans—and anyone else who disturbs the situation in their colonies—away from Samoa. There are reports of shots already fired between the navies. I fear the Americans cannot stand up to the Germans in a war." His voice trailed off as he added, "We French thought we could."

His eyes misted at the memory of France's defeat seventeen years before, but I concentrated on what he'd said. "There has been a battle already? Where? Who won?"

He rubbed his chin in thought. "Let me try to remember the newspaper article. It was in Samoa. There was a German warship called the *Adler* and an American warship. It was named *Nipso*, I think. I believe the Germans won but cannot remember what it said for certain."

Damn it all! I was too late. It had started. The American ship was Commander Mullan's *Nipsic* but I didn't correct him on the name, for a Canadian businessman wouldn't know that information.

The priest went on. "Also the Germans are being very aggressive toward all other foreigners in Samoa whom they suspect of aiding the Samoan rebels. They even arrested a Britisher named Fletcher, the manager for the MacArthur Trading Company. They also seized a British ship, the *Richmond*, for smuggling arms to the Samoans."

That was significant. If the German consul, Doctor Knappe, who ran things in Samoa, was going after the Brits, he must be desperate and therefore even more dangerous. And now that war was unleashed, the German naval reinforcements would be doubled or tripled. The country that got a large squadron there first would have the decisive advantage. Ours should arrive in Samoa soon, but where exactly were the German reinforcements? They would be steaming easterly from the Straits of Malacca and the Torres Strait, probably passing not far to the south of this very area we were in.

Aukai and I had to get to Samoa as fast as possible. I glanced peripherally at the Hawaiian. His face was tense, as if he was thinking the same thing.

"Father Lambert, have you seen any German warships on your journey?" I asked.

"Why, yes, I saw one just yesterday as we sailed past New Georgia Island. It was moving very fast."

The Germans were steaming through British waters to get to Samoa? Maybe he was confused. "Are you sure she wasn't a British ship?"

He let out a breath, as if he was exercising extreme patience. "Well, I am not a sailor or a warrior, Peter, but I do know what the German naval ensign looks like, and that ship was displaying it on its rear mast."

He closed his eyes to visualize it, then said, "A large black cross over a white background divides the flag into quadrants. In the center of that large cross is a German eagle in a circle. In the upper left quadrant of the flag, there is a small black cross over the German national colors of black, white, and red."

"Very good, sir. She was German, all right. Could you describe the ship in detail, please?"

He hesitated and gave me a curious look, and I instantly knew I'd overstepped my Canadian alias. Why would a civilian businessman want to know details about a German ship?

He finally answered. "The ship had two masts and two smokestacks. Smoke was coming out of both of the smokestacks. A lot of smoke. There was a big cannon on the front of the ship and one at the back and a smaller one on the side. Oh, and the ship also had very large electric lights on raised platforms, the kind that pierce the night for a long distance, one on the front and the other at the back. It was daytime so they were not lit, but I remember thinking how very large they were."

"The ship's direction of travel?"

"It was moving in the same direction as we are sailing, Peter." He stood. "And now, if you will be kind enough to excuse me, I will go to my cabin and rest. I fear it will be my last chance to rest comfortably, for I must be ready tomorrow when I arrive at Guadalcanal. My task there will be difficult, and I will need all my strength."

"Thank you, Father," I replied with a sick feeling in my stomach.

Lambert had described the *Blitz*.

30

Samoa

Offshore of Falealili Bay
Upolu Island, Samoa
4:23 P.M., Sunday
10 February 1889

At last, after more than six weeks, ten thousand miles, and too many delays, I arrived at the target area: Upolu Island in the Kingdom of Samoa. Before me spread the dramatic forty-five-mile-long southern coastline of Upolu Island. Upolu is the centerpiece of the Samoan archipelago, and Apia, on its northern coast, is the kingdom's capital and the center of the German military presence in the area. But on the south coast, for as far as I could see, no sign of modern, nineteenth-century civilization could be discerned. Modern war in that scene was hard to imagine.

Nature, not Germany, was in control of this beautiful scene. A ridge of mountains, clad in various shades of green and soaring more than two thousand feet high, spanned the length of the island. In the higher reaches, several slivers of white-foamed waterfalls plummeted off high cliffs, to be lost in the green carpet of forest below. Mist enveloped much of the ridge, swirling and rolling down the slopes.

The foothills descended to within a mile or two of the relatively flat coast. Black rocky cliffs plunged to the sea in several places, where ancient volcanoes' red-hot lava had met the cool ocean and congealed on the spot. The occasional wisp of smoke from a beachside village drifted up from the forests, to be whisked away by the ubiquitous wind. The sky over the island was laden with heavy clouds.

Before us was an open bay called Falealili. A narrow strip of sand separated the thick tangles of green jungle from the blue and green water inside the reef. Irons pointed out several beachside villages, the oval-shaped huts made of thatch. Each settlement was laid out under a small grove of coconut palms, whose fronds seemed to be in constant motion. He called out their singsong names: Saleilua, Poutasi, Mafautu.

David Aukai added that he had been at the bay on his previous visit and that the people were friendly. He knew a local man who would help us once we got ashore.

The water in these parts is as dramatic as the land, for the reef that encircles Upolu is a shallow buttress of brown coral teeth set in purplish-turquoise water. This barrier holds back the large swells of the bottomless, dark blue Pacific. Even in the calm weather we enjoyed at the moment, the ever-present ocean surf reared up all along the reef. Here and there, the waves would collide against outcroppings in the reef, bursting in explosions of spray. Four or five would erupt at once, giving the impression that a fleet was engaged in shore bombardment practice.

Seamen fear reefs such as these, for they maul ships and kill men, yet we were to somehow go through that perilous reef line. Irons casually remarked to me that he knew a channel, that he'd been through it several times, the last one to deliver Aukai. The Hawaiian made a light quip about it reminding him of the reef at Maui in his homeland, making it sound as if we were on a picnic lark. Neither of their comments improved my attitude, for

I couldn't see any benign entrances at all.

My nerves were on edge. I had come to trust Captain Aukai, but John Irons was another matter. The entire time I'd been with Irons, from that moment in the coal bunker aboard *Australia* until our arrival in Samoa, our relations had been one trial and tribulation after another. I couldn't gauge or predict the man's actions accurately, except to understand that he had something wrong deep inside him that colored his every thought and action.

My concerned mounted until I had been ready to drop Irons overboard when we were still back in the Solomons, for his statements were becoming increasingly nonsensical and his behavior was approaching open insanity.

After landing the Marist priest and his natives on a beach east of Honiara at Guadalcanal Island—Irons didn't want to be seen at that harbor—we'd continued on our passage from the Solomons to Samoa. Stopping at Uki near San Cristobal Island at the eastern end of the chain, Irons stopped to see a trader he knew. Two hours later, we sailed with a small load of tinned beef, nails, and calico cloth to better enhance our role as an innocent inter-island trading vessel should we be inspected.

A post-dinner conference was held the night after the priest left us, with the pendulum of Irons' mood swinging back from a sinister wariness to a positive, almost buoyant attitude. Acquiescing to my demand for no more hindrances, he said there would be no more problems now that he had gotten rid of the last of *his* hindrances, meaning Father Lambert. I inquired about what he intended to do with the prisoners since his original plan to sail them to New Guinea had proven unfeasible. He waved a hand dismissively and replied that they would be put into the ship's launch as soon as possible, well provisioned for safe passage to a nearby island.

I asked where on the Samoan coast Aukai, Jane, and I would be landed, that I preferred a location away from the main German activities. He explained that he knew just the place, near a village called Poutasi at Falealili Bay on the south coast of Upolu Island. There the schooner could get close enough inshore to land the three of us and our equipage and munitions where the Germans had no presence.

He said he would also land Chief Kilim there, for the man had a separate mission to perform for Irons ashore at one of the German plantations. What it was he did not say, but I guessed it was to foment rebellion and escape among the indentured Melanesians. That sounded fine with me, for it would add to the discomfort and confusion of the enemy.

Irons ended the discussion with a note of regret, saying that once put ashore in Samoa, we would never see him again, for he had other places to go in his work to free those people still in bondage. His lamenting of our parting contrasted with my inward relief, for I couldn't wait to have him removed from my list of worries.

We sailed easterly from Guadalcanal, the monsoon wind and rain lessening the farther away from the Solomons we progressed. By the time we were halfway between the New Hebrides Island and the island of Fiji, it was down to an easy breeze. It was there and then that Irons divested himself of the prisoners.

In the middle of the night, one hundred miles northwest of Fiji's outer island of Levu, the schooner's launch was fully provisioned with food, water, sails, and oars, then swung up and over the gunwale. Chief Kilim was sent down into the prisoner hold in full war regalia. Standing there in the light of a lantern, his skin glistening with oils and paint, his maniacal grin drooling saliva, he was the picture of the Devil incarnate for the blackbirders, who immediately thought their end had come.

Climbing down to stand beside the native chieftain, the good reverend explained to his inmates what was about to happen. With a shrug, he said that if they did not cooperate with his orders, then he would merely turn them over to Kilim and the crew. All of those worthies were peering down from the hatch coaming at the Germans, literally licking their lips in anticipation.

The duly terrified Germans were then lashed and blindfolded—so they could not see about them once they got up on deck and later report how the ship had been refitted—and brought up on deck. The crew stood close enough to bathe the faces of the captives with their fetid breath, laughing when the poor bastards recoiled in fear. Having had the wits scared out of them, the prisoners were then informed that their lives were being given back to them in Christian charity and that they would be allowed to sail to freedom in the launch. Irons did not tell them their position but did give them a course to steer for two days.

This was followed by his saying a prayer for their deliverance, adding that he hoped they would change their lives just as the infamous slaver and blasphemer John Newton had done after his life had been spared at sea. Still blindfolded, they were led down the side into the tossing launch and told to sit still for ten minutes. They complied nervously, several visibly shaking as they expected the worst.

Bosun Jack snarled down at the boat, *"Mi baim yupela stilim man gen, katin nek na kilim yupela daiman! Mi laik katim nek yupela . . ."*

Aukai translated for me: "I catch you stealing men again and I will cut your throats and kill you. I want to cut your throat."

Kan then cast off the launch's bow line and our darkened ship sailed away, leaving the German blackbirders bobbing in the inky blackness. Soon they were out of sight.

And now I was standing next to Irons again, looking out at the scene of my deliverance from him, though how it was to be accomplished, I knew not. He pointed toward Falealili Bay. "See that little lump of an island in the bay? It's called Nuusafee. That's where the channel is. We'll go in along the reef. Once past the island, we shoot the channel and head for the beach, just to the east of Poutasi village."

All I saw was a line of spray erupting from the reef and said so.

He laughed off my caution. "Oh ye of little faith. I'm beginning to think you don't trust me, Peter. Perhaps I should call you Thomas."

I was mightily tired of the biblical references by this point and ignored his teasing jest. "I'm going below to help Aukai and Jane get the supplies ready."

I had just turned away when the lookout aloft called down, "*Stimsip!*"

Ahead of us, emerging from a rain shower near the eastern end of Upolu Island, perhaps ten miles away, was a speck with a smudge of smoke above it. Bosun Jack grabbed a long glass and scrambled up to join the lookout.

"*Pait stimsip. Jemeni!*"

It was a German warship. Heading for us.

I did some quick calculations about the possibility of the German warship knowing our identity and recent crimes. We had set the German prisoners adrift three days earlier. If all had gone well with them, they would've reached Levu Island late the next day, more likely the day after that.

The word would go out that the Samaritan pirates were in the area of Fiji. How long would it take to reach the Germans in Samoa? There was no oceanic telegraph line so it would have to be by ship. A sailing ship couldn't have beaten us to Samoa, but a steamer could have.

Irons had the same apprehension. "I doubt they know," he said. "But just in case, I do believe it's time to go inshore and get this done quickly."

He walked over and took the wheel from the helmsman, altering course for the bay. The schooner heeled over as she made for the reef in a close reach.

"Jack!" he shouted. "*Hariap* and haul the sheets and set the topsails. Let's get some more speed out of her. Get that square topsail set too." Then he reinforced his orders with some Tok Pisin so the rest of the crew could understand. "*Hariap, Jack! Satan Jemini kam kwikim!*"—"Hurry up, Jack. The German Satan comes quick!"

Irons next turned to me. "Get everything stowed in the longboat and dinghy and get them ready to be swung out. This'll be a bit close, Peter, and we don't have any time to dawdle."

He was right. The warship was close under the lee of Upolu, right along the reef, and making good speed. Her bow wave was visible now, her range maybe eight or nine miles and closing fast. At the vessels' combined velocity, we had only minutes to get ashore before the warship arrived within gun range. And unlike our previous encounter with the Imperial German Navy, there was no place for us to hide.

I ran below, telling Jane and Aukai about the Germans and to get their belongings in the longboat fast. Kan, Aukai, and I manhandled the three remaining cases of Ballistite up from below, the schooner's pounding into the seas making every step a challenge. Then I brought up my seabag of belongings, money, and weapons.

A ship's longboat, fuller bodied than a launch, is designed to carry heavy loads, but the pile we stowed inside looked too much for her to me. There was no time for alternatives, however, for Kan yelled, "*Lukaut!*"

Look out, indeed, for what I saw was a menacing sight. The German warship had set a huge naval ensign from her masthead, the traditional national signal of sovereign authority to all ships in sight. Fully twenty feet long, it streamed and snapped about in the wind, proclaiming to all in the area that she was serious. Very serious.

31
The Battle Ensign

Offshore of Falealili Bay
Upolu Island, Samoa
4:45 P.M., Sunday
10 February 1889

Now I could see that the German ship had no square yards. She was *Blitz*. I recalled the briefing in Washington, when Lieutenant Rodgers estimated her arrival in Samoa to be the twentieth of February at the very earliest. There is an old saying, attributed to a European general who went up against Napoleon: The first casualty of war is your estimate of the enemy's capability. That always leads to the second casualty: your own prewar plan of action.

Aukai pointed at the ship and huffed, "Ha! Look at that big flag, Peter. Those arrogant Germans are showing off."

"No, they're not being arrogant, David. That's her battle ensign," I explained. "It's a sign to any vessel not to doubt her intentions and authority to use force. She's coming after us, all right. We should see a puff of smoke from her foredeck at any second. It'll be the warning signal to heave to and stand by for inspection. Standard naval procedure."

It happened as I said the words. The Hawaiian artilleryman studied the puff and noted, "Blank round from a large-caliber gun." Then he asked, "What comes next, Peter?"

"Next, a real round will drop somewhere off our bow to show us we can't escape. She's not in range yet but will be soon."

Jane, dressed sensibly in a black cotton smock affair, put the last of her things in the boat. Her hair was pulled into a bun, her eyes shining fiercely. I saw the handle of her derringer in a waist pocket.

"I'm ready," she reported, her eyes focused on the approaching warship. "Will we make it ashore in time?"

Everyone else aboard was obviously pondering the same thing, but no one answered her question. Irons, the only one not clearly tense, stood by the helm, faintly smiling. Like the two other times I'd seen him in action, he seemed blithe, or possibly delusional, as if it was a yachting game.

Ahead of us, the reef's rippling line of watery eruptions stretched right across our course, but Irons showed no worry as he gazed at it. I took the long glass from his hand and peered at the place he was steering for.

I could distinguish the little coconut palm– covered, sand-spit islet Irons called Nuusafee, and presently I saw a narrow gap of calm water, but it wasn't what or where I expected. The reef appeared to the naked eye to be solid across for the whole coastline, but near the island it was set back, en echelon, with the small gap perpendicular to the main line of the reef. If the schooner could weather the outer reef, we could bear off to leeward and shoot through the gap, just as he'd said earlier.

Irons grabbed my arm. "Jack's busy. Get some men to sweat that square topsail brace in more. And the main sheet. Then get the spare throat halyards on the longboat and have everyone ready to haul her up and out—but wait for my word!"

We hauled the sails in some more, increasing our speed.

Solomon's Gold heeled over 'til her gunwale was shipping water. We were fairly racing through the water toward the reef, the wind abaft the beam now and the schooner sliding down the waves. We were doing easily nine or more knots, the bow wave's swishing a constant roar along the lee side. Above the roar, I could hear the rumble of the seas hitting the reef, feel the concussions, like gunfire. If we hit at this speed, our bodies would all be flung off the deck and into those razor-sharp coral maws, to be ripped apart instantaneously.

A plume of water fountained a hundred yards ahead, bits of coral and seaweed and fish flying into the air. A split second later I heard the flat bang of the German gunshot.

Just then we arrived at the reef. Irons muscled the wheel down to port and brought the schooner up luffing into the wind, the sails thudding and spars shaking ominously. He handled her brilliantly.

Our speed allowed her to luff up and steer around the edge of the reef to starboard, then bear off a point behind the reef and refill the sails. *Solomon's Gold* heeled over again as we entered the gap and slid in an S-shaped curve around the next reef edge to port.

Another plume of water erupted, this one dead ahead, wetting the deck and sprinkling it with rocks and fish. Shrapnel skipped across the waves. The German gunners were very good.

The beach was only a half mile ahead. Around us was shallow water in a mosaic of pastel colors. We would have to get the incriminating cargo and people to the beach and hidden in the jungle before the Germans arrived. The warship was slightly more than two miles off, the bow wave like a bright white bow tie contrasting with the deep blue ocean and the black smoke pouring from her funnel.

"Commander Wake, sway the longboat up and over the port side! *Port side*, men, the side away from the warship so the Germans can't see! And get the dinghy launched too," commanded Irons as he eased the helm, reducing her angle of heel and her speed.

After a glance back at the warship, he called to Aukai and me, "Peter and David, as soon as they're in the water, board them and get ashore! No time to hide them in the jungle so sink 'em in the water just off the beach. I'll tack the schooner and take her back out to lead those sauerkrauts on a merry chase away from here. Hopefully, they'll be watching me, not you."

Aukai moved Jane to the rail as I made a last remark to Irons. "You can't win that race. They'll get you easily."

"Who knows that for sure? Only God does, and He works in mysterious ways," he shouted to me, a crazed grin covering his face. "Remember how we met in that coal bunker?" His eyes narrowed for a fleeting moment. "I've killed far bigger men than you, Peter Wake, for doing far less to me than punching my nose. But we met at the right time in my life and in yours, and it's led us here, to that beach in this bay."

He shook his head. "The time for talk is long gone. Get ashore and do your job."

The longboat swayed down and hit the water with a thud, towing alongside by her bow line as Kan and some crew jumped in. Aukai and Jane followed. Others jumped down into the dinghy. They included Chief Kilim, who was in plain attire, meaning only his genitalia's gourd sheath. He carried in one hand a bulky woven bag, presumably filled with his battle implements.

"Cast off the boats and wear the ship around, Jack!" roared Irons to the bosun as he waved a quick good-bye to us. The schooner swept past us, her wall of canvas straining as the booms and gaffs swung across the deck and the sails crackled into their new trim.

In seconds, *Solomon's Gold* was heading in the opposite direction, out to sea and away from us. She was shielding us from the *Blitz*, giving us more precious seconds to get as far as we could while under her concealment.

The smaller dinghy was already in the lead, nearing the beach. In our boat, Kan yelled something in Tok Pisin and the men pulled away fast, their rhythm increasing with each stroke. We sat aft and turned around to watch the schooner broad-reach out through the reef's gap.

Water exploded near Irons' ship. The Germans were aiming for him, not us. Another round hit the reef. Irons tacked again, just past the outer edge of the reef, and I saw his strategy. He was keeping the schooner between the warship and us, hiding our movement for as long as possible.

An air burst exploded ten feet above the water, right where the schooner would have been if she'd held course. I knew that technique, for I'd done it myself to blockade-runners on the coast of Florida. The Germans were trying to destroy the sails and rigging so they could save the hull and gather evidence of the schooner's misdeeds.

I returned facing forward and surveyed the beach. The sand was perhaps a thirty-foot-wide strip separating the water and the jungle. The dinghy crew had swamped their boat so she was out of sight. They were running into the jungle, each man bent under a load of supplies.

The warship was only a mile away from *Solomon's Gold* now, the boom of her gun clear. A new round burst close to the schooner's main topmast, severing it. Another passed through the foresail and out into the reef, exploding there. Irons tacked again but this time slowly, for the main topmast was canted over at a ridiculous angle. The schooner stopped halfway through her tack and drifted to leeward, toward the reef just off Nuusafee Island.

A figure climbed the taffrail on the stern of *Solomon's Gold* and aimed a rifle at *Blitz*. Seconds later we heard three gunshots, puny compared to the sound of the German's Krupp cannon. Three more tiny pops came from the schooner's stern. It was Irons, all right, daring the Germans to fire for effect.

"He's goading them," I said. "Committing suicide."

"Yes, you're right. And they've got the correct range and azimuth now so it won't take long," Aukai said to himself.

The warship altered course to port, heading farther out to sea. Her after guns were now unmasked and able to fire. A cloud of black smoke blasted out from her as a deafening broadside fired simultaneously. The result was immediate: The schooner disappeared.

Where she had been was a roiling cloud of black smoke from which flaming sticks of wood and canvas flew in all directions, some large, others small. Debris rained down everywhere, creating tendrils of smoke and hundreds of splashes. The lighter pieces floated on the wind for a while, falling farther away. Then the smoke blew away into nothingness.

Solomon's Gold, John Irons, Bosun Jack, and the few others who had remained aboard were no more.

Blitz was slowing down as she got closer to her victim's liquid grave, men on her bridge pointing to the debris in the water where the schooner had been. No one was pointing toward us at the beach. Soon the warship's hull was out of sight behind Nuusafee Island, her funnels and masts rising above the coconut palms.

Our longboat's hull crunched on the bottom, and everyone jumped out into knee-deep water. A half mile to the left, I saw the Poustasi village. It looked deserted, probably because of the gunfire. To the right was the swamped dinghy. Kilim and his boat crew had already gotten off the beach and into the trees.

Aukai and the Melanesian crewmen lifted the cases out of the longboat and ran up the beach as Kan pulled the bung from the bilge. Jane sloshed ashore, balancing a lady's suitcase on her head. Kan and I pushed the sinking boat out into deeper water, and then he ran for the tree line. The longboat was underwater when I pulled my seabag up to a shoulder and waded ashore. The beach sand was much looser than I'd anticipated, churned by the others, and was retarding my speed.

I was halfway across the beach when I heard Aukai growl the oath in Hawaiian. At the same time, one of the Melanesians yelled for me to hurry, and I heard Jane shouting, "They're shooting at *us* now!"

Seconds later, I was doubled over that black rock on the beach, cursing in excruciating pain from the machine gun wound. Just five more feet and I would've been safe.

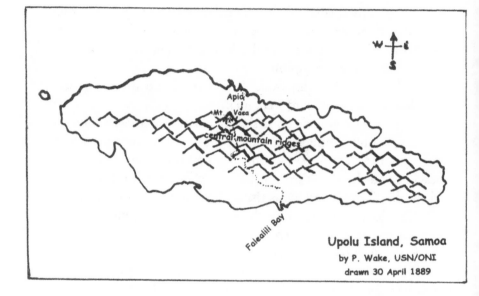

W ⬆ E
S

Apia
Mt. Vaea
central mountain ridges

Faleaiili Bay

Upolu Island, Samoa
by P. Wake, USN/ONI
drawn 30 April 1889

32

Mis Buen Amigos

Falealili Bay
Upolu Island
Kingdom of Samoa
5:20 P.M., Sunday
10 February 1889

The warship loitered off the reef, putting a boat in the water. All the while, those two Maxim guns periodically peppered the beach and jungle with random shots. None was wasted on the seabag or me anymore, presumably because they thought us dead bodies. The Germans' small boat headed toward the beach. It wouldn't be long now.

I called to my friend in the jungle. "David! Get everybody away from here right now. You can't help me so make it to your Samoan contact and get the mission accomplished. Don't worry about me. I'll talk my way out of it with the Germans right after they patch up my leg."

The Hawaiian poked his head out of a bush. "I'm not leaving you here to be captured, Peter."

The image of John Irons' speaking his last words to me came to mind. I echoed them in a command. "The time for talking has gone, Captain Aukai. Just leave and get the job done on those German ships. Now!"

There was no answer, only the stirring of the bushes as he crawled away.

It started to rain. Above me, I saw a squall line from the island's interior. The edge was over me, the rain still just a light shower. But the cloud was dark bluish-gray in the center, and all that water aloft was about to deluge the coast. That gave me an idea.

I turned my attention to the Germans, who were nearing the beach, the oars raising and lowering to the cadence of the coxswain. Several sailors in the bow had their rifles out and were scanning the beach nervously. A taut-faced young officer sat in the stern, glancing first at the squall, then eyeing the huts of Poutasi. None of the Germans appeared worried about me.

I counted the men in the boat. It looked to be about a dozen in all. If I could muster all of my energy to overcome the paralysis, a lunge toward the seabag would get me the shotgun, with which I could rapidly fire five shells of buckshot. That would send forty-five pellets toward the sailors and hopefully remove at least half the enemy from the equation. If I could then somehow crawl into the jungle during the ensuing confusion, I could reload and drop some more of them.

Ultimately, of course, they'd get me. The ship would simply use her main guns and level the jungle. But it would take time for that to happen since the sailors in the boat would have to get out of the line of fire. And the coming downpour would ruin their aiming for a few minutes.

Time was the point, for time was all I had left to give to Aukai and the mission. I hoped I'd have time before the bombardment to bury or hide any belongings identifying me as an American naval officer. It would be better to let them wonder who I was and why I was there.

The German boat grounded thirty feet down the beach from me. The now-black center of the cloud was overhead. It was now or never.

I took three deep breaths and clenched my muscles as hard as I could. Then, with a curse and a growl, I used my arms to launch my body toward the seabag.

The movement caught the sailors by surprise. For a split second, they stood there, half in and half out of the boat. In that instant, I heard a conch shell sound somewhere close by.

From the forest, a deep voice bellowed, "*Sa . . . moh . . . a!*"

A dozen flames leaped out from muzzles along the tree line, the crack of gunfire splitting the air. A bank of gun smoke rolled over me and drifted out to sea. I was draped across the bag with my weaponry but had no strength left to open it.

For a fleeting moment all was silent. The only natural sound was the surf, but seconds later I heard men moaning and crying out. Every German sailor was down, at least half of them dead. The young officer's body was in the same position. His face was frozen in time, still staring off with dead eyes at Poutasi on his left flank.

Another crack sizzled the air with a brain-filling explosion. This time it was lightning. A palm tree a hundred yards down the beach toppled over. Immediately, a cascade of water from above literally pushed me down in the sand.

I heard another shout from behind me. Six massive brown arms reached from behind me and levitated me high off the beach, propelling me rapidly into the darkness of the jungle. I was above their heads, riding atop their uplifted arms, vines and leaves swishing in my face as they trotted away from the beach. The trot became a run when the path got wider, my pain-wracked body bouncing along over them. I couldn't see where we were going or who they were, only the green blur of trees and vines rushing past my head. The inundation of water filled my mouth and nostrils and eyes. My hip was hurting like hell, but I couldn't do anything to alleviate it in that posture, except hope I didn't get dropped.

We went through a large coconut grove, the men running faster. Then we entered the forest again, and the path inclined. The pace slowed but didn't stop. My rescuers were feeling the distance now, with heavy, bass-toned exhales, the sound menacing, almost animal-like. I realized it was in cadence. They were chanting some sort of warrior song in unison to keep their strength up.

Finally, at what I estimated to be a quarter mile from the beach, the men stopped and lowered me gently onto a bed of banana fronds. They then sat down around me, staring at their cargo while they got their breath back. The rain let up but not the humidity. The jungle steamed around us.

There were about twenty of them in all. Every man was more than six feet tall and at least 250 pounds, all of it pure muscle. The brown of their skins ranged from tan to dark mahogany. They wore dark wraparound cloth skirts to their knees, no shirts or shoes, and woven designs in jute around their wrists and ankles. Many had intricate tattoos on their arms and legs, some on their torsos. Except for the men who carried me, they carried shotguns and rifles, and all carried bone daggers or machetes in their waists. Several had vicious-looking wooden clubs shaped like axes.

One of the Samoans was my age, with gray hair and an authoritative mien, whom I presumed to be the head of the group. He was sitting on a fallen tree trunk, his chest heaving, and he looked distinctly unhappy. Next to him was Aukai, who was intently telling him something in the Polynesian lingo.

The head man listened with a grave aspect, then pointed at me and called me a *palangi*. It wasn't said nicely. An animated discussion, or perhaps an argument, began.

Aukai stopped and turned to me, saying, "We are going to get that wound dressed before we go any farther, Peter. Let me have a look at it."

"David, that can wait just a minute. First, tell me what's going on? Who are these men? Where are Jane and the others?"

"Jane and the others should be here at any time. They came by a different path. Chief Kilim went off on his own."

"Irons or Jack get away?"

"No. May God please rest their souls in Heaven."

He gestured toward the Samoan beside him. "Let me explain who this man is, Peter. His name is Toamalosi. In English it would be 'Strong Warrior.' He is the *matai*, the chief, of these men. They are all his family. They live in a village a little way from here, up in the mountains. He and I met on my previous visit so I know that he is a follower of Mataafa and fights the Germans. We can trust him, and he trusts me."

"How the hell did he come to be here, right when we needed him?"

"He heard the warship firing at the schooner and came to investigate. I asked him for assistance. That is why he helped us get you off the beach."

"He doesn't seem too pleased. What's a *palangi*?"

Aukai waved a finger at me. "It just means white man, Peter. Do not worry. I explained that you are a *good* white man, an American, and you were sent to help Samoa."

There was a crackling rumble in the distance as high explosive rounds detonated to the south. The ship was bombarding the beach.

Aukai launched into a dialogue with Toamalosi. Several times, they pointed at me, but I didn't care at that point, for another sharp stab of pain went through me. I spontaneously let loose some regrettable sailor oaths.

"My, my! Not a very gentlemanly thing to say when a lady is present, commander," remarked a bedraggled Jane Cushman as she entered the clearing. Next to her were two Samoan men, and behind them trudged Kan and four of Irons' other Melanesian crew.

Jane knelt down beside me and started ripping the trouser cloth away, poking around my thigh and hip, sending more stabbing pain throughout me. That caused another round of pain-induced curses.

She looked reproachfully at Aukai. "Has anyone seen to this

wound? My God, what are you people thinking of? This needs to be dressed immediately."

"We were about to do that, Jane," I countered.

Nobody else had seen the wound, but they did now, for Jane proceeded to unbuckle and pull off my blood-and rum-soaked trousers. A low groan rose from the gathering when my hip came to view. It was swelling and turning a reddish-purple color already, with several holes where the bullet and flask fragments had punctured the skin.

"This smells like rum," she said in disbelief.

"It hit a flask of Matusalem Cuban rum in my pocket."

"You are very lucky, Peter," observed Aukai as he leaned closer. "Looks to me like that flask blunted it and was turned into shrapnel. You've got several wounds there, but none of them look that bad." His face transformed from concern to mirth when he added, "Peter, you were struck by German lightning, but you were saved by Cuban rum!"

I had to laugh; it was a clever pun. *Blitz* was the German word for lightning. Jane wasn't impressed by the humor, however, and continued to poke around the wound and make clucking sounds. "Stop making jokes. This needs to be taken care of right now!"

She sounded almost as if she had genuine concern for me. I reached out toward her. "Jane, it's not as bad as it looks."

"Listen, you arrogant son of a bitch, you're the one who blackmailed me into this hellhole in the first place. And you're the only white man around right now. So I damn well am *not* going to sit back while the boys have a gab session and let the wounds get infected. You are my ticket out of this mess so get this thing taken care of right now."

Hmm. So much for any affection on her part.

"Jane is right," admitted Aukai. "Let us examine the wounds in detail."

He and Toamalosi examined my hip, which incited more spirited Polynesian discussion between them. Several of the Samoan warriors now added their opinions, and soon a serious medical debate was under way. Well, I hoped it was a medical debate.

Finally, Toamalosi made some sort of pronouncement to his men and the entire discussion ended. Two men jumped up and trotted off somewhere as Aukai casually informed me, "I will get that bullet out of you, and afterward Toamalosi will pack the wound."

"Pack it with what?" I asked dubiously. I didn't fancy a witch doctor stuffing his potions inside my body.

"Natural plant medicines, Peter, made from the double-red hibiscus, the ti plant, and the 'ava pepper plant and mixed with pure coconut oil. Do not worry. I know they will work to heal you and prevent infection."

"Sounds terrible."

"You know something? The traditional war axes of Samoa and Hawaii produce far worse wounds than you have, and Polynesians long ago learned how to treat them. We cannot stay here for long so I will start as soon as the men return with more *ava* for you to drink."

"What the hell is *ava?*"

"A mild sedative broth, called *kava* in Tonga and some other Polynesian islands. You must drink many cups, and it will numb the wound's pain and also your mind's worry."

Five minutes later the men returned, carrying an ornately decorated wooden bowl more than a foot across that had eight-inch-long legs carved from it. They all gathered in a circle as Toamalosi intoned some serious-sounding words, clapped three times, used a small coconut cup to taste the contents in one draft, then spilled a little on the ground. He nodded his approval to his subordinates, and the bowl was brought over to me. The liquid inside was the same color and consistency of used bath water. *Very* used bath water.

Aukai clapped one time, then dipped a small coconut cup into the bowl and held it to my lips. It tasted bland with a mildly bitter aftertaste. He said to gulp it down. I did so and started choking. Another four cups of the stuff were fed me in rapid order.

By the sixth round of drinks, I still felt no anesthetic relief of my pain and began to doubt the wisdom of the whole procedure. After the eighth, I wondered if it only worked on Polynesians. I lost track of the drinks at number fourteen, but I still wasn't keen on the idea of my Hawaiian friend digging around inside my leg without a decent painkiller and some clean surgical instruments.

Damn it all. Why hadn't I brought some laudanum along in the seabag? I chastised myself. A major omission, inexcusable for a veteran like me. Maybe there was some other way to deaden the pain to come?

I wasn't given time to contemplate, much less argue with, Aukai's plan, however, for Jane was suddenly pulled away from me and taken out of sight. The Hawaiian said women weren't allowed to be present for what was to come. That didn't sound good, but I did think it a bit intriguing in an odd way. I also noticed Aukai was speaking slower and more mush-mouthed for some reason. Perhaps he'd had some sips of the 'ava drink to steady his hand.

Without any warning that I can remember, four of the stoutest Samoans proceeded to sit on my legs and arms. Interestingly, I didn't feel them at all. In fact, I thought the hulking brutes looked a bit silly sitting there, holding down my relatively puny form, and I told them so.

Aukai produced a folding knife from his pocket, which elicited envious remarks from the Samoans, and without any further preamble dug into the wound.

I asked if he would stop tickling me.

He translated for the Samoans. They laughed and pounded me good naturedly on the shoulders. I caught the pleasant sounding words, "*Palangi leilei!*"

I thought that a very nice thing for my new friends to say, whatever it was, and answered in my best Spanish, which came out slurred as well. "*Muchas gracias, mis buen amigos!*"

That comment met with a roar of approval and clapping. Then I realized they weren't complimenting me. They were congratulating Aukai, who was holding up a small misshapen slug of lead for all to see. There were other bits of shrapnel lying in his open palm, pieces of the flask that had been in my pocket.

"Your hip is not broken," he reported. "Because of that rum flask, the bullet was not able to penetrate very far inside. It broke apart and tumbled, though I believe I got everything out. And I am glad your flask had no glass insulation, for shattered glass would have been harder to extract."

I'd have to pass that opinion along to my friend Rork, who gave it to me at the end of the war to celebrate our survival. "Yeah, it was a cheap flask from an old friend."

Aukai continued. "But the hip is badly contused, and I think the nerves and muscles that operate your leg were affected by the impact. Perhaps with rest, you can allow them to return to their normal state and regain your ability to walk."

Toamalosi appeared with a cup of some sort of green powder. Aukai said it was pulverized medicinal plants and flowers. The chief stuffed it all into the wound and bound it with banana leaves and sisal string, tickling me more than Aukai's surgical efforts.

A faint gong sounded. Toamalosi, the clan *matai*, looked up at his companions and solemnly announced, "*Sa*."

All of the Samoans got up off me and quietly walked away without any explanation. Aukai bent down and explained, "It is six o'clock and time for the evening Christian devotions, Peter. We will be back in a few minutes. In the meantime, you are going to go to sleep for a while. Jane will be brought back here to watch over you."

Then I felt a light knock on the head just behind my right ear, and all awareness ended.

33
Saint Valentine's Day

Fafinelelei Village
Upolu Island
Kingdom of Samoa
9:30 P.M., Thursday
14 February 1889

It was a scene from one of Pierre Loti's romantic novels. A nearly full, rum-colored moon hung low over the swaying pandanus palms and candlenut trees, fanned by a light breeze scented with frangipani and gardenia. I had the numb taste of *'ava*, balanced by sweet mango, in my mouth and felt the touch of a soft hand caressing my brow.

I was reposed in a *fale*, the oval-shaped, thatched communal hut of my host, Toamalosi, the *matai*, for I was now in his village in the high country. My nurse was his granddaughter, a beautiful native girl of perhaps sixteen, clad in her best blue calico dress, a red hibiscus flower over her right ear. Her long black hair glistened in the reflection of a nearby bonfire in the center of the village.

The ladies of Samoa constantly wear flowers, are quite

feminine, and have the beautiful and most expressive eyes in the world. You know exactly what the ladies are thinking, for their eyes openly show the different shades of mirth or love or anger. That evening, the girl's were pools of amber tranquility as she knelt next to me and hummed a slow melody, accompanying the warriors closer to the fire.

One of the giant Samoans who had carried me from the beach was the lead singer. He was performing a love song, full of long lamenting notes, with other men filling in the harmonious background with slow chants. Silhouetted by the fire, wearing his clan's blue *lavalava*, the sarong of Samoa, the star performer moved his limbs and torso in sympathy to the mood of the song, surprisingly graceful for so large a man.

Though I was on a mission of war, I felt totally at peace right then, very much at home among people who understood the real values of civilization. The pain in my twisted leg and back, bruised shoulder, and perforated hip was still there but much subsided.

I knew that I wouldn't have very long at the village to regain my strength. But what little time I did have was filled with complete relaxation, for Toamalosi had so decreed it to be so. My every need was attended to, immediately and with tender care. It was much better medicine and care than any Western hospital could provide.

Sedated by the *'ava* and the music, my mind drifted back to when we arrived in the village.

I didn't have an idea of what to expect, but I did know I was helpless without the care of the Samoans, for I couldn't even walk.

Those four days of recuperation had done incredible wonders for my body and spirit. Discomfort and aches remained, to be sure, but the body-wracking, stabbing pains disappeared. My twisted and dislocated muscles regained their power day by day.

On the third day, I ventured forth using a bamboo cane. By the fourth, I progressed to walking without its support for short distances. I was still walking slowly, but at least I could move. Fruit, fish, vegetables, and pork were my steady diet. *'Ava* was had every night, sending me into blissful sleep, only to be woken by the sun's greeting rays.

The open wounds on my hip had me worried. Infection of wounds is a great killer in jungled lands. However, Aukai's efforts with a needle and thread, donated from Jane's valise, proved effective in closing the punctures. Best of all, the wound showed no sign of contamination and, amazingly, began to heal nicely, assisted by native lotions involving the oil of coconut meat, certain red flowers, and some sort of greenish powder I never understood. My escape from tropical infection was a mystery to me.

I'd asked Aukai about it when we first arrived in the village. Aukai displayed an enigmatic expression and said, "Do not be troubled, my friend. You will not get the infections. The wound is being kept clean. It is part of *Fa'a Samoa*."

He smiled at my confused reaction and said, "The lifestyle of Samoa. We Polynesians know things that Americans and Europeans do not. It goes back a thousand years, and the lessons are passed down through the generations through long stories. Maybe someday you will understand, if you take time to respect and learn our ways.

"Now, Peter, I must insist you use the time in this village to rest and gather your strength. You are progressing well, but you are not in full *manuia* yet. You must be able to meet the Germans in combat."

I was learning the lingo quickly, but that one was new to me. "*Manuia?*"

"It means good health. I think it will take you four days, maybe five. Then we will go to war."

That memory brought me back to the reality of the moment. The moon had climbed higher, changing into a silvery white light, creating shadows from the trees and huts. The girl caressed my face with a wet *tapa* cloth made from mulberry bark and lifted a coconut cup of *'ava* to my lips. The warrior by the fire sang a tenor part of the love song, his voice echoing among the ridges in the night air.

It would be so easy to live this way, to succumb to the life of Samoa, but I was a warrior myself. *Don't get used to this, Wake,* I reminded myself. *It's all a fantasy, so use it and move on.*

What was happening in the real world on the other side of this island? We were running out of time to accomplish the mission, and I couldn't lie there forever. The village was in the center of the island, near the crest of the highest ridge, nearly two thousand feet above the distant sea. We were isolated from the main battles in the civil war that was raging elsewhere on the north coast of the island. But for how long?

The Germans stayed on the north coast, in and near the capital of Apia and the surrounding plantations of the Firm. They seldom dared to venture far into the interior. But the forces of their installed king, Tamasese, had no fear of jungle or mountains. They ranged through their kindred clans' areas with impunity, occasionally foraying into Mataafa's territory.

Aukai briefed me each day on the rumors coming from the coast: where the German ships were, what the German leadership in Apia was doing, what the latest movements of the Tamasese forces were, and where the Americans' ships were. We learned that open warfare had not yet broken out between the Americans and Germans, but everyone expected it at any moment.

"Say, what day is it, David?" I asked at one point, for I'd lost track of time. "We need to get going soon. I feel stronger now. Maybe tomorrow morning."

"Today is Thursday, the fourteenth of February, Peter. Saint Valentine's Day, I believe."

February fourteenth? I'd thought it was the eleventh or twelfth.

"Already the fourteenth? Then we need to get going early in the morning. I can make it."

He shrugged. "There is no need for that, Peter. The Germans and Tamasese's forces have been quiet in this area, so we are safe here for a little while longer. Besides, I have just received word that we have been successful in our request to meet with Mataafa. He is coming here tomorrow afternoon to discuss the situation with you. The *matai* is going to have a *fiafia*, a celebration, in honor of the event, and has asked the high chiefs of the area to be the official hosts. All will be done in *Fa'a Samoa*, the Samoan way."

"So you got through to Mataafa himself, eh? Very good work, Captain Aukai."

When we'd first arrived up in the mountains, my Hawaiian colleague arranged to send word to the rebel leader, with an appeal for us to meet him. Aukai met him on his mission the previous year, but it had been a passing acquaintance. My friend expressed doubt the requested meeting would come to fruition, since Mataafa was distrustful of all *palangi*, but it now appeared that I would be able to gauge the Samoan freedom forces for myself and see just what might be doable with them.

A *fiafia* was a great celebration, featuring the best of the village's food and entertainment. I hoped it would put Mataafa in a positive frame of mind to cooperate with me.

"All right then," I said, infused with the Hawaiian's optimism. "We'll stay here tomorrow for the event and leave the next day."

"It will be a good meeting, Peter. You will be impressed with Mataafa. He is very good at unifying the people, for politics is a Polynesian art form. He can be of real help to our joint mission."

Aukai left me to rest, but I couldn't, for I dwelt on one thing he'd said offhandedly. I felt my heart breaking and tears filling my eyes. Knowing what was coming, I told the girl I was tired and for her to go away to her *fale*. I didn't want anyone to see me this way.

My mind wasn't on Samoa, or Mataafa, or war with Germany. It was on the date. More specifically, on what had happened on that very day eight years earlier. That was the day my dear wife, Linda, had died of female cancer in Washington while I was away on assignment in South America.

Since 1881, Saint Valentine's Day has been a day of private grief for me.

34

Manuia

Fafinelelei Village
Upolu Island
Kingdom of Samoa
10:25 P.M., Friday
15 February 1889

Mataafa's entourage arrived at sunset, right after the evening *sa* devotional prayer period. The heat of the day was gone and an evening breeze was cooling us nicely.

I leaned against a palm on the edge of the village's communal area and watched the column of warriors' entry. It was quite a parade, led by forty scouts in simple Samoan rigs: *lavalavas*, clubs, machetes, axes, and bone daggers.

Those were followed by five hundred troops, more heavily armed, led by drummers and a color guard carrying the flag of the deposed king, Malietoa Laupepa, who was languishing at Saipan Island in the German-held Marianas Islands. This flag—a white cross on a red background with a white star inside the upper left quarter—was a rallying symbol for the phrase "Samoa for the Samoans."

These warriors had the same dour look as regular soldiers on field campaign everywhere. Springfields, Enfields, and some Winchester repeaters were their main armament, but each carried a dagger or machete as well. They wore regular shirts over their *lavalavas,* with accoutrement belts for the ammunition and other implements. The weaponry and supporting gear appeared to be in good shape and maintenance.

I looked for but didn't see John Klein, the American newspaper reporter for the *New York World* who had become a mercenary advisor for the Samoan rebels. I asked Aukai if the man was still fighting alongside Mataafa. He said he thought not, but in any event the Samoan chief would not admit it even if the reporter was still out there in the jungle helping him, for Aukai had heard that Klein had pressed Mataafa to keep his involvement and whereabouts clandestine. Interestingly, while Tamasese had German advisors with his troops, I didn't see any foreigners with Mataafa's army, not even the ex-pat Brits and Americans who lived in Samoa. I was the only *palangi* around.

The welcoming ceremony was wholly a Polynesian affair held at the village's communal *fale.* European protocol, solemnity, and sophistication had nothing on the Samoans. By the light of numerous torches and a small bonfire, I observed all this from a ringside seat in my personal *fale.* I think the reader of this account will better appreciate this fascinating society with a description of what I observed, so kindly allow me the honor.

This soiree was pure upper crust, and all participants were in the Samoan version of full mess dress uniform: breastplates, enormous headdresses, anklets and bracelets, and elaborate *siapo* cloth aprons over their finest *lavalavas.* Occasional glimpses of their hidden tattoos, the intricate and painfully installed designs of the *pe'a,* could be seen on thighs and torsos.

Each man there had proved himself in war and peace, and each conducted himself with self-confidence and quiet poise. None of it was false affection, for unlike the upper classes of North America and Europe, in Samoa a dilettante never made it to this level.

The host committee, as it were, was led by the senior man of the area, the high-orator chief, or *tulafate*. This regal soul carried with him the ceremonial emblems of his elevated office: the thirty jute-tailed whisk, called a *fue*, which looked like an old-fashioned cat-o'-nine-tails to me, and the *to'oto'o*, a six-foot-long, beautifully carved walking stick.

The *tulafate* had grouped around him the high chiefs of the area, the *ali'i*. Behind them were the various chiefs of the families, the *matai*, including my rescuer, Toamalosi. As a visiting Polynesian who was well versed in *fa'a Samoa*, David Aukai had been given a place of honor with the *matai*.

Mataafa had his own similar entourage of senior officers. They too were decked out in full rig. Introductions were made and old acquaintances renewed, done with an air of gravitas. No laughs, no light-hearted quips.

This all took some time. Once the senior staffs were welcomed, the rank and file did their ceremony. Local men and visiting men stood in separate formations facing each other and proceeded to demonstrate, with unnerving hostile shouts and belligerent stances, their individual close-quarters combat capabilities. It was impressive, to say the least. I've never seen a Western army able to do the same.

After their warrior skills were clearly confirmed, the lower ranks went on to show their amity. By the end these giants, the largest warriors in the world, were all laughing and trading jests like brothers. Thus ended a remarkable illustration of Samoan manhood and war-making aptitude.

Next came dinner, a lavish affair that had been a major production on the part of the host village. Tropical fruits and vegetables such as breadfruit, lemons, taro, yams, sweet potatoes, and arrowroot were the accompaniment for main entrées: roasted chicken, pork, and fish. Each part of the cuisine was wrapped in banana and taro leaves and prepared for hours inside rock-lined earth ovens known as *umu*.

Fruits such as coconut cream, banana, papaya, and limes were mixed into a sweet sauce for the final product, which was a bit on the heavy side but tasted delicious. Plates were tightly woven palm fronds, and cups were hollowed coconuts. And as they did in medieval England not so long ago, we all used our fingers instead of utensils.

The *fiafia*, the entertainment part of the evening, followed. It consisted of the best drink, which included some of the ill-famed "square-face" German gin and rotgut Australian rum. Not everyone partook of the alcohol, for the devout Christians, of whom there are many in Samoa, declined any of it. I am a Christian but do not preclude a dram of rum from my diet, so I did have some.

The entertainment consisted of intimidating demonstrations of the manly arts of Samoan warfare, followed by ladies' dances depicting the far more tender themes and sensibilities of the fairer sex. It is widely thought by outsiders that the giant Samoan men control familial destiny, but after living among them, I know that the women have complete dictatorship over their spouses and offspring.

One may wonder about Jane Cushman. She wasn't asked to the celebration, for unlike her victories in Western high society, the Samoans were not impressed with her, especially the women. So dear Jane sat this soiree out in her hut, probably the first time in her life she failed to secure an invitation to a prestigious social event.

After the dinner, which I ate with the lesser villagers in the outer ring of attendees, I was invited into official seating arrangements of the inner circle for the *fiafia*. Following a brief introduction to the great man himself, who gave me an indifferent gaze, I was quickly ushered away to my spot before I, the ignorant *palangi*, could do or say something stupid and ruin the evening's ambiance.

My place was in the back, next to Aukai. As always in Samoa, we sat on the slatted floor of the *fale*, everyone's legs drawn up under him. I was given permission to keep my right leg straight but covered by a mat because of my wounds and status as an uncoordinated foreigner. During the time of the feast and entertainment, no official business was conducted. My every move and expression were closely scrutinized by Mataafa's lieutenants.

The war council took place after the *fiafia* was over and the village had collapsed into an *ava-* and alcohol-induced stupor. No such rest was intended for the leadership, however. Now the real dialogue would start between Mataafa and me, for I was the reason he'd come—to see the *palangi Amerika* in person and evaluate my worth to the cause of Samoan freedom from German domination.

For this session, lower level persons removed themselves from the *fale*. Only the *tulafale* and *ali'i* remained. They did not participate but sat there staring at me with open mistrust.

Mataafa and I, with Aukai next to us, sat on special woven mats, thicker and softer than most. Far to one side sat a nervous Toamalosi, whose reputation was on the line, for he had saved my life on that beach and subsequently forwarded Aukai's petition for an audience with the great Mataafa.

Toamalosi's reputation was one thing, but my mission was paramount and this moment was crucial. I needed Mataafa's help to succeed, and this was the time to impress him with my motives and my skills. One can imagine the pressure upon me not to fail.

I was well acquainted with the *'ava* ceremony by then. We sat around the *tulafale's* large *tanoa* wooden tub, carved from a single tree, which stood on ten-inch-high legs carved from the tub. The *tulafale* dipped a small cup into the *tanoa* and filled it with *'ava*, then passed it to us one at a time, starting with Mataafa. When you received the cup, you held it out straight from your body with both hands and said, *"Manuia"*—"Good health." Then you downed most of it in one gulp, with just a little left over in the cup to be tossed onto the floor.

This is not a drinking contest to get drunk in the Western way in a bawdy tavern. There is no loud boasting or shouting. *'Ava* is consumed with deliberate care. It is a time of quiet reflective philosophy and bonding when great issues are discussed.

And so it was that I came to sit with Samoan nobility in a

fale on a mountain, under clouds of stars in an inky South Pacific night, drinking '*ava* and speaking about that most serious topic among men.

War.

35

Mataafa

Fafinelelei Village
Upolu Island
Kingdom of Samoa
11:45 P.M., Friday
15 February 1889

The reader may recall at this juncture that the rightful King of Samoa, Malietoa Laupepa, had been deposed by the Germans two years earlier and sent into exile at their colony on Saipan Island in the Marianas Islands. He languished there, a proud man incommunicado from his Samoan people in a strange non-Polynesian land three thousand miles away in the north Pacific.

That afternoon, before Mataafa's arrival, Aukai had given me some background of the drama in which I found myself. It seemed that Mataafa had long been an adversary of Malietoa Laupepa in the incessant political bickering that was Samoa. Therefore, it had been logically assumed by the Germans that Mataafa would be supportive of their ousting of Laupepa.

But Teutonic logic isn't applicable in the South Seas. Mataafa didn't side with the Germans. Quite the contrary. Yes, his long-standing feud with Malietoa Laupepa was very real and heartfelt, but his anger at the arrogant foreign intervention was even more heartfelt. Mataafa was a Samoan first and foremost. Compared to the despised German *palangi*, the deposed and exiled king was a brother Samoan of the first order.

While Mataafa and I drank *'ava* and talked, I studied the great man himself. Even in his advanced age, which I never determined precisely, Mataafa was an imposing figure, far more so than any politico I'd ever met in Washington or London. The strength of his bronzed warrior physique, the intelligence in his eyes, and the decisiveness in his tone all contributed to present an image of barely constrained personal malevolence, should he decide to employ it. That was balanced by his receding white hair, broad white mustache, lined face, measured manner, and kind disposition toward the servants and guests at the *fiafia*.

Mataafa was well known for his devotion to the Roman Catholic faith. On Sundays there was to be no fighting, and he would invariably attend church. He was also well known for caution and sagacity in his dealings with foreigners. No one who ever met Mataafa would think him an ignorant savage, and only a fool would underestimate him.

I instantly understood that this man could be my worst enemy or best friend and that he was impervious to the usual Western flattery or coercion. He was a Polynesian warrior at war, the last defender of his Samoan people and their rights, and had no time for minor social sweet talk, especially from a foreigner whose motives he didn't fully comprehend and certainly didn't trust.

Therefore, after thanking him for coming to see me, I started off with a blunt statement of my mission. "I will be candid with you, sir. You have sent word to my nation, asking if the United States would honor our treaty from years ago to prevent any outside nation from taking over Samoa. Germany and the United States are arguing the point, and many people in both nations are calling for war. The warships in Samoa are ready for war. We Americans do not want war, however. In fact, I was sent here by our president to try to prevent a war between my country and Germany."

I stopped to let Aukai's translation catch up. Mataafa just sat there watching me.

Aukai paused and I went on. "But please understand this. If I cannot prevent a war or if it has already begun, I am to win it immediately by destroying all of the German warships as fast as I can. Sir, I am the enemy of your enemy and, thus, your ally."

I let that part sink in for a bit, then continued on to my main point.

"Tomorrow, Captain Aukai and I will go across the mountains and down to the north coast. There we will begin our duties, for both the King of Hawaii and the President of the United States have a similar goal: to stop the Germans. But before Captain Aukai and I start on our mission, I have a request of you. I need to know what is happening. You know more about the German forces and Tamasese's warriors than anyone on the island. Will you tell me what you know about where they are, how many men they have, what they are armed with, and what they are doing?"

There was a long silence after the translation ended. I heard some Mataafa subordinate leaders speaking quietly to themselves in negative tones, but their commander said nothing. He just sat there and stared at me. Samoans, unlike people in many cultures in the nether regions of the world, look you right in the eye and are not shy about staring at you before answering.

Mataafa's reply was measured. So was the tone of interpretation, which included a command, not a request.

"Yes, Commander Wake, I will help you with information about the Germans and Tamasese's men. Then you will fully answer my questions about the American forces and their intentions in Samoa. And you will tell me the exact place and time of your operation."

It was quite a *quid pro quo*. He knew when he had the upper hand. Otto von Bismarck had nothing on Mataafa when it came to shrewd bargaining.

"Thank you, sir. I agree and will tell you our intentions to the best of my ability. Now, please tell me where the German sailors and marines are ashore on Upolu Island right now."

Not checking with staff for the information, Mataafa instantly answered and Aukai put it into English. "Fifty-seven marines are guarding Tamasese's royal palace at Mulinu'u peninsula near Apia. They have four field cannons. Forty-three sailors are the police of the town of Apia. That is all that are on the island at this time. The Germans sent landing parties ashore at villages on the north coast last week, but they all are back on their ships now."

"And Tamasese's men? Where are they?"

"Three hundred of them, armed with old shotguns and rifles, are around Apia. Fifty, not armed with guns, are out enforcing laws and taxes at Fasitootai at the west end of the island. One hundred fifty-five, armed with German rifles and under the command of the German, Captain Brandeis, are walking through the forest, heading this way. They left Apia this morning and are at Vaea now, readying themselves on the warrior mountain. They are following the main trail across the island. Tomorrow they will climb Mount Fiamoe and rest there. The next day they will be at Papapapai-tai and gather their strength, adding another fifty men with Samoan weapons from the villages around that area. On the next morning, they will attack you here at this village, for they know you are here."

That was disconcerting. "How do they know I am here?"

"It is no secret that German sailors tried to kill American *palangi* landing at Falealili. The Samaritan *palangi* was killed on the schooner, along with his Melanesian crew, but two *palangi*, a man and a woman, got away and were rescued by Toamalosi's men. Everyone on Upolu Island knows this. The German plantations are guarding their blackbirded Melanesian laborers very closely, for word has spread that the Samaritan's ghost has come to the island and will liberate them."

Everyone knew about us? That was even more disconcerting. The good news was that the imagined ghost of Irons, in conjunction with Chief Kilim's efforts, might prove to be a useful diversion.

Mataafa was starting to look perturbed by my obvious ignorance of the enemy's dispositions and intelligence, so before his patience ran out, I asked, "Where are the German warships right now?"

"*Adler* is in Apia. *Eber* is at Pango Pango, over at Tuitila Island. *Olga* is at Savai'i Island."

"Where is the one named *Blitz?*"

"I do not know that ship."

I asked Mataafa if there were any American ships at the island. His eyes widened in bewilderment, then hardened into wariness, for he obviously expected me to know such things. He said no, that the one small American warship, name unknown, had left.

That didn't look good to the Samoans, but it was prudent for the ship. A lone gunboat was no match for the German squadron. I told Mataafa that the Americans were waiting until they could return in force, and that would be soon.

I needed to know more about the German ships. When and where would they concentrate, as in attacking a village? That would be the time and place to use the Ballistite to maximum effect, for surprise was the key element of my plan and I needed to get them all at once. But first I needed detailed intelligence.

"Do you know their plans for the warships? Are they planning a battle?"

He shrugged. "No battle. A *fiafia*. They will all be in Apia the day after tomorrow night for a celebration of a war in their past. It will go into the night."

After translating, Aukai asked me the reason for the traditional German celebration on February seventeenth. I had no idea. To my uncertain knowledge it wasn't a Christian festival, but I wasn't well versed in Lutheran ways. Perhaps a past naval victory, but that didn't make sense. Prussia and, later on, Germany, weren't involved in many naval battles. Their martial skills were on land.

Then I remembered a report from our ONI man in Berlin the year before. It mentioned a military ceremony on February 17th. It was in honor of the day they declared victory over the French in 1871 and held a big parade in occupied Paris. The German military commemorated it every year with a military display and evening gala. Our ONI was always able to glean theretofore unknown information about the German military, especially their vaunted artillery, from attending the various functions in the celebration.

This was exactly what I needed. They would all be in Apia harbor that day and evening. Stuck out in the middle of the Pacific, twenty thousand kilometers away from home and all that was normal for them, the Germans would be like anyone else. They would recreate their homeland in food and drink and music, and the party would go long into the evening.

Mataafa, having done his part of our agreement, asked where the American ships were and when the U.S. army was going to land in Samoa to help him fight the Germans. I repeated my earlier statement that the warships would be coming soon, but they had a very long way to go. That did not please him.

I then said the land battles would be for the Samoans, for they were better land warriors in the jungle than the Americans, who were clumsy in jungles, like the Germans. That didn't please him either, but he seemed to understand it, put in that way.

He asked when and where I was going to attack the Germans. I replied that I did not know when and where yet, for I needed a spy inside their camp. I added that when I did attack them, it would be against their ships, for their ships' guns did the most damage against the Samoans.

Mataafa wasn't delighted with any of my answers but didn't seem overtly angry. I think he appreciated that I had spoken factually with no false promises. He said an approving phrase in Samoan and turned to his staff, rapidly informing them of the situation. They continued to regard me dubiously, clearly not impressed with the *palangi*'s vague statements.

Despite the lack of cheer on the part of my new allies and the fact that evidently everyone on the island knew my location, I was in a better frame of mind, and it wasn't from the *'ava* and rum. At last, I had good intelligence of the enemy and a new affiliation with the senior local leader, and my tiny force was intact and ready to move.

Personally, my *manuia* was regained and I was ready— or as ready as I could be right then—for the rigors of a march across the mountains. And best of all, I had a unique and perfect opportunity to slip a spy inside the enemy's camp and gain some operational intelligence about their true intentions, directly from their leadership's highest levels. Were they readying for war, or did they want a peaceful solution to the conflict?

Jane was about to earn her money.

36
Manaia Fafine, Tane Valea

Imperial German Consulate
Mulinu'u Peninsula
Apia, Upolu Island
Kingdom of Samoa
9:45 P.M., Saturday
17 February 1889

The town of Apia is the national capital of the Kingdom of
Samoa. "National capital" is the politically polite phrase for
the place, but in the interest of accuracy I will state that it is far
too grandiose a term.

Actually, Apia is a collection of a hundred or so native *fale*
huts and several European structures strung along a sandy pathway
known as Beach Road. The road parallels the half-moon–shaped
rocky beach that forms the southern shore of Apia Harbor.

The harbor is an open bay that faces the ocean to the north.
Its wide expanse is deceptive, for there is only a small anchorage
area at its center. The rest of the bay has a coral ledge concealed
just below the surface, ready to consume any vessel that blunders
into it.

The Samoans' *fales* are grouped into several tiny villages. From west to east they are Mulinu'u, Soni, Savalalo, Matafele, and Matautu. Several families live in each village, the community being ruled by the village *matai*.

Germans of all stripes—political, commercial, clerical, and military—are concentrated on the west side of the town. Their consulate, living compounds, stores, main plantation, commercial house, the harbor's main docks, and a copra factory are on or near Beach Road to the west of a small bridge over the rivulet called Mulivai Stream, which carries rainwater from the mountains out into the harbor. There is also a small French convent that serves the Roman Catholic church on the eastern side of the town.

The stream also marks the social and political dividing line between the foreign contingents in the town: Germans are to the west; English and Americans to the east.

The Germans have an additional factor, one of great importance. They are concentrated closest to the Samoan royal houses—more accurately described as very nice *fales*—on the Mulinu'u Peninsula, which forms the western side of the harbor. The shoreline of this peninsula is guarded naturally by a treacherous reef on the harbor side and by thick mangrove swamps on the other side. It has only one land approach through its narrow connection with the main island, and that is right where the Germans built their community.

It is a neatly done setup. To get to the native king, you have to literally go through the Germans.

On the eastern half of the waterfront lie the Roman Catholic Church, the rather dilapidated Samoa Hotel, the British consulate, and the Anglican church. Farther to the east, near the village of Matauta, is the American consulate. Missionaries, traders, beachcombers, ne'er-do-wells, and sea captains who've come ashore are the predominant occupations among the Anglo-Americans of Apia, almost all of whom live on the eastern end of Beach Road. I say Anglo-Americans, but the truth is that there are only twenty or thirty Yanks balanced by fifty or sixty Brits. For the more than two hundred Germans in Apia, this side of town is where the troublemakers are.

There are two major centers of German life in their side of Apia, the German consulate and the Firm's commercial offices, which are conveniently located next to each other just outside the Samoan royal estate at Mulinu'u, the better to control their minions, the native rulers. The reader will remember the diminutive appellation "the Firm" being the far easier nickname throughout the Pacific islands for the vast company formed in Hamburg officially entitled *Deutsche Handels und Plantagen Gesellschaft der Sud See Inseln zu Hamburg.*

For me, Apia's eastern side was of no immediate importance to my mission, for I could not chance revealing my presence and true identity, even among people who I supposed were of like-minded views. The German side was the objective of my mission. The task at this point was not to attack but to listen and gain insight into the Germans' plans, specifically the political architect of the conflict, Dr. Knappe, and his right-hand men, Commodore Fritze and army Captain Brandeis.

To that end, I dispatched my unenthusiastic secret weapon, Mrs. Jane Cushman. I sent Aukai and one of Mataafa's Samoan warriors along to guard her. In addition, Mataafa supplied a woman who knew the layout of the German area.

Samoan women are not demure creatures. They are larger than the average Western female, used to physical challenges, and of quick and decisive intelligence. This particular Polynesian lady, Mika, had penetrated the German area many times to meet her cousins, who had menial jobs there, hence becoming one of the various sources of Mataafa's information about the enemy. Performing the role of personal maidservant, Mika would watch over Jane and transmit messages from her.

Aukai and his man would stay on surveillance outside to receive messages from Mika and provide an emergency egress if things went badly. Aukai was also there to provide a latent menace for Jane to have in the back of her mind should her loyalty to our cause waver and she consider switching sides.

I did not go to Apia with the others. Instead I stayed with

Mataafa, for he was the logistical key to our success. It was he who would provide the men and canoes. He just didn't know it yet. His main force was on the move, outflanking Tamasese's column that was heading for our village.

We saw them at one point, crossing a cocoa field in the high mountains, flying their white flag with a black German cross and red canton with white star, but they didn't see us. We could have hit them with advantage, but Mataafa declined. Instead we let them plod on toward where they thought we would be. He wanted them to be tired and frustrated. I thought it a judicious decision.

I walked next to the great commander, communicating with him by my rudimentary Samoan and through Joseph, one of his underlings who spoke fairly good English, having been taught at the Catholic school. It was important for me to cement my relationship with this man, who would necessarily be the prime support for my operations.

It wasn't easy. We marched for a day along the high ridges—a considerable strain on my hip and leg—and ended up at last in the new camp. Mataafa picked wisely. It was an idyllic bivouac with all we needed, overlooking the Tiavi Waterfall. This cataract plunged three hundred feet to disappear in a verdant gorge below us. Our position was militarily sound, protected by cliffs on three sides, with two escape routes down the fourth. No enemy could approach unseen, but we could disappear into the rain forest labyrinth should it be wise.

My plan was to wait there for the results of Jane's espionage assignment, then decide on where and how to begin the sabotage attack on the German ships.

Why did I not attack them the night of the German celebration in Apia, when their ships were concentrated, one might fairly ask? The reason is simple. We weren't ready. I did not have the supply apparatus set up yet, nor the mode of attack.

It would be soon, of that I had no doubt. For the more Mataafa thought about it, the more keen he became on my concept of ending the German naval gunfire against the Samoans. His men were fearless and effective in close-quarters battle, but warships standing a mile off the beach and raining death down on them was something they couldn't counter by themselves.

We drank 'ava late into the night and spoke of life and women and Samoa. I described my family. His own ainga, or family, was enormous, fully 180 or 190, he thought.

He asked of my career, and I of his. We spoke of past battles and foes. He asked about the United States and why we were in the South Pacific. He wanted to know everything about the outside world that had encroached on his culture. I answered candidly, though it did not cast us palangi in a good light. His reaction was grim silence. He knew the Germans weren't the only outsiders that Samoa would have to deal with in the future.

The celebration of the German victory over France eighteen years earlier started off with a parade of sailors, marines, and bandsmen from the warships. The procession, led by Herr Doctor Knappe, the chief politico, and Commodore Fritze of the Imperial German Navy, started at the Firm and went around the streets to end at the consulate. It was followed by an afternoon picnic under the coconut palms, several speeches, a concert of popular music by the navy band, and some sporting events, all held in the manicured gardens around the consulate.

During the daily rain shower in the late afternoon, everyone retired home to rest and to change into the evening's attire, for the grand gala was to start on the verandah and grounds of the consulate just before sunset.

As dusk gathered, Aukai, led by his Samoan military counterpart, found a nice little observation point in the bushes near the consulate. Jane Cushman arrived at the party in full regalia, exactly one hour later, after the waltzes had started and the gin, beer, and champagne had begun to flow. The arrival was by a hastily chartered carriage, the only one for hire in Apia.

She was fully equipped for her type of battle: green satin dress showing just the right amount of décolletage, face and hair done up to enhance her eyes and minimize her age, and enough jewelry to proclaim her pedigree but not so much to be gauche. This amazing transformation had been accomplished in an hour in Jane's hastily arranged room on the second floor of the Samoa Hotel on the English side of town.

The initial difficulty would be to explain her sudden presence in Apia. This she accomplished by that most ancient of social stratagems: an arrogant and demanding demeanor.

Jane immediately stepped right up to Doctor Knappe. Consul General Knappe was a middle-aged man with a mostly bald head. He sported a large mustache and had kind, dark eyes, and one's first impression was that he was probably a successful clerk, not the leader of Germany's effort to take over the islands of Samoa, with guess-who as the imperial governor. Jane met him as he was greeting guests near the large flagpole at the center of the consular compound. Aukai was in excellent position to see and hear this entire performance and later reported it to me with genuine admiration for Jane's skills of manipulation.

After introductions, mild-mannered Jane Cushman became Attila the Hun, astonishing the consul general of the German Empire in Samoa with the following inquiry/accusation.

"So *you* are the famous Dr. Knappe? Hmm! I have been told that *you*, sir, are completely responsible for the kaiser's policies in Samoa. If that is true, then please tell me why, in God's good name, there is no decent transport in this part of the South Seas, either by water or land? I thought the great German Empire was here to *civilize* this area and to correct those deficiencies and, by the way, to end this scourge of piracy that seems to be considered sport around here!"

Poor Knappe never had a chance. "Madame Cushman, I do not understand."

"Well," she huffed, "I'll just tell you right now so you *do* understand, Doctor! I am bound for Fiji, but yesterday I was put ashore at the wrong island—this island—by the incompetent, half-breed, French pirate scum on the schooner that I innocently made the mistake of engaging in Papeete."

Her eyes flared indignantly, then leveled again at her hapless victim.

"Those despicable liars blatantly told me that this island was Fiji and then proceeded to land me at one of *your* collection of hovels called Lahoolee or some such sounding name. And I must say, sir, a more primitive place I have never seen. It was like being marooned in Africa. The natives didn't speak any civilized language, like English or German, at all. In fact, it didn't look like *your* people had ever even *been* there, much less civilized those savage brutes. They put me in a donkey cart to take me here to Apia. A donkey cart!"

It was a clever ruse by Jane. Everyone on Upolu knew that *palangi* had landed on the south coast of the island. Lauli'i was on the north coast. Knappe made a tactical retreat, recoiling a step before replying, "Do you mean Lauli'i? They sent you ashore at the village of Lauli'i? I had no idea this had happened, Madame Cushman! What an ordeal for you, my dear lady. That is eight kilometers from here on the coastal road, which is not yet improved. I am sorry you had to go through that. It must have been a very difficult journey for you."

In desperation, Knappe spun around and called out while snapping his fingers, "Commodore Fritze! Please come here. You must listen to this tale of maritime crime!"

That was exactly what I had hoped for, that Jane's tale of skulduggery at sea would come under the purview of the navy, thereby gaining her the instant status of damsel in distress—a damsel in acute need of Commodore Fritze's protection and tender loving care.

Commodore Fritze came over, along with several others who had heard the outburst. This was pretty exciting stuff for Apia's gossip set. The head man was being berated by an American woman. Word spread through the crowd quickly. Soon Jane had quite an audience, and they presently heard the story in even more dramatic detail—how the half-native, Creole-speaking skipper of the schooner had joked about the German navy and how easy it was to avoid them, how she had lost most of her luggage in the surf, and how the hotel room she was given in Apia had bugs the size of rats, rats the size of cats, and was absolutely filthy.

The ladies were predictably aghast at such treatment, the gentlemen dutifully enraged. Several disparaging comments were made about the French and their unreliability.

Jane had been to Apia three years earlier, before Fritze and Knappe had been assigned there. Just in case an old hand should recognize her, Jane now launched into her essay on the kindness, moral decency, and strength of the German people, particularly the gentlemen of their global empire who brought modern civilization to pagan lands.

This she knew well, she explained to the captivated audience, because she had had the good fortune to have visited Samoa and Kaiser Wilhelm Land before. In fact, she added, she had even learned some German, a beautiful and strong language, on that previous visit to Apia. Polite phrases of her hosts' lingo were then uttered to the appreciation of all, and soon the bond between the marooned white lady and her white German saviors was set in stone.

Nevertheless, Jane Cushman was a perfectionist in her art form, and she still had to present the *pièce de résistance* of her performance. In the next thirty seconds she did so, managing to smoothly mention the fact that she just happened to be widowed for three years and was sadly alone in the world but was wealthy enough to live quite comfortably, with homes in San Francisco and Monte Carlo.

As an added bonus, by the time Jane ended her tale of woe, she had her right arm firmly entwined in Commodore Fritze's left. Her sad blue eyes looked up at his steely visage with utter awe, while at the same time those shapely breasts pressed against the braid of his uniform sleeve. It was the feminine equivalent of a wrestling takedown, the check before the checkmate. As he passed all of this along to me later, Aukai was in a state of open wonder at what he'd seen.

But that part didn't work, for Commodore Fritze was made of far sterner stuff than your average older man far away from home in the middle of nowhere.

Fritze deftly sidestepped the lovely, rich, lonely Widow Cushman and put her hand into that of his staff aide, Lieutenant Kramer, who had been obediently standing by his superior and watching the show. The lieutenant, a baby-faced young man with not a whisker or wrinkle on his face, was completely taken aback but smart enough to catch the glint in Fritze's eye.

Kramer took the lady's hand, clicked his heels, and said, "Lieutenant Hans Kramer at your service, madam."

Her focus having shifted to the lieutenant, Jane caressed the underside of his hand, stroking his index finger. He smiled shyly, not believing his luck as he surreptitiously caressed her hand in return.

The commodore cleared his throat, lifted his chin high, then announced to Jane and the crowd, "Mrs. Cushman, I am moved by your terrible tale and will immediately take steps to find the scoundrels who perpetrated this crime against you. And I can assure you, madam, that in the kaiser's *German* Empire, justice always prevails!"

He curtly nodded toward his aide.

"In the meantime, Lieutenant Kramer will be your escort and liaison with the squadron. He speaks fluent English, having studied at Dartmouth in Devon for two years. I must be off on naval business, but Kramer is based here at the consulate in Apia. He will be of assistance to you in finding passage onward to Fiji, as well as in attending to your needs here. Do not fear anymore, Madame Cushman, for you are safe and among friends now. Our community is the most civilized place in the South Seas."

Knappe, having recovered from his initial surprise at Jane's appearance, took the opportunity to score some points of his own with the ladies of the German community in Apia.

He stepped back into the proverbial limelight. "Madame Cushman, I want you to know that all we have here in Apia is at your disposal. I completely agree that the hotel over there on the English side is utterly abysmal and certainly not a place fit for a true lady to reside. Therefore, I must insist that you stay at the consulate's guesthouse, which I trust you will find not only comfortable but entirely hygienic. Please, I beg of you, do us that honor. I know the ladies of our community will want to make your acquaintance, show you true German hospitality, and hear in detail your remarkable story of adventure. There are several here who might remember you from your earlier visit."

The blue eyes lost their sadness, now filling with tears of joy as she gazed at the consul general with near hero worship. "*Danke. Danke. Vielen dank.* Thank you so much, Doctor Knappe. Your hospitality is all that I hoped for from the German people. It is not too much to say that you have truly saved my life. And, of course, it is a pleasure for me to accept your kind offer of safety and comfort. "

Lieutenant Kramer, who may have been inexperienced with women but recognized opportunity when it caressed, then offered to take Jane to the hotel, where her things could be collected, and then to her new abode. She graciously accepted his offer and within the hour had established her base of operations right in the heart of the enemy camp.

Aukai, listening from the bushes, whispered his amazement to his Samoan companion. The man shook his head and summed it up in four Samoan words: *manaia fafine, tane valea.* Beautiful woman, stupid men.

37
Crypto-Communications

Tiavi Waterfall
Upolu Island
Kingdom of Samoa
Wednesday
27 February 1889

Refining the plan but keeping it as simple as possible, we finally came up with the solution. From the seventeenth until the twenty-fifth of February, Jane was true to her agreement with me, using the art of persuasion to a clever degree I'd not seen—and I've seen some extremely clever operators.

First, she persuaded the German political leadership and their *haus frauen* who ran the society circles to accept her alibi and entrée into their community. It was an amazing feat since by all rights she should've been relegated to the American consulate across the bridge.

Next, she persuaded Hans Kramer to stay interested in her romantically, even though she never carried through on her implied promises.

That desire on his part was further enhanced by her oft-displayed affection for him and utter fascination with his staff work. This rapt attention was something new for Hans and difficult for him to ignore, for his staff work bored most people he described it to. It bored him mightily. He wanted the action and glory of the deck officers on the squadron's ships, an assignment so far denied him.

Jane was a fantasy come true for a lonely, young man far from home. Yes, she was almost old enough to be his mother, but that meant she was a real woman, not some fickle little girl in Hamburg. This foreign woman made him feel like a successful man, a *leader* of the German Empire, one with an exciting career ahead of him. That he had no real sea experience, no combat experience, and little amorous experience was suddenly lost to his thoughts.

For a week, Jane listened to him over late-night schnapps or cognac. She held his hand. And most salient of all, she not-so-subtly hinted that before she left Apia on the next passenger steamer, she would teach him things about lovemaking that he'd never known or dreamed.

This was how Jane explained it to me later. I believed her insistence on the boundary she did not cross with Hans Kramer. By this point in our extended ordeal, which had begun under such strained and distrustful circumstances, I had come to know the person beneath that pretty exterior and haughty manner. I knew when she was candid.

Jane Cushman was a complicated lady, the compilation of many influences over her convoluted life, from a troubled youth to a spoiled middle age. I never saw her lose her confidence or poise, however. Not even when I blackmailed her in Auckland to buy her feminine skills at persuasion. No, she grudgingly accepted that misfortune and proceeded to deal with it. Of course, the promise to give her the money she needed to prolong her accustomed shipboard lifestyle sweetened the deal and made it more palatable for her. The money was the carrot, balancing the blackmail's stick.

In spite of her faults and failings in life and her seemingly shallow façade, I'd grown to admire Jane Cushman. And in her own way, she'd grown to trust me.

Did our relationship evolve into something more intimate? No, there was never any romance. Both of us were too pragmatic for that, and neither had the lust or romanticism of youth to cloud our judgment. But there did grow a definite unspoken fondness between us. In another place and time, it might have bloomed somewhat. But this was wartime Samoa, love was a luxury quite unaffordable to the likes of us, and Jane Cushman was still only a tool for me to use.

Why Hans Kramer, one might logically ask, when there were so many senior Germans about Apia? Commodore Fritze was not in the running, as we have seen. But Dr. Knappe, the warship captains, managers at the Firm, Captain Brandeis, and many others were of the right age and strata. Some had no wives to impede the process. Theoretically, these men, including the married ones, would be even more susceptible to Jane's charms than young Hans and far more productive in terms of actionable intelligence.

All rational points, of course, to the person inexperienced in my particular business. In the field of espionage, however, one rapidly learns that position and power do not necessarily confer widespread knowledge. It usually means the opposite, that the man has a minimal amount of knowledge and is solely about his individual component in the greater scheme of things.

Yes, the ship captains knew what their particular vessel was doing. The Firm's managers knew about the plantations and commercial enterprises. Captain Brandeis knew about Tamasese's forces. And Dr. Knappe knew the confidential relations with Tamasese and the international goings-on. None of them, though, knew the whole picture on a day-by-day, hour-by-hour basis.

None, except one person: Lieutenant Hans Kramer, Imperial German Navy. For he was the crypto-telegraphist in Apia. Hans was the one man in Samoa who deciphered all of the coded commercial, diplomatic, and naval messages that came to the Germans via warship from the nearest telegraph station at Auckland.

Leaders make decisions that are transformed into orders. Staff officers do the work to transform and implement those orders. And some staff officers, like Kramer, handle the dissemination of the orders and the information that leads to them. Communications is the nexus of information in any organization. It is also the weak point. Penetrate that weak point, and you have all of the information from all of the components. Continue your operation unimpeded, and you continue to own that information on a constant basis. Eventually you will understand even more about his forces than the enemy commander himself.

Over the next several days I received notes from Jane, smuggled out by Mika, who gave them to Aukai. The Hawaiian read them and then gave them to a Samoan runner. Once that man reached Mt. Vaea, he handed them over to another runner, who got then to us at Tiavi.

Jane and I had worked out some basic code words before she went to Apia. "Cane man" was me, referring to the bamboo cane I was using to get around. "Albert" meant Dr. Knappe. "Salty" was Fritze. "Blood relations" was the Anglo-American community. "Hometown team" was Berlin. "Ben" was London. "Vicky's people" were the British. "Daddy" was Washington. "Dinner" was Apia. "Sam" was the U.S. Navy. "Puppet" was Tamasese. "Geronimo" was Mataafa. Jane was "mother." "Word" was telegraph messages. "New one" was *Blitz*. Captain Brandeis, the artillery expert and the one German on land I feared, was "Nick."

There were others as well. Normally, one makes up code words that have no resemblance to the meaning of the actual word, but for an amateur like Jane, I had to keep it simple and easy to remember.

When I read the first note I couldn't suppress a grin, for my *femme fatale* had modified the spelling in our code to further confuse any Germans or Samoans who might intercept it. I received the note on the eighteenth, but she was smart enough to put no date on it.

Cain man—My aficionado is the 1 who sends the word out to everyone. He is bord, but his work ain't dul and has useful stuph. I think this wil wurk out wel and wil send yu some dayly bred.

Aukai sent along an additional note with his observations, including that Jane had been rebuffed several times by Fritze but was firmly latched onto a young staff officer, name unknown. From the "word" reference in Jane's communiqué, I surmised one of that staff officer's functions: the German cryptologist in Samoa.

Inadvertently, Jane Cushman had discovered a gold mine. And to her everlasting credit, she instantly realized it that first evening when she and Hans sat on the verandah of the consulate guesthouse, sipping *digestifs* with dark chocolate and looking into each other's eyes.

The second message came on the nineteenth and contained very interesting information.

Cain man—Not shutin between salty and sam yet, but Albert sur dos want it. Word is interesting. Albert got padled by hometown team a weke ago for being 2 advers to Vicki's people. Albert is very frustrated and thinks hometown team is naive. He wants salty to do something deciciv. Salty is getting help soon and wants to wate for it. Pupet peple are not doin wel and are embarasd. Blood relations sens oportunity, but salty is stil siting on them hard.

It took a while to understand. No shooting between the German and U.S. navies yet. The telegraph traffic is interesting. Knappe got reprimanded by Chancellor Otto von Bismarck—it must have been him, for he was the only one in Berlin who had the power to do so—for harassing the Brits in Samoa. Knappe was frustrated and wanted Fritze to attack. Fritze was getting reinforcements and wanted to wait for them. Tamasese's forces had setbacks and were losing face. And the Anglo-Americans in Apia sensed an opportunity, but the German Navy was still in control through the enforcement of martial law.

I thought about the implications. So Knappe got reprimanded by Bismarck? That was unexpected and crucial. Or was it unexpected? There had been rumors of discord between Bismarck and the Kaiser as far back as October of the previous year. What was young Kaiser Wilhelm II thinking? He'd been on the throne for only a year and was eager to prove himself.

Over the past fifteen years, Bismarck had defused several potential wars with Germany in Europe. Commercial domination was what he wanted, not military conflict. Money for the Junkers industrial elite, not spilled blood from the masses, was his goal. In fact, since the Prussians had overrun France in '70 and then returned most of the land taken, Bismarck had not allowed Germany to expand its European borders. Was he trying to defuse this conflict? Who was really in charge in Berlin—the young militaristic kaiser or the elderly mercantile chancellor? Was there even still time to stop this pending war?

The message for the twentieth only added to the uncertainty.

Cain man—Albert got cariage ride for mother ate dase hence. She's glad to put it all behind but needs that shiny that sam's not so fair haired son promised. Oh, and gues what? Dear ol' Jonny's protégé Kilim was seen at a farm, off toward frisco, doin what Jonny so loved to do. Whole gaggle of Kilim's compatriots are on the run now, seting a most bad exampel for the othurs. Sad news—salty lost the new one. It got sick and went toward India. Only has three children now but is keping them bizy teechin people toward frisco to be polite and ignore Kilim's ideas. Al salty's children are comin to dinurr on the ides—should be a grate shebang. And Pupet really wants to play with yur budie, and he's sendin his friends and all his toys.

This one contained a personal update and some astounding information. Jane's message said she was leaving. Knappe had arranged passage on a steamer for her in eight days, which would be on the twenty-eighth. She said she needed the gold I'd promised her.

On a positive note, evidently Chief Kilim had been seen at a plantation on the east side of the island, liberating some of the Melanesian blackbirds there. Kan and his fellow Melanesian/Malayan/half-breed members of the crew had asked my permission to leave and seek out Kilim a week earlier. Knowing they were far more comfortable with their own kind, I instantly agreed and wished them luck. Presumably, they were part of Kilim's operation.

And there was other positive news: *Blitz* was no longer in the picture, heading west for some repairs, probably toward the Royal Naval station at Singapore since the Germans didn't have a repair yard in the Pacific yet.

Then a sad report: Fritze's other three warships were bombarding Samoan villages in the east in retaliation for some transgression, most likely Kilim's raid. Fritze's ships were going to gather on the "Ides," the fifteenth of March, for another celebration of some sort.

Finally, Tamasese was looking to attack Mataafa, had many men, and was bringing German artillery—that meant Brandeis too—with him.

38

The Best-Laid Plans . . .

Tiavi Waterfall
Upolu Island
Kingdom of Samoa
Wednesday
27 February 1889

I decided to wait until the last possible moment to part with the gold. Accordingly, on the twenty-first, I sent a verbal reply to Jane's request for the gold. The runner told it to Aukai, who repeated it to Mika. *CM says sunrise your last day for the gold.* That would be the twenty-eighth.

A day went by with no message from her, then another, and another. Aukai arrived in camp and reported that Jane was fine and still doing the social circuit during the day and seeing Hans Kramer in the evening. He didn't know the reason for the absence of notes from our spy but saw no indications of duress, nothing out of the ordinary.

At last, we received a note from her on the twenty-fourth

Cain man—Sams son, the 1 who damags things maliciously, came for dinerr last night and he looks pretty irait. Word is that dady and the hometown teem are trying to be nice, but that is just wat the rags ar saying. No one heer agreas with that idea. They want to play hard. By the way, Nic is gon. I think he rijoynd the hometown team. Pupet is excited and reddy to play with you and brot lots of friends to help. I think he's comin right to yur house to give you a bear hug.

It took some deduction but I realized that meant the first American naval reinforcement, a vague synonym for a "vandal," had arrived and was ready for battle. That would be U.S.S. *Vandalia.* The old wooden ship was no match for the three German ships in Samoa, but she was a start. The message traffic included information from the newspapers that Washington and Berlin were trying to be nice—to defuse the conflict?—but the local Germans wanted to play hard. That meant war. There was no way to dissuade the local leadership.

The reference to Brandeis intrigued me. So he had gone home to Germany even as Tamasese was pushing his main army toward us? Was he recalled in anger, part of the German effort to de-escalate the situation? Or was he sent back by Knappe's orders to spur Berlin into backing up the consul general's aggressive plans for Samoa and the Pacific? Either way, it was past the time for a peaceful solution. I couldn't afford to wait any longer, for *Vandalia* was vulnerable. I would have to make the Ballistite attack.

There was another complication. Tamasese was definitely heading our way. The "bear hug" reference was not one of our prearranged codes, and I assumed it meant an enveloping attack on our position.

Aukai and I told Mataafa that news straightaway, but he just acted annoyed at me and said he already knew of the enemy's approach. He ended our brief interview with a dismissive wave and one word, which I happened to know.

It was *lama.* Ambush.

I didn't like it. Mataafa's attitude smacked of dangerous complacency. He had won several encounters in the last six months. He was gathering strength and now had almost six thousand men in villages all over the islands loyal to him.

But this wouldn't be the usual Tamasese-Mataafa skirmish, for the pro-German king had been losing the civil war and desperately needed this victory. He would make an all-out push. He had to. This was it. Tamasese's reputation was on the line, and his future on the throne, perhaps his very life, depended on complete victory.

Plus, there was something in Mataafa's eyes that disturbed me: disdain.

Over the previous week he had asked me several times, his dissatisfaction clear, when I was finally going to attack. He plainly could not comprehend my *palangi* reasons for delay, even though I'd explained them each time. I felt that he was close to abandoning me.

Well, to be fair, I never gave Mataafa any of the details for fear of Samoan boasting or loose *'ava* talk at night. Operational secrecy is always vital, especially when you have only one chance to attack successfully and surprise is the keystone. Modern military commanders, who deal with myriad aspects of campaign logistics in our mechanical world of locomotives and telegraphs and steam warships, entirely understand the need for compartmentalized confidentiality. But Mataafa, for all of his qualities, was not a modern commander.

He would learn the details at the last possible moment but with enough time to fulfill his part. That was what I'd hoped, at least.

I must admit, it was a brilliant scheme. The original idea came to my Hawaiian friend while sitting on the hill overlooking the town during the day. Aukai noticed the local canoes racing at sunset.

These, however, were not the typical small canoes one sees on lakes in the United States.

Oh, no, not at all. These racing canoes, called *fautasi* by the Samoans, are at least one hundred feet long and manned by no fewer than fifty strong paddlers. Under the rhythm of a drummer in the bow and steered by a coxswain in the stern, they move at a swift eight to ten knots. The Germans were used to seeing them in the harbor so there would be nothing unusual about seeing them competing near their squadron anchorage.

Refining the idea but keeping it as simple as possible, Aukai and I finally came up with a workable plan. The attack would be launched just before sunset on March fifteenth, when the German squadron would be gathered again.

Knappe's martial law in Apia was the first hurdle to cross. To get the Ballistite explosives into Apia, past the German navy's police patrols around the town, we would take them aboard a small bateau down the Vaisigano River. It was a small river that flowed from the foothills down into the harbor at the eastern, or somewhat friendlier, side of town. Aukai didn't think the Germans were checking the river itself, only the land approaches and the town's interior.

Once near the harbor, the explosive would be transferred to two of the huge *fautasi* canoes that race each evening. They would be beached just above the mouth of the river on the bay. This would transpire as the sun was setting, the usual time of the contests. Samoans friendly to our cause would then race the two canoes against each other at full speed, coincidently heading very close to the anchored German ships, using them as turning marks.

Aukai would be in one canoe and I in the other. There were six packs of explosives left after the journey to Samoa. Each canoe would have three separate packs of Ballistite explosives wrapped in waterproof oilskins and suspended from coconut floats. As the canoe passed under each warship's stern, a float would be dumped overboard near the ship's rudder post. The Ballistite would have a thirty-second, oilskin-wrapped fuse lit just prior to immersion.

The ensuing explosions, using the magnifying effect of water by being suspended below the surface, would cripple the ships' rudders. They wouldn't be able to steer and would thus be *hors de combat*.

In addition, there would probably be a minimum of casualties since the damage would be directed at the extreme aft ends of the ships. The stern is the area of the officers' staterooms—"officer country" in American parlance—so what internal damage or casualties that might ensue would be of greater value than if the effort was directed elsewhere on the ship.

The entire operation for both canoes, from dumping the first explosive to dumping the third, would take approximately thirty to forty-five seconds. Each warship would receive two Ballistite floats, doubling our chances for success. The canoes would never stop or slow down, continuing to speed away on a course out of the harbor and around to the east, toward the pro-Mataafa village of Vaiala just outside of Apia.

There the canoes would be set adrift to float offshore, and the crews would disappear into the jungle. Aukai and I would return to Mataafa's camp to personally report to the man. And after that, I would return to Apia, where I would show up on one of our vessels and rejoin the U.S. Navy as quietly as possible. Only Admiral Kimberly, ONI, and the president would eventually get to know what had truly happened on the Ides of March in Apia harbor.

Early on, I decided that the American ships would not take part in any of this effort, making their subsequent denials of involvement more genuinely believable to the German authorities. However, they did need to be warned so they knew that the attack was not aimed at them and they could be ready for any German retribution. Therefore, any U.S. warship in the harbor would receive a brief courtesy message addressed as urgent for the senior officer aboard, delivered by native bumboat one hour before sunset. The message would simply say that there was an anti-German action planned for that night, and it would be signed only "The People of Samoa."

This would be a false-flag operation, for the Samoans of Mataafa would naturally get the credit. Tamasese and the Germans would be humiliated in the eyes of the Samoan islanders. Hopefully that *fait accompli*, more than all of the diplomatic palavering that heretofore had yielded nothing, would end the escalation into full-blown war between our countries.

It was the best we could come up with, and I felt confident about its success.

Obviously, Aukai and I needed help to carry it off. Three days ahead of the operation, on March twelfth, we planned to brief Mataafa and get him to use his influence to prepare the way. His assistance would be vital, for he needed to arrange for some porters to help us get the Ballistite down to Malifa Village, situated on the river outside of Apia; have the bateau waiting in place at the village; and most importantly, ensure loyal crews for the big canoes who would listen to commands from Aukai and me.

Unlike when the German squadron had gathered ten days earlier in the harbor, this time we'd be ready. If all went well, by the morning of March sixteenth, the German Navy in Samoa would no longer be a threat to anyone, Samoan or American.

But that was still two weeks away. First we had to deal with a new problem, one that arrived at our camp the evening of the twenty-seventh of February in the form of a breathless young messenger.

It was Joseph, my earlier interpreter with Mataafa. He had been one of Aukai's assistants on the surveillance in Apia, and when the Hawaiian came back up to the mountain camp, Joseph was left in charge in Apia.

Joseph didn't wait for protocol but came up to Aukai and me as we were having our sunset dinner of roasted taro, yams, and pork. In great agitation, he blurted out my nickname among the Samoans, Wounded Warrior. "Toa Manu'a! Toa Manu'a! We have a terrible problem!"

I looked at Aukai, who was as bewildered as I. Our preliminary intelligence effort had gone well. We hadn't even started the actual operation yet. No one besides Aukai and I even knew of it. What could've gone so wrong?

I motioned for Joseph to sit down. "Take a breath first, and then tell me what's happened, Joseph."

He didn't sit. "Mrs. Cushman has disappeared!"

39
Questions and Answers

Tiavi Waterfall
Upolu Island
Kingdom of Samoa
Sunset, Wednesday
27 February 1889

We interviewed Joseph closely. He explained that he last saw Jane around 9 P.M. on the evening of Sunday, the twenty-fourth, the day of her last message to me. She was sipping wine with Kramer on her verandah. Kramer left for his quarters shortly afterward. There was no apparent disagreement between them that Joseph could see at the time. From what he saw and heard from Mika, Lieutenant Kramer had never spent the night in her room, nor she in his.

Mika told Joseph that when he saw Mrs. Cushman the next morning at her room, just after breakfast, the lady seemed tense, as if worried about something. That was the last time any of our people had laid eyes on Jane Cushman. She disappeared around 8:30 on the morning of Monday, the twenty-fifth. She didn't take her belongings. This was three days before she was due to leave on a steamer.

The daily *sa* devotional time had begun, but we didn't stop our interrogation of Joseph. His answers were given in an anguished tone. Yes, Kramer was still seen arriving and leaving the consulate. But, tellingly, he wasn't stopping at the consulate's guesthouse anymore, wasn't out searching, wasn't asking around for Jane. There was no increase in security or activity at the German consulate, no change in anyone's behavior. Mika had asked around of the servants at the German community. None of them had heard anything regarding the American lady or where she was.

The German seamen on police duty hadn't been asking anyone about a missing white woman; neither had the pro-Tamasese Samoans. Joseph added a curious piece of news about the police: Dr. Knappe had revoked the order of martial law in Apia. I thought that significant, but why had he done it?

Checking with the Samoan servants on the other side of town, Joseph found that there was no talk about Jane among the British or Americans or the French nuns at the convent. It was as if Jane Cushman had never existed in Apia.

I asked about ships in the harbor and was told that no passenger steamer had arrived in Apia yet. The *Rockford*, out of Auckland and bound for Honolulu, was due to arrive the next morning. She would be the only passenger steamer for several weeks.

He reported on the current occupants of the harbor. There were several trading schooners at anchor near the German side. *Vandalia* was anchored off the U.S. consulate. One of the German warships had departed a few days earlier, and one of them was lying to her hook near the German consulate.

I couldn't think of anything else to ask. Joseph was visibly distressed, almost to the point of being incapacitated, as if he'd been responsible for Jane's disappearance and possible death. Wondering that very thing, I'd been studying him as he answered our questions. His sorrow seemed authentic, though, and in the end I concluded there was no duplicity on his part. Of the other Samoans involved in the surveillance, I wasn't sure.

I told Joseph he wasn't at fault but left it at that, for I didn't have any idea who or what was the reason for the lady's vanishing. I also told him to keep the news to himself, that Aukai and I would tell Mataafa. Then I dismissed him.

Once we were alone, Aukai quietly asked, "So what do you think happened?"

"I don't have a clue, David, but this isn't accidental. Jane wouldn't leave without the gold; it was funding her future. So she was either abducted or fled. Either way, it was probably because her façade was destroyed somehow. We've got to get down there and get her."

My friend cast me a dubious look. "Can you move well enough to do this? It is much rougher country than what you have seen so far here."

Good question. "I'll have to manage. We leave in ten minutes, right after I tell Mataafa what we know. He won't be happy to hear it, but he might be happy to get me out of his camp for a while."

Mataafa received the news with smoldering resignation. I could see his view of things. So far this American *palangi* had produced nothing but a woman to connive information, and now even that was a dismal failure.

At 8:00 on the evening of the twenty-seventh, Aukai and I, glad to be away from Mataafa's silent glare, began our trek. We were accompanied by Joseph and two other Samoans. They were older men, scarred and tattooed full warriors with cold, emotionless eyes. Mataafa had insisted on the escort, saying it was a dangerous pathway at night even without Tamasese's people out and about. Once down the mountains to the outskirts of Apia, he said our escort would help in any manner we deemed necessary.

The route was only six miles as the crow flies but at least triple that on the steep and winding rocky path. It seemed even longer. I was exhausted after the second hour, my hip rebelling with increasing pain at every step. In addition, the seabag with my weaponry and that damned gold was getting heavier with every hour.

We took a brief intermission at the next morning's sunrise, mainly for my benefit. It was at a beautiful place on the northern slopes of Mt. Vaea that Joseph recommended.

"The view from this magical place will restore your heart, Toa Manu'a. It is a place of ancient warriors and will give you strength for what is to come. In addition to those qualities, it is an excellent observation point to watch the Germans in Apia from a distance."

He was right on all counts. Singing birds and several rushing brooks provided a soothing auditory background for the view, which was truly magnificent. Standing under candlenut and tamarind trees, surrounded by wild croton bushes and hibiscus flowers, you could see all of Apia, the harbor, and the nearby area. Mt. Vaea was the kind of spot that sailors dream of building their home on, a place to live one's final years among nature's bountiful gardens.

So, after thirty minutes of blissful reverie, we resumed the march. It was now all downhill, straining a different set of muscles in my legs. At midmorning we reached our separation point on the outskirts of the town, more than fourteen hours after we had started out from Mataafa's camp. It was now the twenty-eighth, the last day of February.

Following another rest in the shade of a banana grove, I took young Joseph with me and reconnoitered the English side of town. Aukai took the other Samoans to the German side. We would meet again to compare notes at 3:00 under the banyan tree on the west bank of the Vaisigano River, a quarter mile upriver from Malifa Village.

My comrade and I saw and heard nothing of note. I sent him into the back door of every establishment, including the U.S. consulate, to ask the native servants what they'd heard from the American *palangi*. Nothing. At 3:00 Joseph and I met Aukai at the banyan.

He was alone. His bleak expression said volumes.

"A white woman in a muddy dress was seen two days ago on the path in the mangrove swamp west of Fugalei Stream. A group of Tamasese men was in the same area, but they were from another part of Upolu and had no reason to be in that swamp. It has to be her, and they are searching for her. I sent my two men to find her."

"Two days ago, you say? That would be the day after she disappeared. Where is this swamp?"

"About half a mile west of the big German plantation at Savalalo, which is just outside their main settlement. A very arduous place for anyone to traverse." Aukai sighed grimly. "Peter, the only reason a *palangi* woman would go in there is to flee something truly terrible . . ."

He didn't finish the sentence: ". . . like being arrested and executed for spying."

Jane was in mortal danger. The Germans had turned the Samoans loose to find her. Did Knappe know? Or was this all Kramer's doing, keeping her disappearance quiet to minimize his own culpability?

My heart pounded in my chest as I tried to sound confident in front of Auki and Joseph. "Very well. So now we have something. Let's get to Fugalei Swamp and get her out of there."

40

Beeilen Sie Sich!

Fugalei Swamp
West of Apia
Upolu Island
Kingdom of Samoa
7:45 P.M., Thursday
28 February 1889

It was still light when we got there but gloomy inside the mangroves. Joseph led the way. I brought up the rear. The trail was muddy with tidal water and no wider than the width of one man. On each side was a solid, leafy wall of twisted mangrove limbs. Mosquitoes were the dominant force, their whining filling the air, their buzzing in our ears and eyes infuriating even Joseph.

We were at least half a mile inside the swamp when we first heard angry shouts. They were in Samoan and dead ahead. Joseph whispered that they were calling out to each other the location of the *matamata*, the spy.

Gunshots popped. A couple of old Springfields by the sound. They were coming from in front of us on the trail. More shouts. This time they were deep-toned war chants in unison. Primordial sounds. Terrifying in that dark confined place.

We stopped and listened. They were almost at a twist in the trail, twenty feet ahead of us. There was no room to set up a flanking maneuver or run away to either side. It would take too long to move through the tangled maze.

I could hear Jane's pursuers grunting and growling in their disgust. Some of them were apparently trying to move through the mangroves and not doing well.

Then we heard it: a woman's gasp, followed by soft cursing in English. Then, heavy thudding footsteps.

I pulled my Spencer shotgun out of the seabag and knelt, telling Aukai, "We'll get low right here on the trail and fire up into them from the prone position. You take the front and left side. I'll take the front and right side. Joseph, you get down and watch our backs for anyone coming up the trail from behind."

Aukai and I stretched out in the muck. He had his revolver leveled on the path in front. It was the same one he'd used on Starkloff. My Merwin "Skullcrusher" forty-four revolver was shoved in my belt. Then I readied more shells in the shotgun's stock bandolier, making sure they would extricate easily.

"Hold your fire, David," I whispered. "I'll fire first with the shotgun. You start firing when I have to reload after six shotgun rounds. But, remember, we have only a small amount of ammunition so make each shot count."

The sound of desperate panting came through the whine of the mosquitoes—the men right around the bend. The first one in sight was a huge Samoan in a black *lavalava* and nothing else, armed with club and machete.

He lumbered around the curve into full view and stopped in midstride, his eyes on my shotgun's barrel not a pace away from his chest. My finger was drawing back on the trigger when I recognized him as one of the escorts whom Aukai had sent to find Jane. I took my right hand away from the weapon's trigger guard and motioned for him to get down behind us.

Jane was next, carried by the other Samoan. My heart stopped when I saw her. She was limp in his arms and seemed nearly dead. Her face was swollen and misshapen, a mass of ugly dark bruises. The Samoan was wounded badly, with blood pouring down on her from a gash in his forehead.

More thudding feet. The crack of a rifle, then two. Very close, only feet away.

The Samoan didn't need directions. With Jane in one arm he leaped over Aukai and me. He grunted in pain when he fell. Jane gave out a pitiful cry when she hit the ground, but it meant she was still alive.

The next man around that bend would be an enemy. I closed my right eye to save my night vision and fired when the form appeared. He was moving at a trot, but the blast blew him backward into number two in line, who dropped his rifle and stood stunned for an instant. I fired into him as well.

The third man slowed and was searching for us, his rifle at the shoulder point position, ready to fire when he saw me. But he wasn't looking down at the ground. The Germans hadn't trained him for that, for their European enemies stood in orderly lines, so he was traversing his weapon, looking for a chest-high target. My third shot went up into him.

Number four made the same mistake. He was the last one.

Joseph called out in terrified English, "I hear more of them behind us, coming here fast."

I heard them now too. A lot of them. They were running in unison down the trail. Disciplined. A platoon of thirty, maybe more. We had to move.

No one else came around the bend to our front. According to Aukai's briefing to me earlier, in that direction was more swamp for a quarter mile until you arrived at shallow Vaiusu Bay. Tamasese's Mulinu'u Peninsula base was to the right. The German plantation was to our rear. There were no Germans at Vaiusu Bay since it was too shallow.

I got up from the ground, adrenalin masking the pain in my hip, and began trotting forward. We would get to the bay and wade our way along the shore to the west, as far from the Germans and their Samoan forces as possible.

The rest followed me, a half-conscious Jane carried in the arms of the unwounded Samoan now. We had no time to determine her wounds, if any. The wounded Samoan was badly hurt and was losing a lot of blood from that head wound, but he grunted and charged on.

When our pursuers found their comrades behind us, a great howl went up. There would be no quarter for us, that I knew. I also knew that somebody was going to have to do a rear-guard action to allow the rest to escape. That would have to be me. I had the weapons and experience.

It was critical that Aukai survive. He was the only other one who knew the plan. His language skills, Ballistite knowledge, and Polynesian cultural bonds were crucial to carrying it out. Unlike that desperate time on the beach, when I thought all was lost, this time we had a chance for success. But it all rested on the Hawaiian getting out of the swamp.

There were no other options. I wasn't needed anymore. And I had a debt to pay to Jane. I was out of steam anyway.

I stopped, bent over, gasping for air, and told Aukai, "I'm staying here to lay a trap for these bastards. You lead everyone to the bay, then follow the shore to the left and eventually get up to the hills. I'll cut across the mangroves, reach solid land, and meet you at the banyan tree either tomorrow or the following day at sunset."

He started to protest. That irritated me mightily. Didn't he see what was important? I straightened up and shoved him in the shoulder.

"Just do what I say and be a professional, Aukai. Get the Ballistite and finish the friggin' job. And make sure Jane gets away from Samoa."

He stepped close and clasped my hand, pressing it to his chest. "Banyan tree, sunset tomorrow." The others were already gone. He turned to join them.

The enemy was gathering strength. Soon they would be

charging down the path, looking for vengeance. Mangroves are hellish areas for an attack. They are naturally advantageous for defenders. I decided to use an old Seminole Indian tactic from a war thirty years earlier.

Taking a pliable branch, I bent it backwards across the path until it was barely restrained by a limb on the other side. That would stop them for a few minutes while they determined whether it was a trap.

Another twenty feet up the trail, I bent another branch, this one at ankle height, across the trail. That also would stop them. Not for long but long enough for my purposes.

I went up the trail another thirty feet, then into the mangroves on the west side, covering my tracks with leaves where they left the trail. Then I carefully circled through the maze of aerial roots and limbs, creeping under them at one point, climbing over at another, until I reached a position where I could cover the place I'd bent the second branch across the trail. The warriors reached the first barrier and were discussing it heatedly.

I was only five or six feet from the edge of the trail but had no fear of being seen. The night was pitch black now, for even the usual starlight didn't penetrate the mangrove canopy above me.

All manner of bugs crawled across my face and in my ears, and I was drenched in sweat. I balanced the shotgun on a large root and waited, forcing my brain to ignore the pain in my hip and leg, the bugs, the sweat. I'd have to aim by the sound, but a shotgun is the best weapon for that. I slowed my breathing to be able to hear, swiveling the shotgun as I swiveled my head so they would be coordinated when the time came.

The first man tripped on the second branch at ankle height. He roared a curse as his followers ran into each other. About seven or eight, by their sounds. They were so close I could smell them and the square-face on their breaths.

The lead man was on the ground to my left. I swiveled slightly to the right to catch his companions who were coming up. This would have to be done very fast. In seconds.

I plugged both ears by shoving in spare revolver rounds from my pocket to preserve that sense, then closed both eyes for the same reason and fired the first shotgun shell from the Spencer. Keeping my eyes closed, I pumped the shotgun to eject the spent shell, swiveled left, and fired again. I repeated the process another five times, using up all of the shells in the shotgun.

Only then did I open my eyes and take the bullets out of my ears while I reloaded. I found both senses operating, but I saw and heard nothing around me, not even mosquitoes. I smelled the cloud of gunpowder smoke that hung in the air, the only indication of what had happened.

There was no moaning from the wounded. I realized there were no wounded. They were all dead. But more were just up the trail, and they would be at the dead bodies very soon.

It was time to shift my position. The Tamasese men would assume I'd continue to retreat down the trail, setting ambushes as I went. But that wasn't what a Seminole would do. Seminoles would let the reinforcements go by and advance into the enemy's rear areas, where they'd least be expected. That would force the enemy to turn around and abandon the trail ahead to defend the trail behind.

I began crawling slowly east, back the way we'd come. The rest of the Tamasese platoon came up the trail, and I let them go by. There were German voices further back toward the plantation. My German is rudimentary, but I could tell they were issuing orders to their own men.

I had to assume that Aukai's group had reached the bay and were moving along the shoreline, looking for a way to get inland and up to higher ground. Time and ammunition were running out for me, but I had to do one more attack to keep the combined enemy to focus on me, not on the escapees.

I heard the clanking of modern equipment. Germans were running toward me from the east. I'd lost track of where the trail was by then and was concentrating on not deviating from my easterly course. They seemed very close, so I plugged my ears and closed my eyes again. Then I sent two blasts in their direction.

Either the range was too long—more than fifteen feet in thick mangroves is too far; buckshot gets stopped by the tangled limbs— or I misgauged the direction. A thunder of rifle fire replied, the hail of bullets shredding the jungle around me.

A German officer yelled something like "Halt!" Then he furiously yelled it again, adding, *"Beeilen Sie Sich! Die feldkanon! Beeilen Sie Sich!"* I knew that much German—"Hurry up! The field guns! Hurry up!"

The men shouted down the trail to their Samoan comrades who'd gone ahead. I heard an acknowledgment, then running. The ones I'd let pass me came back at full speed up the trail, cursing the braches hitting them in the face, stumbling in the dark. They ran east right past me toward their German comrades. I heard them meet the Germans, then more running, men in boots and some barefoot. It was clear to me what had happened.

The Germans weren't going to lose any more men. They'd evacuated the whole swamp so they could level it with a bombardment.

Guessing where the trail would be, I crawled as fast as anyone can in a mangrove in the dark, dragging a lame body and a heavy bag. When I emerged back onto the open trail, the shelling started. Two field guns, by the sound. They were smart, using beehive rounds with fuses set to explode at fifty feet off the ground. It's a tricky problem to gauge and fuse that properly, but Germans are experts in the use of artillery.

Heading for where I thought the bay was, I started down the trail in the dark void. One hand holding the bag, the other out in front to warn of a tree limb or bend in the path, my hip hurt like hell, but I used the pain to spur me onward, cursing and praying at the same time. The airbursts were all around the swamp, blasting out hundreds of pieces of shrapnel that shredded the mangroves into kindling. Debris began hitting me. The bursts were getting closer.

I started running for my life.

41

A Most Reluctant Guest

Fugalei Swamp
West of Apia
Upolu Island
Kingdom of Samoa
9 P.M., Thursday
28 February 1889

The bombardment stopped, making an eerie silence just as the trail opened up around me. I couldn't feel the trees brushing me on either side anymore. That gave me hope I was near the bay. Once I reached the water, the starlight would show me the way along the shoreline. I felt a tiny glimmer of hope.

It was short lived.

I realized I was running the wrong way when I heard a polished tone call out to me from the darkness. It dripped with mock politeness, as if we were at a cocktail party.

"*Guten Abend, mein Herr. Und Wie geht es Ihnen?*"

When I heard him, I immediately dropped the seabag in the bushes beside me but kept on going, albeit at a slower trot, mentally counting the paces away from the bag. I was stopped completely a few feet later when a bayonet showed up in front of my face and another poked me in the back.

Soon a torch was lit and brought over to illuminate my face, just as the artillery began firing again into the swamp. The men around me weren't Samoan. They were naval infantry. German marines.

The voice called out again from the darkness. "So *you* are the one. I thought you would be younger and bigger. Oh, where are my manners! Please allow me to introduce myself, sir. I am Lieutenant Hans Kramer of His Imperial German Majesty's Navy, specifically the Naval Intelligence Branch. I am so honored and pleased to have you as my guest, Mr.—hmm, let me remember exactly the name—ah yes, Mr. *Cain Man*. And may I present my professional compliments on the moniker. How very biblical of you. Traditional and predictable but quaint all the same."

"Uh, Cain who?" I said, buying time, evaluating my situation and foe. "Hey, what the hell's going on around here? This place is crazy!"

So this was little Hans Kramer, of German naval intelligence, no less. I still couldn't see him, but his voice didn't sound as inexperienced and uncertain as the depiction from Aukai and insinuation from Jane's messages. In fact, this fellow seemed very much in command. His was the voice I heard giving orders earlier.

Another barrage of five shells exploded over the swamp. I could tell the range and direction of the battery now. It was the German marines' field battery half a mile away at Mulinu'u, the same battery that guarded King Tamasese's royal headquarters.

Kramer didn't go for my dumb foreigner ploy. Actually, I didn't think he would. I just needed to stretch out the time.

His British-learned English was fluent, with little trace of a German accent. That told me he probably understood some of the subtle nuances of Jane's messages. He was still standing outside the circle of light from the torch, a disembodied voice in the dark.

He answered my feigned ignorance with, "Come now, sir. I already know you are *Cain Man*, the correspondent of Mrs. Jane

Cushman. Before we continue on this topic, let me say that I admire your gallant attempt to rescue the lady tonight. A noble but futile gesture. As you can see, the swamp, and Mrs. Cushman inside it, is being systematically destroyed by our field guns, as we speak. It is excellent practice for our marines."

"Look, there must be some kind of mistake here, Lieutenant Kramer. My name isn't Cain Man, and I don't know any lady named Jane. I'm Peter Wake, a Canadian businessman touring investment opportunities in the Pacific for a syndicate back home."

Kramer was enjoying this. "Really? You must be very busy then. I thought all of your time was taken up with spying."

Good. I wanted him to be overconfident. He'd be easier to kill. I assessed my circumstances. The torch was blinding me, but I sensed a dozen or so men around me. I could hear them grumbling in German. I'd killed their comrades.

They hadn't searched me yet, and I hadn't heard anyone find my seabag. I surmised I had perhaps twenty or thirty seconds of verbal delay left before both of those things were accomplished. According to the pattern so far, the next artillery volley would be about then also. That could be beneficial.

My Merwin revolver, still stowed in my right side of my waist, had six large-caliber rounds in the cylinder. Each one would stop any threat at close range. I had another twelve bullets in my right trouser pocket.

When forced to engage in close combat by fate, I normally fire what is called a "double tap": two rounds for each target. This is not standard Navy procedure, but my friend Rork and I have found it works quite well as a last-ditch defense. In fact, five months earlier to the day, Rork and I were forced to do just that in a similar predicament in Havana.

This time, however, I was alone and vastly outnumbered, so one round each would have to suffice. The bayonet men would be first, then the torch man. I needed the Germans to be blinded in the darkness.

I turned toward Kramer's voice. "Lieutenant Kramer, I am

ROBERT N. MACOMBER

from Ontario, Canada, and a subject of Her Britannic Majesty, Queen Victoria, your Kaiser Wilhelm's grandmother, by the way. I'm here to invest in German cocoa and copra plantations because they are said to be the most efficient in the world."

The torch man had backed away by this time, so I slowly closed my eyes, hoping they wouldn't notice, but kept talking. "I am staying at the Samoa Hotel over near the British consulate. This evening I went for a walk and wandered down the wrong lane, and suddenly all hell started. My God, I could've been killed!"

I slowly slid my right hand toward my waist. "What the hell were you people thinking? Why would you have artillery practice at night near a crowded town without warning the residents?

"And your treatment of me is outrageous! I don't think your kaiser or his grandmother, my queen, will be impressed by your behavior tonight. I assure you, they will hear about it immediately, so I suggest you begin acting like an officer and a gentleman and assist a fellow white man instead of harassing him."

Kramer's voice came closer. I heard his hands clapping. "Very good, Cain Man. The best defense is always a good offense."

At that point, I decided to make Kramer the primary target. His arrogance had earned him the promotion. The bayonet men would be the second and third rounds. Torch man would be fourth.

Kramer's last words were, "But now our little charade must regrettably come to an end, and you, my reluctant guest, will be . . ."

Boom! The first round ended his sentence. I fired again. Boom! The second round knocked down the bayonet man in front. I crouched straightaway and spun completely around, firing. Boom! The bayonet man behind me dropped.

Right then, the next airbursts from the Mulinu'u battery exploded only two hundred feet away. By now I didn't know where the torch man was, so I opened my left eye and found him fumbling, trying to both hold the torch and fire his rifle.

Boom! A round to his chest ended his dilemma. My last two rounds were fired from waist level in the direction where I assumed the other Germans were.

288

The aforementioned action took five seconds, the result of repeated practice over the years. Therefore the enemy was a bit stunned and slow to respond, but they were regaining their wits now. A German began shooting from my front, the flash lighting up others to his right. His shot wasn't aimed well, however.

Most soldiers are right-handed and naturally choose to traverse to the right as they fire. So after my last shot, I'd dodged to my right, their left. While I did so, my left hand pulled back the slide button on the Merwin to eject the spent shells, and my right dug in my pocket for fresh bullets. I got behind a bush and took a look around, all the while willing myself to reload slowly and carefully.

The torch had fallen into a puddle and was sputtering out. It was chaos in the dark. Germans were shouting orders. Several wild shots were fired. I heard a man choking for air. Probably a throat shot to the front bayonet man.

But where was my seabag? It had my loaded Spencer shotgun. I'd need that to escape through the Germans to the hills. I tried to remember how many paces I'd stepped off since dropping it, but my mind went blank. I'd have to go back down the trail and search by groping through the damned bushes.

Keeping my right eye closed, I got on the ground and belly-crawled back to the pathway. The Germans' rounds were too high. They were putting out suppressive fire but it wasn't coordinated yet. It would be in seconds, though. They would extend their flanks and advance, trapping me.

I found the seabag not where I left it but near the spot where I'd been stopped. It was still full of my things. So they had found it and put it down but hadn't looked inside yet, probably stopped by my shooting. A very close-run thing.

The Germans were calling out orders I couldn't understand, but I heard the voices spreading out. Then they began firing volleys into the bushes, area by area, starting to my left. Torches were lit far behind them. I saw Samoan warriors coming up to join the fight.

A lantern was brought up and hung by a branch. Under the

limb, I saw a saddled horse, tethered to the tree trunk. An officer's horse probably. Between the horse and me were six or seven German marines in a group. They stood facing my direction with their rifles at the bayonet position, waiting for orders and peering out into the gloom for me.

I, like most sailors, am not a horseman. But there are times when one has to make do with what's at hand. That horse was my way out of there.

I fired four blasts as I charged, while, in an effort to confuse them, yelling the only German that came to mind, *"Beeilen Sie sich!"*—"Hurry up!"

That downed or scattered the Germans in front of me, but it also terrified the horse, which began shrieking and pulling at his line lashed to the tree limb. Three Samoans, machetes ready to slice off my head, ran toward me out of nowhere from the left. German marines in the platoon who had been shooting into the jungle now shifted aim toward me but couldn't fire without hitting the pro-German Samoans.

It was hardly a sprint, but I made it to the horse and jerked the rein off the tree. The animal's eyes flared wide at that and he tried to buck away, but I was taking no guff and yanked the reins down hard to show him who was in command. With a painful effort, I mounted the beast—one hand on the reins and the other hoisting my seabag—and kicked him in the gut to get his steam up and under way.

The beast took off as the first Samoan arrived and made a looping swing with the machete. It caught the tail, severing it, and provided more motivation than I ever could. The horse instantly went to full speed, headed east along the sandy lane. I held on for dear life, hunched over with the bag across his shoulders as we raced through the copra plantation.

The marines, no longer encumbered by their own allies being near me, fired with remarkable accuracy in the dark, one round hitting the seabag, another nicking the horse's flank. Their guttural curses filled the night air, echoed by others passing the word around the community. It didn't take a translator to know they were sounding the alarm for everyone in the German area to come outside and shoot me.

The horse was completely beyond any control by then, producing a velocity that was insane in the dark with coconut palms all around. We barely missed several, the horse swerving at the last second, nearly throwing me overboard.

We made it to Beach Road, and he began to slow to a gallop as we approached the lantern-illuminated bridge over Mulivai Stream. Four German sailors in whites were on police picket there. They jumped up in surprise and readied their rifles as we headed for them. There was no attempt to capture the spy who had caused all of this death and pandemonium. They simply knelt down and started taking potshots at me like everyone else.

From my bouncing perch, I fired the last rounds in the Spencer toward them while trying to hide behind the horse's head. My shots produced no effect, not even a pause in the sailors' firing.

Their shooting was more successful. The horse shrieked again and stumbled, then went down hard on his left side, throwing the seabag clear. I landed under the damned creature, which kept shrieking in pain until another rifle round shot him dead.

Everything in my body hurt, but what hurt most of all was my left leg, pinioned beneath the horse. With a curse and a snarl, I extricated it and lay there, gasping for breath and strength, trying to come up with a way to get out of there. Nothing came to mind.

The sailors approached me slowly, calling loudly for their reinforcements to come fast. Relying on pure instinct, I pulled out the Merwin I'd reloaded earlier and fired five rounds toward the sailors, not even taking time to aim. The sailors, who'd been out in the open on Beach Road, were no fools. They scattered and ran for the nearest cover.

I didn't wait for them to regain their wits. As my fifth round went off, I tottered toward the stream, dragging that blessed seabag on the way. My objective was only thirty feet distant, the Mulivai Stream. I headed far to the left of the bridge, for I needed to stay out of the lantern light on the bridge itself.

The sailors fired some rounds, one of which hit my Spencer, then made a rush. I fired my last Merwin bullet at them, gaining another few seconds as they went to the ground.

I felt the ground sloping downward and heard rushing water. That was it. Jumping in despair, I landed in starkly cold water that had rushed down the stream from the mountains. My feet and the seabag, tethered by the cord around my left wrist, were swept away just as a tree limb hit me hard in the back, nearly drowning me.

Somehow I managed to spin around and grab on before I went under permanently. In terror of drowning, I used the last of my legs' muscular power to climb into the limb's mass of branches. There I lay, exhausted of all remaining strength, as the swift water carried me the hundred feet to the stream's mouth in seconds. The current continued to push me away from the shore and out into the open water.

Suddenly a fusillade of gunfire sent up geysers from the stream behind me, but the German sailors were shooting where I had gone into the water. Propelled by that stream, I was already two hundred feet away, drifting into the darkness of Apia Harbor.

My body had ceased to operate by then, but my mind still had enough function to realize that the mountain stream's current had pushed me out into the ebb tide. The water was getting warmer. I was being taken out to sea. There was no wind or cloud above me, and glittering stars carpeted the sky as I floated along in a stupefied trance.

A German warship was off to my left. Deck lanterns were being lit. The decks were full of men. A boat alongside was being loaded with sailors. The boat shoved off, rowing toward the mouth of the stream. Another boat was being swayed out. They would start the search for me near the stream, then work around the harbor, probably checking the area around the American warship first.

U.S.S. *Vandalia* was anchored only five hundred feet away from me. Deck lights illuminated the mundane scene aboard. I could see the officer of the deck leaning on the rail of the bridge, watching the German ship. He probably wondered what all the commotion and shooting was about, an unusual event inside the German-held town. The tide took me past *Vandalia*, but I was too weak to call out that far. Swimming the distance was completely beyond me.

There were no other ships between the open ocean and me. I remembered that the nearest land in that direction was the Tokelau group of islands, four hundred miles away. There was nothing I could do anymore. It was over. My life was done. I would be out in the ocean soon. I hoped David Aukai and Jane Cushman had escaped to safety.

I decided to think of something more pleasant for my final hours of life. Joyous times with my wife, Linda, and our children drifted through my mind as I closed my eyes. I'd soon see Linda again, if God didn't bar me from Heaven for what I'd done on Earth.

42
Reunion

Upolu Island
Kingdom of Samoa
Saturday
9 March 1889

My body floated on the sea for three days. I have no recollection of that time. Indeed, I've permanently lost nine days from my memory, and I only know what I was later told by Aukai. That was at a pro-Mataafa village somewhere on the northern slopes of Mt. Vaea, near that overlook I'd loved.

When I'd emerged from semiconsciousness and recovered my senses, I at once asked Aukai about his and Jane's escape from the swamp, but my friend postponed, insisting on first telling the tale of my three miracles. Here is what he told me, nine long days after my dream of meeting my dearest Linda again in Heaven.

"You are nothing short of a legend around here, my friend. The man who received three miracles from God."

Legend? I didn't feel like a legend. I was thankful to be alive but felt like a punching bag. An old, feeble punching bag.

"Yes, Peter, it is absolutely true. The first miracle happened on the third day of March, three days after your skirmish at the swamp. A fisherman named Pita found you drifting far out at sea, tangled in a dead tree, along with that old seabag of yours.

"He thought you were as dead as the tree, probably a heathen *palangi* beachcomber who got drunk and fell into the water. He took your seabag and was going to let your body sink away. Looking through your bag, he found your American Navy uniform and medals, and that changed his perception of you completely. By the way, guess what the English translation of the Samoan name Pita is?"

"No clue."

"It is Peter! He was named after the saint, like you. Coincidence? I think not. The hand of God is in this tale, from beginning to end. And it gets better, my friend, much better.

"You see, this fisherman is from Lauli'i, the village on the north coast. That is the place the Germans were bombarding last year when the American warship *Adams* interposed itself, thereby saving the lives of the people there. The villagers never forgot that and have kind thoughts for your country because of it.

"So this man Pita, a Methodist, now understood you were not a drunken beachcomber but a man of honor and a friend of his village. So he decided to give your body a proper Christian burial at sea, with your medals pinned to your chest and a prayer for God to look after you. As he disentangled your body from the tree, the second miracle happened: Your parched lips mumbled the word 'Mataafa.'"

Aukai beamed with delight.

"You were alive! And you had uttered the name of the man his village supports in the civil war against the German puppet king. The fisherman knew exactly what he must do: Sail you to Lauli'i and get you to Mataafa's people, who would know what to do. It took Pita two days to sail to his village, for the winds were rising and contrary to his course, and during that time he gave you his coconut water and fruits to keep you alive. But he could not understand how you would survive, for you could not move, or eat or drink much at all, or even talk. You just lay there in his boat, dying.

"Finally, on the fifth of March, he made it to the village just as a tropical storm unleashed its fury on Samoa. It was a close call, my friend.

"The word went out at Lauli'i, and soon warriors arrived from the mountains to take you away. It was pouring rain and the streams became torrents, but they covered you with a tarpaulin and carried you up the mountain, reaching here that same night.

"Mataafa came to see you and had a real doctor summoned here. He examined you and said it was hopeless, that your body's organs had shut down due to dehydration. Death was only a matter of time. Mataafa became quite upset and sent the doctor away. He ordered everyone to pray to Jesus for your life and for the village here to administer the traditional Polynesian restorative treatments of hot rocks, cool waters, fruit broths and mountain water, plant potions, 'ava, and muscle massages.

"For three days everyone prayed to Jesus and treated you with the old ways. During this time you were delirious, sometimes whispering to a lady named Linda, sometimes laughing and sometimes crying. And then yesterday it happened: You opened your eyes fully and spoke strong words for the first time, saying, 'I am hungry.' You lived. That was the third miracle! Mataafa proclaimed it as such and has ordered a *fiafia* for when you feel better. He has also given you a new name, Toa Uso, Warrior Brother. As in *his* brother."

I didn't comprehend that part at all. The big man had long disdained me for my failures. And I still hadn't ended the threat of German naval gunfire.

"So Mataafa likes me now?"

"Like you? It is far more than that, Peter. The two Samoan warriors with us that night in the swamp were his favorite grandsons, his heirs. They lived. We all did. You saved all of us with your skills and courage. You sacrificed yourself for us to get away. Polynesians do not forget such things. You are now a member of Mataafa's family, a true brother, a hero to the people of Samoa. You are called Toa Uso, Warrior Brother, the *palangi Amerika* about whom tales will be told for all time."

"Did everyone get out?"

"All are safe, including Mika, who fled to the hills before Kramer could find her."

"What happened to you and Jane and the others that night?"

"We heard the gunfire of your ambushes. I could tell it was your shotgun, so I told them to keep running. We found Vaiusu Bay and followed the shoreline to the west, then made our way up Pesega Stream inland to a friendly village that Mataafa's grandsons knew. When I heard that artillery barrage, I thought the enemy finally got you. How did you get out of that?"

"Luck. God's help. I don't know. . . ."

He listened quietly, then said, "There are rumors that Kramer was one of those killed that night."

I didn't have the energy to go into the whole episode, so I only said, "He was a cocky bastard, enjoyed calling me Cain Man, trying to humiliate me by showing how smart he was. But he let his guard down and I killed him and got away. So continue with your story. What happened after you got to that village?"

"We waited for two days, then went up into the hills and rejoined Mataafa's men. When we heard you were found, we came here to be with you. Jane has been helping take care of you. She has been with you constantly."

"What happened to make her disappear?"

"She was getting more worried about Kramer deducing her real intent, but it was just a feeling. He had not said or done anything to alert her fully. The morning she disappeared, Kramer stopped by her apartment after breakfast. He must have already figured her out by then, for he began to look through her belongings without an explanation, ignoring her protests. He searched in her purse and found her next note to you. It said she was worried that Kramer was becoming mistrustful of her. He saw through the code words and knew he'd been duped.

"He was instantly enraged, threatening to have her executed as a spy. She told him doing that would be stupid, merely exposing his own weakness and incompetence to his superiors. And that, she told him, would lead to his own arrest for treason.

"Kramer lost all sanity at that moment and hit her hard in the face, which caused the wound we saw when we found her. Then he threw her down, knocking her head on the floor of the guesthouse. She pretended to be unconscious while he went to the verandah and called for the guard watch to come and get her. She fled out a back door and ran through the German area until she was in the swamp."

"Why didn't she run to Joseph at the surveillance spot?"

He shrugged. "She panicked and just started running."

I thought of my own panic on the trail in the swamp, running the wrong way, right

into the enemy. "Understandable. So she ran into the swamp."

"Right. She hid there, with no water or food, until our Samoans found her in a greatly weakened condition. I think she was close to dying. They had to carry her on our escape out of the swamp and up into the hills. She is doing much better, but her beautiful face now has a scar from Kramer. He must have had a large ring on his finger when he hit her to make that kind of wound. The scar will not go away. She is embarrassed, I think, for you to see her now."

My heart sank with the weight of my guilt. I was the one who had forced Jane into this whole situation through the despicable means of blackmail. But she wasn't the person I had initially thought she was on the ship when I'd come up with the plan to use her. I'd been wrong—so wrong—and had to make some kind of amends.

"I need to talk to her, David. Alone."

"I understand, Peter, and will tell her. By the way, tomorrow will be a day of thanksgiving for your healing. Mataafa's priest is coming to lead everyone in prayers."

"Tomorrow. . . . What day is it now?"

"Saturday, the ninth of March. Yes, I know what you are thinking. We still have six days to go. I have the Ballistite here and ready to transport."

Six days, and I was physically weak as a kitten. Damn it all. And now we had additional worries caused by Jane's rescue. I needed a situation report.

"Any repercussions from Jane's escape and our skirmish?"

Aukai nodded. "Yes. The Germans are saying it was an ineffectual raid by renegade Englishmen who support Mataafa. They protested to the English consul, Colonel de Coetlogon, who denied it. There are now two German warships in the harbor, *Eber* and *Olga*. The flagship, *Adler*, is somewhere on the north coast right now, and there are rumors she is confronting the American ship *Nipsic*."

"Are patrols in town and around the harbor increased?"

"The sailors on police patrol have been doubled. They are more heavily armed and roam the Anglo side at all hours. Knappe was threatening to reinstate martial law again and impose a dusk-to-dawn curfew on the east side of town, but he has backed away from that now. I have no word of increased boat patrols in the harbor. I think the Germans do not gauge Mataafa capable of mounting an attack on the water."

That evening Jane came to my *fale*. She was dressed in a faded, green, flower-print dress, the type Samoan ladies wear. Her black hair was done up in the native style, with a white frangipani flower over her right ear, the sign of a woman whose heart is not yet taken.

A single coconut-oil candle cast a dim glow, but I could tell the swelling in her face had gone down. Then I saw the scar. Her skin was spilt in a purplish line across her left cheekbone. It would've taken more than a fist to do that.

Her expression serious, she whispered, "First things first, Peter. I have something for you that I saw inside Hans' valise while he was indisposed. It's a telegraph message sent to him from the station at Auckland. I don't understand it. I think the numbers are code for words. No one else here knows I have it."

She handed me a short section of telegraph strip, which read:

00311 18399 21656 10782 06330

Jane was right. It was numeric code, arranged in five five-digit groups. It appeared to be a variation of the standard Slater Code, a commercial telegraph code that has been adopted and modified by various governments. The code consists of twenty-five thousand words in a dictionary, each of which is represented by a five-digit number from 00001 up to 25000. You add or subtract the code key number from each five-digit number to get the correct five digits and thus the real word. Sometimes the code key number was hidden in the message, usually in the first or last group. It's a simple operation, far easier to use than our U.S. Navy Secret Code and far easier to decode.

I sat up and reached out for her hand. "Thank you for the good work, my dear. It is a coded message and maybe an important one. While I'm lying here recuperating, I'll try to decipher it. Jane, is it your impression the Germans here want a fight?"

"Many Germans here are worried, but they're quiet about it. Some in the leadership here are openly spoiling for a fight. They're humiliated by the failure to end Mataafa's rebellion. They're irate about the ex-pats' support of Mataafa and about the American interference with their bombardments. They're absolutely sure they can scare us out of the Pacific with a quick victory over our ships that will make us negotiate a peace. They think we're too busy with Latin America to really care about this area." She let out a long sigh. "It worked for them back in the sixties with Denmark, Austria, and France, didn't it?"

"Thank you. Unfortunately, that's my impression too."

Jane looked at the ticker strip, her eyes misting. I reached for her hand. "And thank you for helping me recover, Jane."

I wanted to make her smile. She had such a pretty smile. "I hear you're quite a good nurse. I'm sorry that I probably wasn't so good a patient."

The smile never came. Instead, she tightened her hold on my hand. "You saved all of our lives in that swamp, Peter. We all thought you'd been killed. It was heartbreaking."

I said what I should've said long before. "Back in Auckland, I was bluffing on the blackmail. I never thought it would get this bad for you. Jane, I'm so sorry for all I've put you through. I'll get you out of Samoa safely and make sure you'll be able to start a comfortable new life."

Her reply had a pessimistic tinge. "Yes, well, thanks for saying that. As for a new life, it's hard to imagine that right now, isn't it? Get some rest, Peter."

She turned to leave, but I didn't let go of her hand. There was something I needed to say. "Jane, I wish things were different for us. . . ."

"I know you do, Peter. I can see by your eyes what's in your heart. I wish that things were different too."

"Maybe in the future, when this is over. . . ."

"The future? The future is too far away for me to even think about. Now please get some sleep."

She walked away, our moment of intimate connection over.

43

Confusion and Delight

Upolu Island
Kingdom of Samoa
Sunrise, Thursday
14 March 1889

On the evening of the ninth, reports from Mataafa's Samoan sources showed that events had begun to develop quickly, several of them producing unexpected results.

The first one was welcomed by all: peace feelers put out by both Samoan sides in the civil war. An uneasy and undeclared truce settled over the island. No one knew how long it would last, but everyone in Apia hoped it would hold. The gruesome realities of two years of intra-Samoan warfare had drained all enthusiasm for a continuance of the bloodshed.

Equally positive was a new stance by the local German officialdom. Consul Knappe's previously arrogant behavior toward British and American residents had dissipated, making me wonder what the recent cable traffic from Berlin contained. Had Bismarck calmed the hotheads at home who wanted war?

Then, late on Sunday, the tenth of March, came the news that dashed hopes for a peaceful settlement of the Samoan crisis. We learned that Germans in Apia were rejoicing the news that *Adler* had sunk *Nipsic* in battle. The global war between Germany and the United States had begun. The Americans and British in Apia, and Mataafa as well, were stunned. I resolved to begin my operation earlier than planned and also determined that it was time for me to shed my anonymity and contact the U.S. consul, Mr. Blacklock, for his assessment of the situation.

Later that night, after hours and hours of dissection of those numbers, I had an idea of what Kramer's coded message meant. The first set of numbers, 00311, was simply the date of the German secret dictionary code key to be used, the code for the third month, first week of that month, first day of that week. The dictionary code key changed every day. I, of course, had no idea of the German code key and had no copy of Slater's Code with me, though I did recall the number key for certain words with naval significance.

The last set of numbers was the mathematic operation to be applied to the code key. After trying various combinations, I realized that subtraction of that number, 06330, from the other numbers was the applicable operation, the key to opening the code.

The middle three number sets were the actual message. I applied the mathematical operation to them. The first set of numbers looked familiar, from my vague memory of Slater's Code. It was the number code for "reinforcements." Two words followed it. The second number set I didn't recognize. The third one I did know. It was the number set for "soon."

A chill went through me. *Vandalia* was alone. The Germans were getting ready to sweep across the Pacific. First Samoa, then possibly Hawaii?

The pendulum of sentiment swung back the next day, for *Nipsic* steamed into port under a morning rain shower. Her reported demise had been a gross German press deception designed to manipulate public feeling in the fatherland. Was Knappe responsible for that report? I had no way to know.

My view from the idyllic spot at Mt. Vaea was perfect for watching the harbor. *Nipsic* passed by *Vandalia* and anchored close in to shore, off the mouth of the Vaisigano River on the east side of town. The English-speaking population breathed a sigh of relief. I returned to the original date of March fifteenth for the attack.

Later the same day, U.S.S. *Trenton* arrived in Apia. She was a relatively new ship but was unarmored with a wooden hull, an obsolete under-powered engine, and ancient muzzle-loading guns. Aboard her was the commander-in-chief of the U.S. Navy's Pacific Squadron, Rear Admiral Lewis Ashfield Kimberly, an officer highly regarded in the navy. Best of all, Rork was supposed to be aboard as well.

The admiral was taking no chances. The American ships anchored in a line so their fire was mutually supporting and could target the German side of the harbor.

Theoretically, Kimberly had received word of my mission from Washington and was the only American official in Samoa who knew.

By trusted Samoan courier, I sent a message to Admiral Kimberly: *Sir, I am here. Will finish my job from Walker soon. Please send Rork to me. Another note forthcoming. Wake*

The Samoan government under Tamasese, faced with this barely restrained naval confrontation in the harbor, announced that Apia would be a neutral area and no fighting between foreigners would be allowed. Knappe, who told the local government what to say in the first place, instantly agreed on behalf of Germany. Kimberly complied but kept his ships' guns manned, as were the German warships'.

Commodore Fritze's cruiser, *Adler*, came into the harbor on Tuesday, the twelfth. She anchored in the center of the German battle line, between the *Eber* farther inside the anchorage and *Olga* on the outer end. Thus the entire German squadron was assembled and anchored a bit earlier than I'd anticipated. I kept the original date of my operation. The Ides of March was three days hence, on Friday.

The Royal Navy arrived on the twelfth also. Their senior man in the South Pacific, Rear Admiral Henry Fairfax, sent one of his best ships, H.M.S. *Calliope*, to Apia. She was a modern, steel-hulled cruiser under the command of a Captain Kane. He wisely anchored at the outer end of the German line of ships, away from the line of fire from either side. Kane had the unenviable job of neutral observer, forbidden to take sides in the heightening international drama. *Calliope* was the farthest out from the town and nearest to the open ocean.

Half a dozen schooners rounded out the harbor's densely packed maritime population, most of them anchored in the shallow water on the German side, since they were contracted or owned by the Firm.

~~~

While the cocks were crowing at a tomato-red, misty sunrise on Thursday, the fourteenth, my professional world changed radically for the better. A boisterous Irish brogue woke me from my blissful, *'ava*-enhanced slumber.

"Well, now. Jus' lookee here! Me eyes don't believe what they're seein' afore them, for if it ain't Commander Peter Wake, senior officer o' ever-so-secret special assignments section, hidden well inside the Office o' blooming Naval Intelligence o' our blessed Uncle Sam's bloody-awful, friggin' navy, loungin' about like he was his majesty, the dusky heathen Sultan o' Zanzibar himself!"

A long finger stabbed the air for emphasis.

"Oh, me boyo, 'tis a good damned thing ye've got the likes o' *me* around here now to keep yer puny old bones out o' trouble, your holy honorship, Commander Peter Wake."

Boatswain Sean Aloysius Rork, United States Navy, had arrived. I was delighted.

The big brute stood over me, peering down and examining my carcass with concern in his eyes. Well, that sort of attitude wouldn't do at all, for we had a job to get done. So I set the tone properly from the start.

"Rork, you sorry Gaelic laggard of a bosun, you took long enough to get here. I've had to carry this whole damned thing 'til now. Though I'll freely admit it's been pleasant not having to run the usual interference between the fathers of the local girls and your old lecherous self. Now, if you're done gawking at me, are you ready to bear a hand and get a dicey assignment completed? Be warned, it's not one for faint hearts."

The concern vanished, replaced by my old friend's famous grin, which had charmed ladies around the world and led to more than one bar fight.

"Aye, sir, dicey jobs're me specialty, so Bosun Rork's standin' here ready to bear ye a hand. An 'tis a good bloomin' thing one's all ye want, for one hand's all me got. As fer me takin' so long, it's ten thousand bloody miles to get here!"

A knowing look came over his face as the finger wagged at me.

"Me ears've heard that yer already risen up to a right lofty height with the senior locals. Honorary brother of the head fellow, are ye? Oh, the natives were talkin' mighty fine about you, sir, when they took me walkin' up this here mountain. Even treated a ruffian such as me like minor royalty, once they knew yer me friend an' ancient shipmate."

A Samoan girl delivered us cups of juice and silently departed. Rork admired her walking away and commented, "An' 'tis positively amazin' how friendly the lassies can be here. Ye've done well indeed, boyo."

That impish look in his eye implied more than he said. It worried me.

"Yes, I've made some friends among them. These Samoans're good sailors and decent people, Rork. Now, before anything else, I'm telling you to please ignore the girls here, even when they invite you to do otherwise, which they probably will, knowing you. Consider that an order, Bosun Rork. I'll not have a repetition of what happened on the Mekong River. Understood?"

Rork assumed his innocent expression, which didn't fool me in the least.

"Aye, aye on the lassies, sir. Ye know me, though. 'Tis always business afore pleasure. Always."

Then he straightened up and snapped his fingers. "Ooh, speakin' o' orders, Admiral Kimberly knows our orders an' says to say hello to you, sir. Told me to say if you can end this mess peaceable-like, all the better. But he's expectin' serious help from us if'n push comes to shove."

"What's happening onboard the ships in the harbor?"

"Aye, push is likely comin' to shove, sir. Them bastard Kraut officers're openly laughin' at our wood hulls an' old smoothbores when they have their boats row 'round us. Ooh, aye, the struttin' Teutonic buggers're jus' itchin' to make our lads swim home. Bloody damned infuriatin'. Kimberly's walkin' a fine line with the poxied bastards."

"Yes, he surely is. They outgun him."

"That they do. But it jes' means our lads're more the ready to fight, to show 'em what Americans can do with what they've got. Aye, me boyo, from admiral to cook, we're all thinkin' it'll come at any time. 'Tis pretty grim in that harbor right now. An' the limeys'll be no help to us, o' course. Queen Vicki made her bed with the Heinies years ago, literally."

I didn't have time for him to launch into his usual anti-English diatribe about wrongs done to the Irish, so I switched topics to one I worried about.

"What's the weather look like to you? Looks odd to me."

"Ocean's lookin' greasy to me. Swells out o' the north an' east, breakin' on the reefs around the harbor. Every ship at anchor is rollin' her guts out. The glass is fallin' but the wind's still low. Started rainin' light an hour ago, but me thinks that's jus' the beginning' o' what's to come. Mark me words, sir, gonna be some serious rain an' wind soon. Maybe a full gale in a couple o' days. The squadron will need to set to sea to weather it."

The Samoans told me the same thing the day before, saying an *afa* was coming. I didn't know that word. Aukai explained that *afa* meant hurricane, far worse than a gale. Even if a storm of that magnitude was on the way, I wasn't worried. We'd get our work completed before the brunt of it struck. A month of preparation and ordeal had gone into getting everything set for the Ides of March. I'd be damned if I would be deterred by some wind and rain. And after we'd done our work, Kimberly's squadron wouldn't be needed in Samoa. They could leave and weather the gale, or whatever was coming, in relative safety at sea.

"A little rain tomorrow will be helpful to conceal our efforts."

The grin returned as he cocked an eyebrow and lowered his voice to a conspiratorial tone. The Irish always love a good conspiracy.

"Ooh, me knows that glint in yer eye well, Peter Wake. So what's it to be, sir? Killing some o' them nasty-arsed, kraut-eatin' Heinies afore the bastards can sink our ships, are we?"

"You're damned close, Rork. It's false-flag sabotage on their entire squadron at once, hitting their rudders with explosives as simultaneously as we can. Minimal casualties and damage to the Germans. Hopefully none of them will be killed. I don't want to make them martyrs. And not a bit of any of it will be traceable to Uncle Sam. The Mataafa Samoans will get all of the credit."

He rubbed his hands together in glee. "Aye! Sounds right delicious to me, sir. So when does all this fun begin?"

"We get under way from here in a few hours and head for our rendezvous point. Main action will be tomorrow evening at sunset. Now it's time for you to meet your new Hawaiian shipmate. Have the girl outside call for Captain Aukai to come in here. We'll go over the plan in detail."

"An' methinks there's a billet for a salty bosun in this plan, right?"

"Rork, I can't believe you just asked such a silly question.

Since when have I ever left you out of the action? And you're really going to like this one, my old friend, for you just joined the crew of a Samoan *fautasi.*"

And having said all that, I began to explain to Rork all that I had experienced and done on the mission until that day. He never said a word the entire time, just sat there stunned, his expression getting grimmer with each revelation.

44
All of the *Palangi*
Ships Will Die

Apia Harbor
Kingdom of Samoa
Sunset, Friday
15 March 1889

I never saw the sun rise on the Ides of March, because an hour
before it was due to peek over the eastern horizon, a solid wall
of rain descended from a bruised and angry sky. This was no usual
daily tropical downpour but an incredibly heavy flow of water
from above. Hour after hour, the cascade never stopped flowing
down, as if the island had drifted under some gargantuan waterfall.

I began the operation anyway. Rork, Aukai, Joseph, and I led
the column of Samoan porters lugging the Ballistite down Mt.
Vaea for our rendezvous with the bateau at Malifa Village on the
Vaisigano River. Jane stayed in Mataafa's camp overlooking the
town, awaiting our return the next day.

The storm's most salient elements, the rain and wind, became
an incessant frontal assault on all of our senses, rapidly debilitating
our strength through attrition. The noise of it crashing down upon

trees, huts, and the ground was a continual roar. I had to yell to be heard even a few feet away.

The weight of this falling water was overwhelming, literally filling the air to the point that it was hard to breathe. Driven by the rising wind, it felt like hail on our skin. The impact on our eyes made us perpetually squint, and we dared not turn our ears broadside to it. Visibility was limited to a matter of yards, and the peculiarly acrid smell of electrified air and jungle detritus was everywhere.

The rain pounding down completely changed the island as well. Our column slipped and slid down animal paths that had become flowing creeks. Every rut and indentation turned into a watercourse. Where two joined, they became a wild stream. Normally lazy creeks turned into raging rivers. Danger was in every step of our journey.

When we arrived at the Vaisigano River, I was dismayed. It had turned into a frightening vision of a watery hell. Carts, huts, horses, pigs, bushes, human bodies, trees, boulders—anything and everything was flung along that torrent as it ate its way down through the earth and rock, consuming all in its path to the harbor.

I had to admit the reality of my situation. There was no way to use the river for transporting our munitions down to Apia, thereby circumventing the German land patrols. My reservations mounted regarding the operation, for the weather was getting worse far faster than I'd expected. And if it was this bad a couple of miles inland, what was the harbor like?

Could the mission even still de done? I needed to see the harbor myself before making that decision. So onward we trudged, leaving the paths and joining the main cross-island track. This road was now the confluence of several paths-turned-watercourses, and at several places it was three feet deep in fast-moving water.

The river option was out, so I determined we'd carry the explosives by foot right into Apia. The more I thought about it, the more I realized that the German sailors on police patrol wouldn't be a problem. Not in that weather. They'd all either be

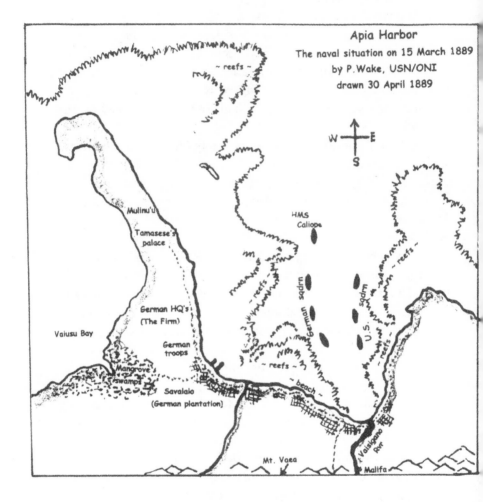

Apia Harbor
The naval situation on 15 March 1889
by P. Wake, USN/ONI
drawn 30 April 1889

~ reefs ~

W ← → E
S

Mulinu'u

Tamasese's palace

HMS Caliope

German sqdrn

U.S. sqdrn

~ reefs ~

German HQ's
(The Firm)

Vaiusu Bay

German troops

~ reefs ~

Mangrove swamps

~ beach ~

Savalalo
(German plantation)

Vaisigano Rvr

Mt. Vaea

Malifa

back in their barracks or, more likely, sent back to their ships. No one would predict an attack in that weather.

Down the mountain we went, passing entire villages with their thatch blown away, their livestock scattered, and their crops flattened. Most disconcerting, we saw entire families lashed to palm trees, fully expecting worse conditions. They shook their heads at us, saying we were fools.

At last we reached the coastal plain. At just before 6:00, we slogged into the eastern side of the town, much of which was flooded by the overflowed banks of the adjacent Vaisigano River. Sure enough, we were never stopped by anybody. In fact, we never saw a German, only the few Brits and Samoans who were boarding up the Anglican church. The tide was higher than normal, already beginning to flood the town.

By now the storm had piped up to at least a full gale, and the velocity, fifty knots or more, was still rising rapidly from the north. With the wind blowing straight into the harbor from the open ocean, debris was flying through the town. It was only with handholds on trees and buildings that I could move, all of my various injuries screaming for attention. Every step was in pain.

I hugged a coconut palm and peered out at the harbor. I couldn't see any ships, though the nearest, *Nipsic*, was only two hundred yards away. I did see several streams of black smoke scudding through the air. The ships hadn't put to sea, where they would be away from the dangers of the reefs and far safer. It was too late to leave now. The American ships weren't powerful enough to steam into the wind. Instead they were steaming ahead, trying to relieve the strain on their anchors. A new gust hit me, much stronger than the previous. It was a hurricane. And it wasn't getting better.

Why didn't the warships all go to sea, a far safer place to weather a storm? That was standard practice for seamen. Rork gave his opinion: Neither side wanted to be the first to flee the harbor. Pride. Now the ships were in mortal danger, trapped on a leeward shore, surrounded by coral reefs, without room to set more cable out for their anchors.

One look at the harbor told me it was suicidal and idiotic to even contemplate an attack. The harbor was far worse than the river, with ten-foot-high surf smashing down on the waterfront, washing away Beach Road right in front of me. There was no way a *fautasi* could survive in those conditions or even get out into the harbor through the mouth of the river.

I decided to check on the Samoan attack force, whom we'd planned to meet at the second curve of the river inside the mouth. I presumed they had decamped due to the storm, but since we were close by, I'd make sure. We made our way behind the church and waded east through the flood of rain water from the hills, looking for where the bank of the Vaisigano used to be.

The scene we found was incredible. There on a little hump of higher ground—lashed by the wind, pummeled by the rain, fending off debris—were the crews of the two *fautasi.*

One hundred proud, young Samoans stood waiting for Toa Uso, the *palangi* warrior brother of the great Mataafa, to arrive. If I'd had any other nickname or benefactor, they would've used their common sense and gone home long before. But I didn't, and they would never abandon Mataafa or the foreigner he respected enough to name his brother.

Their two eighty-foot-long canoes, one painted yellow and the other green, were resting upside down at the water's edge. Each was ready to be righted and launched into the frothing cauldron that was now the Vaisigano.

The men stood silently watching me, waiting for my decision.

Aukai and I, followed by Rork, approached the oldest man in the group. By his creased face and snow-white hair, I guessed he was even older than I. This fellow evidently was the skipper of one of the two canoes.

Old he might have been, but the man wasn't frail. Still built like a wrestling champion, standing with arms akimbo, the man's face was a picture of defiance toward the elements. The wind wasn't even buffeting him. His *lavalava* whipped in the breeze, showing his legs and torso to be completely covered from his knees to his navel in the painfully inflicted tattoos of Samoa's warrior seamen. One look in his squinted eyes and you knew this ancient, South Pacific man had seen and done far worse than what was happening around him then. He was fully ready to lead his men out there against the German occupiers of his island. I had no doubt that every one of them would follow his lead. It was a dramatic demonstration of raw courage.

Rork stood there, clearly awed, and yelled in my ear, "Sweet Jesus, Mary, an' Joseph. These lads're on *our* side? Me eyes've nary seen the likes o' this fine lot o' men."

"Samoan loyalty, Rork."

Aukai introduced me to the head man. His name was Anetere'a, which my friend translated into English as Andrew, as in the biblical fisherman and saint.

Aukai glanced questioningly at me for my decision.

I shook my head and said, "No attack."

He told the man in Samoan that Toa Uso was greatly impressed and appreciative of this show of devotion to Mataafa by the brave men of Samoa. But no attack could be successful because of the storm, and therefore he could send his men home.

The man nodded his understanding and replied that he would send those with wives and children home, but he would also ask for volunteers to stay in the town. Their help would be needed by the sailors on the ships in the harbor, he explained, for this was an *afa mata'utia*, a most terrible hurricane.

Aukai suddenly paused in his translation of the man's final words. When he resumed, he did so quietly. "Anetere'a says it was very foolish for the ships to stay in the harbor. He says all of the *palangi* ships will die. Many *palangi* sailors will die too."

I'd been thinking the same thing.

Most of the Samoans volunteered. After taking their *fautasi* canoes onto even higher ground, they returned and stood on the harbor shore, watching the harbor, waiting to help when the time came.

Calling Aukai over to the shelter of a kapok tree, I told him to send our porters back up the mountain with the Ballistite, for we couldn't chance losing it in the town and needed it hidden somewhere safe. I ordered him to go too, explaining that Rork and I were going to stay in Apia for a while during the storm. My purpose in remaining was to visit the U.S. consul and confer with him.

Aukai respectfully suggested that the Samoans could get the Ballistite to safety without him, and he would check on it later. He added that I needed him along with me to translate for the locals in the town. Aukai ended his proposal by adding that when I visited Consul Blacklock, he would pretend to be a Samoan servant of mine, since none of the foreigners in Samoa were to know of his identity, much less his nationality and mission.

That sounded good to me. I was glad to have him with us. We all could go back up the mountain together in the morning when the storm had passed. Then we would come up with another attack plan, for I was certain that the Germans weren't going to back down in their confrontation with the United States and that Samoa was just the first round in the fight.

45

Battling the Tempest

Apia Harbor
Kingdom of Samoa
Friday Night
15 March 1889

Aukai and Rork decided to stay outside, under the lee of the building, when we arrived at the nondescript consulate-residence of the U.S. representative in Samoa. My introduction at Consul Blacklock's front door didn't include my mission or my occupation within the navy, only that I was a supernumerary with the squadron caught ashore by the storm and unable to return to the flagship. I asked if I could seek shelter for a moment at the boarded-up consulate.

He welcomed me graciously and apologized for the lack of amenities due to the conditions. He and his family were planning to evacuate to a friend's house on higher ground, he said, but first he would rest a bit before fighting the wind outside since he'd already had a long, exhausting day. One of his children brought a lantern into the parlor, which was soaked from a dozen leaks in the ceiling, and we sat for a few minutes.

Blacklock, originally an Australian, had become a naturalized American in California before settling in Samoa. He was a part-time representative for the U.S., his main occupation being that of a mercantile businessman. He struck me as a hard-working, calm, decent sort. The man understood the Samoan culture well, for he was married to Apele Tietie, a well-known Samoan woman. Several of their children were running around the house.

Unlike many career State Department diplomats I've met, I liked and respected Consul Blacklock immediately. He was a man grounded in reality.

Part-time though he may have been, this backwater consul had been thrust into the center of world attention. The President of the United States read his reports. The Germans and British would have loved to read his reports. High-stakes decisions were being made based on his advice. It was Blacklock's communiqué several months earlier that had finally captured the Washington press's attention and mobilized U.S. naval reinforcements to the area.

Following the required polite conversation about his family, his business, and the shoreside preparations for the storm, I eased into my main reason for contacting him, asking what his predictions were about war between the United States and Germany over Samoa and what the German strategy would be if it came to that.

He was refreshingly honest enough to say he didn't know for sure. The arrival of the American Navy had dampened local German bellicosity, to be sure, but there were too many outside variables, of which he had no up-to-date knowledge. Those mainly revolved around the national political motivations in faraway Berlin and Washington.

As for German war plans, he was candid again, saying he had no knowledge of them. I thanked him for his time and candor and told him I thought he'd done a very good job under extremely difficult conditions.

A powerful gust rocked the frame home, the wind screeching through the seams. Blacklock cast a worried glance at the wall. The lantern flickered, making shadows dance around the room.

He waved a tired hand and said, "The Samoans were right. This storm is a full hurricane out of the north, our worst nightmare in Apia."

Another blast of wind shook the house, producing a prolonged rattling and squeaking of rafters and walls. Children in a back room screamed in fear. Blacklock jumped up and ran to see what had happened, followed by two servants. I heard him tell his family it was time to go.

I took leave of the consulate without saying good-bye. Aukai, Rork, and I groped our way through the knee-deep water in the dark to where the Samoans waited, ready to assist the sailors.

An hour later, I saw *Nipsic's* lights in the rain, for she had dragged and was very close to the shore. The other ships were dragging closer too, their lights circular looms of gray in the black.

"*Nipsic's* steamin' ahead to reset her hooks," said Rork into my ear. "Look at that smoke pourin' out! The ol' girl's usin' all the power she's got but makin' only a knot at most against this wind."

He pointed to our right and yelled, "Shipwreck!"

It was the harbor pilot cutter, Aukai explained. A wave picked the wrecked hull up and washed it onto the beach, which was now a hundred feet inland of where it had been when we'd arrived earlier. The bodies of two Samoan crewmen were tangled in the cutter's rigging. The hull split apart on the next wave, and the bodies were flung away into the surf.

The wind had risen to the point where I couldn't stand against it, even with a secure handhold. Even Rork and the Polynesians could barely stay put in one spot. Verbal communication was a thing of the past. The hurricane sucked all sound away except for its own menacing roar.

We waited in the lee of trees and buildings, for there was no longer a way to project assistance out to the ships. Our only function would be to wait for them to be driven downwind to us as shipwrecks. Then we might be able to help get some survivors ashore through the current and surf. It was too late to try to find our way to higher ground anyway. There was no road anymore, and no one could see. The night was a complete void.

In the pitch black, the wind brought us snatches of the sailors' battle to live: a fragment of shouted orders and screams of pain, the ominous thudding crash of colliding ships, acrid smokestack gases, canvas and spars and deck fittings flying through the air.

It was a terror-filled night. Men like us were dying out there while we huddled and waited.

Dawn on Saturday, the sixteenth, brought no harbinger of better weather. The wind—that unseen but lethal wall of air—had increased in velocity. The thing was now a full-blown major hurricane.

The sky grew perceivably lighter and the visibility increased, but it showed a dismal scene. *Eber* had disappeared, sunk. Part of her bow was on the western reef. In front of us, *Nipsic's* hull was slashed and splintered. Everything normally on her sides—boats, booms, chain plates, davits, braces, and shrouds—was gone, for *Olga* had smashed into her twice. The smokestack was thrown down on deck, and billows of black smoke erupted from her hull as if she was on fire. I saw with alarm that *Nipsic* was holding to only one anchor and that one barely, for she was quickly drifting astern as we watched.

The Germans had fared worse. *Olga* was shipwrecked on the reef near *Eber's* remains. *Olga* had fortunately gone ashore sitting upright. The German flagship *Adler* was not so lucky. She was on the reef, completely capsized onto her port side, her hull dented and ripped open by the coral.

Calliope, Trenton, and *Vandalia* were still out there, but all were dragging downwind. *Vandalia* was making no smoke. Her engine was out of action, a death blow.

A blast of exhaust gas belched from *Nipsic,* and she slowly moved forward. Rork put his mouth to my ear and yelled, "They're beachin' her!"

Ten minutes later she hit the reef by Blacklock's consulate, which had been turned into a ruin itself. Another few waves shoved *Nipsic* farther ashore, and she came to rest in the shallow water behind the reef, sitting upright on her lines as if she was docked. It was a neat piece of seamanship.

Then they made a mistake. They lowered a boat to take a line ashore. Normally it was the proper thing to do. But Apia harbor wasn't normal anymore. The tide had turned and was ebbing fast. The tremendous outflow of the Vaisigano River, filled with the combined rainwater runoff from half the island, joined the ebb tide to produce an incredible rip current moving against the hurricane winds. That created waves in the harbor of monstrous proportions—fifteen, twenty feet—that no boat could navigate. *Nipsic's* boat capsized, throwing the sailors into the water. They all were swept out to sea by that malevolent current as everyone watched from ships and shore.

Vandalia was next. Her last hook came loose, and she careened onto the reef and sank there, instantly smashed open by seas sweeping right over her main deck. Her masts still stood somehow, now filled with men clinging to the ratlines like flies caught in a spider's web, awaiting their deaths. Many went into the water and tried to get ashore, only a couple of hundred yards away. They were swept away by the current.

Trenton was making sternway slowly but still had some steam up. Then we didn't see smoke issuing forth from her anymore. Her demise was only a matter of time.

Calliope, a modern ship with real power—unlike the American ships, which had only auxiliary engines—was swinging close to *Trenton* on one side and the reef on the other.

We spent the morning helping the Samoans rescue sailors, German and American, from the reefs and shipwrecks. Time was a chaotic blur, measured by the waves smashing around us. Dozens of seamen were just out of reach as they were swept away, desperately shouting things we couldn't hear, their eyes locked on us until they went down.

At noon, we saw *Calliope* begin using all of her power, a continuous stream of black smoke pouring from her stack. She could usually steam along easily at sixteen knots. But in that tempest overwhelming her, the best she could do was one knot.

I assumed she was easing the strain on her anchor cable. Then I realized there was no cable off her bow. The Royal Navy's white ensign was sent up to the gaff and streamed aft. Rork and I exchanged looks. It was a daring decision by Captain Kane. *Calliope* wasn't steaming to ease the load on the anchor and ship. She was getting out to the sea and freedom.

The British were fighting back against the hurricane.

It was a thrilling sight. Her flag was ripped to shreds, but another white ensign went up and instantly sheeted out hard in the wind. The bow heaved thirty feet up in the air with each wave, then plunged down under the water. Her hull came within a hundred feet of *Trenton*, and it looked as if a collision was certain. But *Calliope* still kept moving, smashing against and through the solid mass of wind and water that opposed her.

Rork slapped my shoulder, put his mouth to my ear, and shouted in grinning admiration, "God bless those damned limey bastards! They're doin' it!"

A rare lull in the gusts allowed a fleeting sound to reach us. Rork said, "What the hell . . . ?" I couldn't believe it either. Was that men cheering?

It was indeed.

"*Cah . . . lie . . . oh . . . pee! Cah . . . lie . . . oh . . . pee!*"

Trenton's doomed men were up on the main deck, hundreds of them, sending cheer after cheer toward the Brits as *Calliope* fought her way by them. Slowly, foot by foot, she edged past the

Americans. Her agonizing journey took more than two hours. At last, she made it the half mile around the maws of the reef ahead of her.

We saw her make the turn downwind in deep water, away from the lee shore and death. Every soul on that body-strewn beach—Samoan, American, British, and German—cheered the Royal Navy.

The Brits had beaten the tempest.

46
Heroism

Apia, Upolu Island
Kingdom of Samoa
Saturday Afternoon and Evening
16 March 1889

*T*renton held out longer than we thought she could. All afternoon she dragged astern, her men desperately keeping the bow to the wind, pumping the rising water in her holds, repairing damages, fighting with every skill they had to keep her afloat. But the inevitable happened at sunset. *Trenton* was wrecked on the reef next to her sister *Vandalia*, whose men still clung to the rigging, unable to swim ashore against that hellish current. Each man waited to fall to his death, weakened from exhaustion or that terrifyingly evil wind that tried to pry him loose.

In late afternoon the wind lost its highest velocity, still gusting to hurricane force but allowing more lulls down to a mere full gale. Onshore we did our best.

The Samoans were the true heroes, showing incredible courage and skill. Far stronger than us *palangi*, they waded out into that current, in water up to their necks, to rescue the foreign sailors. They brought them to dry land on their shoulders, gently laid them down, and then returned into the water to do it all over again, hour after hour.

A weighted messenger line was thrown to us by *Nipsic*. Several Samoans swam out and retrieved it. After it was hauled ashore, a hawser was bent on and sent over, to be secured around several palm trees. After that, every single man from *Nipsic* went hand over hand along the hawser to the shore, the captain leaving the ship last. Several fell into the water, into which Samoans dashed, got them before the current did, and carried them to safety.

Many sailors weren't so lucky. Bodies were washing up everywhere. Hundreds of them. Each was examined for signs of life and taken to the Protestant church, where volunteers from the Wesleyan Methodists and the London Missionary Society—denominations not always on good terms with each other in the South Pacific—banded together and ran a makeshift hospital. The dead were laid close by, arranged by nationality and rank, adhering to naval discipline even in death.

Trenton swamped and sank to the bottom, but with her hull still intact and main deck above the water, she was in better shape than the quickly decomposing *Vandalia*. *Trenton's* men fired line rockets to the sailors in *Vandalia's* rigging and eventually got them all off her. Fifteen minutes later, the wreck finally caved in and *Vandalia's* masts collapsed. The Americans were then taken ashore from *Trenton* by Samoans, usually carried in their arms because of injuries sustained or because the torment aloft rendered the sailors' leg muscles utterly powerless.

By 10:00 that night, almost all of the Americans had been rescued from the shipwrecks. Survivors were grouped together on the beach by ship's company. Each crew rested under sails spread out to shed the rain and was given food and water by the local British and American residents. German sailors were taken to the Firm's building, where they were cared for by the company's employees and the German residents.

The wind started to lay down at nightfall but not the rain. Our work on the beach continued throughout the night. My companions and I collapsed late that night under a tarpaulin near the church. The adrenalin of the day and evening wore off an hour later, and most were fast asleep. My body's aggravated pains forbade any such bliss for me. I tossed and turned, while Rork snored until dawn.

Sunday arrived with anticlimactic gentility, for the hurricane had left us and moved on to other prey. It was as if there'd never been a catastrophe at all. The sky was bright blue, with not a cloud to be seen, and only a light breeze ruffled the water. If you looked aloft, you would think it a beautiful day in paradise. But if you dared to lower your eyes and survey the scene around you onshore or in the harbor, you saw death littering every view.

Dead ships, dead men, dead animals, dead trees were everywhere.

The smell was beginning, and haste was necessary to prevent disease. Once again, we started examining every body for life, hoping for miracles. A few were found and hastened to the makeshift hospital. The rest were taken to the temporary morgue. Ghoulish work. The kind that forbids recounting in detail.

Jane Cushman reported for volunteer duty at the hospital that morning. She'd walked all the way down the mountain with Mataafa's entourage. We didn't even have time to converse, just a quick smile of appreciation that the other had made it through the ordeal.

Upolu was a shattered island. The weight of the hurricane, added to two years of internecine war, exhausted any appetite for more bloodshed. The peace feelers from a week earlier now became peace offers. I heard rumors that Mataafa and Tamasese would meet to talk.

I was summoned to Rear Admiral Kimberly at 1:00 in the afternoon. I changed into my ragged uniform. We met in a tent the admiral was using as a headquarters. The poor man was haggard. He politely cleared the tent for a private talk with me. His staff complied begrudgingly, sending me suspicious looks on the way out, for they'd not seen this strange naval officer before. Who was I, and what was I doing in Samoa?

Kimberly didn't have the time or energy for the usual preambles.

"Commander, as you know, I was fully briefed on your mission before I assumed command of the Pacific Squadron. Unfortunately, we never got the chance to go over that mission after my arrival in Samoa, but I understand you've been here for some time and needed to stay away from the squadron for clandestine reasons. Obviously, the situation has changed in Apia and with our squadron."

He stopped abruptly. I got the impression he was about to modify that to "former squadron," but he didn't.

He started again. "Yes, well, obviously, I'll be ashore here for a while and will have to deal closely with the Germans. Fortunately, the hurricane trumped their war talk, and they've been very cooperative. The storm ended the animosity."

Kimberly's worn-out voice drifted off for an instant. "But still, I need to know, were you able to conduct any preemptive sabotage against the German ships? Are there any . . . *complications* . . . that might arise that I need to know about in my interactions with Doctor Knappe or the German commodore?"

It was delicately put. I replied in such a way as to protect him with deniability.

"Sir, there were some skirmishes with their naval intelligence people, specifically a Lieutenant Hans Kramer. Kramer is dead, and I am sure they won't want to raise the issue. As far as sabotage goes, my main mission against their anchored squadron, which would've been a false-flag operation, was planned for Friday night at sunset. The storm's arrival prevented it."

"False flag?"

I decided not to give details. "A *ruse de guerre* in espionage, sir. The anti-German Samoans under Mataafa would've carried it out and gotten credit. Nothing could've been tied to us."

Kimberly thought about that for a while. Then he said, "What would this action have accomplished?"

"It would've eliminated all of their ships' ability to maneuver, sir."

The admiral's surprise at my answer was evident. He knew I was holding back but as a professional could guess that I meant the ships' rudders.

In the end, he merely said, "Hmm, very intriguing indeed. Someday I'd be interested in hearing the details. But for now, commander, it appears your skills are no longer needed here, since the German squadron has ceased to exist."

I prepared to exit, but he had more. "However, you can still be very useful to me. A native schooner just put in to port. You will charter her to Auckland and carry my confidential dispatches. There you'll cable my report to Washington about what happened here. My signal officer has encoded it already."

I'd seen the schooner he'd mentioned. It was a small trading vessel, maybe sixty feet and probably barely seaworthy after the storm. I wasn't worried. With Rork along, we could get her squared away and make it to Auckland.

"Aye, aye, sir. It'll get done. A simple request, sir?"

He sounded exhausted when he said, "Yes, Wake, what is it?"

"I have my noncommissioned aide, along with a foreign ally and an American operative here in Apia. All of them were crucial to my operations here and in the rescue of the sailors. Do I have permission to take them with me to Auckland?"

The squadron flag lieutenant ducked under the tent flap and said, "Sir, the German commodore is here. He's on crutches. Broken leg from *Adler*'s shipwreck."

Kimberly's brow furrowed as he stood, my cue to leave. He absentmindedly told me, "Yes, go ahead, commander. Take your people out with you."

The admiral reached inside his coat and handed me an envelope. It was water stained and still damp, the addressee on the outside smeared.

"Alright, here's the message. Good luck, commander."

Looking him in the eye, I saluted. "And to you, sir."

47
Honors Rendered

The American Beach Camp
Apia, Upolu Island
Kingdom of Samoa
Sunday
17 March 1889

On my way out of the American bivouac on the beach, I met the prime foe of the U.S. Navy in Samoa. Commodore Fritze, accompanied by one of his staff officers, was on his way in to see Admiral Kimberly.

Kimberly's flag lieutenant, still curious about who I was, introduced me to the German commodore. "Commodore Fritze, may I present to you Commander Wake, a supernumerary with our squadron staff. Commander, this is Commodore Fritze, commanding the Asiatic Squadron of the Imperial German Navy."

Though Fritze didn't look his best, standing there in a tattered uniform, right leg splinted straight, and arms bent around hastily constructed crutches, the man's commanding presence was very much intact. An imposing man to have as an enemy.

The commodore was senior to me, so I saluted and spoke the requisite words of respect. "A privilege to meet you, sir. We all watched your brave fight against the storm and are sorry for your losses. Our navy stands ready to assist in any way we can."

Fritze stared hard at me, his hands tightly clenching the crutches. "So you are alive, Commander Peter Wake. I thought you were dead . . . *twice*. A valuable lesson to be relearned again: Never believe the first after-action reports you receive. It is very good to meet you in person finally."

His manicured British accent was impeccably polite, his tone unmistakably intimidating. He knew everything: John Irons' schooner delivering me to the beach, Jane working Hans to compromise German communications, my gunfight at the swamp. I was the man behind several minor but persistent irritations.

But did he know about the planned Ballistite attack? It might have killed or maimed *him* if he had been in his cabin during the explosion.

I gestured at the wreckage around the harbor. "It appears, commodore, that God has had His say in this. So it's all ended between us now, isn't it, sir?"

The flag lieutenant's jaw dropped at the conversation so far. He quickly interposed, saying to the German commodore, "Ah, sir, . . . Admiral Kimberly's tent is this way."

Fritze ignored him and gazed at the harbor, lingering on the hulk of his ruined flagship, *Adler*. His hands loosened their grip on the crutches. His next words lost their edge. "Yes, commander, neither of us has won. God has indeed stepped in, and we both have paid a terrible price. Two hundred of our countries' sailors are dead, maybe more."

He sounded sincere, so I expanded on the theme. "Well, sir, I think the toll between us would've been far worse if the hurricane hadn't come here. You would've won the battle, of that there is no doubt. But the war wouldn't have ended in Samoa."

Fritze nodded thoughtfully. "You are correct, commander. The war would not have ended here. The great powers would have chosen sides—Germany's traditional enemies in Europe would ensure that—and soon it would have spread around the world. To Europe, to the Americas. A long, bloody, modern war fought with machinery and science."

The flag lieutenant cleared his throat nervously. "Sir, the admiral is ready. . . ."

Commodore Fritze smiled and nodded at the lieutenant as if he'd just noticed him. Then he returned his gaze to me, his tone almost friendly. "Commander Wake, thank you for your candid words. I must go and meet with your admiral now. The next time you and I meet, we should enjoy a glass of schnapps and discuss our experiences in Samoa. Until then, commander."

Following usual naval custom, I saluted Fritze first, looking him in the eye. He returned the salute smartly. It was mere seconds, but it made a lasting memory for me: honors rendered between two foes who tried their best to stop each other.

The commodore then swiveled on his right crutch and hobbled off to meet the admiral.

The next morning, on Monday, 18 March 1889, Rork was rowing me out to the schooner in a dinghy. Aukai and Jane were already aboard, waiting for us to arrive. All of our meager possessions were stowed, and the vessel was ready to get under way. Since peace had settled in Samoa, Aukai brought out the remaining case of Ballistite to take back to Hawaii, the others having been ruined by the storm.

Halfway to the schooner, near *Adler's* wrecked hulk, Rork stopped rowing. He had that look on his face, the one he gets when he's about to do something wicked.

"Got an idea in me head, sir."

"Which is?" I replied warily.

"Remember when we was on the beach an' saw that longboat

from *Adler* capsize on the second day? She went over right about here. We helped the Samoans rescue some o' the Heinies from that boat. Bunch o' officers, they were. One o' 'em had staff braids on his shoulder."

"Right. What of it?"

"Them officers were mighty upset about losing what was in the boat. One young officer, the one with the staff braids, let slip it was a book. Then he knew he'd said too much an' clammed up tighter than a virgin at Curry's Saloon on Duval. But that's the word he used: book. Now why would just a book cause all that? A logbook? Nay. They're important but not *that* important. That lad was scared witless, he was."

He paused for effect, his eyebrows flickering upward in delight. "So maybe he was the squadron signal officer and that lost book was their *code* book."

"Hmm, very good point, Rork. And we just happen to be right over where it would be, don't we? I imagine the Germans have recovered it by now, though." I looked over the dinghy's side. The water looked about eight feet deep.

"Well, me thinks one o' us should go for a swim, jus' to make sure." He grinned. "An' since yer gimpy, that would be me, sir."

"Rork, you really are a pirate at heart, aren't you? The odds are against us, but have at it anyway."

I glanced at the beach a hundred yards away. The Germans had set up their bivouac there. Several were watching us.

"Make it look like you're drunk and fell in," I told my friend.

"Ooh, me thinks that'll be easy as a Dublin tart on a Friday night!"

Rork always had a theatrical ability, and he employed it fully now. Raising his slurred voice in Gaelic song, he slipped over the side and plunged to the bottom. The bubbles rising to the surface showed me his course. Soon his head appeared. "No luck yet." That said, he went down again.

He repeated this several times while I made a pretense of trying to haul him aboard, for the Germans ashore were starting to focus their attention on us. Soon they would be coming out in a boat, either to help us or stop us from loitering near their shipwreck.

Rork's head came up again, this time with a smile. "Found it," he said before heading down. A boatful of German sailors started heading our way from the wreck of the *Eber*. I began laughing, as if it were all a joke between drunks, but that didn't deflect their attention one bit.

They were seventy yards away when an officer at the stern shouted in English, "You there! What are you doing?"

"Oh, my friend is drunk again and fell in the water. No problem, sir. I'm getting him out."

Several officers on the beach were staring. At that distance, I couldn't tell who they were, but one was on crutches.

The water on the bay side of the dinghy, out of sight of the beach and the German boat, began foaming with bubbles. Rork broke the surface, his legs working furiously to keep him up, and gasped for air. He shoved an oilskin waterproof canvas bag up to the gunwale. It was weighted with at least twenty pounds of lead. I grabbed the damned thing and put it down in the bilge, under the thwart.

"Get the hell in the dinghy fast, Rork," I whispered. "The Germans are almost here and they don't look happy."

As Rork heaved himself up and over the gunwale, I waved at the German boat, where the officer was standing to get a better look at us. "He's aboard now. No problem! We don't need your help." I shook my head while smiling and yelled my version of German, "*Nein helpen. Nein helpen.*"

Rork, grinning idiotically, waved at them as well. The boat slowed, then headed for the beach, where the officers were still studying us.

"Say, would you mind rowing, sir? Ooh, me arms're bloody damned tired."

"It would be my pleasure, Rork. Well done."

Half an hour later, at my instigation, our schooner weighed

anchor earlier than the skipper had planned. We sailed around the eastern end of Samoa, then set a course to the south and Auckland. When we arrived in six days, the world would learn via telegraph of the disaster in Apia on the Ides of March.

No one else aboard the schooner was told of Rork's find, for it was highly sensitive. In the locker below my bunk was my seabag. At the bottom of the bag, below my weaponry, was a large-format book, six inches thick, with a lead-lined green cover. The title on the first page was in ornate Gothic printing and said it all:

Kaiserliches Deutsches Marine Codebuch
Zahlen Sie 18 von 187
15 Oktober 1888
Hamburger Flottenstation

Rork's efforts had yielded the 18th of 187 copies of the Imperial German Navy's secret codebook—the newest edition, from six months earlier—issued at Hamburg Naval Station. It was an espionage treasure trove with an ironic twist: The receipt stamp in the lower right corner had the signature of Lt. H. Kramer. My German wasn't sufficient to read the rest of the book, but I didn't need to. ONI had several men at headquarters fluent in the language.

Secrecy was paramount, however, for if the Germans attributed the codebook's loss to the storm, they would continue to use the code. But if they attributed it to us, the code would be changed as soon as Berlin learned of its capture.

At sunset that evening, I thought about Commodore Fritze's suggestion to someday drink some schnapps and talk over our experiences in Samoa. No, I decided, that probably wasn't going to happen.

48

Consequences

Commodore John G. Walker's Office
Chief of the Bureau of Navigation
Naval Headquarters
State, War, and Navy Building
Washington, D.C.
2 May 1889

C ommodore Walker frowned and leaned back in his swivel chair, stroking his forked beard with one hand and drumming the fingers of the other on his desk. He'd read my official written report that morning. I'd just finished giving him my unofficial verbal report, which contained information that might be considered politically unpalatable.

His tone was incredulous. "So let me get this straight, Wake. You were within an hour of blowing up the German squadron, using Ballistite from Italy, furnished by a Hawaiian army officer, who was himself on clandestine assignment in Samoa, with the attack to be done by a bunch of natives in a big canoe."

"Two big canoes, sir."

He stared at me as if I was crazy. "All right, Wake, it was

two big canoes. And all this was after you had already played rich businessman in Hawaii, helped to kill a German colonel and dumped his body overboard on a steamer in the middle of the Pacific, blackmailed an American citizen into being a female spy, participated in piracy with a religious lunatic, attacked and killed German sailors and marines, killed a German naval officer, and befriended some savage rebel chief . . ."

"Excuse me, sir, but Mataafa is no savage. He's a devout Christian. Goes to church every Sunday."

"Right, he's a *Christian* savage rebel chief who made you his brother, of all things. Very touching, Wake. And after the storm, Rork found the German naval codebook, the one bright spot in this litany of odd decisions that would give the politicos around here heart attacks if they ever find out. Then, when your steamer stopped in Honolulu on the way home, you took complete leave of your senses and accepted this Hawaiian native king fellow's invitation to be some sort of a big man in his royal order. I suppose he's a Christian too?"

"King Kalakua is very much a Christian, sir. He invested me as a Grand Officer of the Royal Order of Kalakua, a prestigious award, for saving Captain Aukai's life in the fight at the swamp. It turns out Captain Aukai is a nephew of the king. I agreed, thinking it would be beneficial for us to have some goodwill with the Hawaiian royalty. We haven't had much of that in Hawaii lately."

Walker sighed. "Did that effort to get goodwill have to include getting drunk with the king and that international reprobate, Stevenson, whom you are now bosom pals with? You were seen performing some lewd pagan dance with both of them. I've seen the complaints that were sent to Washington by the Missionary Society. Our new boss, Secretary of the Navy Tracey, was not amused to receive them on his first month in office."

Complaints? That was news to me. I didn't remember any missionaries at the party. But, then again, my memory was blurred a bit about that evening.

"Robert Louis Stevenson is an acclaimed novelist, sir. He is a close friend of King Kalakua and now me. He wanted to know whether he should build his final home in Samoa, and I told him of a spot on a mountaintop that I knew. He is very pro-American in the Pacific and will be a good ally. And yes, sir, at the beach *lu'au*, what we call a picnic, the king and Robert asked me to join them in a *hula* dance. Quite harmless stuff, sir. Some of the prudes in town must've been offended the next morning when they heard about it. The king very much appreciated my participation."

The commodore ignored my comment and went on, the frown becoming a scowl. "And there's more, for after going native in Samoa and Hawaii, you gave this woman you blackmailed previously *all* of the greenbacks and gold you had left over, almost *five thousand dollars*. And you then had the temerity to put this blatantly improper diversion of funds down on your voucher report as a 'confidential operative expense.'"

"Jane Cushman did her job and deserved it, sir. She's disfigured because of me and needs the money to start life over in Australia. It is a matter of honor."

His quarterdeck voice—the thunderous one that brooked no impertinence—was emerging. "Peter Wake, I've been in the navy for forty long years. I've seen and heard it all, but you get into the craziest, stupidest, most unexplainable and indefensible predicaments in the navy. And this assignment takes the cake over all of your others, even that Cuban caper in eighty-six.

"Allow me to summarize, commander. In addition to cavorting with the natives out there, you've committed conspiracy of homicide after the fact, blackmail of an American civilian, piracy against a foreign government, and grand theft of U.S. government funds. Do any of these behavioral decisions sound a little odd to you?"

Hmm. I had to admit that, put that way, my decisions did sound a little less than by the book. Although, compared to the criminal issues, the missionary complaints about *hula* dancing with the king of Hawaii seemed insignificant.

"Ah . . . well, sir, they really seemed the right things to do at the time. You had to be there to fully understand, sir. It was complicated."

He glanced up at the ceiling. "Thank God, I *wasn't* out there."

Walker exhaled slowly, then folded his hands in front of him.

"Commander Wake, I have run interference for you around here for seven years. And for some reason that I can't explain even to myself, I'm going to do it again with the accountants and the politicians. But this is the last time. Understood?"

"Fully, sir. Thank you, sir."

"You know I'm going back to sea this fall, commanding the new squadron of steel ships. I've gotten permission to bring you with me as the staff signal and intelligence officer. And yes, before you ask, Rork is going too. It's time all three of us smelled the ocean from the deck of a warship. I've no choice, because if you stick around here much longer, you'll probably get us both into the kind of trouble even I can't escape."

I couldn't believe my ears. I was returning to sea aboard a warship. Better yet, I'd be in the new squadron of steel-hulled ships being commissioned. It was the dream assignment of every officer in the navy.

"You've got me surprised, sir. Thank you very much, sir."

"You're welcome. And please do me one huge favor, Peter."

"Yes, sir! You name it."

"You've still got several months to go in ONI. Lie low and stay out of *any* controversy until we get ourselves out of this building, will you? We've got a new executive administration now, and I've completely run out of excuses to defend you. That is all for now."

I jumped to attention. "Aye, aye, sir!"

As I walked down the passageway from his office, the import of what had just transpired hit me. Finally I would be away from the shadowy world of espionage and its skulduggery and paranoia, employing questionable behavior and dealing with the dregs of human existence. I would never again feel the need to treat a woman as I had Jane Cushman and feel the self-loathing afterward.

I would live in the sunlight again, doing the proper job of a naval officer, an honorable job that required no obfuscation.

I would be back in the United States Navy.

Lt. Sean Wake, U.S.N.
U.S.S. Olympia, Pacific Squadron
27 May 1897

Dear Son,

Now you are one of the few who know what really happened out in the Pacific in '89. It was a very close-run thing. Would war there have spread around the world? Yes.

Fortunately, the hurricane that killed 221 seamen and injured more than 150 cooled the hot heads in Berlin and Washington. Along with the British, we Americans and the Germans met in conference in April 1889, deciding that Samoa should be ruled over by all three equally and that Malietoa Laupepa would be reinstalled as king. No Samoans attended.

Chancellor Bismarck, who restrained Kaiser Wilhelm II in '89 and set up the conference, left office in '90. I am worried because there are no such restraints on the kaiser today, for he is surrounded by men with far less wisdom and fortitude than Bismarck.

Spain is our major adversary today, but, mark my words, in the future that will change. Germany's aggression is mounting unchecked. She has long coveted Latin America and the Caribbean, so keep a weather eye out for trouble on the horizon. We aren't weak now, as we were back in '89, but a war with Germany would be horrific.

You might wonder what happened to the people I met in the Pacific. I will start with the one thing I regret. I misjudged Jane Cushman completely and should never have coerced her into working for me. Her anger surfaced on our return to Honolulu. She told me she would never forgive me for the terror she endured and the scar that reminds her of it. That is why I gave her all of my remaining funds. We silently parted ways in Honolulu. I later heard she started a new life as a merchant's wife in Fremantle, Australia.

King Kalakua died in '91. His sister, Lili'uokalani, assumed the throne, only to be deposed in '93 by the same American-Hawaiians I met that afternoon at Royal Hawaiian Hotel. David Aukai tried to defend his queen with his life, but she forbade bloodshed. He refused to join the new army formed afterward and lives quietly on the beach at Waikiki.

Robert Louis Stevenson moved to the little spot in Samoa that I suggested the night of the lu'au. *He lived and wrote there—calling it Vailima—until his death a couple of years ago.*

Blacklock is still U.S. consul in Apia. Knappe and Fritze were recalled to Berlin, their careers not impaired. Malietoa Laupepa is still king but is in ill health and is locked in bitter conflict with Mataafa Iosefo. Rear Admiral Kimberly, a good man and sailor, retired to Massachusetts. My mentor, Admiral Walker, just retired after 47 years of honorable service and now runs the Nicaragua Canal Commission. And your father returned to ONI in '93 because of events in Cuba. As you know, a month ago my old friend Theodore Roosevelt was appointed Assistant Secretary of the Navy, so I work directly for him now. Predictably, it hasn't been dull.

With all of my respect and love,
Your proud father,
Peter Wake

Endnotes by Chapter

Chapter 1: Dying a Deniable Death on the Far Side of the World

Hiram Maxim (1840–1916) was an American inventor who couldn't convince the U.S. government to buy his new automatic firing weapon, so he went to England, formed a company, and sold it to the British. It changed world history.

For more about Wake's 1874 adventures in Africa, read *An Affair of Honor.*

Chapter 2: The View from Washington, Six Weeks Earlier

The State, War, and Navy Building housed the diplomatic, army, and navy branches of the executive branch of the U.S. government. It was right next to the Executive Mansion, which has been known since Theodore Roosevelt's administration as the White House. The navy's offices were closest to the president's office, and naval officers were frequently summoned there to provide information regarding foreign countries, leaders, and capabilities. The State, War, and Navy Building is now known as the Eisenhower Executive Office Building (EEOB).

Room 272 of the EEOB was the traditional office of the

secretary of the navy. It is now the ceremonial office of the vice president. It was restored in the mid-1980s, along with many other areas of the building, to its 1880s' appearance.

Commodore John Grimes Walker (1835–1907) was a legend in the U.S. Navy. From 1881 to 1889 he was the Chief of the Bureau of Navigation, the main operations branch of the navy and, as such, he implemented the Office of Naval Intelligence in 1882 and fostered it until 1889. In that year, he was given command of a squadron of the navy's first steel-hulled warships—a considerable honor—and became an innovator of squadron and fleet tactics.

President Grover Cleveland (1837–1908), a New York state Democratic governor, was president of the United States twice, from 1885 to 1889 and from 1893 to 1897. The inauguration in those days was on March 4th. The XX Amendment in 1933 changed it to January 20.

Secretary of the Navy William Whitney (1841–1904) of Massachusetts has a very good historical reputation and is generally regarded as one of the leaders who modernized the U.S. Navy.

Lieutenant Raymond Rodgers (1849–1925), the head of ONI from 1885 to 1889, came from a family of sailors. He was a son and brother of admirals and a grandnephew of two commodores. He went on to become a distinguished naval officer in his own right, eventually retiring in 1911 as a rear admiral.

Commander Richard Leary (1841–1902), a combat veteran of the Civil War, later commanded U.S.S. *San Francisco* at Cuba in the Spanish-American War and was naval governor of Guam (1899–1900). He retired as a rear admiral in 1901 and died shortly after.

Commander Dennis Mullan (early 1840s–1928) was a Civil War combat veteran who fought in Korea in 1871 and served until 1901, when he retired with the rank of commander.

Chapter 3: Friends and Foes
The British royal house had a very close relationship with Germany. In fact, it was called Saxon-Coburg and Gotha up until World

War I, when it was changed to the more English-sounding House of Windsor, which it has retained to this day.

Admiral David Dixon Porter (1813–1891) was also a legend in the navy, with many political enemies. By the 1880s, though he was the senior officer and the second full admiral of the navy (his adoptive brother, David Farragut, was the first), he was winding down his active leadership role. In those years he concentrated on writing, producing eight books, both histories and novels. He died in 1891, after serving his country for 62 years.

For more about Wake's 1886 espionage mission in Cuba, read *The Darkest Shade of Honor*. For his 1888 mission in Cuba, read *Honorable Lies*.

Benjamin Harrison (1833–1901), a Republican from Indiana, was a grandson of President William H. Harrison (president from March 4 to April 4, 1841) who became a general in the Civil War and subsequently governor of his state. He was inaugurated as president on March 4, 1889, and lost his reelection bid four years later to Grover Cleveland, who was voted back into the presidency for a second time. Harrison is chiefly remembered for championing for economic policy and African-Americans' civil rights.

Chapter 4: Disturbing Intelligence
Pago Pago is pronounced in Samoan as Pango Pango.

Chapter 5: A World at War?
Rear Admiral Lewis Kimberly (1830–1902) was originally from New York state and joined the navy in 1846, becoming one of the first graduates of the naval academy. He commanded the Pacific Squadron from 1887 to 1890. He retired in 1892, after serving for 46 years.

For more about Linda Wake's illness and death, read *A Different Kind of Honor*.

For more about Wake's love affair in Haiti, read *Honor Bound*.

Chapter 7: Orders

José Martí (1858–1895) is the most famous Cuban in history. He was a writer and revolutionary leader, who first met Wake in *The Darkest Shade of Honor*. Their friendship was truly cemented in *Honorable Lies*, and continued until Martí's death in Cuba in 1895.

S.S. *Australia*, built in 1875, was a famous ship that plied the Pacific for three decades. Her end came in 1905, when she was chartered to the Russian government in the Russo-Japanese War and subsequently sunk that year by the Japanese cruiser *Suma*. Wake will be involved in that war, on personal assignment from President Theodore Roosevelt, who afterward will receive the Nobel Prize for bringing the two parties to the peace table.

Chapter 8: A Lecture on American Liberty

Sanford Ballard Dole (1844–1926) was born in Hawaii to Protestant missionaries there. A lawyer, he was appointed by King Kalakua to the Hawaii supreme court and by Queen Lili'uokalani to her privy council. When Lili'uokalani was deposed in 1893, Dole ended up being the president of the new government after Lorrin Thurston declined. Dole's goal was to convince the U.S. to annex Hawaii. However, newly elected to his second term, President Grover Cleveland refused. When the U.S. finally did annex Hawaii in 1898, Dole became the first governor of the territory. He was a U.S. District Court judge from 1903 to 1915. His cousin James Dole founded the Hawaiian Pineapple Company in 1901, which later became the world-famous Dole Food Company.

King David Kalakaua (1836–1891), also known as the "Merrie Monarch," reigned from 1874 until his death from kidney disease at age 54 in 1891. He had no children, so his sister took the throne. He built the Iolani Palace, which still exists. The Merrie Monarch Hula Festival is still held in his honor, and the Hawaiian national (later, the state) anthem was written by him.

Chapter 9: Crown Princess Lili'uokalani

Crown Princess Lydia Lili'uokalani (1838–1917) became queen in 1891 upon the death of her brother, King Kalakua. She continued his policy of rediscovery of traditional Hawaiian culture, which had been banned by foreign influences over the kingdom. She wrote the iconic Hawaiian song "Aloha Oe."

Washington Place still exists and is located at 320 Beretania Street, two blocks from the Iolani Royal Palace. After being deposed in 1893, Queen Lili'uokalani lived there until her death 1917. From 1918 onward, it was the executive mansion of the governors of Hawaii. It is still being used by the governors for ceremonial purposes. There are weekly public tours.

Chapter 10: Cocktail Intrigue

Iolani Palace still exists and is located at 364 South King Street in downtown Honolulu. It was built by King Kalakua for a huge sum and completed in 1882. After neglect and misuse for decades, in the 1980s it was beautifully restored to its late 1880s' appearance and is open for public tour. Everyone in Hawaii should visit this very impressive place.

Robert Louis Stevenson (1850–1894) was a proud Scotsman and probably the best-known novelist in the world in the 1880s. His debilitating tuberculosis (then commonly called "consumption") led him to forgo the cold, damp Scotland that he loved and search the Pacific for healthier environs where he could live and work during his final years. He ended up at Upolu Island in Samoa at the end of 1889 and built his dream home at a place he called Vailima, "place of the five waters." He lived there, beloved by the Samoans, until his death in 1894. He was buried high on Mt. Vaea by 200 Samoans who forged a path to his grave known as the Trail of Grieving Hearts. When I researched and wrote this novel, I lived just down the mountain from there. I urge everyone to visit Vailima, which is open to the public.

Chapter 13: Complications
For details of Wake's "shady operation" in the Bahamas in 1888, read *Honor Bound*.

Chapter 14: The Offer
Flogging in the Royal Navy officially ended in 1881, though it had fallen into disuse by the 1860s. The U.S. Navy outlawed flogging in 1850.

Chapter 21: Surprises
For more about Wake and Rork in Southeast Asia, read *The Honored Dead*.

Ballistite was invented by Alfred Nobel in 1887, and the Italians got one of the first contracts, ordering 300,000 kilograms. Mostly, it was used for rifle ammunition, but it also had larger explosive applications. Nobel (1833–1896), whom a French newspaper called "the merchant of death," was worried about his legacy. A year before he died, he wrote into his will to have his estate fund prizes recognizing positive contributions to mankind, hence the famous Nobel Prize.

Chapter 22: A Not-so-Good Samaritan
Tok Pisin is a phonetic language based on local native, English, German, Dutch, and French words. It is used in Melanesia and particularly in Papua New Guinea to this very day as a broad working language to unite many different lingual subgroups.

Chapter 23: A Leap of Faith
German New Guinea, or Kaiser Wilhelm Land, is now known as Papua New Guinea. The Germans lost it to the Australians in World War I.

Chapter 30: Samoa
Poutasi Village still exists. I visited the beach in the story while researching this novel.

Chapter 32: Mis Buen Amigos
Wake is using some phonetic spelling with his Samoan to make it simpler for the reader. The actual Samoan word for white person is *palagi,* which is pronounced palangee. As in Pago Pago, the letter G is always pronounced *ng* as in song.

Chapter 33: Saint Valentine's Day
Pierre Loti was the pen name of French naval officer and novelist Louis Viaud (1850–1923). He and Wake became friends during the Battle of Hue at Vietnam in 1883. Read *The Honored Dead* to see what happened there.

Tapa cloth is also called *siapo* in Samoa. Made from the bark of a mulberry tree, it is considered a Polynesian art form across the Pacific. Some of the more ornate tapa pieces can be very expensive and are family heirlooms.

Chapter 44: All of the Palangi Ships Will Die
The Vaisigano River mouth is next to the well-known Aggie Grey's Hotel (built in the 1930s), made famous by James Michener. In addition to its intriguing bar, lobby, and gardens, it has great *fiafia* celebrations on Wednesday evenings. I recommend it.

Chapter 47: Honors Rendered
A copy of the 1888 Imperial German Navy Secret Codebook exists today at the NSA library. It is a fascinating look into the field of intelligence in the 1880s.

Acknowledgments

Academic Research

This project took seven years to complete. It was not only interesting for me but great fun as well.

There are two types of research done for my novels in the Honor Series. The first is academic research. This research is a treasure hunt to find memoirs, official reports, maps and charts, and press stories from the period and locale of the book. In addition, I peruse modern historical references, interview contemporary experts on the subject matters within the project, and study modern sailing guides for the area. This provides me with the facts and structure of the project.

I am assisted in all of this academic research by a wonderful band of happily kindred souls around the world. I call them my Subject Matter Advanced Resource Team (yes, that spells SMART). In the inner core of SMART are Randy Briggs and his team of biblio-sleuths at the Lee County Library System. They unfailingly locate, provide, (and also suggest) hard-to-find research texts. They include Lillian Bradley at the Pine Island Library and Eileen

Downing and Jo Starr at Processing at Library HQ. America is very fortunate to have free public libraries—not many countries in the world do—and Florida has some of the very finest.

Other SMART people who assisted in the project include NSA veterans Ron Kemper and Richard and Susan Rolfe, all of whom are extremely well versed in foreign languages, cryptocomms, and cryptanalysis, having worked in that arcane world for decades. Bill Milne and Rene Stein at the NSA's National Cryptologic Museum at Fort Meade, Maryland, were very valuable resources. Bill is an encyclopedia of cryptologic history. Rene, the chief librarian, allowed me inside the codebook room where the late-nineteenth-century codes are located, a treasure trove of material, including the 1891 German naval codebook. Captain Jack Orzalli, U.S.N. (Ret.), did research for me at the Kittery (Maine) Historical and Naval Museum, locating the century-old memoirs of several American naval participants in the events described in this story, particularly the hurricane, a crucial component of the research on this project.

The following is a list of some of the research material I used in this project to understand the rapid political, naval, and international changes that were occurring in the United States and the world in 1889:

American Gunboat Diplomacy and the Old Navy by Kenneth Hagan
Gold Braid and Foreign Relations by David F. Long
The Naval Aristocracy by Peter Karsten
The Office of Naval Intelligence by Jeffery M. Dorwart
Letters from the Asiatic Station by Frank Emory Bunts
By Order of the Kaiser by Terrel Gottschall
Navalism and the Emergence of American Sea Power by Mark Russell Shulman
Naval Customs and Usage by LCDR Leland P. Lovette
The Old Steam Navy, Volume One, by Donald Canney

Admirals of the New Steel Navy by James C. Bradford
Dictionary of the Admirals of the U.S. Navy, Vols. One and Two, by William B. Cogar
The Records of Living Officers of the U.S. Navy and Marine Corps by Lewis Randolph Hamersly (1899)
Conway's All the World's Fighting Ships 1860–1905 by Robert Gardner, Editorial Director
The 1885 ONI Report: *Characteristics of Principal Foreign Ships of War*
The 1889–1909 reports of the ONI on *Coaling, Docking, and Repairing Facilities of the Ports of the World*
Everyday Life in Washington by Charles M. Pepper
The Code Breakers by David Kahn (1967)
An excerpt from a lecture series by William Friedman of the NSA, one of America's greatest cryptanalysts (1950s)

Information about Hawaii, the Samoan Islands, the German colonies across the Pacific, and the situation in that region in 1889 was gleaned from the following sources:

The Story of Laulii, a Daughter of Samoa by William H. Barnes (1889)
My Consulate in Samoa by William B. Churchward
My Samoan Chief by Fay G. Calkins (1971)
History of Later Years of the Hawaiian Monarchy . . . and the Revolution of 1893 by W.D. Alexander (1896)
The Hawaiian Islands, an 1896 Report of the Foreign Affairs Dept. of the Republic of Hawaii
"Our Relations to Samoa" by George H. Bates in *Century Magazine* (May 1889)
"Samoa: Isles of the Navigators" by Hervey W. Whitaker in *Century Magazine* (May 1889)
A Footnote to History: Eight Years of Trouble in Samoa by Robert Louis Stevenson (1892)
In the South Seas by Robert Louis Stevenson (1896)

Robert Louis Stevenson in the South Seas (Stevenson's letters 1888–1890) by Alanna Knight
Stevenson's Germany: The Case Against Germany in the Pacific by Charles Brunsdon Fletcher (1920)
German Colonization in Oceania by Hephaestus Books
"The Tuscarora's Mission to Samoa" by Henry Erben in *Century Magazine* (May 1889)
"Monthly News" of *Harper's New Monthly Magazine* (March 1889)
Disputing the Samoa Islands with Germany by Harry Thurston Peck (1889)
Blackbirding in the Pacific by Louis Becke
Blackbirding in the South Pacific by William Brown Churchward (1888)
"The Fiji Islands" from the *Pall Mall Gazette* in *The Living Age Magazine* (June 1874)
"Samoan Hurricane" by RADM L.A. Kimberly, U.S. Naval Historical Foundation (1890)
Eyewitness memoirs (unpublished) of the Samoan hurricane by Lt. John Hawley, Lt. Louis Hewlett, and Lt. Earnest Sanstrom, U.S.N., courtesy of the Kittery (Maine) Historical and Naval Museum and Captain Jack Orzalli, U.S.N. (Ret.)
The article "Six War Vessels Sunk" in the *New York Times* (30 March 1889)
The Earth and Its Inhabitants—Oceanica by Élisée Reclus (1898)
Coral and Cocoanut: The Cruise of the Yacht Fire-Fly to Samoa by Frank Frankfort Moore and W.H. Overend (1890)
Thirty Years in the South Seas by Richard Parkinson
Samoa mo Samoa by J.W. Davidson (1967)
Amerika Samoa by CAPT J.A.C. Gray, U.S.N. (1960)
History of Samoa by John William Hart, Glen Wright, and Allan D. Patterson (1971)
An Outline of Samoan History by Sylvia Masterman (1980)
Tales of the South Pacific by James Michener (1957)

John Garret's 1974 *The Journal of Pacific History* article "The Conflict between the London Missionary Society and the Wesleyan Methodists in 19th Century Samoa"
An essay on the Samoan spirit world by M.D. Olson in *The Journal of the Polynesian Society* (1997)
A Simplified Dictionary of Modern Samoan by R. W. Allardice
A Walking Tour of Historic Fagatogo by John Enright
Islands of Samoa (maps) by James A. Bier (University of Illinois)
The period-contemporary Pacific maps in the Perry-Castañeda Map Collection of the University of Texas

Eyeball Recon

The second type of research in my projects is eyeball recon. In this phase, I go (usually by ship) out to the locales in the book, meet the people, see the terrain and ocean, and immerse myself as deeply as I can into the culture of the area. This kind of hands-on investigation is invaluable, providing me with a true "flavor" of the places and people I write about so I can describe them more vividly in the story. For this particular novel, I steamed through Polynesia and Melanesia on four different ships over the past seven years and learned a huge amount about that beautiful and intriguing part of the world.

My eyeball recon in the Pacific was fascinating. There are still a lot of intriguing characters out there. First, let me thank the passenger lines that carried me to the South Pacific. The famous Cunard Line of Great Britain had me as a guest author and lecturer aboard *Queen Mary 2* and *Queen Victoria* on their voyages through Polynesia in 2007–2009.

The Silver Sea Line took me on as a guest author to the islands of Melanesia and ultimately up into the mountains of Papua New Guinea, formerly known as Kaiser Wilhelm Land. There I met the impressive warriors of the Dani Sentani tribe and learned firsthand about the culture. I also steamed with Silver Sea through eastern Polynesia in 2010.

I was helped in my understanding of the history and culture of New Guinea by John and Joan Colman, Australians who have lived and worked in that fascinating place for most of their lives. They were my shipmates when I visited New Guinea in 2009.

Mary Thomas, the best-known coordinator of international lecturers in the business, arranged my most recent voyage to the South Pacific as a guest author onboard the incredible, private-residence ship *The World*, as she steamed through Polynesia in the spring of 2012.

As my six-week Polynesian journey in 2012 evolved, I lived in Apia on Upolu Island—just down the mountain from Robert Louis Stevenson's home—where I finished writing this novel. Jeanelle Harrison of Geraci Travel in Florida arranged my transport and lodging in Upolu, Pago Pago, and Honolulu and for the route home. Not an easy task.

During the years of researching this novel and traveling throughout Polynesia, I became enamored with Samoa and *Fa'a Samoa*, the Samoan way of life. My affection for the people, culture, and islands of Samoa started in 2007, when I first visited Pago Pago at Tutuila Island in American Samoa. I gained a wonderful introduction to the culture during an afternoon with the gracious Princess Avisa of western Tutuila Island. The Jean P. Hayden Museum of Samoan Culture helped me on Samoan bush medicine. Over the years, the lovely ladies at the legendary Sadie Thompson Inn, my favorite haunt in Pago Pago, helped me understand what a liberty bar was like for U.S. Navy sailors in the turn-of-the-century Pacific. I always stay at Sadie's when I'm in Pago Pago, and I urge you to do the same.

At Upolu Island in Samoa, I have many people to thank. David Wong-Tung, special advisor to the prime minister, helped me on politics and history, including a dynamic discussion one evening at Aggie Grey's; Foketi Imo Evalu of the Ministry of Finance explained the local economics; the entire staff at Insel Fehmarn Hotel, my home in Apia, showed me the incredible hospitality of their culture; Palo Vaaelua helped me on Samoan names and meanings; the *fiafia* crew at Aggie Grey's Hotel assisted my understanding of traditional life; Nitrosene Matealona of Robert Louis Stevenson's home and museum at Vailima spent a morning with me discussing RLS's life and love of Samoa and Hawaii; Fetaiaimauso Gauta, research material librarian at the Nelson Memorial Public Library of Apia, found excellent reference works for me; and Lumepa Apelu, interim head of the Museum of Samoa, patiently answered all of my cultural-historical questions during several visits.

In Hawaii, the wonderful staff at Iolani Palace also patiently answered my questions during my five visits. Everyone visiting Honolulu needs to see this important place in Hawaiian history. Ala Moana and the Mission House Museum were a great help in Honolulu as well.

Dear Friends Who Helped

Thanks also go to my dear friends Mark and Christine Strom, who allowed me to write the beginning of this novel at their wonderful sanctuary at Maramonte in the mountains of North Carolina.

Randy Wayne White, a fellow islander and *New York Times* bestselling novelist, has been a friend and mentor for many years. In addition to dispensing very decent rum, he also helps me with business advice.

I am very blessed to have the lovely and brilliant Nancy Glickman of Pine Island in the center of my life. In addition to being a gifted amateur astronomer and naturalist and an excellent critical reader, she is a constant source of energy, wisdom, and encouragement during these long projects.

And, of course, I have the Wakians around the world. They

give me the motivation to keep steaming onward and upward and the strength to take on the next project that lies just beyond that distant horizon.

Thank you all so much,

Robert N. Macomber
The Boat House
St. James, Pine Island
Florida
2013

THE HONOR SERIES
"Sign on early and set sail with Peter Wake for both solid historical context and exciting sea stories." —U.S. Naval Institute Proceedings

At the Edge of Honor. This nationally acclaimed naval Civil War novel, the first in the Honor series of naval fiction, takes the reader into the steamy world of Key West and the Caribbean in 1863 and introduces Peter Wake, the reluctant New England volunteer officer who finds himself battling the enemy on the coasts of Florida, sinister intrigue in Spanish Havana and the British Bahamas, and social taboos in Key West when he falls in love with the daughter of a Confederate zealot. Winner of the 2003 Patrick D. Smith Literary Award for Best Historical Novel of Florida.

Point of Honor. In this second book in the Honor series, it is 1864 and Lt. Peter Wake, United States Navy, assisted by his indomitable Irish bosun, Sean Rork, commands the naval schooner *St. James.* He searches for army deserters in the Dry Tortugas, finds an old nemesis during a standoff with the French Navy on the coast of Mexico, starts a drunken tavern riot in Key West, and confronts incompetent Federal army officers during an invasion of upper Florida. Winner of the 2004 John Esten Cooke Literary Award for Best Work in Southern Fiction.

Honorable Mention. This third book in the Honor series of naval fiction covers the tumultuous end of the Civil War in Florida and the Caribbean. Lt. Peter Wake is now in command of the steamer USS *Hunt* and quickly plunges into action, chasing a strange vessel during a tropical storm off Cuba, confronting death to liberate an escaping slave ship, and coming face to face with the enemy's most powerful ocean warship in Havana's harbor. Finally, when he tracks down a colony of former Confederates in Puerto Rico, Wake becomes involved in a deadly twist of irony.

A Dishonorable Few. Fourth in the Honor series. It is 1869 and the United States is painfully recovering from the Civil War. Lt. Peter Wake heads to turbulent Central America to deal with a former American naval officer turned renegade mercenary. As the action unfolds in Colombia and Panama, Wake realizes that his most dangerous adversary may be a man on his own ship, forcing Wake to make a decision that will lead to his court-martial in Washington when the mission has finally ended.

An Affair of Honor. Fifth in the Honor series. It's December 1873 and Lt. Peter Wake is the executive officer of the USS *Omaha* on patrol in the West Indies, eager to return home. Fate, however, has other plans. He runs afoul of the Royal Navy in Antigua and then is sent off to Europe, where he finds himself embroiled in a Spanish civil war. But his real test comes when he and Sean Rork are sent on a mission in northern Africa.

A Different Kind of Honor. In this sixth novel in the Honor series, it's 1879 and Lt. Cmdr. Peter Wake, USN, is on assignment as the American naval observer to the War of the Pacific along the west coast of South America. During this mission Wake will witness history's first battle between ocean-going ironclads, ride the world's first deep-diving submarine, face his first machine guns in combat, and run for his life in the Catacombs of the Dead in Lima. Winner of the American Library Association's 2008 W.Y. Boyd Literary Award for Excellence in Military Fiction.

The Honored Dead. Seventh in the series. On what at first appears to be a simple mission for the U.S. president in French Indochina in 1883, naval intelligence officer Lt. Cmdr. Peter Wake encounters opium warlords, Chinese-Malay pirates, and French gangsters.

The Darkest Shade of Honor. Eighth in the series. It's 1886 and Wake, now of the U.S. Navy's Office of Naval Intelligence, meets rising politico Theodore Roosevelt in New York City. Wake is assigned to uncover Cuban revolutionary activities between Florida and Cuba. He meets José Martí, finds himself engulfed in the most catastrophic event in Key West history, and must make a decision involving the very darkest shade of honor.

Honor Bound. Ninth in the series. In 1888 Wake, U.S. Navy intelligence agent, meets a woman from his past who begs him to find her missing son. Wake sets off across Florida, through the Bahamian islands, and deep into the dank jungles of Haiti. Overcoming storms, mutiny, and shipwreck, Wake discovers the hidden lair of an anarchist group planning to wreak havoc around the world—unless he stops it.

Honorable Lies. Tenth in the series. In September 1888, Commander Wake has five days to rescue his two captured operatives from a dungeon in Spanish colonial Havana. But his plan quickly falls apart when the head of Spanish counter-intelligence springs a deadly trap. Huguenots, Freemasons, the beautiful actress Sandra Bernhardt, the re-election of President Grover Cleveland, and Cuban patriot José Martí are all part of the action.

CPSIA information can be obtained
at www.ICGtesting.com
Printed in the USA
BVHW07s2143170718
521861BV00001B/3/P